They all stood as one, raising their glasses in salute.

"To the future," proposed Barrington.

"The future," the rest echoed, then downed their drinks in one go.

Montrose watched them leave one by one, shaking hands and smiling. Once they had cleared the room, he made his way to the doorway, then to an adjoining room. His visitor stood, the painting on the wall still askew to reveal an observation hole.

"You heard?" asked Montrose.

"I did," his mysterious visitor replied.

"What do you think? Will it work?"

"I think your plan solid enough for now," the stranger replied, "though we may have to take more overt action in the future."

"You have something specific in mind?" asked Montrose.

"Not at this time, but I rather suspect that our young princess will be resilient to your efforts."

"She's just a young girl," replied Montrose.

"No, she's a young woman," corrected his visitor. "I've underestimated her once already, I'll not do it a second time."

"Come, come now," added Montrose, "you can't possibly believe she can outsmart us."

"Only time will tell," the visitor replied.

BURDEN OF THE CROWN

Heir to the Crown: Book Six

PAUL J BENNETT

Also by Paul J Bennett

HEIR TO THE CROWN SERIES

SERVANT OF THE CROWN

SWORD OF THE CROWN

MERCERIAN TALES: STORIES OF THE PAST

HEART OF THE CROWN

SHADOW OF THE CROWN

MERCERIAN TALES: THE CALL OF MAGIC

FATE OF THE CROWN

BURDEN OF THE CROWN

MERCERIAN TALES: THE MAKING OF A MAN

DEFENDER OF THE CROWN

FURY OF THE CROWN

MERCERIAN TALES: HONOUR THY ANCESTORS

WAR OF THE CROWN

TRIUMPH OF THE CROWN

MERCERIAN TALES: INTO THE FORGE

GUARDIAN OF THE CROWN

ENEMY OF THE CROWN

PERIL OF THE CROWN

THE FROZEN FLAME SERIES

AWAKENING | ASHES | EMBERS | FLAMES | INFERNO

MAELSTROM | VORTEX | TORRENT | CATACLYSM

POWER ASCENDING SERIES

TEMPERED STEEL | TEMPLE KNIGHT | WARRIOR KNIGHT | TEMPLE CAPTAIN | WARRIOR LORD | TEMPLE COMMANDER

THE CHRONICLES OF CYRIC

INTO THE MAELSTROM | MIDWINTER MURDER

THE BEAST OF BRUNHAUSEN | A PLAGUE IN ZEIDERBRUCH

Dedication

To Carol

My wife, best friend, and great love of my life.
I am so delighted to be with you as we make this journey together.

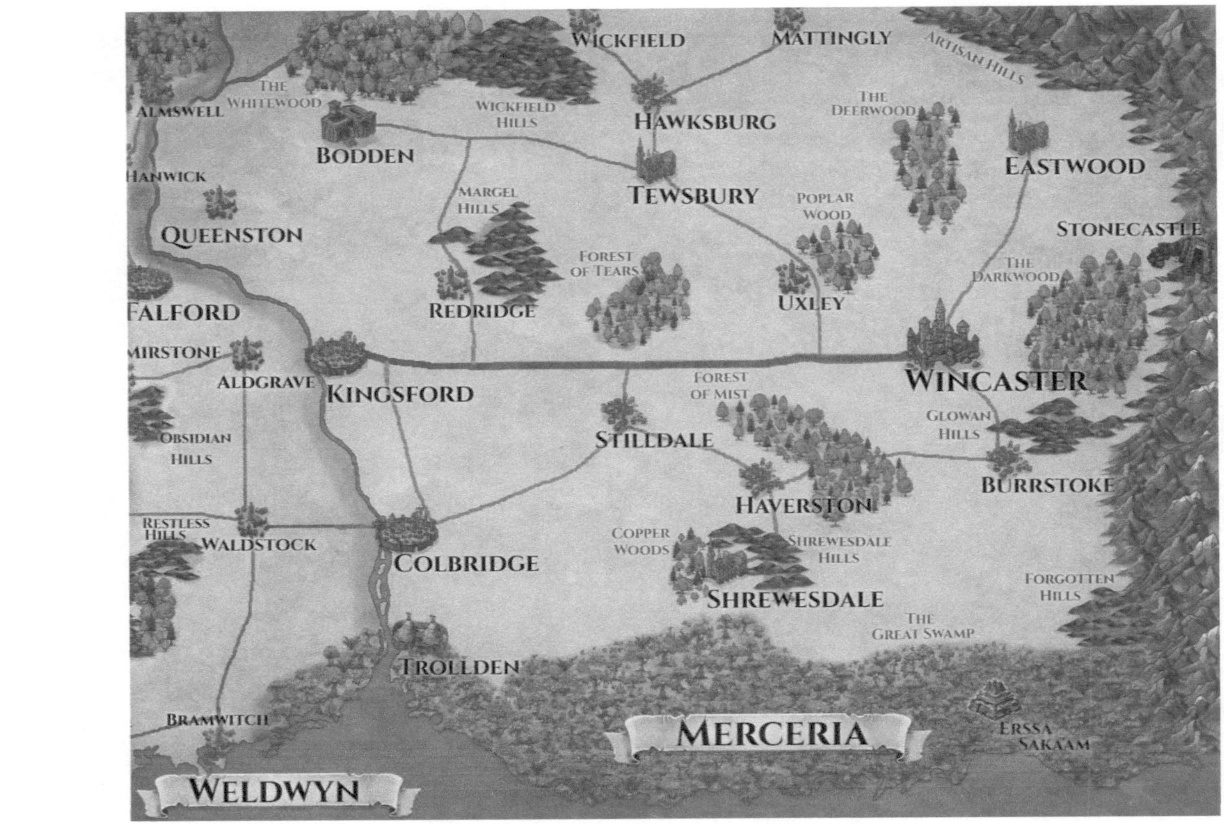

ALMSWELL
THE WHITEWOOD
HANWICK
WICKFIELD
WICKFIELD HILLS
MATTINGLY
ARTISAN HILLS
BODDEN
HAWKSBURG
THE DEERWOOD
EASTWOOD
QUEENSTON
MARGEL HILLS
TEWSBURY
POPLAR WOOD
STONECASTLE
FOREST OF TEARS
THE DARKWOOD
FALFORD
REDRIDGE
UXLEY
MIRSTONE
ALDGRAVE
KINGSFORD
FOREST OF MIST
WINCASTER
OBSIDIAN HILLS
STILLDALE
GLOWAN HILLS
RESTLESS HILLS
HAVERSTON
BURRSTOKE
WALDSTOCK
COPPER WOODS
SHREWESDALE HILLS
COLBRIDGE
SHREWESDALE
FORGOTTEN HILLS
THE GREAT SWAMP
TROLLDEN
BRAMWITCH
MERCERIA
ERSSA SAKAAM
WELDWYN

ONE

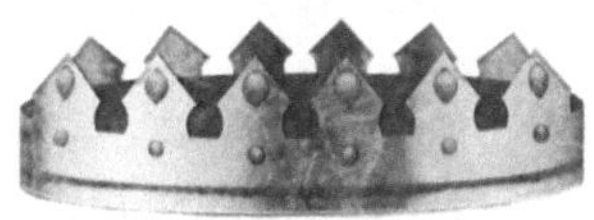

Wincaster

FALL 962 MC* (MERCERIAN CALENDAR)

Lord George Montrose, the Earl of Shrewesdale, paused momentarily, pulling down his shirt to expose the sleeve beneath his tunic. Pleased with the effect, he grabbed the door handle with a firm grip and opened the door to see a room with a group of four men assembled. Instantly recognizing Lord Clive Barrington, the earl made his way towards him, his hand extended.

"Lord Barrington," he exclaimed, "so good to see you."

"Not at all," responded Barrington, "it is I who have the honour. I was overwhelmed to receive the invitation."

Montrose released his firm grip on the man, "And who do we have here?"

"Let me introduce you," said Barrington, turning to the rest. "This is His Grace, Lord George Montrose, the Earl of Shrewesdale, though I suspect you're all familiar with him, at least by reputation."

The remaining three men nodded their heads in agreement.

"This," continued Barrington, moving to the first, "is Lord Landry Pearson, second cousin to Lord Alexander Stanton, the Earl of Tewsbury."

"How do you do?" said Lord Pearson in greeting.

"Fine. How fares your cousin?" asked Montrose. "I hear he's not well."

"He is old, nothing more," replied Pearson. "Though I rather suspect he's not long for this world. He's already outlived most of the family."

"Sorry to hear that," offered Montrose, "but we're glad to have you here in his stead."

Barrington steered him to the next visitor.

"Rowan!" said Shrewesdale with a smile. "I haven't seen you for years."

"Yes, cousin," replied Lord Webster. "I'm glad I could make it, for these are dark times."

"They certainly are," agreed Montrose, "but I look forward to your counsel. How is the family?"

"They are well," said Webster, "thank you for asking. And yourself?"

"Never been fitter," said Montrose, "though I'd be happier still if we didn't have a young girl on the throne."

"Your Grace," interrupted Barrington, "I don't believe you've met Lord Markham Anglesley, the new Duke of Colbridge."

Montrose looked at the plump nineteen-year-old in surprise. He was youthful, but still had the look of determination for which his father had been renowned.

"May I say," offered Montrose, "how tragic it was to hear of your father's death."

"Thank you," replied Markham, showing little emotion. "I know that would have meant a lot to him."

Montrose turned his attention to address the group as a whole. "Please, gentlemen, sit. Let's have some refreshment shall we, there's no need to stand on ceremony here."

Barrington handed out the drinks that were waiting nearby. The Earl of Shrewesdale paused until everyone was seated before continuing.

"Gentlemen," he began, "I have invited you all here today to seek your counsel. As you know, the war that has ravaged our land for so long has finally been put to rest, and a new ruler has taken her place upon the throne."

Murmurs of protest echoed throughout the room, but the earl held up his hand to forestall them. "We may not agree with the result, but her army was victorious in the end. Let us not dwell on the past, but on the future and what we might make of it."

"What do you have in mind?" asked Barrington.

"Before I discuss my own ideas," replied the earl, "I'd like to hear your thoughts on our new queen."

"She's not queen yet," objected Barrington.

"True," said Montrose, "but, regardless of her title, she sits upon the throne. Even as a mere princess, she wields considerable power."

"Is there no one else who can claim the crown?" asked Pearson.

"What about the elder sister, Margaret?" asked Webster.

"Gone, I'm afraid," supplied Montrose, "with little hope of reappearing, I'm told."

"Too bad," grumbled Pearson, "it would have been an elegant solution. I'm afraid we're stuck with this snivelling child, Anna."

"Yes," agreed Webster, "but if we can't remove her, then might we be able to control her?"

"You have an idea?" asked Barrington.

"No," admitted Webster, "but I rather suspect Lord Montrose does. How about it, Your Grace?"

"I have some thoughts I've been mulling about," admitted the earl.

"Do tell," prompted Barrington.

"It has become quite evident to me," continued Montrose, "that our princess is not much more than an impressionable young girl with a close-knit group of advisors that she relies on. These men and women exercise considerable control over her. It is that group that represents the real danger to Merceria, not Anna herself. The princess is only a figurehead."

"So what do we do about it?" asked Pearson.

"We must insulate her from those that would control her, then, when she is at her lowest, we replace her advisors with our own."

"An excellent plan," offered Barrington, "though I rather suspect it will be difficult."

"It will indeed," nodded Montrose, "and one that will take considerable time. This is a long-term plan, not an immediate solution. We must bide our time for the near future. Once we have lulled the princess into a false sense of security, we shall begin removing the influence of her advisors, one by one."

"And how do you propose we do that?" asked young Markham.

"It's rumoured," said Montrose, "that she'll be handing out titles to her friends."

"And?" asked Barrington, eager for more details.

"And titles come with lands. I propose that these lands develop problems that keep them from court."

"We are but a small group," noted Pearson. "How do you suggest we do that?"

"Fear not," offered Shrewesdale, "I have influence beyond these walls, though I won't go into details at this point. In the meantime, we need to expand our group. Be on the lookout for anyone disaffected by the actions of our new princess. She's bound to make decisions that people don't agree with, and we may find that our enemy does our recruiting for us."

"You're a clever man, Your Grace," offered Barrington. "I'm glad you're on our side."

"As are we all," added Pearson, the others nodding in agreement.

"Are there any other questions?" asked the earl.

Colbridge held up his hand, causing the others to wince at the young man's immaturity.

"Yes, Markham?" said Montrose, his voice polite.

"Might I make a suggestion?" the young man enquired.

"By all means," replied Montrose.

"My father once proposed a union between myself and the princess. I could make the offer again, surely she'd see the wisdom in using marriage to unite the factions of the court."

"An excellent idea," commented Pearson, "and one that would save us a great deal of effort."

"How so?" asked Webster.

"Once married," explained Pearson, "young Markham here would rule as king. Technically, we wouldn't need the princess at all."

"We'd need her long enough to produce an heir," added Markham, "distasteful as that might be."

"What do you think, Your Grace?" asked Markham.

"I think it worth a try," agreed Montrose, "and it would save us all a lot of work."

"When, do you think," asked Markham, "would be the ideal time to suggest such a union?"

"I believe it best we float the idea about the court first," said Montrose, "without using your name. If we can convince the other nobles of the wisdom of our logic, then we'll bring it up with the princess."

"I hear we've all been summoned," said Webster.

"Yes," said Barrington, "we're all to be at the Palace this very afternoon, in fact."

"What would you have us do?" asked Pearson, looking to the earl for guidance.

"For now, just listen," Montrose replied. "We need to know how she intends to move forward. When we know that, we can adjust our own plans accordingly."

Once again, they all nodded their heads in agreement. Montrose looked at each in turn, trying to judge their level of commitment. Satisfied that they were dedicated to the cause, he continued, "I must remind you that the task on which we are about to embark might be considered treasonous by some. It is imperative that you speak of this to no one outside of these walls."

"But you asked us to recruit others sympathetic to our cause," protested Webster. "To do so would require us to reveal our plans."

"No," said Montrose, "if you think you've found a new member for our little group, you must first bring it to our attention. It will be for all of us to decide who to include in the future, are we clear?"

They all nodded.

"Very well," he continued, "then I suggest we prepare for court. After all, we must endeavour to make a good impression on our new ruler. We'll meet back here tomorrow evening."

They all stood as one, raising their glasses in salute.

"To the future," proposed Barrington.

"The future," the rest echoed, then downed their drinks in one go.

Montrose watched them leave one by one, shaking hands and smiling. Once they had cleared the room, he made his way to the doorway, then to an adjoining room. His visitor stood, the painting on the wall still askew to reveal an observation hole.

"You heard?" asked Montrose.

"I did," his mysterious visitor replied.

"What do you think? Will it work?"

"I think your plan solid enough for now," the stranger replied, "though we may have to take more overt action in the future."

"You have something specific in mind?" asked Montrose.

"Not at this time, but I rather suspect that our young princess will be resilient to your efforts."

"She's just a young girl," replied Montrose.

"No, she's a young woman," corrected his visitor. "I've underestimated her once already, I'll not do it a second time."

"Come, come now," added Montrose, "you can't possibly believe she can outsmart us."

"Only time will tell," the visitor replied.

TWO

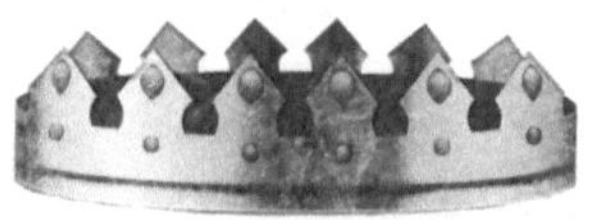

The Gathering

FALL 962 MC

Gerald opened the door just a little, enough to peer through at the assembled guests.

"How does it look?" asked Anna.

"Crowded," he observed. "You're the one that wanted commoners invited, and they're packing them in as tightly as they can."

"It's important," she replied. "They need to know that I'm doing things differently."

"I think they got the message," said Gerald, "I only hope things don't go sideways. Crowds can turn suddenly, without warning. I'd hate to see what would happen if this lot got upset."

"They won't," promised Anna, "and I'm counting on them to keep the nobles in their place."

He turned from the door to look at her in surprise. "You what?"

"The nobles secretly fear the mob. They won't try a power play if the commoners are here."

"It's a gamble," he said, "but I suppose you're right."

"Are the guards all in place?" Anna asked.

"They are," he replied. "Beverly is waiting for your arrival. I only wish we had more knights we could trust. The war may be over, but I can't say I feel safe with Knights of the Sword guarding you."

"I know," she said, "but we've had little time to do much of anything."

"Nervous?" he asked, noticing her wringing her hands.

"Terribly," she replied. "I've never done this before."

"Nonsense," said Gerald, "you held court in Summersgate when you took the oaths of the Kurathians."

"This is different," she defended. "That was all arranged ahead of time. When I go out there today, it will be the first time they hear of my plans. What if they don't like them?"

"They'll like them, don't you worry. Now, let's have a look at you."

Gerald walked around Anna, fussing with the sleeve of her dress. "There, perfect," he pronounced. "There's only one thing missing."

"What?" she asked, her voice squeaking out in fear.

In answer, he stepped across to the other door, opening it wide to reveal her maid, Sophie.

"Did you bring him?" asked Gerald.

"He's right here," Sophie said, then called out, "Tempus!"

The large Kurathian Mastiff bounded down the hall, halting at the door to stare at his mistress, his tail wagging.

"There," soothed Gerald, "now you're all set."

"I can't take Tempus with me," Anna argued, "he'll scare them."

"Nonsense," he replied, "he's docile. And besides, no noble's going to argue with you if he's present."

Anna held her arms out towards Gerald, and the old soldier stepped forward, embracing her.

He could feel her trembling and tried to soothe her. "It'll be all right, Anna," he promised. "We're all in this together." He waited until she gathered her composure before he let go. "Now, let's get you out there, shall we?"

She nodded her head in approval as Tempus took up his place beside her. Gerald peeked out into the great hall again and spotted Hayley close by, their eyes locking for an instant as he nodded his head. The ranger whispered to the steward, and then a horn sounded, the chatter in the room tapering off into silence.

"Announcing," boomed a voice, "Her Royal Highness, Princess Anna of Merceria."

Gerald opened the door, standing to the side as Anna and Tempus entered the hall. There were a few gasps from the audience at the sight of the great dog, but they were quickly drowned out by cheers. It seemed the commoners loved their princess.

He watched as she made her way to the throne at the end of the hall, where Beverly stood with a line of knights and soldiers in front, facing the crowd. As the young princess approached, Beverly turned to bow in her direction, then took up a position to the right of the throne.

Gerald felt someone just behind him and turned to see Sophie peering over his shoulder.

"Come on," he said to her, "let's go inside and get a better view, shall we?"

They stepped through the door, closing it behind them and watched, mesmerized as Anna took her place before the warrior's throne. She held her hands up in front of her to still the voices, and after a bit, the cheering finally subsided.

"Mercerians," she began, "we stand here, today, after a savage civil war. With that conflict concluded, it is time that we band together to build a new future, one free from oppression and corruption. As your new sovereign, I wish to make it clear that under my rule, things will change. When I first took up arms in defence of this realm, it was to protect the common folk, for without you, there can be no nobility or even royalty. It is the obligation of the nobles to look after the commoners, and I intend to do just that."

She glanced towards Gerald, and he could see the sweat on her brow. He nodded at her, watching her take a deep breath even as her left hand sought the head of Tempus.

"As victor and rightful ruler of Merceria," she continued, "it is my duty and pleasure to reward those that have been so instrumental in our success. First, I call upon Lady Aubrey Brandon."

There was a bit of a stir as the young mage pushed her way through the crowd to come before the princess, bending down upon one knee.

"Be it known," Anna continued, "that from this day forth, you shall be recognized as Lady Aubrey Brandon, Baroness of Hawksburg." She waited a moment for the applause to die down, then continued, "Arise, Lady Aubrey."

Aubrey stood, and Anna embraced her, exchanging some quiet words. The baroness backed up, then turned and resumed her place in the crowd.

"That's no surprise," muttered Gerald.

"Wait, there's more coming," whispered Sophie.

Gerald looked at her in surprise, "Really? Tell me."

"Shush, now," said Sophie, a wicked grin on her face, "she's about to speak again."

Gerald returned his gaze to the ceremony.

Now that Aubrey had returned to her previous position, Anna looked like she was seeking someone else in the crowd. Gerald noticed a smile appear on her face as she spotted Prince Alric. The young man was surrounded by a group of his own guards, many in commoner's clothes so as not to create a stir. Gerald knew that Anna and Alric would eventually marry, but they had both agreed that she must put her kingdom to rights first. For now, at least, Alric was just a friendly face in the crowd and a staunch ally.

"I call on Hayley Chambers," declared Anna.

"What?" called out the ranger in surprise. Recovering quickly, she continued, "I mean, yes, Your Highness." Hayley had been standing with the other knights that formed the princess's guard and now turned, moving to kneel before her sovereign.

"Dame Hayley," Anna proclaimed, "from this day forward, you shall be Lady Hayley Chambers, Baroness of Queenston."

Gerald chuckled as Hayley's eyes bulged. Even Sophie failed to stifle a laugh.

"Well deserved," said Sophie, once she caught her breath.

Hayley stood to be embraced by Anna. Gerald wondered what the nobles thought of this, for he knew that King Andred would never have touched a subject, let along embrace them in public.

Before the ranger was allowed to leave, however, Anna spoke once more. "In recognition of your new title and elevation to the ranks of the nobility, we entrust you with this coat of arms."

Two servants came forth, bearing a covered shield. They held it up, facing the crowd, as Anna pulled the cover loose. The cloth fell to the floor, revealing the shield's heraldic symbol, that of a gryphon.

Even from the door, Gerald could see the tears in Hayley's eyes. The young ranger gratefully took the shield, returning to the crowd and her mage, Revi Bloom.

"And now," Anna continued, "with today's proclamations behind us, I have one more announcement. I call on every noble of the realm to assemble here, in Wincaster, by the end of the month to pledge their oath of allegiance. Word shall be sent throughout the kingdom that any who fail to show themselves, without just cause, will be stricken from the ranks of nobility."

She nodded to Beverly, who then gave a command. All the knights snapped to attention, garnering the interest of the crowd. The horn sounded once more as Anna left the room, heading directly for Gerald, who opened the door and followed her, along with Sophie. The young maid closed the door as Anna sat down on a nearby chair.

"How was it?" the princess asked.

"You did well," said Gerald. "They loved you."

"I'm not so sure of that," Anna replied. "I saw several disgruntled nobles out there. Do you think they'll all show up for the oath?"

"I should think so," mused Gerald. "Nobody wants to throw their title away. What was that bit about just cause?"

"That was for Baron Fitzwilliam's benefit," she said. "I need him back in Bodden, keeping an eye on things. I did mention it to him beforehand. Beverly will take the oath on his behalf."

"The other nobles won't like that," said Gerald. "She's not the baron, AND she's a woman."

"They'd best get used to it," she replied, "things are going to be different around here from now on."

"That's the old Anna I know," he said, "but don't try to rush too much through too quickly. We've only just won the war, remember. There's likely still a lot of hard feelings going around."

"I know," she said, "and I'll take it slowly."

"So now that your big debut is over, what's next?" he asked.

"Simple," she replied, "we go and mingle."

"Mingle?" he said. "Surely not, it's too dangerous!"

"I insist," she said. "I'm the people's princess. I want to be amongst them, and no one's going to try to kill me in front of so many witnesses."

"She has a point," offered Sophie. "The crowd would rip any would-be assassin to bits."

"I suppose," said Gerald, "but I must insist you have protection at all times."

"Of course," said Anna, smiling at him, "that's what you're here for."

Gerald moved towards the door again, making ready to open it.

"Not yet," said Anna.

"Why not?" he asked.

"I want to change into something more comfortable first. You wait here with Tempus. Come along, Sophie."

They exited the room, leaving the old warrior alone with the great mastiff. Gerald looked down at the beast and rubbed his head in fondness. "Well, my old friend," he said, "what do you think?"

Tempus's bark echoed in his head.

Prince Alric of Weldwyn looked about the great hall. "Well, Jack," he said, "I'd say the princess made quite an impression."

"I'd have to agree," said the cavalier, "though I was a little surprised when she handed out two baronies. If I'd known they were up for grabs, I'd have put my name in the hat."

Alric chuckled, "You're already in line for a viscountcy, Jack, a barony would be a step-down."

"Yes," the cavalier agreed, "but they come with young women, don't they?"

"Is that all you ever think about?" asked the prince.

"No," he admitted, "I also think about jousting. Why, is there more?"

Alric was just about to respond that there was, but the smirk on the cavalier's face told him he had taken the bait. "What shall I do with you, Jack?"

The cavalier's attention was suddenly occupied by Lady Aubrey, who was moving towards them.

"Baroness Brandon," said Jack in exaggerated tones, "so good of you to come slum with us common folk."

The young woman looked shocked at the comment, and Alric had to act quickly to rectify the situation, "He's just jesting. Please don't take offence."

"Of course not," she said, recovering swiftly. "Her Highness wanted me to make sure you had received your invitation to dinner."

"I did," replied Alric, "and I shall be delighted to be there. Tell me, is it to be a private affair?"

"Only if you think a dozen or so people is private," shared Aubrey. "Though, I daresay that in the coming days, you'll have ample opportunity for 'alone time' with the princess."

"Ah yes, alone," said Alric, "that usually means just the two of us along with half a dozen bodyguards."

"We must protect her," defended Aubrey. "There's still a lot of bad blood from the war."

"Of course," he replied, bowing, "I meant no disrespect. Please, let her know I'll be there."

"You can tell her yourself, if you like," said Aubrey, "she'll be returning here once she's changed."

"Alas, I cannot," responded Alric. "I have letters to write, and we agreed that we should not make our relationship known officially. To the court, we are just allies. I think it easier to maintain that facade if I were to be absent for the rest of this celebration. Please convey my apologies."

"Of course," said Aubrey. "How about you, Lord Marlowe?"

"Much as I'd like to stick around," said Jack, "my place is beside my prince."

"Then I shall see you both this evening," said Aubrey, "and I bid you good afternoon, Your Highness."

"And to you, Lady Aubrey," said Alric.

Revi Bloom smiled back at Hayley, her happiness contagious. "Congratulations," he said, "you've earned it."

"Did you know anything about it?" she asked.

"No," he admitted, "it was a complete surprise to me."

"I would never have expected it. What would my father have thought, I wonder?"

"I expect he'd be as shocked as you," offered the mage. "Imagine, a poacher's daughter now a baroness."

"It isn't as strange as you might think," offered a voice.

They turned to see Commander Lanaka, the Kurathian warrior and leader of the light horse.

"Why would you say that?" asked Revi.

"I've been learning a lot about you Mercerians," he answered. "There were no nobles in the original founders, you know. It was simply mercenary captains giving themselves titles."

"He's right," agreed Revi, "though that was quite some time ago."

"Tell me, Lanaka," asked Hayley, "now that the war's over, what do you intend to do?"

"Settle down, of course," he replied, "and maybe bring the word of the Saints to you heathens." He grinned to indicate he meant no offence.

"So you're going to find yourself a nice little wife and put the horses out to pasture?" asked Hayley.

"No," he replied, "I'm already married. A group of us are going home to retrieve our families. The princess promised us land grants if we settle. This is a rare opportunity for us."

"Why?" asked Hayley. "Don't you have land for sale back home?"

"No," Lanaka replied. "In the Kurathian Isles, there is no land available. It was portioned out long ago, and the islands are overcrowded. That's why we became mercenaries in the first place, to try to accumulate wealth."

"How's that been working out for you?" asked Revi.

"Not well, I'm afraid," confessed the mercenary, "but now you've given us a home. It means a lot."

"And if the Kurathians invade us at some point in the future, will you fight them?" asked the mage.

"Of course," he replied, "we are Mercerians now. We have pledged our service to the princess."

"Well, I, for one," said Hayley, "am glad to have you on our side."

"As am I," added Revi. "Now tell me, do Kurathians drink?"

"Do fish swim?" asked Lanaka. "Of course we drink, I'd have thought you knew that by now."

"Then maybe you might like to drop by later and share a drink with us?" said Revi.

"With us?" said Hayley in surprise. "As in, we're sharing a house now?"

"Well," said Revi, blushing slightly, "that is if you want to? I don't want to pressure you or anything."

In answer, she turned back to Lanaka, "Yes, do come and visit US, Lanaka. I need witnesses."

"I should be delighted," he said, "though I fear it will be after the council meeting."

"Oh, yes," said Revi, "I'd forgotten about that. It'll probably go quite late."

"We could do it tomorrow night," suggested Hayley.

"Yes," agreed Revi, "right after I meet with the Mages Council."

"That won't work," the ranger complained. "You're just setting it up, you'll be there all night."

"How about the next day, then?" asked Revi.

"I have to deal with reorganizing the rangers," said Hayley, "I told you that already."

"Not to worry," said Lanaka, "we shall arrange it when we are all available, we are at peace now, after all. Don't worry, eventually we'll find time for merriment."

Sir Arnim Caster, Knight of the Hound, looked over his soldiers. They were lined up in the hallway, waiting to take up their guard positions under his watchful eye.

"Now, remember," he said, "the war might be over, but you must still be vigilant. If anything appears out of the ordinary, give a shout of warning. Is that clear?"

"Yes, sir," they all replied.

"Arnim," called out a familiar voice.

The knight couldn't help but smile as his wife, Lady Nicole, entered the hallway.

"There you are," she said, drawing closer. "What are you up to?"

"I'm seeing to the Royal Guard," he explained. "This is no time to be lax about these things. There could be enemies at loose in the Palace."

She looked at him in understanding, then continued with her interrogation. "Surely these men can deploy themselves? They've been at it now for weeks."

"It is my duty," Arnim replied obstinately. "Why do you ask?"

"I'm waiting for you to come and dance with me, husband," she said.

"I'll be there as soon as my duty permits," he replied. "I promise, Nikki."

A smirk fell across the face of one of the guards. Arnim wheeled on him suddenly, his face a mask of fury, "Something funny, Baker?"

The man's face became set in stone, "No, sir. Sorry, sir."

"Very well," Arnim said, eyeing the man carefully. He waited a moment longer before looking back to his wife, "I'll be along directly, my dear, as soon as I've seen to these..."

"Soldiers?" she supplied.

"Yes," he agreed, "though I'm loath to apply the name to them."

Nikki watched as Arnim marched them down the hall and then turned the corner, disappearing from sight. She sighed and then resumed her journey to the great hall.

Lord Richard Fitzwilliam watched as Princess Anna made her way through the crowd.

"She looks so regal," said Albreda, "far older than the little girl I first met."

"Indeed," said Fitz. "Did I ever tell you about the first time I met her?"

"No," lied Albreda, who had heard the story many times before, "do tell."

"I was visiting Uxley," he continued, "and Gerald and the princess played a prank on me, pretending she was a hunchback."

"You should have known better," said Albreda, "and what if she had been? Would it have made any difference?"

"Well, no, I suppose not," he sputtered.

He was saved from further explanation by the arrival of the princess and Gerald.

"Baron Fitzwilliam," said Anna, "so good of you to be here."

"Your Highness," said Fitz, "it is my privilege."

"Albreda," added Anna, "your presence is also greatly appreciated. I hear you'll be joining the discussion this evening?"

"I shall," said Albreda. "This Mages Council sounds interesting."

"That reminds me of something," said Anna, motioning to Sophie, who stood nearby. The young maid came forward, scroll case in hand. The princess took it, passing it to the druid.

"What's this?" asked Albreda.

"A Royal Pardon," replied Anna.

"A what?" asked Fitz.

"It came to my attention," said the princess, "that years ago, Albreda was found guilty of the crime of witchcraft."

Fitz turned to the druid in surprise, "Is this true?"

"It is," she admitted, "though I must confess I give it little thought these days."

"I read the transcripts of the trial," said Anna, "and I must say it was a grave miscarriage of justice. I have used my prerogative to overrule the charges and to issue the pardon. You are now free to visit any part of the realm you wish, though I daresay you could have done that at any time without it."

"I don't know what to say," admitted Albreda, "you've found me at a loss for words."

"I'll take it," offered Fitz. "We can frame it and hang it somewhere for all to see."

"Don't be ridiculous, Richard," said Albreda, "who wants to look at a pardon?"

"I would," said the baron. "It will remind me of you when you're away."

She smiled, "Very well, I accept your offer, Princess."

"What do you plan to do now that the war's over?" asked Gerald.

"I had thought to stay in Wincaster a little while," answered the druid, "then join the baron back in Bodden. I'm fascinated by this idea of a magic council. How do you see it working, Highness?"

"I should think much like the one in Weldwyn," offered Anna. "In that kingdom, mages are not allowed to rule. Instead, they carry out their magical studies and act as a source of information for the crown."

"A most logical way of organizing things," agreed Albreda. "I also thought I might pass on some of my knowledge, it appears some of our mages are lacking the basics of the craft."

"You're speaking of Revi Bloom, aren't you?" said Gerald. "He's mostly self-taught."

"So was I," defended Albreda, "and it didn't stop me from developing more power."

"I wish you luck, then," offered Gerald, "you'll have a hard time dragging him away from the magical flames, or temples, or whatever it is we're calling them these days."

"I believe the correct term is magical portals," offered Albreda, "though each mage seems to prefer their own name."

"And what do you make of our mages?" asked Anna.

"It's a diverse group," observed the druid. "A good choice to make up a council of spellcasters. I'm much impressed by Lady Aubrey, she has come a long way in her studies in rather a short time, the mark of a great mage. I look forward to working with her."

"And the rest?" pressed Anna.

"They are all men, and like most male mages, are consumed by their studies. I find women see the larger picture."

"Which is?" asked Fitz.

"We must establish a system of apprenticeship, or all of our knowledge will die with us. We can hardly return to the days before the war."

"In that, we are in agreement," said Anna. "I know that Revi is proposing a school of some sort. I was planning on funding it, but with the expenses incurred by the war, that will have to be put on hold."

"An academy," said Albreda, "I hadn't thought of that. I shall have to give it some consideration."

"In the meantime," suggested the baron, "might I tempt you with a little Hawksburg red?"

THREE

Reforms

FALL 962 MC

Gerald looked around the table, taking in the faces of everyone present. Although technically it was the princess's advisory council, in reality, it was more like her family. He sat to Anna's left, with Tempus on the floor between them, gnawing away at a massive bone. To the other side sat Prince Alric, then the cavalier, Jack Marlowe. Anna had insisted on their presence since, as allies of Merceria, they would wish to be kept apprised of what was happening.

Continuing down the table was Sir Arnim Caster and his wife, Lady Nicole, while just beyond them sat Captain Lanaka and the Kurathian mage, Kiren-Jool. On Gerald's other side sat Beverly, then her father, Baron Fitzwilliam and Albreda, along with Lady Aubrey. Rounding out the group was the Life Mage Revi Bloom and Dame Hayley. No, he corrected himself, she was Lady Hayley now.

Gerald turned to Anna. "We're missing a few by my count," he said.

Anna smiled. "You're correct," she agreed. "Our allies have returned to their respective homes, but they'll be back in due course."

"When do you intend to introduce them to the court?" he asked.

"All in good time," she said, rising from her seat, "but we have other matters to deal with first."

Those in the room went quiet, looking to their princess to commence the proceedings.

"I'm glad you're all here," Anna began. "The war has left us in a difficult situation, one which we must address immediately."

"Which is?" asked Gerald.

"I'm sorry to say," she continued, "that the kingdom is rather short on funds. My brother, Henry, used what little remained to shore up his army, leaving us, as the victors of the war, with little left to run the kingdom."

She paused, inviting feedback.

"What are we to do?" asked Aubrey.

"A good question," said Anna, "and one to which we have several options, but I'd like your opinions before I make any decisions."

"We'll have to reduce the army," said Fitz. "Maintaining a force of this size is too expensive, and as you've already indicated, the war IS over."

"But we can't!" argued Arnim. "If we show weakness, the Norlanders will attack."

"Then we need a compromise," said Gerald. "Keep the north armed and reduce troops in Wincaster."

"Precisely my thoughts," said Anna. "I also wish to reorganize the army and make it more efficient."

"What about our allies?" asked Fitz. "We have Dwarves, Orcs and Elves that helped us. What is to happen to their troops?"

"The Elves have marched back to the Darkwood," explained Anna, "though Telethial will return shortly to represent her people in Wincaster."

"And the Dwarves?" asked Arnim.

"They have also returned home," Anna continued. "I have sent Herdwin to meet with their lord in the hopes of forging a more lasting bond."

"Wait a moment," said Beverly, looking around the room, "I don't see Lily, where is she?"

"She has undertaken a diplomatic mission to Erssa Saka'am to reconnect with her people. It is my desire that she eventually return to us to represent their interests."

"And the Orcs and Trolls?" asked Arnim.

"The Orcs have moved north," answered Gerald, "to patrol the border near Wickfield and Mattingly. They'll be based out of Hawksburg and help with the rebuilding effort, but will be able to respond quickly to any threat in the north. Captain Lanaka will be joining them once his horsemen have recovered."

"I thought everyone was healed?" said Aubrey.

"They are," replied Gerald, "but they have to break in new horses before they march. If you remember, they lost quite a few at the Battle of the Crossroads."

"Yes," added Anna, "and the Trolls have moved into the swamp south of Colbridge. They'll be setting up a village at the mouth of the river and begin clearing it. With any luck, we'll be able to sail ships to the sea by next summer."

"But we don't have any seagoing vessels!" argued Arnim.

"WE do," said Alric, "and I can guarantee you they'd love to ship goods to Merceria, it's a whole new market for them. I would suggest you impose an import tax, nothing too severe, but it'll help defray some of your costs."

"An excellent idea," agreed Anna, "and eventually, I'd like to see Mercerian ships returning the favour."

"I'm sure the shipyards of Southport would love to sell you vessels," offered Jack.

"A welcome offer," said Anna, "but one that will have to wait until we can afford it. Now, getting back to the army, I'm pleased to announce that I'm naming Gerald as marshal-general."

"Surely the baron is better suited," deferred Gerald.

"Nonsense," said Fitz. "You led the army to victory, you've earned it."

"Then I'll accept, under one condition," replied Gerald.

"Which is?" asked Anna in surprise.

"The old organization doesn't work well. Instead of a marshal-general, I shall be just a marshal, with generals beneath me in the chain of command. That will allow us greater flexibility in the future. I'd like the army to be less dependent on a single leader."

Anna nodded her head in agreement. "I like that," she said. "Who would you name as general, then?"

"Baron Fitzwilliam," suggested Gerald, "if he would agree."

"I would be honoured," said Fitz.

"Of course," continued Gerald, "we'll have to draw up a list of responsibilities and such. I'd also like to appoint Beverly as commander of all horse troops."

"And what would that entail?" asked Anna.

"The complete reorganization of our cavalry forces. With few exceptions, our Mercerian horse is woefully under-trained. I thought we'd organize our light cavalry in a manner similar to the Kurathians. I know Beverly has some ideas on the subject, as well."

"What say you, Beverly?" asked Anna. "Will you accept the position?"

"I'd be delighted, Highness," replied the knight.

"Anything else, Gerald?" asked Anna with a smile. "You seem to be particularly well-organized tonight."

"I've been giving the rangers some thought," he replied.

"As have I," confessed Anna. "In fact, I'd already approached Hayley with the idea of making some changes. Tell me what you have in mind, then I'll share my thoughts."

"The rangers should be an important part of an army, acting as skirmishing troops, mounting pickets, watching for enemy troop movements and so on. This, of course, would only be during a time of war, but during peace, they'd have to train in these tactics."

"I agree," said Anna, "and it would fit nicely with their current skill set."

"Excuse me," interrupted Prince Alric, "but can you explain to me how rangers work? We have no such organization in Weldwyn."

"Certainly," replied Anna. "The King's Rangers were originally created to protect the roads back in 600's. Banditry was rife, you see, and trade was grinding to a halt. The king hand-picked them to enforce his laws."

"So they were like a town guard?" said Alric.

"Yes," she said, "but with more authority. These days, though, they have the power of judge, jury, and executioner."

"Isn't that little extreme?" asked Jack.

"It has grown to be so," said Anna, "and that has led to corruption and abuse of their power. That's why we need to implement changes."

"So who's in charge of them?" asked Alric.

"I am, now," said Anna. "They report directly to the reigning monarch."

"You say they patrol the roads, I take it they do that individually?"

"Usually," said Anna, "though perhaps Hayley can tell you more."

"I'd be happy to explain," said Hayley. She pulled forth her ranger medallion that was hanging around her neck. "This,' she started, "is a ranger token. One side has the symbol of the rangers, the other, my number."

"Your number?" said Jack. "What's that mean?"

"Each ranger is issued a number," Hayley explained. "They're never repeated and are given out sequentially. It's the closest thing to rank that rangers have."

"They have no rank?" said Alric in surprise. "How are they organized during war?"

"When two or more rangers work together," she explained, "the lowest number is considered senior."

"I see a problem with that," said Jack. "It only looks at time served. Surely some rangers are more capable than others."

"True," said Anna, "but most rangers operate alone. The system has worked well for more than three hundred years. It is only under King Andred's reign that corruption has emerged on a large scale."

"So how do you propose to change that?" asked Alric.

"I intend to create the office of High Ranger," Anna explained, "and award the position to Hayley. All rangers would report directly to her, and she, in turn, to me. Of course, in wartime, they would be seconded to the army command. What do you think, Hayley?"

"I think it's a grand idea," the ranger replied, "but are you sure I'm the one to command them?"

"You're the most honest ranger I know," said Anna, "and trust me, I've met the worst example. I want the rangers to regain the respect they deserve. No more of this judge, jury, and executioner business. In future, all rangers must bring their charges to a court."

"Understood," said Hayley, "and a welcome change it will be. Will I have the discretion to discharge those that break the rules?"

"Yes," said Anna, "and revoke their lifetime ranger status. I'll leave the details up to you."

"Very well, Highness," said Hayley, "I look forward to the challenge."

"Don't rangers work by seniority?" asked Revi.

"They do," agreed Hayley. "Each ranger has a number, the lower the number, the higher the seniority."

"Well then," said Anna, "I shall issue an immediate order. From now on, Lady Hayley Chambers will be ranger number one."

"What else have we to discuss?" asked Gerald.

"The mastiffs," said Anna.

"Oh yes," said Gerald, "we've sent them to Queenston, the open space there is much more suitable for them. Unfortunately, we have no way of replacing them."

"Yes, we do," said Anna, smiling.

"We do?"

"Yes, we've sent for some breeding stock."

"How did we arrange that?" asked Gerald.

"With Captain Lanaka's help," said Anna.

"Care to explain?" said Gerald, turning to the Kurathian.

"Most certainly, my esteemed friend," the cavalry commander replied. "Many of my men travelled back to Weldwyn to take a ship home. They will return with their families, to make a life here in Merceria, and bring back the coveted breeding stock for the mastiffs, though it will likely take some time to do so."

"How long, do you expect?" asked Gerald.

"Perhaps a year, maybe more," said Lanaka. "The trip alone will take six months, but the courts of Kurathia are notoriously slow in handling requests."

"I don't understand," offered Arnim, "why would the courts be needed?"

Lanaka stroked his beard a moment before replying, "The Kurathian Isles are ruled by individual princes, each holding court separately from the others. They are constantly vying amongst themselves for power and influence. You see, each is an absolute ruler, controlling much of life for the average person. In order to bring back our families, we will need permission from our princes, but it will take considerably more effort to convince them to release hounds to our care."

"But you think it possible?" asked Gerald.

"I do," Lanaka replied. "The breeders have been asking for exports for some time."

"I'd have thought they'd like to keep the mastiffs exclusively for their own use," suggested Arnim.

"The mastiffs were not originally Kurathian," explained Lanaka, "but came to the islands after being captured on the battlefield."

"How interesting," said Anna, "I'd love to know more."

"Alas, so would I," offered Lanaka, "but I'm afraid Kurathian history is not my strong point."

"Let's return to this reorganization you mentioned," interrupted Arnim. "How would it work?"

"Men would still be organized into companies," explained Gerald, "but a larger, more fixed framework would be used in times of war. Baron Fitzwilliam and I have discussed some ideas. Would you like to comment, my lord?" He looked to Fitz.

"Saxnor's sake, Gerald!" the baron exclaimed. "You can't keep calling me 'my lord' if I'm going to be working under your command. You must call me Fitz, or at least just Baron."

"Now, now, Richard," soothed Albreda, "we're all new to this. You must give him time."

"Please continue, Baron," said Anna.

"If you remember," began Fitz, "when we marched on Eastwood back in '60, we organized the army into brigades. It is my suggestion that we formalize that structure. Each brigade would be assigned elements of a supporting nature, such as smiths and wagons and such. In peacetime, the brigades would hold nothing but these extra troops, but in times of war, they would be assigned companies as needed."

"And these brigades," said Beverly, "would take care of all supply matters?"

"Yes," the baron agreed, "precisely, my dear."

"It will take some trial and error," added Gerald, "but the baron and I agreed we'd start in Bodden, forming the first such brigade there."

"Yes," agreed Fitz, "it will let us smooth out the wrinkles and make changes as we go. Once we've reached something that works, we'll duplicate our success elsewhere."

"It sounds like our plans for the army are well in hand," offered Aubrey, "but what of other things, the Nobles Council, for example?"

"That is a little more complicated," replied Anna. "As sovereign of

Merceria, I can do as I please with the army, but I need the approval of the Nobles Council to change the laws of the land, and that includes adding new seats to said council."

"You wanted to add our allies to the council, didn't you? How do you plan to proceed?" asked Aubrey.

"Slowly," said Anna. "I can appoint nobles to fill vacancies, but I must be cognizant of the inheritance laws. My first priority is to convince them to change the laws of succession."

"I'm not sure I follow," said Lanaka.

"At present, in Merceria," the princess continued, "only men may inherit unless there is no male descendant. I intend to change the law to allow the eldest to inherit, regardless of gender. It also means I'll still rule as queen once I'm married."

"I'd be interested to know how Prince Alric feels about that," said Arnim.

"I've discussed this with Anna a few times," said the prince, "and I have no problem with it. I was raised as the third son of the King of Weldwyn, and I have no expectations as far as the crown is concerned. In fact, we're going to hold off the announcement of our engagement until the princess can amend the laws. In the meantime, I can at least help with your army problem."

"How so?" asked Revi.

"I'll place my personal army under the command of the marshal here."

"How many troops is that?" asked Arnim.

"One hundred horsemen," said Alric, "not including my personal guards who I'll still need to protect me on occasion. My father has also agreed to send some troops to help bolster your defences until you can get things in order."

"I would have thought he'd just allow us to use the soldiers you brought to Wincaster for the siege," said Arnim.

"No," replied the prince, "those men didn't volunteer for long term duty. With the war over, they want nothing more than to get back to their families. Those that come in future will be expecting a longer stay."

"It's greatly appreciated," said Fitz. "We owe you a great debt, Prince Alric."

"It's my pleasure," replied the prince. "My father also expressed an interest in a treaty of defence."

"Which is?" asked Hayley.

Alric looked to Anna, allowing her to explain. "It's an idea that I've read about," she said. "Both kingdoms would agree to come to the other's aid in times of war."

"So we'd be permanent allies," said Arnim.

"Only in regards to defence," clarified Anna. "If we were to take aggressive action, attacking Norland, for example, they would not be bound by it. If, however, we were attacked, they would come to our aid, as we would if the situation were reversed."

"It certainly gives us some breathing room," said Gerald, "and the men of Weldwyn would be welcomed in Merceria. They were very much appreciated during the war."

"The defence agreement isn't signed yet," warned Anna. "I have to be crowned first, and there's still much work to be done before that can happen."

"Then when can we expect the coronation, Highness?" asked Aubrey.

"That depends on the Nobles Council," Anna replied, "but I should like to have it next summer. That is the traditional time for an enthronement. Now, I've kept you here for quite some time, and I know there's a lot of work still to do. I shall let you be about your duties."

They all rose, making their way from the room. The princess had made it known that these meetings were to be as informal as possible, eschewing the normal practises of court, and so they drifted off, each deep in conversation with their peers.

The room cleared, save for Anna, Gerald, Aubrey, and of course, Tempus.

"That went well," commented Aubrey.

"Yes," agreed Anna, "though I rather suspect most knew what to expect. I haven't exactly been quiet about the changes I'd like to make."

"So what's next?" asked Aubrey.

"Gerald, here, will take care of the changes to the army while you and I delve into Mercerian law."

"That sounds about as exciting as breaking a leg," responded Aubrey.

"Yes," agreed the princess, "but at least you can heal a broken leg with a spell. I fear making changes to the laws will be much more difficult."

FOUR

Beverly

FALL 962 MC

Beverly halted Lightning and stared. The barracks of the Wincaster Light Horse stood before her, looking much as it had all those years ago when she had been their captain. She remembered the miserable state she had initially found it in and all the work that had gone towards improving it. Now, she wondered how much of that still remained.

Urging her mount forward, the great beast responded instantly, perhaps recognizing the area himself. Halting in the practice yard, she waited, knowing full well that her presence could not help but be noticed.

Sure enough, a soldier exited the offices, and as he drew closer, she recognized him as Sergeant Hugh Gardner, the very same man that had served her back in '54. He walked across the yard, halting just before her and stood smartly.

"Captain," he said, a smile on his face, "good to see you again, ma'am."

"And you, Hugh," she responded. "Tell me, how have the men been?"

"As well as can be expected," the sergeant replied, his tone hesitant.

"That doesn't fill me with confidence," she said. "Let's have a look around, shall we?"

Beverly dismounted, leaving Lightning to make his own way to the water trough, while Sergeant Gardner led her towards the company's offices.

"Are you here to resume command?" asked the Sergeant.

"No," she responded, "I'm the new commander of all cavalry forces. This company is under my chain of command now, though your captain remains responsible for all company matters. Tell me, is Captain Eldridge still here?"

"He is," confirmed Gardner, "not that we see much of him these days."

Beverly halted a moment, causing her guide to also stop. "When was the last time you saw him?"

"Almost a month ago," said the sergeant. "He tells us he's a busy man."

"Busy doing what?" asked Beverly, resuming her march.

"I have no idea, ma'am," said Gardner. "I asked him once, but he told me it was no concern of mine."

"You still have officer's quarters here?" she asked.

"We do," he confessed, "but the captain spends no time there."

They entered the company offices, and Beverly looked around. It hadn't changed much since she left; there was a desk and some shelves, but little else of interest save a couple of chairs. She sat at the desk to see the company ledger open before her.

"Is this up to date?" she asked, pointing at the book.

"It is," said the sergeant, "or at least it was yesterday."

She looked through the entries, paying particular attention to the last few pages. It was hard to read, and she struggled to make out the words written in the awful penmanship.

"Whose writing is this?" she enquired. "It's almost illegible."

"Mine, I'm afraid."

"Why are you doing this?" she asked. "That's the captain's job."

"The captain hasn't been here," the sergeant replied, "and someone had to do it, or we wouldn't be able to collect our pay."

"There are several mistakes here," said Beverly, in an irritated tone.

"Sorry, ma'am," said Gardner.

She softened her tone, "It's not your fault, Sergeant. You never should have been put into this situation."

She closed the ledger, returning her gaze to Gardner.

"So tell me, Hugh, how are the men, really?"

"Well enough," the sergeant replied, "but I'm afraid things haven't been the same since you left."

"Do they still follow the guidelines I left behind?"

"I'm afraid not," said Hugh. "The captain ordered them thrown out. Took too much effort, he said. I hate to speak ill of the man, but he shows no interest in us at all, other than collecting his pay, that is."

"I see," said Beverly. "I shall have to have a chat with this captain of yours. He has a house somewhere in the noble's quarter, doesn't he?"

"He does," admitted the sergeant. "If you examine the orders book, you'll see he's had men dispatched there on occasion."

"Why would he do that?" she asked.

"He uses the men to supplement his staff when he has parties."

"He what?" she asked in shock.

"Here, let me show you," said Gardner. He retrieved the orders book from the shelf, placing it on the table, then skimmed through its pages, stopping when he found what he was looking for.

"You taught us to record all orders we received," he continued, "a habit we've kept up with over the years. You can see an entry here." He turned the book for Beverly to view.

She looked at the entry. Twelve men had been assigned to an address not far from the Palace.

"I take it this is the captain's address?" she asked, pointing at the entry.

"It is," the sergeant confirmed.

"Good, I think I shall pay him a visit."

"What do you want us to do, ma'am?" asked Gardner. "Do we still call you ma'am?"

"Commander will do," she replied, "or you can call me Dame Beverly. I'd like you to prepare the captain's room."

"For what, Commander?"

"Either Captain Eldridge will be taking up residence here, or you'll have a new captain by dinner time."

"I'll get right on it," promised the sergeant.

Beverly returned to the Palace, intending to walk to the house of Captain Eldridge. She saw to Lighting first, then continued on her way, still in full armour. It wasn't a far distance, and she soon found herself staring at a well-situated house, embellished with carved white bricks. To the side was a carefully manicured garden, indicating that great care had been taken in the upkeep of the grounds.

She advanced to the door, where a brass knocker was visible. It was highly polished, so much so that she could see her reflection on it. She grasped the knocker, using it to rap three times on the door.

Footsteps approached, and then a man who looked to be in his forties opened the door.

"Yes?" he said.

"Is your master home?" asked Beverly.

"He is," the man responded, "but he is entertaining a guest. Might I enquire as to who you are?"

"My name is Beverly Fitzwilliam," she replied, "Commander Beverly Fitzwilliam."

If she had expected him to recognize the name, she was deeply disappointed. The servant simply stared at her as if she were a merchant.

"And the nature of your visit?" he pressed.

"I am his new commanding officer," she said, "and I thought it best to introduce myself." She had remained polite, though the servant's lack of deference annoyed her.

"Very well," the man said, sounding as if this was a major inconvenience, "if you'll come with me, I'll show you to the sitting room."

He turned his back on her, annoying her further, but she stifled the urge to yell at him, instead following him into the house. Beverly was led down a hallway into a small room off the eastern side. The servant opened it, beckoning her to enter.

"You can wait here," he said, "and I'll let my master know you wish to speak with him."

"Will Captain Eldridge be long?" she asked, as politely as possible.

"I have no idea," the man replied. He left, closing the door behind him.

Beverly looked about the room at what appeared to be comfortable chairs, as well as a window, but what drew her attention the most were the artifacts. It seemed Captain Eldridge liked the military life, for there was a collection of swords and shields mounted on the walls, and even a suit of well-worn chainmail, decorating a mannequin, sitting in a place of honour.

She moved towards the fireplace to warm herself on this cool autumn afternoon. Above the mantle was a large painting. She had seen paintings before, of course, for Bodden held a very lifelike representation of her mother, but the picture here depicted a battle of some sort. She was examining the details when she heard voices in the hallway, and a moment later, the door opened, revealing Captain Eldridge and another man she didn't recognize.

"I know you," said Eldridge, "you're that Fitzwilliam woman. Beverly, wasn't it?"

"Yes," she said.

He turned to his companion, "I took over the Wincaster Light Horse from her back in '54."

"That's correct," said Beverly.

"What brings you to my estate?" Eldridge asked.

"Matters of the army," she said, looking at his companion. "Are you going to introduce us?"

"Pardon my manners," said Eldridge. "Landry, this is Dame Beverly Fitzwilliam, Knight of the Hound. Beverly, this is Lord Landry Pearson, second cousin to Lord Alexander Stanton, the Earl of Tewsbury. Have you met before?"

"No," said Beverly.

"Charmed," replied Lord Pearson.

"Please," asked Eldrige, "have a seat, will you? You too, Landry. Some wine, perhaps?"

"I still have mine," said Pearson, "though perhaps the lady would care to imbibe?"

"No, thank you," said Beverly.

"Now," said the Captain, "what is it you'd like to talk to me about?"

"The Wincaster Light Horse," she said.

"What about them?" asked Eldridge.

"You are still their captain, are you not?" she asked.

"I am," he nodded. "Why?"

"I just came from their barracks. It seems their books are in poor shape.

"What if they are?" asked Eldridge. "It's of no concern to you?"

"I beg to differ," she said politely. "It is of immense interest to me."

"Why would my company be of interest to you?" he asked. "You gave up that command years ago."

"I see your confusion," she said. "I forgot to mention that I am now commander of all cavalry in Merceria."

"You're what?" said Eldrige in astonishment.

"I am the Commander of Horse," she clarified, "and your direct superior."

"I was not informed of such," he protested.

"I'm informing you now," she said, "and I'm informing you that in future, you will billet with your men one out of every two days."

"I'm to what?" he stammered. "You can't order me about like this."

"I can, and I am," she replied.

"This is highly irregular," he argued. "You can't be my superior, the Wincaster Light Horse reports directly to the marshal-general."

"Changes are being made to the army of Merceria," she said, remaining calm. "You must adapt or surrender your command."

"What in blazes are you talking about?" Pearson interrupted.

"This doesn't concern you, Lord," said Beverly. "It is a matter of military discipline."

"You wouldn't know discipline if it hit you in the face," accused Eldridge.

"Are you familiar with my career?" she asked.

"I can't say that I am," said Eldridge, "though it matters little. I know my rights."

"Your rights?" queried Beverly.

"Yes," he admonished, "I shall take it to your superior, the marshal-general."

"Which is it?" she asked. "The marshal or the general? The ranks have been split, you see."

"Then I shall take the matter to the marshal himself," the captain vowed.

"You're welcome to do so," she said, pleased with herself for not losing her temper. "Now, gentlemen, if you'll excuse me, I have other matters that need my attention. Good day, Lord Pearson, Lord Eldridge, I'll let myself out."

She bowed her head slightly then left the room, making her way to the front door. It would be interesting to see what Gerald made of the man's request, she thought. She must remind herself to check in with him later to learn of his decision.

Gerald looked down at the map spread out before him on the table.

"I suppose we could split the Kurathians between Bodden and Hawksburg," he said.

"I wouldn't," advised Fitz. "They operate better as a group, and I don't really need any more cavalry, I've still got the Bodden Horse."

"A good point," said Gerald. "What else have we got?"

In answer, Fitz looked down at his list, just as there was a knock at the door.

"Enter," commanded Gerald.

A young soldier poked his head in, "A visitor for you, sir. A man named Eldridge, a captain, I believe."

"Very good, Hill," said Gerald. "Send him in, will you?"

"That's unexpected," said Fitz.

"Yes," agreed Gerald, "it seems I'm popular today."

"Indeed," said the baron, "shall I leave?"

"No," said Gerald, "we still have lots of work to do. This will likely only take a moment. Probably someone wants a promotion or something."

Once more, Hill opened the door, revealing a very well-dressed man.

"Captain Eldridge?" asked Gerald.

The captain entered, surprised by the sight of Gerald. Although the man was the marshal of the realm, he wore simple clothes, and within the safety of the Palace, he had even eschewed his regular chain mail shirt.

Fitz looked at the visitor. "Speak, man," he commanded.

"Sorry, my lord," said Eldridge, turning his attention to the baron. "I was expecting the marshal. I was told he was here?"

"He is," said Fitz, pointing at Gerald. "This IS Marshal Matheson."

"I'm sorry, sir," apologized Eldridge. "I didn't realize."

"What can I do for you today, Captain?" asked Gerald.

"I'm here to register a complaint," said the visitor.

"Interesting," mused Fitz.

"What type of complaint?" asked Gerald.

"I have been treated in a most uncivilized manner," the man sputtered.

"Go on," urged Gerald, "I'm listening."

"I was ordered to take up residence in a barracks, my lord."

"Marshal," corrected Gerald.

"Pardon?" said Eldridge.

"I'm not a lord," explained Gerald, "you call me sir or marshal, not Lord."

"Sorry, sir."

"Now, tell me about this treatment of yours. What were you ordered to do again?"

"Live in the barracks with the men," complained the captain.

"I see," mused Gerald, "and who gave you this order?"

"A woman," said Eldridge, disgust evident on his face, "Dame Beverly Fitzwilliam."

Gerald turned to the baron, and with a smirk, asked, "Have you heard of this woman, General?"

"I have a passing acquaintance with her," Fitz admitted. "I hear she can be quite stubborn at times."

"I've heard that too," agreed Gerald, looking once more to their visitor. "Tell me more, Captain."

"She claimed to outrank me, sir, and proceeded to order me about like a common soldier."

Gerald nodded his head in understanding. "I see," he said. "Anything else?"

"Yes," the man exclaimed, "the woman had the gall to come to my home, of all places!"

"How terrible for you," commiserated Gerald.

"The nerve," added Fitz, enjoying himself far too much.

"And she said if I didn't comply," added Eldridge, warming to the task, "that I'd have to resign my position as captain!"

"Ah," said Gerald, "now I see. You've come to offer your resignation." He turned back to the baron, "I think that's your responsibility, General."

"Is it?" replied Fitz. "I don't think so. Surely, as the marshal, that's yours?"

"I'm not here to resign," interrupted Eldridge, "I want the situation resolved."

"And you want us to resolve it for you," said Gerald, "is that it?"

"Yes, sir."

"And you will abide by our decision?" asked Fitz.

"Of course, my lord," swore Eldridge.

"Very well," said Gerald, "tell me, General Fitzwilliam, what are your thoughts on this matter?"

Eldridge's eyes almost popped out at the mention of the baron's name.

"I think the answer is quite clear, don't you?" suggested Fitz.

"I'd have to agree," said Gerald, turning to the captain one final time. "Captain Eldridge, Commander Beverly Fitzwilliam is your commanding officer. Since you have seen fit to question her orders, I will accept your resignation, effective immediately."

"But you can't," objected Eldridge.

"I can, and I have," said Gerald, "and if I hear any more complaints from you on this matter, I shall have you arrested."

"For what?" sputtered Eldridge.

"For disobeying the lawful order of a superior officer," explained Gerald.

The man paled even more, and for a moment, Gerald wondered if he might pass out.

"Hill!" called Gerald.

The door opened a moment later, "Yes, sir?"

"Have guards escort this man from the premises, would you? And if he gives you any trouble, feel free to use force."

"I must object," said Eldridge.

"A lively one," commented Fitz.

"You are free to go over my head if you like," said Gerald, "but I doubt the princess will have time to see you, she has much more important matters at hand. I suggest you accept my decision with grace and humility. Take him away, Hill."

"Yes, sir," promised the guard. Hill waved his hands in the direction of the door then followed as the ex-captain was escorted from the room. The door closed, leaving Gerald and Fitz once more alone in the room.

"That was interesting," noted Fitz.

"He's another Captain Walters," said Gerald.

"Ah, yes," said Fitz, "the man that caused the riots back in '53. I do hope this one proves to be less troublesome."

"You think I handled that badly?" asked Gerald.

"No, my dear fellow. I think you handled it admirably. We need less of those spoiled rich officers and more professionals in this army of ours. Now, shall we get back to work?"

FIVE

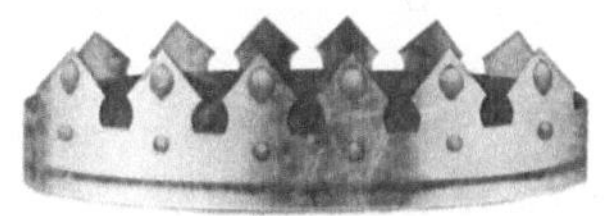

The Mages Council

FALL 962 MC

Aldus Hearn reached across the table, grabbing the wine bottle then sat back, pouring the amber-hued liquid into his goblet.

"Would you like some?" he asked Aubrey, sitting to his right.

"No, thank you," she replied.

He took a mouthful, savouring the taste, then swallowed, placing his goblet back onto the table.

The Kurathian Enchanter, Kiren-Jool, looked to the head of the table where Revi Bloom was reading over his notes.

"Are we ready to begin?" the Kurathian asked.

"Yes," added Albreda, "we've been waiting for some time. Are you ready, Master Bloom?"

In answer, the Life Mage looked up from his notes. "Yes," he said, "I believe I am."

He made a show of straightening his papers, then looked at the assembled mages.

"This is to be the first meeting of the Royal Council of Mages," he began. "I propose that we establish some basic rules and then open things up for discussion. Shall we proceed?"

He looked around to see them all nodding their heads.

"Very well," he continued, "it has been suggested to me that we create this organization similar to that of our brethren in Weldwyn. As some of you know, mages there are not allowed to rule in any capacity, but act as experts to the crown in all matters pertaining to magic."

"I suggest we amend that," interrupted Albreda.

"How so?" asked Revi in irritation.

"Young Aubrey is a baroness. I should hate to force her to give up that position just because she casts magic."

"How do you suggest we amend it?" asked Hearn. "That is to say, what should we change?"

"I think that mages should be banned from seeking the crown, a very clear distinction."

"I shall take it up with the princess," promised Revi. "I can't say what her thoughts would be on this matter."

"What's next on the list?" asked Hearn.

"I'd like to turn our attention to the gates," said Revi.

"The gates?" said Aubrey. "Surely there are other, more pressing matters to discuss?"

"They are of immense importance!" countered Revi. "Am I the only one to see that? What could possibly be of more concern?"

"Lots of things," suggested Albreda.

"Such as?" demanded Revi.

"Well," she continued, "the gates are useful insofar as they can be used to traverse great distances, but we have a far better solution before us."

"Which is?" asked Aubrey.

"The spell of recall," said Albreda.

"I've heard of that," said Hearn, "though I've not used it myself. How does it work?"

Albreda continued, "It allows a mage to travel great distances, though the destination must always be a circle of power."

"You mean a magic circle?" asked Aubrey. "There's one in Hawksburg."

"There is?" uttered Albreda. "I didn't know that. I was thinking of the stone circles in the Whitewood."

"They must be like the one in the Forest of Mist," suggested Revi.

"Another circle?" said Albreda. "How interesting. I must seek it out sometime."

"This spell of recall," said Aubrey, "is it limited to Earth Mages?"

"No," replied Albreda, "that is to say, I don't think so. I believe it's a universal spell."

"Fascinating as that is," said Revi, "there are a rather limited collection of circles we can use. Far better, I think, to focus our attention on the gates."

"Couldn't we make new circles?" asked Kiren-Jool.

They all turned to look at the Kurathian in surprise.

"Well, it only stands to reason," he continued. "After all, someone had to make the circles in the first place. You don't think Hawksburg grew one on its own, do you?"

"I hadn't really considered that," said Albreda. "Tell me, do any of you know how to create a magic circle?"

They all shook their heads.

"Well, somebody must know," said Aubrey. "What about the mages in Weldwyn. Do they have any?"

"Yes," said Revi, "at the Dome."

"The Dome?" queried Albreda. "What's that?"

"The Grand Edifice of the Arcane Wizards Council," said Revi. "It's called the Dome because it has an immense copper dome over it."

"I like the name," said Hearn. "Can we have one of those?"

"In time, perhaps," suggested Revi, "but let's stick to the topic, shall we?"

"Do they have a magic circle there, or not?" asked Aubrey.

"They do," confirmed Revi, "though it's likely been there for centuries. I have no idea if they still know how to make them."

"Unfortunate," said Hearn, "you had us going there for a moment."

"Not so unfortunate," offered Aubrey. "I remember chatting with Roxanne Fortuna just before we left Weldwyn. She mentioned they have an extensive library. I bet the information we'd need would be there."

"An interesting thought," said Albreda. "It sounds similar to the Great Library."

"You mean the Library of Kendros, in Shrewesdale?" said Hearn.

"It's the same thing," said Aubrey.

"Perhaps the answer would lie there, instead?" Aldus suggested.

"No," said Albreda, "I've been there, years ago, I would have remembered."

"You were there?" asked Hearn in surprise. "When was this?"

"Back in '21," she said. "It's not a place I'm eager to return to."

"That's when I began my apprenticeship to Mezin, the scholar," said Hearn.

"It was," added Albreda, "and you were most rude, if I recall."

"I was?" replied Hearn. "I don't remember meeting you."

"It wasn't really a meeting," she retorted, "you barged past me in a rush to get to your master."

"Did I? I don't remember that," defended Hearn, "but I apologize if I did."

"Apology accepted," said Albreda, "even if it is more than forty years late."

"I think the Dome is our best option," interjected Aubrey. "For one thing, it's run by mages, and they're far more likely to be helpful."

"Who shall go there?" asked Kiren-Jool. "I'm afraid it can't be me. Weldwyn doesn't like us Kurathians much, I doubt they'd give me access."

"I agree," said Revi, "but I can't go, I'm far too busy with my studies here. What about you, Aubrey?"

"I wish I could," she replied, "but I have to see to the rebuilding of Hawksburg."

"I'll go," offered Albreda, "but before I do, I'll teach Aubrey the recall spell."

"That would be lovely," said Aubrey. "What can you tell us about it?"

"In order to use it," explained Albreda, "you have to be familiar with the target circle. That requires careful study, which can take hours."

"That's rather annoying," noted Revi.

"It is," agreed Albreda, "and yet, at the same time, it prevents outsiders from using them to gain entry."

"Fascinating," added Aubrey, "I had no idea. How is this studying carried out?"

"We'll talk after the meeting," said Albreda, "I think there are other things to discuss today."

"I look forward to it," said Aubrey. "What's next on the list, Revi?"

The Life Mage consulted his notes once more, then pursed his lips, "It seems Her Highness wants magic circles built in all the major cities."

"Hah," said Aubrey, "I knew she'd think of that, I was just about to mention it myself."

"We've already talked about them," said Hearn, "can't we move onto the next topic?"

"We've talked about finding out how to create them," said Aubrey, "but what about guarding them?"

Hearn stared at her, a confused look on his face. "Why would we need to guard them? Surely only a mage would be capable of using them?"

"But if what Albreda tells us is true..." began Aubrey.

"It is," confirmed Albreda.

"Well, then," Aubrey continued, "we'd have to make sure that foreign mages didn't get the chance to study them."

"An interesting thought," said Kiren-Jool. "How would you propose we do that?"

"I'd suggest guards," said Revi. "Isn't that how you normally protect things?"

"I'd say it's a bit more complicated than that," insisted Aubrey. "You'd need the circle in its own room, with a single entrance. Guards would have to be posted to prevent anyone, without authorization, from entering the room for more than a few moments, that way they wouldn't have time to study it."

"Sounds good," said Revi, making a note on his list. "I'll forward this to the princess for consideration. Would anyone else like to comment on the subject? No? Good, let's move onto the next topic, shall we?"

"Which is?" asked Aubrey.

"Establishing a magical academy," said Revi. "A school of magic, if you will."

"How would that work?" asked Kiren-Jool. "I thought everyone used the apprenticeship method?"

"While there's nothing wrong with apprentices," added Aubrey, "we can maximize our training by combining our collective knowledge."

"You're beginning to sound like Master Bloom," said Hearn.

"We'd have to establish some sort of curriculum," Aubrey continued, "and start by teaching the new students the magical alphabet. That could easily be done by a single person, and why not have a group of students rather than just one. That's the way they teach things in the army, isn't it?"

"It is," agreed Hearn, "but it's taken generations for them to come up with their current system."

"So why can't we do the same thing with mages?" asked Aubrey.

"We wouldn't have enough books," complained Revi. "We'd have to create things from scratch."

"I've already started," confessed Aubrey.

Albreda looked at her in surprise, "You have? What a clever girl you are, Aubrey, I should like to see what you've written."

"I'd be happy to show you," the young mage replied.

"Just a moment," said Hearn, "I just thought of something."

"What now?" asked an annoyed Revi.

"It's about the circles," said Hearn.

"We're done with the circles," said Revi. "We can't do more until Albreda gets back from Weldwyn."

"Let him speak, Master Bloom," said Kiren-Jool.

"Very well, Aldus, tell us your concerns."

"Magic circles are tuned to the magic of their creators, aren't they?" asked Hearn.

"What in the Afterlife are you talking about?" demanded Revi.

"I mean," the old man continued, "that they're likely to be a circle of fire, or water, or of life, is that not true?"

"Yes," admitted Aubrey, "the circle in Hawksburg is attuned to Life Magic, or at least, I think it is. Why?"

"Well," continued Hearn, "it is my understanding that a mage cannot use a circle from a different school of magic."

"That's not quite true," offered Albreda, "a mage can use another school's circle, but at a lesser power level."

"Meaning?" asked Kiren-Jool.

"Meaning," continued Albreda, "that Aubrey, for example, could use the stone circles in the Whitewood, but would not be able to call upon as much power from them as I would. It's also my understanding that one cannot use a circle from an opposite element. In other words, a Fire Mage couldn't use a magic pool, nor an Air Mage use a stone circle."

"We don't have Fire or Water Mages in Merceria at present," said Revi, "so I think it's safe to say that isn't an issue."

"Yes," agreed Aubrey, "but it might not always be so. We must look to the future."

"All of this makes for an interesting discussion," said Albreda, "but until we can make these circles, it is of no use to us."

"Agreed," said Aubrey, "so where does that leave us?"

"After this meeting," said Revi, "Albreda will begin teaching Aubrey the recall spell and show her how to study the stone circles and the Hawksburg circle. Once she's satisfied with Aubrey's progress, Albreda will then proceed to Summersgate, the capital of Weldwyn. I'll give her a letter of introduction to the Dome."

"And the rest of us?" asked Kiren-Jool.

"I think it best," said Revi, "if Aldus returns to the north. It would be handy to have a mage with the army should the Norlanders prove trouble-some, and he's most familiar with the area."

"And me?" asked Kiren-Jool.

"You should remain here in Wincaster, we may have need of your knowledge. We'll reconvene when Albreda returns from her trip. Are we in agreement?"

He looked around as they all nodded their assent.

"Good, then we shall consider this meeting dismissed. Good day, mages."

Albreda was halfway down the hall when Aubrey caught up with her. The druid heard the footsteps approaching and turned, halting her progress.

"Aubrey," she said, "I was just thinking of you. Shall we begin your training?"

The young mage, caught by surprise, asked, "So soon?"

"There is no time like the present," said Albreda, "and I'd like to head off to Weldwyn knowing I've passed on the knowledge."

"How long will it take?" asked Aubrey.

"A few days at most. I thought we'd recall to the eastern edge of the Whitewood first. I'll show you how the spell works, and you can practice a few castings, then we'll move on to Hawksburg. That's the longest part of the trip."

"Why so?" asked the Life Mage.

"We'll have to travel overland, and I'm afraid it's quite some distance. Once we arrive, you can show me this magic circle of yours. We'll also need to put some guards on it."

"What about the stone circles?" asked Aubrey. "Won't they need guards?"

"They are guarded by the woods," explained Albreda. "I doubt anyone could study them without my say so."

"I must say I'm a little leery of letting people into my circle. Not that I object to you using it, but I'm not so sure about others."

"I feel the same," said Albreda. "I have reservations about letting all these mages have access to the Whitewood, though I have no fear where you are concerned. Let us take it one step at a time, shall we?"

"Yes," agreed Aubrey, "but I should at least send word to the princess to let her know I'll be gone for a while."

"A good idea," said Albreda, "and perhaps, while you're doing that, I'll get some nice raw beef."

"Raw beef?" said Aubrey in surprise.

"Yes, it's one of Snarl's favourites."

"Who's Snarl?" asked the Life Mage.

"One of my oldest friends. When I first came to the Whitewood, I was befriended by a pack of wolves. My dearest friend at that time was a wolf named Fang. Through the years, I have kept track of his line. Snarl is one of his descendants. He keeps an eye on things for me while I'm away."

"I should love to meet him," said Aubrey.

"You will," the druid promised, "he loves visitors. I believe the last time he met an outsider was when he met Aldwin."

"Beverly's smith?" said Aubrey in surprise.

"You know of him?" asked Albreda. "I'm surprised, I thought she kept her relationship with him quiet."

"She did," Aubrey confessed, "but since the war, it's out in the open."

"Yes," admitted the druid, "and her father has given his permission for them to marry. It's only a matter of time now."

"Where is Aldwin?"

"I believe he's still here in Wincaster," said Albreda, "but he's due to return to Bodden with the baron."

"She'll miss him," offered Aubrey.

"Yes, but she doesn't need the distraction at this time."

"What does that mean?" Aubrey asked.

"I have visions," said Albreda, "and I think something is brewing here in Wincaster."

"Surely not," the Life Mage retorted, "we drove the Dark Queen out."

"It is not the Dark Queen that threatens the throne this time," Albreda replied, "it is the princess, herself."

"I don't understand," said Aubrey.

"Nor do I, entirely," explained Albreda. "These visions come to me with no explanation. Only the future will reveal the true meaning of them."

Aubrey exited the Palace, walking through the lush Royal Gardens, where Albreda stood waiting for her.

"All set?" the druid asked.

"Yes," said Aubrey, "though I wasn't sure what we'd need to take."

"We shall not need anything," said Albreda, "unless you want a change of clothes?"

"Horses might be handy," suggested the Life Mage. "We have some distance to cover to eventually get to Hawksburg, don't we?"

"Tell me, Lady Brandon, can you ride without a saddle?"

"Of course, my father bred horses," Aubrey defended.

"Then we will be fine. I'll arrange mounts once we arrive at the White-wood, though they may not be what you're used to."

"What kind of mounts?" the young mage enquired.

"You'll see," said Albreda. "Think of it as an adventure. Now, are you ready to learn recall?"

"I'm all ears," said Aubrey. "Where shall we begin?"

"I'll use recall to get us to the Whitewood. Just watch for now, and I'll explain everything else later, once you've had a chance to study the stone circle."

"Does the spell take long to cast?"

"It's a ritual," explained Albreda, "one that takes much longer than a standard spell. Recall consists of two parts, the first determines how many people are being recalled, while the second determines the distance to be traversed. Since there are only two of us, the first part doesn't need much power, but the destination is some distance away. The farther the distance, the more power is required."

"I see," said Aubrey, "and what happens if you fail to cast the second part of the ritual?"

"You would fail to transport. Don't worry, there would be no harm to you, you would simply expend the energy and remain where you started. You could continue the attempt, but it would require the expenditure of more power."

"How far can the spell take you?"

"It depends on your expertise," said Albreda. "I am quite experienced in spell casting, so I can travel great distances."

"Could you recall to Summersgate?" asked Aubrey.

"The capital of Weldyn?" said Albreda. "I suppose so, though I think that would require most of my energy. Of course, I'd also have to have a magic circle memorized there as well."

"This sounds much better than the Saurian Portals," commented Aubrey.

"Yes," agreed the druid. "Now, shall I begin?"

"Please do," said the Life Mage.

Albreda raised her hands and started uttering the words of power. When the air began buzzing with magical energy, Aubrey felt her hair trying to escape its braid. A swirl of wind developed about them, and then small particles of dust and grass seemed to rise from the ground, forming a circular wall that blocked the sight of everything beyond it. Moments later, Albreda's incantation ceased, and the wall collapsed, revealing thick woods and a circle of stones that glowed briefly with magical runes.

"We're here," announced the druid.

"That was... amazing," said Aubrey. She moved towards the stones, examining them closely. "These are magical runes," she observed, "but this is nothing like my magic circle."

"And yet there are similarities," added Albreda. "I rather suspect the runes here will match those in Hawksburg."

"Yes, now that you mention it, they do," confirmed the Life Mage, "all except for this one." She stooped, looking at a rune that lay near the bottom.

"I was never able to identify that one," said Albreda. "There was no record of it in the Great Library."

"That's because it's not magical in nature," offered Aubrey. "It's the mark of the Meghara."

"Meghara?" said Albreda in surprise. "You mean the ancient sorceress? I recall Beverly telling me of her. She said it was a title the Orcs gave to their mightiest spellcasters, wasn't it?"

"Something like that," said Aubrey, "though I suppose the Orcs would have a more complete understanding of it. It seems this circle was made by her. They found her mark in the Forest of Mist, as well."

"Fascinating," said Albreda. "It seems the Orcs were well advanced in their study of magic. We, Humans, appear to have spent years trying to catch up to them."

"I think magic was more common in those days," offered Aubrey. "I would have to say that magic has ebbed since the coming of humankind."

"Nonsense," said Albreda, "the only reason magic has ebbed is because Humans initially feared what they couldn't understand. Even now, there are those amongst us that fear magic. When I was younger, I was accused of being a witch."

"Why?" asked the young mage.

"I manifested my powers. People feared me because I was different. I'm a wild mage, Aubrey. I didn't have a master to teach me what I was."

"That's terrible," commiserated the Life Mage.

"It's long in the past," said Albreda. "Now come, and I'll show you how to study the stones so that you may recall to them. Once we've done that, we'll move over there," she pointed at a spot off in the distance, "then have you cast the spell."

Aubrey proved to be a quick study and was soon using the spell with no help at all.

"What's next?" she asked.

As if in answer, a distant howl echoed through the woods.

"What's that?" asked Aubrey.

"That's Snarl," said Albreda, "I'd know his howl anywhere. He'll be along shortly, and then we can set out for Hawksburg."

"We're walking?"

"No, I'll call on some of my woodland friends."

"Surely you don't expect me to ride a wolf?"

"No," said Albreda, "of course not, but how do you feel about riding an elk?"

"An elk?" said Aubrey in surprise. "Truly?"

"Why not? Though I daresay, it takes a little getting used to."

"And these elk won't mind having Snarl around?"

"Of course not," said Albreda, "wolves only prey on the sick and old." She turned her attention to the trees, "Did you hear that?"

"I didn't hear anything," confessed the Life Mage.

Albreda turned to the north and crouched as a large wolf entered the clearing. It padded over to her, licking her face as she stroked his head. The druid then stood, turning to Aubrey, "This is Snarl, would you like to say hello?"

The young mage moved towards the wolf, holding out her hands hesitantly.

Snarl moved a step closer, licking her fingers.

"He likes you," observed Albreda.

"What's not to like?" asked Aubrey. "I get along with everyone."

The druid chuckled, "So you do. Now, let me summon some mounts for us."

"Didn't you get beef for Snarl?"

Albreda looked down at the wolf, a furrow creasing her brow, "I'm sorry, old friend, I completely forgot. Perhaps I'll bring you some from Hawksburg."

"Isn't he going with us?"

"That's up to him," said Albreda. "What do you say, Snarl? Care to accompany us on a little trip?"

In answer, the wolf sat, then let out a long howl that echoed through the woods.

"It seems we have his answer," Albreda said.

"You can understand that?" asked Aubrey.

"Of course, I'm an Earth Mage."

"Does that mean Master Hearn could as well?"

"I'm not sure about that," mused Albreda. "Aldus Hearn concentrates more on plants and such. If he applied himself, I have no doubt he'd be capable of it, but every druid is unique in their own way, much as you are different from Master Revi Bloom."

"That makes sense, I suppose. It's fascinating, watching what you do."

"What I do?" said Albreda in surprise. "It pales compared to your potential. You can heal the sick, Aubrey, that's no small feat."

"I suppose you're right," admitted Aubrey, "I hadn't really given it much thought. I do so love to help people."

"That's where we differ," added Albreda. "Where you like the comfort of others, I generally detest it, though I must admit there are some exceptions."

"I'll take that as a compliment," said Aubrey, "but shouldn't we be on our way?"

"Of course," said the druid, "just wait a moment."

She cast a spell, this time holding her hands out to the side. It was a short casting, and then a gust of wind began to radiate out from the druid, rustling leaves as it dissipated. It took mere moments for the creatures to arrive, two great elk that made their way into the circle of stones, lowering themselves to the ground before them.

Aubrey looked on in astonishment as Albreda moved up beside one of them.

"They can be a little tricky to mount," offered the druid, "and you should sit back a little farther than you would on a horse, but I think you'll find that once you're used to it, it can be quite a pleasant experience."

She climbed onto the impressive creature's back, then waited as Aubrey did likewise. Albreda nodded her head, touching her hand to the elk's neck as she did. Both stately mounts rose to their feet.

Aubrey's horsemanship served her proud, allowing her to quickly adapt to this strange mode of transportation.

"Shall we?" asked Albreda.

"Lead on," said Aubrey, her face all smiles.

SIX

Parting

———————

FALL 962 MC

Beverly watched as the carriage was finally loaded with everyone's trunks. The first part of the trip would entail a relatively short ride to Uxley Hall. From there, Revi would open the portal to Queenston, making her father's journey to Bodden much shorter. Going with the baron was Aldwin, and, if truth be known, the smith was the only reason for Beverly's presence on the first part of the trip.

Fitz walked around the carriage, stretching his legs, waiting impatiently for the arrival of Revi and the smith. Aldwin appeared first, riding a horse, much to Beverly's delight. The smith smiled as soon as he saw her and Beverly felt her heart skip a beat. After all they'd been through, she still felt excited by the prospect of his company, even if only for a short time.

He rode up beside her, his steel-grey eyes twinkling in the morning light, his smile making the dull weather seem perfectly sunny.

"I'm going to miss you," Aldwin said.

"And I, you," remarked Beverly, "but we'll be together soon, I promise. My father has approved our marriage, and we've waited for what feels like forever."

"I would gladly wait an eternity for you," he said.

"My goodness," said Beverly in surprise, "you're turning into quite the poet."

He blushed slightly. "Albreda suggested I read Califax."

"Truly?" exclaimed the red-headed knight. "You're just full of surprises."

She looked around the area searching for Revi Bloom. The mage was late, which had become a common occurrence these days, and she wondered what might keep him so occupied. She soon saw two riders approaching and instantly recognized the mage and his partner in crime, Dame Hayley. Everyone else's attention turned to the new arrivals, leaving Beverly with an opportunity.

"Aldwin," she said quietly, "come here."

He moved his horse closer until they were stirrup to stirrup. She leaned to the side, kissing him as he did likewise. They parted lips just as her father gave out a call.

"There you are, Master Bloom. I was beginning to get worried."

"Don't worry, Baron," replied Hayley, "I had to drag him away from his studies, but he's here now."

"I'll ride in the carriage," said Revi, dismounting.

Hayley looked over at Beverly and Aldwin, a smile crossing her lips. "I'll join you," she said. "Let me just tie the horses behind the carriage."

"What do you say, Aldwin?" asked Beverly. "Shall we lead or follow?"

"Lead, I think," the smith answered, "it's a bit more private."

Beverly blushed slightly. They had known each other since childhood and had been through so much, and yet when she was around him, she felt so much younger than she was. She heard the crack of the whip, and then the carriage started moving without them.

"Come on," she said, laughing, "we'll lose our position!"

She raced off, making sure Lightning didn't gallop too fast. It would be terrible if Aldwin were unable to catch her, after all.

By noon, they were well on their way, Wincaster left far behind.

"How's the hammer holding up?" asked Aldwin.

"Nature's Fury? Quite well," she replied. "I've been trying out some new moves with it."

"You'll have to show me sometime, I'd love to see your moves." Aldwin, suddenly realizing what he had said, blushed furiously.

She laughed, "And I'd like to show them to you. What are you going to get up to, now that the war's over?"

"It'll feel good to get back to my smithy," he replied, "though I'll miss you."

"Well, I suppose you'll get more work done without me," she said.

"I don't know about that. I like working when you're nearby. Some of my fondest memories are of you sitting in the smithy while I hammered away, but you serve the queen now."

"She's not the queen yet," reminded Beverly. "She has a lot of work to do before the coronation."

"Then I'm surprised she let you accompany us as far as Uxley."

"Even knights are allowed time off every now and again," Beverly said, "and she wanted me to check up on Uxley."

"Check up?"

"Yes, see how the villagers are doing and visit the hall. I've even got a bundle of letters to drop off."

"You get along with her quite well, don't you?" he asked.

"I do," she confessed, "it's like having a cousin."

"Like Aubrey?"

"Not quite the same," Beverly said, "but I feel like I can be myself around the princess. Of course, it's different if it's an official function, but in the privacy of the Palace, she's quite easy to get along with."

"Who would have thought that the Rose of Bodden would become body-guard to a queen."

"Rose of Bodden? Is that what they're calling me these days?"

"It is," remarked Aldwin, "but they mean it in the best possible way. You should be flattered."

"I am," she said, "and it's much more preferable to the names they called me in Shrewesdale."

"Don't pay attention to them," said Aldwin, "they don't know anything."

"Perhaps one day," she continued, "I'll just be known as the smith's wife."

Aldwin laughed, "I very much doubt that. You shall always be the Mistress of Bodden, no one would ever call you that."

"I wouldn't be offended," Beverly said, "though I know you're right, of course. If it were within my power, we'd already be married."

"If it was within your power," said Aldwin, "we would have been married when you were only thirteen."

"True enough," she admitted, "but I'm glad we waited. Our relationship has matured."

"I agree," he said, "and I'm very thankful to your father, I owe him a great deal."

"He likes you a lot, Aldwin," she said. "In some ways, I think you're like the son he never had."

"He doesn't need a son, Beverly, he has you."

"That's sweet of you to say, but I can't continue the family name."

"Why not?" he asked.

"Well, for one thing, you're a Strongarm, that's the name my father gave you."

"I don't think he ever really gave me that name, it's just what he called me. Certainly, the smithy isn't in that name."

"It's not?" Beverly asked in surprise.

"No, I'm simply listed as Aldwin, with no last name at all."

"But what does that mean?" she asked.

"It means," he continued, "that when we marry, I can't give you a last name. You'll remain a Fitzwilliam."

"Does that bother you?" she asked.

"Not at all, why would it?"

"I would have thought that most men would wish their wives to take their name."

"I've loved you for years, Beverly," he said, "and I know you've felt the same way. Our union was an impossible dream, and yet through circumstances I still don't understand, we are to be married. I don't care what your name is, as long as I'm able to hold you."

"I believe that's the sweetest thing you've ever said to me," said Beverly, "though I think we'd do more than just hold each other."

He laughed, finally relaxing. "That too," he admitted.

"There you go," she said, "you've finally let go of all the tense muscles. Do I intimidate you?"

"No, but your father does, at least when you're around. I feel like he's constantly watching me."

"That's because he is," she said. "Don't worry, I'm sure it'll stop once we're married. He just doesn't believe we should be... intimate until we're joined in matrimony. He's very old fashioned that way."

They stopped that night at an inn called the Gryphon's Rest. Hayley thought the name highly amusing and couldn't help commenting on the inaccurate portrayal of the beast on the sign. Beverly was forced to share a room with Hayley, while Revi did likewise with Aldwin. The baron, as befitting a man of his station, was given his own.

They headed out early the next day, turning north onto the road that ran through Uxley itself. Revi and Hayley rode ahead, allowing Beverly and Aldwin to spend some quality time with her father in the carriage.

It was late afternoon when the village came into view.

"It hasn't changed much," said Beverly, looking out the window.

"No, I suppose it hasn't," agreed Fitz. "Do you remember the first time you visited?"

"I could hardly forget," she replied, "the rebellion had just begun. Little did I know what I was getting into."

"Any regrets?" asked the baron.

"None," she replied. "You?"

"A few, actually," he said, surprising his daughter.

"Oh," said Beverly, "like what?"

"Well, for one thing," he continued, "I should have told you that I loved you more often."

"I know how much you love me, Father, it doesn't need to be said."

"Yes, but I always felt you missed your mother's touch."

"This isn't like you, Father, you're growing melancholy."

"Sorry," he replied, "I'm just getting old."

"I think it's more than that," said Beverly, breaking into a grin. "I think you're missing Albreda."

"What?" he said. "Nonsense!"

"Oh come now, Father, it's obvious how you two feel about each other. Having a relationship with Albreda is not a betrayal of Mother, she died years ago. You deserve to be happy."

"What do you think of Albreda?" asked Fitz.

"I quite like her," she said, "though I doubt I'd ever be able to call her mother, she's too much of a friend for that."

"What about you, Aldwin," asked Fitz, "what do you think?"

"Me?" the smith said in surprise. "What have I got to do with any of this?"

"You're marrying into this family," he continued, "I'd value your opinion."

"You would?"

"Of course, why wouldn't I?"

"I'm just a smith," said Aldwin.

"Don't be silly, my boy, you're much more than that. Tell me, what do you think of Albreda?"

"She's nice," he said, "though she can be a bit brusque at times."

"Brusque?" said Fitz in surprise. "That's a strange word for a smith to use."

"He's been reading Califax," explained Beverly.

"Ah yes, the Bard of Shrewesdale. No doubt that was Albreda's doing. She's obsessed with the man's writings."

"Is that a bad thing?" asked Aldwin.

"No," said the baron, "I have to admit he has a way with words. Oh look, there's the Old Oak."

They rolled past the tavern, Beverly waving to Arlo and Sam as they did. Crossing the stream, they trundled up the road towards the estate, anticipating the comfortable beds that awaited them.

The Hall soon came into view, its white stone standing out against the green of the grounds.

"Quite the house," said Aldwin.

"Yes," said Fitz, "it was built years ago as a hunting lodge for the Royal Family. Now, it's a favourite of the princess. I suppose it'll become her country estate soon enough, a place to get away from the intrigue of the court."

The carriage rolled to a stop, and a couple of servants rushed forward to unload their trunks. The baron stepped out, followed by Beverly, and a very uncomfortable looking Aldwin.

"What's the matter?" asked Beverly.

"I'm just a smith," he said. "They shouldn't be waiting on me."

"You're my future husband," said Beverly, "you'd best get used to it. Don't worry, they won't bite you."

They were met by Hanson, the old steward, his white hair draped across a mostly bald head, lending him an air of eccentricity.

"Lord Fitzwilliam," the man greeted, "how nice to see you. Word was sent ahead of your arrival, so we have rooms prepared for you and your guests."

"Thank you, Hanson," said Fitz. He turned to Beverly, whispering, "Do they know about the gate?"

"Hanson does," said Beverly. "The princess thought it best a few people here were familiar with it, though I doubt they've ever seen it."

"Very good," said Fitz, turning his attention back to the steward. "We shall only be here the one night, I'm afraid. I will be travelling through the gate with Aldwin and Revi Bloom, but the rest will remain here until the mage returns. I believe my daughter also has some correspondence for you. We'll see to all of that once we're settled in."

"As you wish, my lord."

The next morning found them all standing before the underground portal. The ancient temple had been discovered over two years ago, and it had taken the mage, Revi Bloom, the vast majority of that time to figure out how it worked. He stood before it now, his attention completely absorbed watching the green flame.

"Quite remarkable," remarked Fitz. "I've heard about it, of course, but have never seen it."

"I've been through it quite a lot," said Beverly. "The first time you'll feel a little disoriented, but it soon wears off."

"Any tips?" asked Aldwin.

"Yes," she said, "make sure you have a firm stance as you go through. It's best to stand still and just touch the flame."

"Won't it burn?" the smith asked.

"You might think so, but no, it is only a magical flame," said Beverly. "Revi will go through after you, and you'll get to see Erssa Saka'am."

"I thought we were going to Queenston," he replied.

"The gates don't directly connect," she answered, "instead, everything has to go through the main temple that lies in the swamp. Once you're safely deposited in Queenston, Revi will return here by the same route."

"Can't you come with us?" the smith asked.

"I wish I could," she replied, "but the flame takes time to regenerate after it's used. The more people that use it, the longer it'll take to recharge. I'm afraid I'll have to say my goodbye's now."

She took his hand, leading him from the chamber so they could have some privacy. Beverly stood before him, struggling with what to say.

"I..." she began, the words trailing off.

"I know," he said, "but we'll be together again, soon enough."

He kissed her, and she held him tight, his arms encircling her. It felt like she was home, and she didn't want it to end, but then they were interrupted by Hayley.

"Sorry, Bev," the ranger said, "but it's time to go. Your father has already stepped through the flame, and it's Aldwin's turn."

"So soon?" asked the red-headed knight.

"I'm afraid so," said Hayley. "I'll give you two a moment more." She returned to the room where the magical flame waited.

Beverly breathed in his scent then stepped back, relishing the image before her.

"I must go," said Aldwin.

Beverly nodded her head, too emotional to speak. She followed him back into the portal room, green light flickering from the flame.

"You may step through now, master smith," said Revi.

Aldwin nodded, moving closer to the flame. He took a firm stance, then touched it and was whisked away in an instant. The flame collapsed in on itself, then slowly started building up again.

"You all right, Bev?" asked Hayley.

Beverly nodded, wiping a tear from her eye.

Once the flame reset, Revi stepped through, without so much as a wave.

Hayley stood with her hands on her hips, a look of astonishment on her face. "He didn't say goodbye!" she declared. "That's not like him."

"What's that?" asked Beverly, her composure now returned.

"Revi," said Hayley. "He's been a little off lately, but he didn't even say goodbye before he stepped through the flame. That's just not like him."

"He was likely overthinking things," suggested Beverly, "I wouldn't read too much into it. Anyway, he'll be returning before too long."

"I suppose you're right," said the ranger. "Oh, that reminds me, I have something in my pack."

"You do?"

"Yes, I thought that since we have to wait for my errant mage to return, we might as well have a drink." She reached in and pulled forth a bottle of wine. "Here we go, a nice Hawksburg Red."

"A good choice," said Beverly, "one of my father's favourites."

"And that's not all," added the ranger, "I also brought some cheese."

"Please tell me it's not from Hawksburg, I can't stand the smell of that stuff."

"Relax," said Hayley, "it's a nice white Stilldale."

SEVEN

Hawksburg

FALL 962 MC

Snarl ran ahead, while Aubrey and Albreda made their way into Hawksburg. The war had not been kind to the city, and burned-out skeletons of houses lined their progress.

"Good gods," said Albreda, "the city is devastated. I knew they'd torched it, but I didn't expect this level of destruction. Did they leave any buildings standing?"

"A few," said Aubrey, "mostly those without thatched roofs."

"The troops were lazy," said Albreda, "and likely didn't want to take any extra effort. What about the manor, is it intact?"

"It is," said the Life Mage, "but most of the furniture is gone."

They rode up the street, the sounds of chopping wood coming to their ears. Soon, they could make out the manor house, its front courtyard packed with people. Orcs mingled with the Humans, cutting wood into more manageable sizes.

Albreda halted, dropping to the ground. There was no use bringing the elk any closer. Aubrey did the same, and they continued on foot, the wolf trailing behind them.

"Lady Aubrey," called out a rough voice.

The crowd parted, and the Orc shaman, Kraloch, came forward. "It's good to see you again," he said. "It has been some time since you last visited us."

"Good to see you, Kraloch," Aubrey said. "What progress have you been making?"

"We have set up temporary housing in the common," the Orc replied, "and started building more permanent structures. We aim to have a number of them done before winter arrives."

Aubrey looked around at the crowd, Humans and Orcs working together to rebuild the city. "Will it be enough, do you think?"

"Hopefully," said Kraloch, "we started by building longhouses, what you would call barracks. They will hold people until the spring thaw, though it will be crowded."

"I'm surprised by the number of people here," observed the druid. "Didn't many flee when the attack came?"

"Yes," answered Aubrey, "and most of those went to Queenston to settle. I doubt they'll return."

"You still have a sizable population from the look of it," observed Albreda.

"Indeed we do," the Life Mage replied, "but I wish we had some defences."

"The war's over," Albreda reminded her.

"For how long?" asked Aubrey. "If the Norlanders find out how weak we are, they'll make a move against us."

"Defences will have to wait," said the druid. "The people must be protected from winter above all else."

"I suppose you're right," she said. "What can we do to help?"

"Talk to your people," said Kraloch. "That alone will give them hope."

Aubrey turned to Albreda, but words failed her.

"Go ahead," offered the druid, "the circle can wait. See to your people first." She turned to the Orc, "Master Kraloch, how may I be of assistance?"

"What can you do?" asked the shaman.

"I can move earth. Perhaps I can clear away the remains of the burned-out houses?"

"That would help immensely," replied Kraloch, "for it would allow us to concentrate solely on building."

"Show me the way, my friend," said the druid.

The two women worked in Hawksburg for almost a week, clearing away rubble and helping wherever they could. It soon became a common occurrence to see them walking through the devastated area, the large wolf trailing them.

One evening, as they sat on makeshift chairs before the fire, cold winds blew in from the north.

"Winter will be here soon," mused Aubrey. "You need to get on the way to Weldwyn."

"True enough," replied Albreda, "but we haven't looked at this circle of yours. Perchance we should do that first?"

"When?" asked Aubrey. "We seem to have had no time."

"Why not now?"

"Now?" asked the Life Mage.

"Why not?" asked Albreda. "We are merely sitting here, we might as well put the time to good use."

"Very well," said Aubrey, rising. "Come along, and I'll show you the old manor house. It was used by my great grandmother."

They made their way out back, crossing the grounds to the structure. Aubrey led the way, carrying a lantern, while Albreda followed, along with Snarl.

The Life Mage entered the building, turning to the left and what was left of the old library.

"For Saxnor's sake," she said.

"What is it?" asked Albreda.

"They stripped away most of the books, there are hardly any left." Aubrey knelt, picking up a ripped cover and showing it to the druid. "This was signed by Califax himself," she said, "and look at it now, nothing but a ripped and torn cover."

"Why is the bookshelf crooked?" asked Albreda.

"I had to flee in a hurry," Aubrey explained. "I was in the casting room when they came for me. I grabbed the book and ran. I didn't have time to hide anything."

"The book?"

"Yes," replied Aubrey, "the spellbook of my great grandmother. I have it in Wincaster now, safely locked away in the Palace."

"Show me this casting room," said Albreda.

Aubrey walked over to the wooden shelf that was slightly apart from the wall, revealing the stairs beyond. She pushed it the rest of the way, moving to the top of the stairs.

"There's a single room beneath the library, that's where the magic circle is."

"Lead on," said Albreda.

Aubrey took two steps and then stopped. "There's a body here!" she said.

Albreda moved closer, her interest piqued, but then glanced back to the wolf. "Snarl doesn't detect any danger," she said. "He's got a good sense for that type of thing."

Aubrey moved forward, stepping past the body into the room.

Albreda followed, pausing to examine the body in more detail. "He's been burned," she said.

"How did that happen, I wonder?" said Aubrey. "I had no flame here."

Albreda examined the arch over the door. "I suspect it was a trap, I see evidence of a rune. See this scorch mark here?" she pointed.

"How would that work?" asked Aubrey.

"This rune would likely activate if someone passed through the door."

"But I went through, and I didn't activate it."

"True," said Albreda, "but you have magical potential."

"But my father..." she objected.

"He was in close proximity to you," Albreda explained. "But of more interest is the fact that it was a rune of fire."

"Meaning?" asked the Life Mage.

"Meaning that a Fire Mage must have created it."

"We don't know of any Fire Mages in Merceria," said Aubrey, "though I know of at least one in Weldwyn."

"Your great grandmother lived long before either of us," said Albreda. "I suspect there were many more mages in those days."

"What do you suppose happened to them all?"

"I don't know," said the druid, "perhaps they died off without training apprentices."

"There's at least one other explanation I can think of," offered Aubrey.

"Which is?"

"We know Lady Penelope is an Elf, and they're immortal. Could her agents have hunted them down over the years and eliminated them?"

"It's quite possible," said Albreda, "but if that's the case, why was your grandmother spared?"

"I'm not sure," said Aubrey, "but as far as I know, she never passed her gift onto an apprentice."

"No, I suppose not," said Albreda. "But at least she had the foresight to leave her spellbook here, for you to find."

"Perhaps she had visions," offered Aubrey, "like you."

"An interesting thought. Perhaps she knew more than she let on."

"When I first found this room," said Aubrey, "the magic circle was covered by dirt."

Albreda moved into the room, gazing at the floor. "She must have wanted to hide its presence, I can think of no other reason. What do you know of your great grandmother?"

"Not much, I'm afraid. Her name was Juliana, though she was known as 'Nan' to my parents." Tears came to Aubrey's eyes unbidden. "Sorry, this place reminds me of when my father and I first found it."

Albreda moved towards the young mage, hugging her. "I understand," she said, "losing a family is a great tragedy. Believe me, I know."

Aubrey stepped back, looking at her in surprise, "You do?"

"Yes," admitted the druid, "I lost my mother when I was eight, and my father was killed by Norlanders when I was thirteen."

"So young!" exclaimed Aubrey. "How did you manage without them?"

"I found the Whitewood. It became my home, and the wolves looked after me."

"Is that how you discovered you were an Earth Mage?"

"No," said Albreda, "that came later. I didn't understand it at the time, I was still quite young."

"I'm sorry," said Aubrey, "I had no idea."

"It's long in the past now," the druid continued, "and we cannot live in the past. We must continue forward, as they would have wanted us to."

"You're right," said Aubrey, wiping away her tears.

"Now," said Albreda, "let's examine this circle of yours in more detail, shall we? I've never seen a circle of Life Magic before. I assume that's what we call it."

"Why? Is there another name for it?"

"Possibly," said the druid, "I'm not the expert in such things. I know stone circles are used by Earth Mages, and I read somewhere that Necromancers use pentagrams. I would imagine each school of magic has its own terms, but magic circle would apply to all of them, regardless of their actual type. What do you think we should call it?"

"How about a circle of life?" asked Aubrey.

"Life circle might be more appropriate," offered Albreda, "though it matters little. We can call it whatever you like. After all, you're the one that discovered it."

"Then life circle it is," said Aubrey.

Albreda crouched, examining the edge in more detail. It was actually two circles, one inside of the other, with the space in between decorated by magic runes.

"These symbols match those in the Whitewood," observed the druid.

"Yes," agreed Aubrey, "and I think I found the creator's mark."

"Creator's mark?"

"Yes," repeated Aubrey, "just as the Meghara left her mark on the stone circles, so too, did someone mark this one. It's the only rune that isn't part of the magical alphabet."

"So it is," agreed the druid, shifting her position slightly. "Do you recognize it?"

"No," replied Aubrey, "and I saw no indication of it in any of my great grandmother's notes."

"Notes? You found more than just spells?"

"I did," said Aubrey. "Aside from the spells, there was a whole host of additional information, often scribbled randomly in the margins. Most of it was beyond my understanding at the time. I'd only mastered a few spells before Valmar came to Hawksburg."

"What a vile creature he is," said Albreda. "He deserves a terrible death for all the things he's done."

"Agreed," said Aubrey.

"And since then?"

"I've been so busy with the war that I haven't returned to my studies. It still sits, waiting for me to investigate further, and now, with Hawksburg in ruins, I have even less time."

Albreda returned her attention to the floor. "The workmanship on this is masterful. I suspect it must have taken a great amount of effort."

"I noticed that too," said Aubrey. "It looks like it's set in gold. It likely cost a fortune."

"Yes," agreed the druid, rising to her feet. "I suspect the princess's idea of putting circles in all the major cities is going to cost a great deal more than she thought."

"If this is a life circle," asked Aubrey, "can you still use it?"

"There's only one way to find out," replied Albreda. "I'll commit this one to memory, then recall here from close by. I'll stand just outside of the circle when I cast."

"What can I do?" asked Aubrey.

"Some better light would help."

Aubrey cast a spell, illuminating the room with a glowing ball of light, "Is that better?"

"Perfect," said Albreda. "Now I shall get to work, as should you."

"Me? I've already used the circle to cast spells."

"Yes," said Albreda, "but to recall to it, you must memorize it. Now come along, we have a lot of work ahead of us."

It took the rest of the evening to commit the circle to memory. Aubrey found it quite easy to recall to it, but for Albreda, it was a bit more of an effort, no doubt due to the fact it wasn't a stone circle.

They had resolved to return to the Whitewood in the morning, for there was one more location for Aubrey to memorize, and so it was that bright and early the next day, they stood in the basement once more. This time, they had taken pains to close the concealed door that led into the room. Snarl followed Albreda, curling up on the floor within the circle.

"Why are we standing in the circle?" asked Aubrey. "Surely we can cast from anywhere?"

"We can," said Albreda, "but if you cast within the circle, it will amplify your spell."

"I noticed that when casting other spells," remarked Aubrey, "but I hadn't realized it would affect a recall."

"Oh, yes," said the druid, "it will amplify any spell you cast. Even I can feel its effect, and it's not of my school. It must, indeed, be a powerful creation."

"Circles can be of different strengths?" asked Aubrey. "That surprises me, I thought they were all the same."

"No," said Albreda, "they can vary a lot. The two circles in the Whitewood are different from each other. The one in the east is more powerful, though we still don't know how they're created."

"I find this whole topic quite intriguing, I wish I could go to Weldwyn with you."

"I'd like that too," said Albreda, "but you're needed here, there is so much work to be done. Are you ready to return to the Whitewood? We still have a circle for you to memorize."

"Yes," said Aubrey, "though I'd like to return us to the eastern circle first if you don't mind. I want to see how much energy it requires."

"By all means," said the druid.

Aubrey took her place in the centre of the circle and started to cast her spell. The inlaid gold runes began to glow, and then a vertical wall of bright white light shot up from the circle, obscuring their surroundings. As she completed the incantation, the wall disappeared, revealing woods all around them. Snarl let out a howl.

"Someone's glad to be home," said Aubrey.

Albreda was standing perfectly still as if straining to hear something.

"What is it?" asked Aubrey.

"Someone's in the woods," the druid replied.

"Who?"

"Soldiers," responded Albreda. "They've crossed the river from the north."

"Norlanders!" uttered Aubrey.

"Precisely."

"How do you know?"

"The trees told me," said Albreda.

"What do we do?"

"We shall have to investigate," said the druid, turning to Snarl. She placed her forehead to his for a moment and then the great wolf bounded off into the underbrush. "I've sent him to find the pack. In the meantime, keep an eye out, I'm going to cast a spell."

Albreda closed her eyes, uttering words of power. Aubrey felt the magic tingling in the air, then the druid began weaving about, reminding Aubrey of Revi Bloom when he looked through the eyes of his familiar.

"I see them," said Albreda, her eyes still closed. "It looks like two dozen or so, nothing we can't handle."

"I'm a Life Mage," protested Aubrey, "what can I do against that many soldiers?"

Albreda opened her eyes, "Let's see, shall we?"

The two mages made their way through the woods. The farther they travelled, the easier it became to hear the interlopers.

When they halted, Albreda cast a spell. Moments later, Aubrey's dress turned from blue to multiple earth colours, blending in with the background. The druid soon repeated the process on herself.

"You are now blending in with the woods," said Albreda. "Be warned though, if you cast a spell, the effect will be dispelled."

They crouched, watching the men's progress. They were clearly soldiers, cutting their way through the brush with long knives and axes.

Albreda turned to look behind her as a pack of wolves approached. "Ah," she said, "our reinforcements have arrived. Time to take action, I think."

She beckoned Snarl forward then pressed her forehead to his again. Once she released him, he led the pack off to the side, intent on flanking the intruders.

Aubrey watched the scene unfolding before her as they waited, and then Albreda stood and began gesticulating. The trees surrounding them bent to her will, while the branches whipped out, striking the soldiers. Some fought back, but there was little they could do against trees. Albreda cast again, and this time, a small light sailed across the distance to strike the ground in front of the men.

Moments later, vines erupted from the point of impact, and the screams of pain and terror that emanated from the Norlanders signalled the wolves to rush forward, growling. Aubrey couldn't see what was happening, but she could certainly hear as flesh was rent and swords struck out. Soon, the soldiers ran in fear, but Albreda rushed forward, casting once more. A tree pulled itself from the ground blocking the Norlanders retreat with its branches. The noise of fighting soon subsided.

Aubrey rose from her position. "Should I heal them?" she asked.

"No," said Albreda, "there can be no survivors."

"Surely we could take prisoners?" asked Aubrey.

"No," repeated Albreda, "invaders never leave the Whitewood alive.

Their complete annihilation is the price they pay for violating the sanctity of the woods. If any were to make it home with news of what they encountered, they would return equipped to meet us. That must never happen."

A wolf trotted from the fray, limping badly.

"I understand," said Aubrey, "but at least let me heal your wolves."

"Of course," said Albreda, "that would be most appreciated."

Aubrey cast her spell, her hands glowing with energy as she placed them upon the wolf, watching the light absorb into her patient, curing the wounds.

"What now?" Aubrey asked. "Do we bury them?"

"No," responded Albreda, "the woods will see to their bodies. We must travel westward to the other circle and thence to Bodden, the baron must be made aware of this incursion."

"Didn't we leave the baron in Wincaster?" asked the Life Mage.

"We did, but I know he intended to return to Bodden. He's likely there by now."

"And if he isn't?" asked Aubrey.

"Then we'll wait there until his arrival. Don't worry, they'll let us in, they know me there."

EIGHT

Bodden

FALL 962 MC

Baron Fitzwilliam entered the map room, still clutching his drink. It had been a hard ride from Queenston, but now that he was here, he was eager to get back to work. He placed his goblet on the table, making his way towards the cabinet that held his maps. Poking through them, he found what he was looking for and laid it out on the table, using his goblet to anchor one corner.

The map revealed the geography of Merceria, but, he noted, it was badly in need of an update. He sought out quill and ink, then sat, pulling some notes from his tunic.

The baron thought of himself as an educated man, and while he had to admit his maps weren't perfect, he prided himself that they were as accurate a facsimile as could be constructed. He had made careful notes concerning Queenston's location and now sat pondering them with great interest. Content with his observations, he dipped the quill and amended the map of the realm, adding Queenston to its rightful place.

He was pleased. Queenston sat roughly halfway to Kingsford, and with the war over, he could look forward to an influx of trade. Soon, a road would be cleared, and Bodden would no longer feel as though it were all alone in the wilderness.

Fitz sat back, admiring his work, then realized there were other maps now in need of updating. Taking a sip of his wine, he stood, making his way to the window. A cool breeze drifted across the barony, presaging snow, and he knew that it wouldn't be long before the icy grip of winter made itself known once again.

A call from below caught his attention, and he spied two figures off in the distance, heading towards Bodden. That, by itself, was not unusual, for farmers could often be seen returning from their fields, but the presence of a wolf beside them told him that one of them was Albreda. The bigger question was, who was the other?

The baron made his way from the tower, then out of the Keep, confident that he would reach the gates of Bodden long before the druid arrived.

The guards, already alerted by their approach, now manned the walls. They were not expecting trouble, but the baron had drilled into them the necessity of always being on the alert. Having suffered three sieges in his own lifetime, Fitz was not willing to take chances.

He climbed to the top of the gatehouse and peered over the battlements. The travellers were closer now, and the baron could easily make out Albreda's features. He turned his attention to her companion, a look of surprise coming to his face as he recognized his niece, Aubrey Brandon.

"Let them in," he called out, then made his way down to greet them.

"Richard," called out Albreda, "I see you made it back in good time."

"I did," he stammered back, "but I must admit I'm surprised to see the two of you. If I'd known you wanted to visit, I would have had you travel with me."

"Hello, Uncle," said Aubrey.

"You surprise me, Aubrey," he said. "I never would have thought I'd see you in Bodden so soon. I must say this is delightful!"

"I'm afraid we're not here on a social call," interrupted Albreda. "We've come across some Norlanders."

"Where?" he asked, instantly alert.

"In the Whitewood," added Aubrey, "but Albreda took care of them."

"It's odd that they would try to enter the wood," said Fitz. "What do you make of it?"

"Let's go to the map room, shall we," suggested the druid, "and we'll show you where the incursion took place."

"Good idea," agreed Fitz. He looked past the two ladies, "Have you no horses?"

"No," said Albreda, "I've been teaching Lady Aubrey how to use magic to travel quickly."

"Ah," said Fitz, "a subject I must admit is a little beyond my understanding. Come, let me feed you and then you can tell me all about your adventures."

"Perhaps we should eat in the tower," suggested Albreda, "I think time may be of the essence."

"Very well," agreed Fitz, turning to one of his soldiers. "Send for Sir Heward and Sergeant Blackwood. Have them meet us in the map room." He returned his attention to his visitors, "Come along then, let's get you up there. I've just started updating my maps."

"Updating them?" asked Aubrey.

"Yes," he replied, "I thought it best to add Queenston to them. After all, it's not really a hidden base anymore."

"And how do you feel about that," asked Albreda, "having another town so close?"

"It's not really close," said Fitz, "it's still some seventy miles or so distant."

"Yes," said the druid, "but it will, no doubt, increase trade. I suppose you'll have an influx of people, as well."

"Perhaps," he mused, "and Saxnor knows we could use it, but don't worry, the Whitewood will still be safe, I promise you. Now, tell me about these Norlanders."

"We ran across them quite by happenstance. We had just recalled to the eastern end of the wood."

"Recalled?" said Fitz. "What's that?"

"A spell, Uncle. It allows instantaneous travel."

"Ah, now I see," said the baron. "That's what you used during the war. I thought perhaps you had some kind of gate like the princess has."

"No," explained Albreda, "it's a spell, and I've been teaching it to Aubrey. She's proven to be a quick study."

"And so you encountered these raiders," he prompted.

"Yes," the druid continued, "we had just arrived, and my sentinels alerted me to it. We decided to investigate."

"By yourselves?" asked Fitz. "That sounds a tad dangerous."

"We had help, Richard, never fear. The animals of the Whitewood came to our assistance."

"How many were there?" he asked as they began taking the steps up to the map room.

"No more than two dozen, I'd say."

"None of them escaped," added Aubrey.

"None? I would have thought one or two might have run away."

"No, Richard, I can't permit it. If even one were to relay what they encountered, their fear of the woods would be broken."

"Still," said Fitz, "two dozen, that's a sizable party, though not enough to carry out an invasion."

"We thought so too," said Aubrey. "Albreda felt you might have some ideas on the matter."

They entered the map room, taking up positions around the table, just as a couple of servants appeared bearing wine and a promise of food.

"Can you show me where you ran across them?" asked Fitz.

Albreda examined the map, then stabbed down close to where the Whitewood joined the Wickfield Hills. "Here," she said.

"Interesting," he mused. "They likely thought the chance of discovery was low."

"What do you think they wanted?" asked Aubrey. "There's not much of value there."

"No," agreed the baron, "but odds are they were trying to avoid detection by the Witch of the Whitewood. That's what they call you, isn't it, Albreda?"

"Yes," she admitted, "amongst other things."

"But why?" continued Aubrey. "And why such a small group?"

"I suspect they wished to infiltrate our borders in order to get information about our troops. They've always wanted to conquer us."

"Why?" asked Aubrey. "I've never understood why they bear us such malice."

"Norland was founded by a member of the Royal Family of Merceria," said Fitz.

"What?" said the Life Mage in surprise.

"It's true, I'm afraid," added Albreda. "The war we fought wasn't the first rebellion in Merceria. Back in 520, the king's sons fought over their claims to the throne. The defeated son fled north, founding Norland. They've been trying to reclaim the throne ever since."

"But aren't we at peace with the Norlanders?" asked Aubrey.

"Actually," added the baron, "we've never been at peace with them. There is no treaty or agreement between our two realms."

"So we're still at war, after all this time?" said Aubrey.

"We are," he confirmed.

"So what do we do now, Richard?" asked Albreda. "Surely this won't be their only attempt?"

"Likely not," agreed Fitz. "I should like to get word to the garrison at Hawksburg. We'll need to step up patrols and take greater care, be on the lookout for small groups."

"I can carry word to Hawksburg immediately, Uncle," suggested Aubrey. "I can recall there now."

"That is most fortuitous," continued the baron. "I should like to send Heward there to take command, then I'll need you to return to Wincaster and let them know what's going on. What about you, Albreda?"

"I'm afraid I'm off to Weldwyn," replied the druid, "on a matter of some importance."

"I'll be sorry to see you go," he confessed. "Is it anything I can help you with?"

"No," said Albreda, "I have to visit the mages in Summersgate. We'd like to construct more magic circles, and they are said to have the knowledge we need. I doubt your presence would be of any benefit, though I'd welcome the company, of course."

He looked at her a moment before continuing, "I must admit it's a tempting offer, but my place is here, especially with Norlanders hopping about."

Their discussion was interrupted by the arrival of Sir Heward and Sergeant Blackwood.

"You sent for us, Lord?" asked Heward.

"Yes, Heward, we have word of a Norland incursion. A minor one, to be sure, but still of concern. I fear there may be further attempts. I can't shake the feeling that they're preparing for something big, and I'd like to be ready. I'm going to send you to Hawksburg and put you in charge of the area. You'll remain there until the marshal sends word."

"Very well, my lord. When shall we leave?"

"I'll get you there by supper time," said Aubrey.

The great knight looked at her in surprise, "Indeed?"

"I have a circle of magic there," she explained.

"Will I be able to take my horse?" asked Heward.

"I don't see why not," she replied. "It shouldn't strain my powers much."

"I take it," offered Blackwood, "that you want our patrols stepped up, Lord?"

"I do, Sergeant," said Fitz. "Have them start first thing in the morning."

"Aye, sir," said Blackwood. "Is there anything else?"

"No," said the baron, "but let the men know our old foe is up to something, I don't want any surprises."

Sergeant Blackwood left the room, his footsteps echoing back up the stairwell.

"With your permission, Lord," said Heward, "I shall gather my things."

"Very well, Sir Heward," said Fitz, "I'll have Lady Aubrey meet you down by the stables."

The great knight hurried from the room, leaving Fitz, once again, with the druid and his niece.

"Uncle," said Aubrey, "might I ask you a question?"

"Of course, my dear," the baron replied.

"I heard a rumour that you were offered a Dukedom, is that true?"

"It is," said Fitz. "Her highness offered me the Duchy of Eastwood, but I declined."

"Surely not," said Aubrey in surprise, "it would have been a great honour."

"Indeed it would," defended Fitz, "but my place is in Bodden. I have no desire for power, and my life is here." He looked to Albreda, and their eyes met, leaving no doubt as to his meaning.

"I'm sure the princess was disappointed," Aubrey added.

"She was, to be sure," said Fitz, "but Bodden has been my whole life. She understood that."

"Well I, for one, am glad to see you back here, Richard, keeping the north safe," said Albreda.

"I'd have to agree with that," offered Aubrey. "I only wish I'd had more time to see Bodden."

"It can't be helped, my dear," said Fitz. "Though perhaps, before you disappear, I'll give you a quick tour. At the very least, you should see Aldwin's forge. After all, eventually he'll be family."

"I'd like that," said Aubrey. "Any idea how much longer we'll have to wait for that happy day?"

"I don't think it will be much longer," said the baron. "Now that the war's over, there's very little to prevent it from happening."

Aubrey stood ready, watching as Heward rode up.

"You'll have to dismount," she said. "I don't think the ceiling in Hawksburg is high enough for you to remain seated."

Heward climbed down from his seat, leading his mount to stand beside the Life Mage.

"How long will this take?" he asked.

"Not long," she said. "It'll be over and done before you know it."

"I have done this before," he said. "I travelled to the circle of stones in the east of the Whitewood."

"This will take us to the inside of a building," said Aubrey, then paused.

"What is it?" Heward asked.

"I just remembered something. We'll appear in a basement. Will it be a problem getting your horse up the stairs?"

"I don't know," admitted the knight, "I've never tried."

"We'll give it a go," said Aubrey, "but if not, I'll have to return him here."

"Can you do that?"

"Not directly, but Albreda showed me the western stone circle, it's relatively close by."

"Well," suggested Heward, "perhaps we'd best be on our way. I'm ready whenever you are."

"Very well," said Aubrey, "don't move from your present position, it will take me some time to cast the ritual."

She raised her hands, bringing forth the words of power. A white circle appeared on the ground, centred on the mage. As she spoke, a cylinder of light formed around them and blocked their view of Bodden. As the magical words continued to pour forth, Heward noticed the air growing stale. He felt a slight tingling sensation, and then the cylinder of light dropped, revealing a rather small room, that rapidly turned dark.

"Hold on a moment," said Aubrey.

Again Heward heard her speak the strange words, and then a globe of light lit the room.

"It's a tight fit," observed Heward.

"The steps are over here," said Aubrey. "Let me just open the secret door up top." She entered the stairwell, the light following her. Moments later, Heward heard a scraping sound. "All set," she called down.

Heward moved forward to examine the stairwell. "The steps are narrow," the knight observed, "but not too steep. I'll have to lead him." He started up the stairs, the reins securely in his hands.

"A few more pounds and he'd be stuck," said the knight. "If you're going to use this in the future, you might want to consider widening the stairs."

"I think we'd need to do a bit more than that," said Aubrey. "I believe the whole first floor should be gutted, and the ceiling needs to be taller, not to mention guards."

"Guards?" he asked.

"Yes, we discussed this at the Mages Council. We need to guard the circles to make sure others can't use them."

"You need an engineer," observed Heward. "I hear the Dwarves are good at that sort of thing."

"You sound like my cousin," said Aubrey. "Beverly always thinks of Dwarves when some feat of construction is required."

"I'll take that as a compliment," said the knight.

"As well you should. Now come, I'll introduce you to Kraloch, he commands the garrison at the moment."

"You have an Orc in charge of Hawksburg?" asked Heward. "You surprise me."

"They've been helping us rebuild," said Aubrey, "and the townsfolk have become quite fond of them."

"I thought he was a shaman?"

"He is, what of it?"

"Do their shamans command their warriors?"

"Yes," said Aubrey, "why wouldn't they?"

"I don't know," said the knight, "I just assumed that shamans were like mages, and I've never heard of a mage commanding an army."

"My understanding is that a shaman isn't allowed to become a chieftain.

Beyond that, they do the same thing as every other Orc. Kraloch was of great assistance during the war."

"I meant no disrespect," said Heward, "but I had very little interaction with them. They are a fascinating race."

"Agreed," said Aubrey, "and Kraloch speaks our language quite well. You should have no trouble working with him."

When they exited the house, the fresh scent of the woods drifted in their direction, while off in the distance, they heard the sound of hammering and sawing.

"Sounds like you've kept them busy here," Heward said.

"Yes," she agreed, "but there's still so much to be done. The garrison is helping with the rebuilding effort, but with the incursions, you'll likely have to send many of them farther north."

"I'll try not to disrupt things here too much," he promised.

They rounded the manor house, revealing an area busy with workers. Kraloch spotted them immediately and made his way over.

"Greetings," offered the Orc. "I see you have returned."

"I have," said Aubrey. "May I introduce Sir Heward?"

"Good day to you," the knight said, bowing his head slightly.

"And to you, master knight," said Kraloch.

"Heward will be taking command of the frontier," said Aubrey. "There's been an incursion by Norlanders, and we're to be put on alert."

"My hunters are at your disposal," offered Kraloch.

"Hunters? I thought you had warriors?" said the knight.

"They don't use that term," explained Aubrey, "but it amounts to the same thing. Kraloch, I wonder if you might fill Sir Heward in on the local troop dispositions? I'm afraid I must make haste to Wincaster on urgent business."

"By all means, Lady Aubrey," said the Orc, "I shall be delighted."

"Excellent," said the mage, "then I will leave you to it."

NINE

Changes

FALL 962 MC

Beverly watched as the nobles filed through the doorway. They had all come, as the princess had expected, to take their oaths on the morrow, and now each made their way into a banquet that had been prepared in their honour.

The Knight of the Hound nodded her head in recognition of Lord Somerset, the Duke of Kingsford. He, at least, was a staunch ally, but other than her own friends, the rest were mostly an unknown quantity.

Beverly spied Lord George Montrose, the Earl of Shrewesdale, and tried to hide her disgust. He had been one of King Andred's closest advisors, and in her mind, should not be trusted. Their eyes met, but the earl, wisely, did not challenge her. She was here today representing her father, and as such, was wearing courtly attire, a far cry from her armour, though she had insisted on keeping her sword.

Lord Alexander Stanton, the Earl of Tewsbury, was next to arrive. He had been ill of late and was walking with the aid of a cane and two servants who helped him.

Young Lord Markham Anglesley rounded out the top nobles. As the son of the previous Duke of Colbridge, he was the only heir to that position, but his support of King Henry made Beverly wonder, yet again, the wisdom in letting him maintain his title. Perhaps it would have been better, she thought, to have them all executed?

Next in seniority came Lord Emery Chesterton, the Viscount of Stilldale. He had remained as neutral as possible during the conflict and was an unknown factor as far as his support for the princess went.

Lastly was Lady Aubrey Brandon, now the Baroness of Hawksburg and one of only two baronesses in the kingdom, along with Hayley. Beverly fell in beside her cousin as they made their way into the hall.

"I hear you went to Bodden," said Beverly. "How was it?"

"Quite nice," replied Aubrey. "I've never been there before."

"I trust things went smoothly?"

"Quite the opposite," replied the mage, "but I'll have to tell you about it later."

They followed the other nobles past the open door, to enter the dining hall itself. Servants guided them to their seats ,which, due to their lower station, were at the far end of the table. The place at the head was reserved for the princess, with a mat on the floor beside her, intended for Tempus. On either side were seats reserved for the dukes. Under normal circumstances, all four positions would have been filled, but King Henry had not named a Duke of Wincaster before his death, and the Duchy of Eastwood was still vacant after the flight of Lord Roland Valmar. Despite their absences, there were still seats for these two titles. Beyond them sat the two earls, followed by two chairs for viscounts, with only one filled, as the Viscountcy of Haverston had been vacant since the death of Anna's brother, Alfred, back in '60, yet another position that must be awarded.

Aubrey sat in her assigned place, while Beverly, looking down, realized that a spot for the Baron of Redridge sat between them. He had been Lady Penelope's brother, also killed during the war. Eschewing protocol, she sat directly beside her cousin, thus putting her at maximum distance from the Earl of Shrewesdale.

With all the nobles in place, a servant rapped the floor with a cane, drawing everyone's attention.

"Her Highness, Princess Anna of Merceria," he announced.

Everyone stood as she entered, draped in a finely made dress of a rather simple design. Tempus trotted in beside her, growling slightly as they approached the table, perhaps sensing the mood of the room. She stood at the head for a moment, taking everyone's measure.

"Please be seated, gentlemen, ladies," the princess said.

They all sat, keeping their eyes on their new monarch.

"I have invited you here today to address you before the oath-taking ceremony tomorrow. I know that we have been through a lot this last year, but I wanted to assure you that my reign will begin with fairness and civility. I can see that some of you have questions, perhaps we should begin with Lord Stanton?"

"Your Highness," said the Earl of Tewsbury, "may I first say that you impress me with your grace and humility."

"Thank you, Lord Stanton, but perhaps we should dispense with the compliments, or I fear we will be here all day. What is your question?"

"I was wondering," the old man continued, "what is being done about replacing our missing members?" He swept his arm around the room, indicating the multitude of empty chairs.

"They will be filled in due course," replied the princess, "but I fear it will take some time. We are still awaiting a full accounting of our losses, and family trees must be consulted to determine the most eligible candidates."

"And what," spoke up Lord Chesterton, "is the status of our army?"

"A good question, my lord," replied Anna. She turned to the door where her maid stood waiting. "Will you show them in, Sophie?"

Sophie opened the door, admitting Gerald, Hayley, and Revi Bloom. They filed in, standing in an informal line to Anna's right.

"These are some of my advisors," continued Anna. "I know that there are a few of you that haven't been introduced, so let me rectify that. First is Gerald Matheson, Marshal of our Mercerian Army."

Gerald bowed. He appeared extremely uncomfortable in his courtly tunic, and Beverly wondered where Sophie had found such an outfit. It certainly looked strange, seeing him without his customary chainmail shirt, but then again, she, herself, was wearing a dress.

"Also, we have Lady Hayley Chambers, Baroness of Queenston, and head of the Queen's Rangers."

Hayley bowed slightly, as was the Mercerian custom for women warriors.

"Baroness," said Anna, "please take your place at the table."

Hayley moved down to the far end to sit beside Beverly, nodding at her friend.

"Lastly," continued Anna, "we have Master Revi Bloom, the Royal Life Mage and head of the newly formed Mages Council."

The mage blushed slightly as he bowed his head.

"Gentlemen," she said, looking at Gerald and Revi, "please take a position by our most noble dukes. Be advised that they are here as advisors, so that you, the nobles of Merceria, might be able to receive the information you would like in a timely manner."

She waited as Gerald and Revi sat, then turned back to the Viscount of Stilldale.

"Would you be so kind as to repeat your question, my lord?"

"Yes," Lord Chesterton repeated, "I think I can speak for everyone here when I ask what the status of the army is at present? Can we protect ourselves from foreign aggressors?"

Anna nodded at Gerald.

"Yes, my lord," the marshal began. "Currently, we have the bulk of our forces garrisoning Wincaster. We have secured our western border, and don't anticipate any trouble there for some time to come."

"Why is that?" asked Lord Stanton. "Surely we must keep all our cities well garrisoned?"

"Her Highness has concluded an agreement with Weldwyn, my lord, which will guarantee peace with them for the foreseeable future."

"And what was the price of that agreement?" Stanton pressed.

"Yes," added Lord Chesterton, "are we to cede them land?"

"Not at all," interrupted the princess. "Our agreement with Weldwyn is one of mutual trust and admiration. It is also my intention to sign a defensive alliance once I'm queen."

"Alliance," asked Montrose, "surely not! We cannot trust the Westlanders."

"I beg to differ," interjected Beverly, "they have proven to be most trustworthy."

"I must protest the inclusion of this woman," fumed Montrose. "She holds no title and is not fit to sit at this table."

"I am here at the behest of my father, Baron Fitzwilliam," said Beverly, her voice rising slightly. "I have every right to be here."

"I say not!" decried Montrose. "And where is Baron Fitzwilliam, is he to forfeit his title?"

"I have granted him a special dispensation," said Anna, "for the north needs guarding, and he is the most suited to take up that role. In his place, I have allowed Dame Beverly to speak on his behalf."

"There is no precedent," pressed Montrose.

"Actually, there is," said Beverly, standing. "My uncle stood as proxy for my grandfather when King Andred III was crowned. The king invoked the ancient laws of our ancestors, though you can challenge me to trial by combat if you disagree."

"That's true," added Aubrey, "though I might remind you that no stand-ins are allowed. Does anyone here wish to challenge Dame Beverly's right?"

The room fell silent. Montrose was seething but wisely held his tongue.

Hayley grabbed Beverly's hand, whispering, "Come, sit, Bev. Don't let him get to you."

Beverly sat, her eyes boring into Lord Montrose.

"I'm sorry," said Lord Chesterton, looking at Anna. "You said there was trouble up north?"

"Yes," continued the princess, "we have recent accounts of Norland raiders crossing our border."

"How recent?" asked Lord Anglesley.

"Just over a week ago," replied Anna.

"How did you get such information so soon?" asked Anglesley. "Surely, a rider would have taken two weeks or more to make it to Wincaster from the frontier?"

"I brought it," said Aubrey.

"You?" said Anglesley. "And are you the fastest rider in the kingdom?"

"No," she admitted, "though I am a mage."

Montrose looked at her in surprise. "What kind of mage?" he enquired.

"Life Magic," she replied. "I used spells to speed my journey."

"And who reported this incursion?" asked Montrose. "How do we know we can trust them?"

"I was there," Aubrey said, "along with the druid, Albreda. She defeated the incursion."

"By herself?" asked Lord Chesterton. "How preposterous!"

"It's true," she defended. "As I said, I saw it myself."

"It couldn't have been much of a threat if a single woman could deal with it," accused Anglesley.

"You haven't seen her use her powers," said Aubrey.

"I can attest to the powers of Albreda," said Anna, ending all arguments. "I think the point here is that there is a threat in the north."

"Agreed," said Gerald. "In response, we've sent more horses north. They'll be reinforced with foot once we've completed demobilizing our army."

"Demobilizing?" said Montrose. "You mean to reduce our army now, in the face of this threat?"

"We have little choice, Your Grace," said Gerald. "We lack the necessary funds to maintain the forces we have."

"Then we should levy taxes," suggested Anglesley.

"The people of Merceria have already born the brunt of the civil war," said Anna. "I will not see them suffer further."

"How many troops are being disbanded?" asked Lord Chesterton.

"Almost half, my lord," said Gerald.

"Your Highness," spoke up Lord Stanton, "are you sure this man is competent to command the army?"

Anna's voice rose sharply, "Marshal Matheson's abilities in this matter are beyond reproach. He is the reason that my army was victorious in this war. Without him, we would not be here today."

"I would suggest," said Lord Chesterton, "that we let the marshal deal with this problem and move on to other topics."

"Agreed," added Aubrey.

"Very well," said Anna. "Lord Somerset, did you have a question?"

"Yes, Your Highness," said the Duke of Kingsford, "I should like to address the question of your succession."

"My succession?" said Anna in surprise.

"Yes," he continued. "There can be no argument with your sitting on the throne. After all, you did win the war. My question, rather, is what would happen if you should be incapacitated? You have no heir at present. Who would rule in your absence?"

"A good point, Your Grace," she replied, "and something I have given much thought to, of late. If something were to happen to me, I would like someone who I know I could trust to carry out my plans. Someone who would have the support of people that are important to me. Until I bear an heir, I appoint as my successor, none other than Marshal Gerald Matheson."

"This is an outrage!" shouted Montrose. "You can't appoint a commoner as ruler of our kingdom." He turned to Gerald, "I commend you on your military service, Marshal, but that does not make you fit to rule."

"Actually," continued Anna, "you're correct when you say a commoner cannot rule Merceria, that's why I have elected to elevate him to the ranks of the nobility."

"What!" exclaimed Stanton. "You can't just make anyone a noble."

"I most certainly can," said the princess. "I might remind you that when our mercenary ancestors came to this land, there were no nobles at all. Over time, the different company commanders became the leaders, eventually adopting the titles we use today. It is in the spirit of our ancestors that I do so now."

"Fine," fumed Montrose, "so you can make him a baron, that still doesn't give him the right to rule."

"He will not be a baron," said Anna, her voice growing firmer. "I hereby appoint him Duke of Wincaster."

Everyone in the room was shocked into silence, especially Gerald, who was surprised by the statement.

"It is the right of the Monarch," said Lord Somerset. "The Duchy of Wincaster has always been the prerogative of the crown."

"A most interesting development," said Lord Chesterton, "and one which, I think, will likely take some time getting used to. In the meantime, I believe there are other matters to discuss. Might I enquire as to the topic of matrimony? Surely Your Highness should wed?"

"And I promise you, I will," said Anna, "but we have much to deal with first."

"Might I suggest, Highness," said Montrose, "that you pick a noble of Merceria. It would serve to unite an otherwise fractious realm."

"I will consider it," said Anna. "Do you have a candidate in mind?"

"I would suggest," said Montrose, "our very own Lord Markham Anglesley, Your Highness. He offers an excellent pedigree and is close to you in age. I think it would be a most excellent match. What say you, gentlemen?" he looked around at the other nobles, completely ignoring the three ladies at the far end of the table. The men were all nodding their heads in agreement."

"I shall consider it," said Anna, smiling, "though he would have to agree never to rule."

"I beg your pardon?" asked Lord Stanton. "What do you mean he'd never rule? Surely by marrying you, he would become king."

"No," she replied, "the man I marry will never be King of Merceria, I will not allow it. And while we're at it, my firstborn child shall rule after me, regardless of gender."

"You can't mean that?" demanded Stanton. "It goes against all our laws."

"Not anymore," said Anna, "I intend to change the laws."

"This is too much!" declared Stanton. "You invite us here and then dictate these unacceptable terms to us."

"You are free to leave, Lord Stanton," said Anna, "but I remind you that if you fail to give your oath tomorrow, you will forfeit your lands and title."

They all looked around, shock on their faces.

"I think the time for pleasantries is over, gentlemen," the princess continued. "I intend to make sweeping changes to this kingdom. No more will the elite rule at the expense of the commoners. I will bring law to this land, that each person may be treated fairly and without malice, rich or poor. No longer will nobles judge those below them in summary justice. I invite you to participate in this new future or step aside to allow its progress. Those that oppose my reforms will find themselves out of favour."

She stared at each in turn. It was a strange sensation, this young woman staring down these great men of power, but Beverly knew that her predecessors had taken great pains to put all the power in the hands of the crown. The great nobles of the realm had little choice, for the princess's army controlled the kingdom.

"Might I say," said Lord Somerset, timidly, "that I wholeheartedly agree with you. It's about time that reforms were made."

"As do I," said Lord Chesterton, much to Anna's surprise. "I, too, think that the distribution of power amongst the nobles had led to rampant corruption and abuse."

"Thank you, gentlemen, for your kind words," said Anna, rising. "I think this meeting is concluded. I look forward to seeing you all tomorrow. Now, you may leave."

They all rose quietly, making their way to the door. Anna's eyes met those of Beverly, indicating the ladies should remain. She waited till all the noblemen left, then sat back down. Only Anna, Gerald, Revi and the three ladies now sat at the table.

"You shouldn't have done that, Anna," said Gerald. "You've made enemies."

"I already had enemies," said the princess, "but at least now they're out in the open."

"Yes," agreed Gerald, "but you still need support to pass your laws, don't you?"

"Yes," added Aubrey, "you'll need a majority of council votes."

"How does the council work?" asked Hayley. "This is all so new to me."

"Dukes and earls count as two votes," explained Aubrey, "while everyone else gets but a single vote."

"Then surely we have enough?" said the ranger.

"No," said Aubrey, "the vote count is always based on the total seats, meaning the empty seats count."

"I still don't understand," said Hayley.

"Let me put it this way," said Aubrey, "under normal circumstances there are four dukes and two earls, making a total of twelve votes. Add in the two viscounts and three barons..."

"Four barons," reminded Beverly, "you have to add Queenston now."

"I stand corrected," continued Aubrey, "so two viscounts and four barons adds six extra votes, making a grand total of?"

"Eighteen," said Hayley. "And so to pass laws requires a majority of ten votes?"

"Exactly," said Anna.

"How many votes do we have?" asked Hayley.

"Five for certain," said Aubrey, "that includes Gerald at two, then us three women for three more."

"We might have Chesterton," suggested Beverly. "He appears reasonable, so that's another vote."

"Yes," agreed Anna, "and Lord Somerset would count at two, but that still leaves us short at eight."

"At least Montrose and his cronies are short as well."

"Yes," agreed Aubrey, "but that could all change. You have to follow the laws of inheritance for the missing nobility. There's a very real danger that Montrose will win out."

"You think that likely?" asked Hayley.

"Don't sell him short," warned Beverly. "He's despicable, but he's got wealth and influence, and isn't afraid to use it."

"Wait a moment," said Aubrey, "wasn't your brother, Alfred, the Viscount of Haverston."

"He was," admitted Anna, "and I know what you're going to suggest. I could appoint someone to that position, but I'd risk alienating Chesterton or Somerset if they think I'm trying to strong-arm them."

"So what do we do?" asked Beverly.

"I wish I knew," said Anna. "I suppose we'll have to wait and see what tomorrow brings."

"I have another idea," said Aubrey. "Suppose we look into these empty seats. If we could locate the heirs and get to them first, we might get the votes we need. After all, we only need a slim margin."

"A good idea," said Anna, "but I'd guess that Montrose is already looking into it. I'm afraid we have a severe disadvantage, a lack of sufficient funds."

"There has to be a way," said Beverly.

"Maybe there is," suggested Hayley, "but it would take some time."

"What's your idea?" asked Gerald.

"We could dig into the Earl of Shrewesdale's background. There's bound to be some skeletons there. Perhaps there's something that we could use against him."

"Perhaps," said Anna, "I'll get Arnim to look into it."

"He's a murderer!" declared Beverly, a bitter tone to her voice.

"Murderer?" said Aubrey. "Why would you say that?"

"He ordered the death of Olivia," said Beverly.

"Who's Olivia?" asked Anna.

"She was a Knight of the Sword," explained Beverly, "or at least she was until she left the order. Montrose had her sentenced to death for helping me."

"Helping you?" said Aubrey. "Why? What happened?"

"His men attacked me," said Beverly, her eyes looking downward, "while I was sleeping. They tried to... I'm sure you can guess the rest."

"And this Olivia came to your rescue?" asked Anna.

"She did," Beverly continued, "but later, the earl's men came to arrest both of us. I was only spared because I was the daughter of a baron. The earl took all my belongings and forced me from the city."

"That's terrible," said Gerald, shocked.

"How did you get your gear back," asked Hayley, "or didn't you have Lightning then?"

"I did," she said, "but the earl took everything. It was Sir Heward that recovered my things."

"This Olivia," said Anna, "you say she used to be a knight?"

"She did," Beverly admitted, "though I don't see how that helps things."

"I don't either," said Aubrey. "He's quite within his rights as the Earl of Shrewesdale, though I can't condone his actions."

"Revi," said Anna, "you've been awfully quiet during these proceedings, what's your opinion?" She looked across at the mage, who was scribbling something on a parchment. He either didn't hear or refused to acknowledge the princess's words.

"Revi!" yelled Gerald, startling the mage.

"What?" Revi asked.

"Your opinion, man," said Gerald, his annoyance quite evident.

"On what?" he asked.

"On the council," added Gerald.

"It is of little consequence to me," the mage replied, "and I have far more important matters to attend to than juggling nobles and their alliances. I'm afraid the politics of court are a thing I have little interest in."

Gerald stared at him in astonishment.

"I think our mage is tired," offered Hayley. "I know he's spending a lot of time studying the flames of late."

"Perhaps you're right," said Aubrey, "I know how taxing magic can be."

"You are correct, of course," said Anna, "and I know these last few days have been tiring for you all. I'll let you get some rest."

Hayley made her way over to Revi, pulling him from his seat with a gentle guiding hand. They exited, followed by Aubrey and Beverly, leaving only Gerald in the room with Anna.

"What was that all about?" asked Gerald.

"I have no idea," said Anna. "I've never seen Master Bloom like that before. Could he be ill?"

"He's a Life Mage, wouldn't he just heal himself?"

"I don't know," said Anna, "perhaps he's too sick to cast? I'll have Aubrey check in on him."

"It's a good thing we have Lady Aubrey," mused Gerald. "It appears our Royal Mage is becoming a tad erratic in his behaviour."

"Perhaps we're reading too much into this," suggested Anna. "After all, it's been a frustrating day, and we're all on edge. I can't say I blame him for not paying attention."

"Won't we need him tomorrow, for the oath-taking?"

"No, Aubrey will be there. I know you want a healer nearby at all times, Gerald, but Aubrey is almost as powerful as Master Bloom now, at least as far as healing goes."

"A good point," agreed Gerald, "and as the Baroness of Hawksburg, she'll have to be there tomorrow anyway."

"Then it's settled," said Anna. "You should get some sleep, Gerald, it's likely to be a long day tomorrow."

"And you," he replied. "You're starting to get bags under your eyes."

"I'm not sleeping well," she admitted. "There's so much going on here in the capital."

"You can't sleep?"

"I try to, but my mind keeps churning."

"You need something to occupy your mind elsewhere," suggested Gerald.

"Good idea," agreed Anna, "but what?"

Sophie's voice drifted over from the door, "Why don't you have Gerald tell you a bedtime story, Highness?"

Anna's face lit up, "What a marvellous idea, Sophie. What do you say, Gerald? Would you read me a bedtime story?"

"I don't know, Anna. You're the ruler of Merceria now, not a little girl."

"Nonsense," she said. "I've always said you're my father, so I'll always be your little girl."

"But I haven't even eaten yet," he complained. "You broke up the meeting before we had a chance to dine."

"Easily solved," said Anna, turning to her maid. "Sophie, get the servants to bring three dinners to my rooms."

"Three, Highness?" said the maid.

"Yes, of course, you'll join us," she said. "I know how much you like Gerald's stories."

TEN

The Oath

FALL 962 MC

Gerald gazed out the windows of the palace. He was facing south, looking down upon the courtyard that lay below.

"There's quite a crowd beyond the gates," he said. "Are you sure this is a good idea?"

"Of course," said Anna, who sat still as Sophie finished her hair. "I want the commoners to be able to bear witness, it's their kingdom too."

"I agree with your sentiment," he said, "but I don't know if taking the oaths outside is a good idea."

"Nonsense," she said, "it'll keep the nobles on their toes. I doubt any of them will say anything troubling with so many witnesses."

"This is a dangerous game, Anna," he warned. "I saw a mob run rampant at Walpole street, back in '53. You don't want to witness what can happen."

"I understand your concerns, Gerald, but the situation here is quite different. These people are not starving, and they know I have their best interests at heart."

"You seem so sure of yourself," continued the old warrior, "a far cry from the nervous girl that was afraid to talk to them only a short time ago."

"That's because you're here to help me," she said.

She held her head still as Sophie made a slight adjustment to her hair.

"Remember what you taught me, Gerald?" she asked.

"I've taught you many things," he mused. "Which particular lesson did you have in mind?"

"It is the obligation of the nobility to protect the commoners," she declared, "and that runs both ways. A wise man once told me that if you look after your people, they will, in turn, look after you."

"Who was that?" he asked.

"You, Gerald," she said, then smiled. She glanced in the mirror, "Very nice, Sophie."

"Thank you, Highness," said the maid. "I've left it over your ears to keep you warmer. Are you sure you won't wear the wrap? It's a little chilly for this time of year."

"I'll be fine," the princess declared.

"You should have it nearby," suggested Gerald, "just in case."

"Very well," surrendered Anna. "You can carry it, Sophie, just in case I need it. I wouldn't want the Duke of Wincaster worrying about it."

"I'm not a duke, Anna," he protested.

"You will be, once you take the oath," she said, turning in her chair to face him. "And I want you to know, regardless of the oath, I always want you to speak your mind."

"Understood," he said. "Now, hadn't we better be moving? The nobles look like they're all assembled."

"Let them wait a little longer," said Anna, "it'll teach them humility." She rose from her chair and twirled in front of the mirror. "What do you think?" she asked.

"You look beautiful," said Gerald, "and Sophie's done an impressive job with your hair. You look so much older."

"Good," she grinned. "Now, let's go take some oaths, shall we?"

"Very well, Your Highness," he said, moving from the window to the door. He opened it to see Dame Beverly waiting outside. "We're ready," he announced.

Beverly led them downstairs and through the Palace. They exited the structure by means of the massive front doors, and then paused, surveying the area before them. A large wooden platform had been built, topped by the warrior's throne. Steps led from either side, allowing those pledging their oaths to reach the monarch on one side, then withdraw from the other.

"Remind me again why the platform's so tall?" asked Gerald.

"So that the commoners beyond the gate can watch," answered Anna. "Now, where's Tempus?"

In answer, there was a bark from the massive dog, who sat beside Dame Hayley as she stood just behind the throne. No, thought Gerald, it's Lady Hayley now that she was a baroness.

As Anna made her way forward, horns sounded, and then a roar of appreciation erupted from the crowd. Gerald watched as Anna ascended the stairs, towards the throne, then turned and stood before it, looking to her audience.

"People of Merceria," she called out, her voice loud and clear, "I come here today to begin my reign by receiving the oath of allegiance from my loyal subjects." She paused as the crowd, once more, applauded.

Gerald watched the visitors within the gate. The nobles of the realm seemed unimpressed with the spectacle before them, and he wondered how many were already plotting against her. Was he being paranoid to think such a thing?

Anna sat down on the warrior's throne. She had refused to wear the crown until her coronation, so instead, today, she had opted for a simpler display of power, that of the throne itself. It was a seat of stone, with a high back and arms, simple in design, and yet, steeped in history.

When the Master of Heralds stepped forward, horns sounded once more, compelling the audience to fall silent.

Gerald absently listened to the words pouring forth from the man, but was not really paying attention. It caught him by surprise when his name was the first to be announced. He stepped forward, climbing the steps to pass Beverly, who stood with drawn sword. She nodded to him, and then he knelt before Anna, who extended her hand. He kissed her ring, as was the custom.

"I swear my fealty to you, Princess Anna of Merceria, and all your heirs as long as I shall live. To serve you faithfully, and without exception, until the end of my days."

"I accept your oath," she replied, in a formal tone, "and do promise to be a true and valiant sovereign of this realm. Arise, Lord Gerald Matheson, Duke of Wincaster and Marshal of the Realm."

There was only scattered applause from the nobles, and most of that from Aubrey and Hayley, but the commoners beyond the gate seemed thrilled by the announcement and exploded into a cacophony of cheers.

Anna waited until the cheers subsided before continuing. "Come stand beside me, Gerald, so that people may see the esteem in which I hold you."

"Are you sure?" he whispered.

"Of course," she said, "to my right, that's where you belong."

He moved up beside her, turning to face the crowd. He recognized the look of disgust on the Earl of Shrewesdale's face, but there was little he could do about it.

One by one, the Master of Heralds announced the nobles, each one climbing the platform to kiss the ring and proclaim their fealty. The last to do so was Lady Hayley Chambers, the new Baroness of Queenston. This brought some surprise, for many commoners knew nothing of the new town, whatsoever.

Gerald thought the ceremony complete when the Master of Heralds stepped forward again. Was this to last forever?

A commoner walked up to the throne, his head bowed in obeisance. He took the oath on behalf of the commoners of Merceria. A nice touch in Gerald's mind, and one which he hadn't expected. The man's oath complete, he left the platform.

Finally, Anna rose from her seat, marking the end of the ceremony. The herald announced a day of celebration and then Anna held out her hand for Gerald to escort her from the platform. They walked past the guards, and Beverly fell in behind them. Hayley soon followed, Tempus beside her, while the rest of the nobles waited their turn to enter the great hall.

An enormous banquet had been laid out in honour of the day, but this time Anna had insisted on changes to the seating arrangement. Gerald, as always, sat to her right while the huge bulk of Tempus lay to her left. Beside the great dog was Aubrey while Beverly was placed to Gerald's right. Past them, on either side, sat the great dukes and earls of the kingdom with the lesser nobles after them, based on their seniority.

In addition to the nobles, there were quite a few knights in attendance. Anna had issued a general amnesty for those who fought for her brother, but the wording of it had been precise; fighting for the other side was forgiven, but acts of violence towards the populace was not. There had been no reports detailing specific problems as yet, but Gerald thought it likely that in the coming days, stories would soon emerge about atrocities committed in the name of King Henry.

He knew that Beverly, in addition to her military duties, had been looking into the Knights of the Sword. Strictly speaking, they were not part of her command, for they fell under the direct order of the sovereign, but Beverly had been given the queen's authority to investigate them, with an eye to determining their loyalty. They were, after all, the senior order of knighthood in the kingdom, and as such, still deserved to take up their rightful place in defence of the crown.

Gerald looked around the room and smiled as he noticed the guards. They were dressed in the finest armour, but he knew that beneath the chainmail, lay members of the Guard Cavalry, perhaps the most elite troops of the realm. They were armed and armoured as knights, but they were, to a man, born commoners. Most were professional soldiers, with years of experience behind them, while only their leader, Dame Beverly, held a title, that of Knight of the Hound.

There were only three such knights left, and he looked down the table to see one of them, Sir Arnim Caster, deep in conversation with his wife, Lady

Nicole. The last, Dame Hayley, sat in her seat as Baroness of Queenston, beside the Royal Life Mage Revi Bloom. They, too, were chatting together, and Gerald was glad to see the mage back to some semblance of his old self.

"What do you think, Gerald?" Anna asked, interrupting his musings.

"Of what?" he replied.

"Of the ceremony, of course. How do you think it went?"

"Rather well," he said. "That was a nice touch, having someone swear on behalf of the commoners. Who came up with that?"

"I did," she beamed, letting loose the little girl that was still inside her. "The citizens of Wincaster loved it."

"They certainly did," said Gerald, "but some of the nobles weren't impressed."

"You worry too much," said Anna. "I know I'm pushing them hard, but it will all pay off in the end."

"And what is the end, Anna?"

"The rule of law," she said, "where everyone is treated equally when it comes to the courts. I know there will still be nobles, and privilege, for that matter, but the law of the land should be fair and equal for all."

"It's a noble sentiment," agreed Gerald, "but if you move too fast, you'll make more enemies. The kingdom's already divided by old loyalties."

"I know," she said, "and we shall have to find some way to mend bridges. I'm hoping to soften my approach now that they've given me their oath."

"Soften? How do you intend to do that?"

"By seeking their counsel when appointing the empty titles."

"Won't they just take advantage?" he warned.

"Perhaps," she said, "but I'll have to be careful not to give up too much power."

"What about Eastwood?" he asked.

"I had hoped to give that to Baron Fitzwilliam, but he refused."

"Did he? I suppose that's not too surprising, he's always loved Bodden."

"I considered making him the Earl of Bodden, but the town's not big enough," confessed Anna, "so what am I to do?"

"What about the other races?" asked Gerald, keeping his voice low. "If you can get them onto the council, you'd have more influence."

"Yes," she agreed, "but I can't imagine any of the nobles of Merceria wishing to dilute their own power to do so. I'll wait till I'm queen and then make a few changes by proclamation."

"You can do that?" he asked.

"Oh yes," she said, "thanks to King Andred, I can get away with all manner of things."

"Then why not use that to make your changes now?" he asked.

"I want people to embrace the changes, not have them shoved down their throats. If I use force, I'll turn everyone against me. I must try to be diplomatic about this."

"So, you're going to buy their support by appointments?"

"Yes," she confessed, "I know it's not a perfect solution, but it's better than ruling by decree."

Farther down the table, Lord Montrose leaned closer to the Earl of Tewsbury.

"I trust the day finds you in good health, Lord Stanton?"

"It does," replied the elderly duke, "though I daresay I've been better. I'm afraid some of the day's activities have not agreed with my stomach."

"I'm sorry to hear that," said Montrose. "Is there anything I can do to help?"

"I doubt it," replied Lord Stanton. "I suppose we'll just have to weather it out."

"In that, I think we are in agreement," offered Montrose. "How was the trip down here?"

"Pleasant enough," replied Stanton. "I understand you've been spending some time in the company of my cousin. He tells me great things about you."

"Does he now?"

"Indeed, he does. I also have it on good authority that your list of friends is growing."

"You humble me," said Montrose. "I am merely a facilitator."

"Do you remember the Walters family?" asked Stanton.

"Wasn't it their nephew that died at Walpole Street?" asked Montrose.

"It was. It seems the uncle takes exception to the appointment of this new marshal. I might suggest you have someone talk to him, I'm sure his thoughts on the kingdom might align with your own."

"I shall keep that in mind," said Montrose

"Might I enquire if you have any... plans for the foreseeable future?"

"None that I would take seriously," said Montrose. "Why do you ask?"

"I thought I might invite you and your companions to Tewsbury for a visit. Sometimes it's nice to get away from the rigours of court, don't you think?"

"And away from prying eyes?" asked Montrose.

"Precisely," Stanton agreed.

"And when might this visit take place, do you think?"

"I believe the midwinter festival would be a grand time to get together, don't you?"

"I do," said Montrose, "and I look forward to seeing you there, as, I suspect, the rest will."

"Very well then, it's all settled. We'll meet again over the winter."

The Duke

WINTER 962/963 MC

Gerald sat at the table as servants brought him his meal. He looked around at the empty room, feeling alone, despite the presence of servants standing nearby. As the Duke of Wincaster, he was expected to live in a grand estate, a sprawling manor that filled half a city block.

Anna was the ruling monarch now, her time taken up by the running of the kingdom, with little left over for socializing. He, himself, was a duke as well as the Marshal of Merceria, giving him great responsibility that weighed heavily on his mind.

He looked down at the soup before him and grimaced. The staff treated him well, but the cook's choice of food left him somewhat bewildered. He had tried to protest but was promptly told that it was only proper for a man of his station, and so he now sat, staring at the unappetizing bowl before him.

He dipped his spoon, and then put it to his lips, slurping it, much to the admonishment of the servant who stood ready nearby. The first time he had done this, the servant had rushed forward to dab his mouth with a cloth. Gerald had quickly put an end to that sort of behaviour, but he still felt like a little boy, being forced to eat under the watchful eye of his guardian.

He had tried to be friendly with the staff, but after years of serving the Royal Family, they were detached and aloof, eschewing any familiarity. If truth be told, he preferred to spend his days at the marshal's offices in the Palace, overseeing the army, far from the pampered life of a duke. But the princess had wished to honour him with this title, and so he sat there, eating a meal he detested, doing what he thought was proper for a man of his newly elevated station.

Hearing a distant knock on the front door, he laid down his spoon, straining to listen. The measured footsteps of his head servant, Winston, went past the dining room, and then Gerald heard the distinct sound of the front door being opened.

At first, the conversation was muffled, but then Winston raised his voice.

"Trades are to use the back entrance!" he exclaimed.

Eager to discover what had transpired, Gerald rose and exited the dining hall to see Winston standing at the front door.

"Who's there?" called out Gerald.

"A tradesman, my lord," replied the servant.

"I'm not in trades," said a familiar voice, "I'm a messenger and an old friend of his lordship."

"I highly doubt that," declared Winston. "You are nothing more than common riff-raff. Messengers, like other trades, are to use the rear entrance. The front door is for people of quality." He turned to face Gerald, "I'm sorry, my lord, but this man doesn't know his place."

"And what is this man's name?" asked Gerald. "Have you even bothered to ask?"

In answer, Winston turned back to face the visitor, still blocking Gerald's view.

"Well?" he said. "You heard his lordship's request. Out with it, man."

"Edgar Greenfield," the man announced.

"Edgar!" called out Gerald, advancing to the door. "Good to see you, my old friend. Come in, come in." Turning his attention to his servant, who wore a look of undisguised revulsion, Gerald said, "You may go, Winston."

The servant bowed deeply, "Very good, my lord."

"Saxnor's balls, but it's been a long time, Edgar!" said Gerald. "How have you been?"

"I been fine," the old man replied, "an' I daresay you been doin' well, yerself."

"I suppose I have," Gerald replied, "though I think I was happier just being a groundskeeper."

"Is that so?" said Edgar. "I find that surprisin', you 'avin this nice house an' all."

"Don't let the fine trappings fool you, it's nothing but a gilded cage. But where are my manners, you must be hungry?"

"I've already eaten," said Edgar, "an' I'm afraid I can't stay long, I've work to do. I'm sorry to say this is all official and such."

"Oh," said Gerald, a little disappointed, "of course, I should have realized."

"Not that I wouldn't like a visit, mind you," continued the courier, "but the princess 'as us couriers busy these days."

"So what is it you came to see me about?" asked Gerald.

"I've been up north these last few weeks," continued Edgar, "all the way up into Norland, to be sure. Things 'ave been 'oppin about of late."

"More so than usual?" asked Gerald.

"Oh, aye, much more. The King of Norland is gettin' on in years. I reckon he won't last another winter, though I've been known to be wrong on occasion."

"Surely, this is information for the princess?" said Gerald.

"Oh, it is," agreed the courier, "but she told me to fill you in. You see the current king, 'e 'as no heir, so when he finally goes to the Afterlife, it'll be a bloody war for the crown. 'Er highness thinks it might cross our borders."

"A valid point," mused Gerald. "Thank you for bringing it to my attention, I shall have to move more troops to the frontier."

"The princess expected as much," offered Edgar.

"How is she doing? I haven't seen much of her lately."

"She seems in fine form," said Edgar, "though I daresay she's a busy one, what with everythin' that's going on." He reached into his pouch, withdrawing some folded papers. "I 'ave numbers 'ere for you, showing where they 'ave their soldiers."

Gerald took them, opening them to examine the notes. "Good work, as always, Edgar. I see you've even listed some of their troop strengths."

"Aye, those that I could see. I only 'ope it 'elps."

"It will Edgar, it will. Where are you off to now?"

"The Princess 'as me goin' to Colbridge. Wants me to find out more about that there duke."

"Good luck with that," offered Gerald. "I hear he's in Shrewesdale's camp these days."

"Still," said Edgar, "my old dad always said it was good to know as much about an enemy as you can. I'll leave you to get back to yer meal."

"I'd rather not," said Gerald.

"You got yerself loads of coins now, me ole friend. You can eat where you like."

Gerald's face lit up, "I can, can't I?" He turned towards the hallway and called out, "Winston?"

The servant dutifully appeared, a look of tolerance on his face. "Yes, my lord?"

"I'm going out to eat," said Gerald. "If anyone is looking for me, I'll be at the Queen's Arms."

"But your meal is already prepared, my lord" objected the servant.

"Then you eat it," said Gerald, "and share it with the others."

"Yes, sir," replied Winston, though his voice betrayed his annoyance.

Revi Bloom stared at the green flame before him. He was at Uxley, in the ancient Saurian temple that had been discovered there almost three years earlier. At that time, they had little knowledge of its power, but now, after much study, Revi felt his understanding had grown immensely. The flames were magical in nature, the result of energy that crossed the land through ley lines. At Uxley, the lines converged, both the east-west and those that ran north-south, creating a single point of power that far exceeded those elsewhere.

He knew the gates allowed travel between points, that had served them well during the war, but now, staring at the flame, he wondered if there might be more to this? His studies had revealed the method by which the flame was harnessed to transport people across long distances, yet the base, the construction that held the runes, still hid secrets. He was convinced of it.

Why, he wondered, would there be so many runes left unused? Was it merely to confuse those that would seek its power, or was there some other use for them? He imagined lines of force stretching over great distances, allowing them to travel even farther. It was as if the answer was just out of his reach.

As frustrating as all this was, he was still inexorably drawn to the flame. The more he examined it, the more he became convinced that he was on the cusp of discovering its hidden secrets. He scribbled down some notes, intending to elaborate upon them at a later date. Almost the entire book was full of such important details, and though he honestly planned to do something with them, the flame always drew him back.

Lord Alexander Stanton, Earl of Tewsbury, took a seat at the table and lifted his goblet, "Gentlemen, I give you the crown."

His assembled guests grabbed their own drinks, but there was a decided reluctance to toast the object of their disdain.

"Come now," continued Lord Stanton, "it is the crown I am toasting, not the current occupant. Surely you can find it in your hearts to separate the two?"

"Eloquently put," added Lord George Montrose, the Earl of Shrewesdale.

They all toasted the crown, Montrose downing the contents of his in one go.

"I hear you have something to tell us, Lord Stanton," said Montrose.

"I have indeed," said the elderly earl with a grin. "You might say our campaign has begun."

"Could you be more specific?" asked Lord Walters, the newest member of the group.

"Of course," said their host. "If we are to control the crown, we must, of course, win influence over Her Highness."

"We know that," grumbled Harlon Eldridge.

"Captain Eldridge," said Montrose, "I might remind you of your place. Please let the earl continue."

"Sorry, my lord," Eldridge responded, "but I'm not a captain anymore, thanks to that Fitzwilliam bitch."

"Now, now," soothed Lord Barrington, "let's not let our emotions get the better of us."

"Pray, continue, Lord Stanton," said Montrose. "You were saying something about gaining favour?"

"Ah, yes," said the old man, "in order to gain such favour, it's important that we remove the current influencers that she has surrounded herself with, do you not agree?"

"Of course," agreed Montrose, "have you news on that regard?"

"I do, indeed. I have considerable influence amongst the servants of our new Duke of Wincaster. They have managed to effectively reduce the influence of this marshal over the princess."

"This is excellent news," said Montrose.

"Agreed," offered Lord Barrington, "but he is only one of many. How do we move forward from here?"

"I have arranged some of that," said Montrose, offering a smile. "I sent my brother north, into Norland. He is not without influence there."

"To what end?" asked Lord Pearson. "Surely, you don't mean to offer them the crown?"

"That was not my intention," answered Montrose, "but if something should happen to the princess, certainly you wouldn't want that commoner put in charge? If we could arrange a legitimate claim to the throne, we could avoid war."

"And unite the two kingdoms at the same time!" added Lord Webster. "What a marvellous idea."

"Then what is our short term goal?" asked Lord Walters.

"Simple," said Stanton, "with increased activity on the northern border, they'll have to keep their best leaders busy. With Marshal Matheson already occupied in Wincaster, who do you think that would fall to?"

"Lord Fitzwilliam, I should think," offered Webster.

"No," corrected Lord Barrington, "he's needed in Bodden. No, I think his daughter would be the logical choice."

"Exactly," said Montrose, taking a drink.

"Clever," added Lord Markham Anglesley. "You get rid of the bodyguard by stirring up problems on the frontier. But what of the others?"

"Others?" said Captain Eldridge.

"Yes," added Anglesley, "there's still the Royal Life Mage and the ranger."

"Ah, yes," said Montrose, "I was hoping some of you might come up with something."

"What about bandits?" asked Eldridge.

"What about them?" said Barrington.

"Well," the captain continued, "if bandits were to start harassing the roads, surely the rangers would be kept busy. I would suspect that would also include their leader, wouldn't it?"

"A good point," said Montrose, "but where would we locate such bandits."

"Leave that to me," offered Eldridge. "You supply the coins, and I'll see to the hiring."

"Agreed," said Montrose.

"This is all well and good," said Walters, "but I must have satisfaction on this so-called marshal. He was responsible for my nephew's death and cannot be allowed to walk free."

"Give us time," said Barrington, "we don't want to rush things. You'll have your revenge, don't you worry."

"What of the mage, Revi Bloom?" pressed Lord Anglesley.

"From what I hear," said Stanton, "he is of little significance. His studies keep him from the capital for most of the time."

"Then who's left to deal with?" asked Barrington.

"Sir Arnim Caster," suggested Montrose, "but he has a new wife. I'm sure we can apply some pressure there to keep him in check. There's nothing quite like the first bloom of love to keep a man's thoughts from his work."

"And the foreigners?" pressed Pearson.

"Of little consequence," said Stanton. "The Prince of Weldwyn has little say in these matters. He's here as an ambassador, nothing more. I'm confident he won't interfere in internal affairs."

"It seems patience has served us well," offered Stanton.

"Indeed it has," agreed Montrose, lifting his drink once more. "Gentlemen, I give you the new year. May its passing mark an end to the usurper."

TWELVE

The North

SPRING 963 MC

Baron Fitzwilliam halted his horse and waited while the other riders caught up, Sir James being the first to join him.

"Do you see them, Lord, to the northwest?"

"I do," the baron replied, "but it doesn't look like a normal raiding party."

"How so?" asked the knight. "They are armed and in our territory, are they not?"

"They are," Fitz agreed, "but they have people out in front looking for tracks, not the normal actions of raiders, I'd wager."

"They are still in Mercerian territory, Lord," said Sir James, "and as such must be punished. We can't afford to look weak, sir."

"Normally, I'd agree with you," said Fitz, "but there's something very odd about this."

"How do you wish to proceed?"

"We outnumber them," said the baron, "so I think we'll try a more direct approach. Keep the men in close formation, and we'll go and talk. Perhaps a show of force is all that will be necessary."

"Very well, Lord," said Sir James. He barked out orders, and the Bodden Horse spread out to either side to form a disciplined line.

Baron Fitzwilliam waited until all were in their places, then advanced at the trot, directly towards the Norlanders.

Their presence was soon noted, and the enemy troops formed into a rough line. Two men, however, rode forward, under a sign of truce.

Fitz held up his hand, signalling for the line to halt. "An interesting turn of events, wouldn't you say?"

"Indeed, my lord," said Sir James. "Your orders?"

"You're with me," he said to the knight, then yelled out, "Sergeant Blackwood?"

"Sir!" came the reply.

"Sir James and I are going forward to parley. You command the horse."

"Yes, sir," the warrior responded.

Fitz edged his horse forward, and Sir James fell in beside him. The enemy commander had halted halfway between the two lines, but there were no signs of an impending fight, for the Norlanders had no weapons in hand.

As they drew closer, Fitz could make out more details about the Norland commander. He was young, far younger than the baron would have expected, perhaps only in his early twenties. His dark brown hair framed a dusky complexion, topped off by a neatly trimmed beard.

"Greetings," the young warrior called out as they approached. "I am Captain Aden, in service to His Grace, the Earl of Beaconsgate."

"And my name is Lord Richard Fitzwilliam, Baron of Bodden. What brings you to my domain, Captain?"

"I can assure you we mean no harm," the Norlander soothed. "We are merely chasing down some criminals that have managed to evade capture."

"Criminals, you say," said Fitz. "What is their crime?"

"It does not concern you," said the captain. "It is an internal matter."

"I beg to differ," said the baron. "As soon as you crossed the border, it became my concern. Your very presence here is an act of war."

"Come, now," the captain continued, "you and I both know that there is no lasting peace between our two kingdoms."

"True," responded Fitz, "but there is an uneasy truce. Would you have us break into open warfare?"

"I mean you no harm," the captain persisted. "Permit us to retrieve our prisoners, and we shall be on our way."

"That I cannot do. You have violated our borders. You will remove your men to the north of the river, or we shall give battle. Which is it to be?"

"Are you sure there is no way we can reach an agreement?"

"Positive," said Fitz. "I have fought with your people for many years, I see no reason to begin trusting you now."

"Very well," acquiesced the captain, "we shall return to Norland territory, but I warn you, these people we seek are dangerous."

"I shall be the judge of that," remarked Fitz. He looked past the Norland captain to see the men that stood waiting beyond. They represented very little in the way of a threat, but still, the baron didn't trust them. "We shall escort you to the river," said Fitz at last.

"That won't be necessary," offered the captain, "we know the way."

"Not at all," said Fitz. "In fact, I rather insist."

"Very well," the captain agreed reluctantly.

Fitz wheeled about, Sir James following. They soon reached their own lines where Sergeant Blackwood sat, waiting.

"You have news, Lord?"

"We will escort the Norlanders back to the river," commanded Fitz. "Make sure you keep an eye on the beggars."

"Will do, sir," replied Blackwood.

"What about the men they were looking for?" asked Sir James.

"We'll follow up on them soon enough," said Fitz. "How much daylight do you think we have left?"

"Plenty of time to return to the Keep if that's what you're thinking," replied the knight. "Why? What did you have in mind?"

"We'll split off a small group to follow the trail afterwards if we can. The rest will return to Bodden once they've seen this lot off our land. I'd like you to take the bulk of the horsemen back to Bodden, while I take Blackwood and some men with me to track down these fugitives."

"Is that wise, my lord?" said Sir James. "We really don't know what to expect from them."

"If they're wanted by our Norland Earl, that means they may be of use to us. I'd like to find them alive, if possible, but if they resist, we'll use the sword on them."

"Very well," said Sir James.

Baron Fitzwilliam watched as his sergeant deployed the men. There were two groups, each following the Norlanders, one on the right, the other on the left, ready to react should trouble threaten.

The Norlanders, true to their word, returned to the river, and by late afternoon, they had all crossed the ford. They marched off, heading eastward, upriver, and Fitz waited until they were out of sight before issuing his commands. Blackwood, the baron, and twenty men picked up the trail while Sir James took the rest back to the relative safety of the Keep.

It was getting dark, and their progress slowed.

"We're losing the trail, sir," said Blackwood.

"Then we shall halt," Fitz replied.

"Are we going to return to the Keep?"

"No, not yet," he answered. "Once it's dark, we should be able to see their campfires. You think we're close?"

"Yes, Lord," said the sergeant. "I'm surprised we haven't seen them already."

"Very well," Fitz continued, turning in the saddle. "You men water the horses, but be ready to ride when it turns dark."

The Bodden Horse was used to patrolling the frontier, and it wasn't unheard of to camp out of doors, but it was still early spring, and the darkness brought a bitterness with it. The baron dismounted, stretching his legs. He had spent a lifetime of soldiering in the saddle, but now he felt his age. All he wanted was to be back in his comfortable bed, tucked in with a nice book, but it was not to be.

He looked westward, seeing the sun beginning to sink over the horizon. It lit the sky with a reddish hue, promising clear weather for the morning.

It was Sergeant Blackwood that was the first to notice the campfires that sprang up to the southwest, illuminating a group of trees.

"Lord," he pointed.

"I see it," said Fitz. "Mount up, men. Prepare to ride out."

His men, all disciplined warriors, prepared themselves.

"Weapons sheathed, gentlemen," ordered Fitz, "we're trying to be friendly."

"Is that wise, sir?" asked Blackwood. "After all, we don't know how many there are."

"I think we can safely assume there's not too many."

"How can you say so with any certainty?" asked the sergeant.

"You saw the size of the Norland troop," said Fitz. "That was only enough to capture a small group, perhaps a dozen or so. Any more, and they would have needed extra men."

"Sound reasoning," said Blackwood.

"We'll move forward in columns of two," said Fitz, "but we'll take it slowly, I don't want anyone's horse breaking a leg in the dark."

"Very well, sir," said Blackwood, turning to relay the orders.

They were soon trotting forward, the jangle of harnesses echoing across the fields.

As they drew closer, Fitz began to make out figures. There were, perhaps, ten or so individuals and he was surprised to see that at least two of them were children. He pulled his horse up short, yelling out the command to halt.

"What's this?" he asked aloud. "Can that be children?"

"It looks like it, sir," said Blackwood. "Shall I ride forward and check?"

"We'll both go," said Fitz, "but there's no point in taking the entire patrol."

Blackwood barked out the command to wait, and then rode forward, following the baron a tail's length behind.

It was impossible to be quiet on his horse, his armour alone made enough noise as he rode, and so Baron Fitzwilliam elected to ride directly towards the closest fire. People were scrambling about the camp in a mad effort to arm themselves, but Fitz pulled up short, calling out instead.

"My name," he shouted, "is Lord Richard Fitzwilliam, Baron of Bodden. Who is in charge here?"

In answer, a man stepped forward, brandishing a crude pitchfork.

"I am," he said in a timid voice.

"Put down your weapons," ordered Fitz, "I mean you no harm."

The Norlander lowered his pitchfork.

Fitz dismounted, then advanced, leaving his sword scabbarded. "Who are you?" he asked.

"My name's Oakes," the man responded, "and I'm a farmer, or at least I was."

"And why have you entered this land?" said Fitz.

"We mean no harm," Oakes responded, "but we have been driven from our homes."

"Driven, you say? By who?"

"Poverty," said the Norlander. "The earl takes everything we produce, leaving us ill-equipped to last until the next harvest."

"So you're fleeing your rightful liege?" pressed Fitz.

"We are," Oakes replied, "but we beg you not to send us back across the river. The earl won't take kindly to us being returned, it will mean death for us."

"You say you're a farmer?"

"I am," the man agreed, "as is the rest of my group."

"And are you willing to work hard?" Fitz asked.

"Yes, Lord. As long as we are treated fairly."

"Then I give you a choice," called out the baron. "You can return with me to Bodden and become farmers once more, or I can escort you back to the border. Which will it be?"

"We would welcome the opportunity to till the land again, Lord."

"Good," said Fitz, "then you'll come with us. If you work hard, you'll be rewarded, but cross me and I'll see you back across the river once more."

"Aye, my lord," Oakes responded, "and thank you, my lord."

"Don't thank me yet," said Fitz, "there's plenty of planting to be done in the next few weeks. Now, let's be on our way, Bodden is still some distance off."

Early the next morning found the baron in his favourite map room. He was gazing out the window when Sir Gareth entered.

"Ah, there you are, Gareth," said Fitz, eating a piece of cheese. "What do you make of the newcomers?"

"An interesting development, Lord," said the knight. "Are you sure we can trust them?"

"Only time will tell us for sure," said Fitz, "but I think so. Why, do you not agree?"

"I find myself hard-pressed to trust Norlanders, Lord. They've been so problematic in the past."

"A good point," said Fitz, "but this seems very different, somehow."

"Could they be spies?" asked the knight.

"I suppose it's possible," said Fitz, "but we'll take precautions. They'll only be allowed in the village, for now, not the Keep itself."

"A wise precaution, Lord."

"I had a chat with their leader late last night," said Fitz. "He had some interesting news to impart."

"Do tell," said Sir Gareth.

"What do you know of the Earl of Beaconsgate?" asked Fitz.

"He's the southernmost Earl of Norland?, is he not?" said the knight.

"He is," agreed Fitz, "and he's the one behind most of the attacks on Bodden, at least all the ones in my lifetime. Rumour has it that he wants to be King of Norland."

"How would he accomplish that?" asked Sir Gareth. "Surely, there's an heir?"

"Apparently not," answered Fitz. "It appears that the current Norland King's son passed many years ago, leaving no suitable heir to inherit the crown upon his death."

"I take it that's bad news for us," mused the knight.

"Indeed it is," said Fitz, "for you see, this earl's line claims kingship over all of Merceria."

"He's a Royal Heir?" asked the knight.

"If you count a Royal Line that dates back centuries, then yes, I suppose he's an heir, though I doubt that would give him the support he'd require to defeat us."

"I see," said Sir Gareth, "but if he were to take the throne of Norland..."

"Yes," said Fitz, "that would give him all the troops he'd require, especially now, when we are at our weakest."

"What shall we do, Lord?" asked Sir Gareth.

"I shall dispatch word to Wincaster," said Fitz, "though I doubt it will have any effect. Until such time as they cross the border, what else can we do?"

"We could reinforce the border," suggested the knight.

"Already been done," said Fitz, "and Sir Heward is on the lookout for trouble near Wickfield. All we can do now is pray and hope that the King of Norland lives on."

"Strange to think we should wish long life to a Norlander," said Sir Gareth.

"Indeed," said Fitz, "but these are strange times."

Prince Alric made his way through the halls of the Palace in Wincaster. The guards, used to his presence, allowed him entry to the princess's offices, where Anna sat, pouring over notes.

"I see you're busy, as usual," he offered.

She looked up from her work, a smile lighting up her face. "Alric, so good to see you again. It feels like ages since we last spoke."

"It has been some time," he confessed, "but you said it was important to give you some distance."

"And I appreciate that," she replied, "though I've missed you terribly. Have you heard anything from Weldwyn?"

"I have," said the young prince, "and my parents both send their regards. I mentioned the cutbacks in the army, and my father has agreed to send some more troops, if you wish?"

"I do wish," she replied, "though I can't really deploy them here, in the capital. That would give too much ammunition to Shrewesdale and his supporters."

"He sounds like a dangerous man," commented Alric. "Are you sure there's nothing you can do about him?"

"I wish I could," lamented the princess, "but I want laws that are equal for everyone. I can't very well do that and then start making exceptions for myself, now can I?"

"Perhaps you can charge him with something?" he suggested. "A man like that's bound to have a few bodies he's hiding."

"We're looking into something," she said, "but so far, we have no solid proof, at least nothing that would stand up in a court of law."

Alric looked around the room, taking in the extensive collection of books. "I see some things haven't changed," he said, picking a book at random.

She smiled, "Yes, I still manage to find a little time to read if that's what you mean."

"Where's Gerald, I haven't seen him of late?"

Anna set down the paper she was examining, "I'm afraid I haven't seen much of him either."

"Why not?" he asked. "He never used to leave your side."

"He's a duke now," she said, "and he deserves to be able to take things easy. I don't want to burden him with all of my issues."

"Nonsense," said Alric, "he's like a father to you. Surely you've visited him?"

She blushed, betraying her error, "I'm afraid I've been too busy."

"Too busy for Gerald?" he asked.

"I have a coronation to plan, not to mention approving all these appointments." She indicated the mass of papers on her desk.

"I see," he said cooly.

"What's that supposed to mean?"

"You once told me about how you surrounded yourself with friends," he said, "and now, here you are, isolating yourself from their support."

"I suppose you're right," Anna said, "but it's all so overwhelming."

"You need to share the burden," he said, "surely you can delegate things."

"I can't," she said, "or they won't get done properly."

"Won't they?" he countered. "You appointed Gerald as marshal, do you now think he can't lead the army?"

"Of course I don't think that," she defended, "but this is different."

"Is it?" Alric said. "You've lost what it means to be you, Anna. Where's the young visionary that wanted to change the world?"

"Buried beneath paperwork," she confessed. "Oh, Alric, what have I become? How did I get to this point?"

"Better you ask how you get out of this situation you find yourself in," he suggested.

"But how?" she asked.

"The first thing you need to do is get Gerald back."

"I can't," she said. "I can't take away all the rewards I've given him, the manor, the title..."

"Do you think so little of him that you think he would value a manor house over your company?"

"I suppose not," she confessed.

"You know he's miserable," said Alric.

"He is? How do you know?"

"It's reflected in his work. He used to take a great interest in the troops, but now I hear he's too busy to even mount an inspection."

The look of shock on her face told him all he needed to know.

"You need to bring him back to the Palace, Anna," he continued. "Tell him you need his counsel, now more than ever. Tell him to take up residence in the Palace, where he'll always be on call. He'll like that."

"He will?" she asked. "Won't he just think I'm ordering him about?"

"He wants to feel needed, Anna, you've lost sight of that."

"I do miss him terribly," she admitted.

"As you should," he said. "Now, write out an order for him, and I'll deliver it myself."

"I will, Alric," she said, her energy restored, "and tell him I expect him by dinner.

He bowed gracefully, "Your wish is my command, Highness."

A knock summoned Winston. He opened the front door to see a young man, preparing to knock once more. Behind him stood another, wearing expensive-looking clothing.

"Yes?" said the servant.

"I am Lord Jack Marlowe," the visitor said, "representing His Highness, Prince Alric of Weldwyn. We're here to see the duke."

The servant, eyes wild, appeared startled by this revelation. "The Weldwyn Ambassador? Here?"

"Indeed," said Jack. "Now go and get him, fellow, or there'll be trouble."

"Of course, sir," the servant said, closing the door, his footsteps receding.

"That's a strange one," mused Jack.

"Strange indeed," added Alric. "I would have thought he'd at least invite us in."

"Perhaps not as strange as we might think," mused Jack. "Where did Gerald's servants come from?"

"From the previous duke, I suppose," offered Alric. "Why?"

"It seems to me they might have their own agenda."

"You think they're plotting against the crown? That's a leap, isn't it?"

"The last Duke of Wincaster was King Henry, wasn't it?" asked Jack.

"It was," agreed Alric, "and I think I see where you're going with this. Those nobles arrayed against the princess likely have contacts here."

"It would make sense," said Jack. "You know how easy it is to get information when you talk to the servants, especially for one with my charm and grace."

"I suppose it is," the young prince agreed.

The door opened, interrupting their discussion. A surprised Gerald looked out.

"Your Highness," he said, "is something wrong?"

"I have a letter for you, Gerald, from the princess." Alric pulled forth the letter, handing it to the old man.

"For me?" said Gerald. "How strange."

The marshal opened it immediately. Alric had been too polite to read the letter, but its message was clear. Gerald's face lit up, and Alric watched a tear form in the corner of the man's eye.

The duke left the mansion without a backward glance. "I'm ready," was all he said.

"Excellent," said Alric. "Now come along, my good man, we've work to do."

Jack led them back to the Palace while Gerald and Alric made small talk. Through the entrance they went, the guards snapping to attention as they passed. They soon arrived at the dining hall, where another servant opened the doors for them.

Inside sat Anna, at the head of the table. Her eyes lit up, and she rose, running across the room.

"Gerald," she said, giving him a hug, "I'm so glad to see you."

"You are?" he asked. "I thought you wanted me out of the way."

"No," said Anna, "never, but I'm afraid I let my position get the better of me. I'm sorry Gerald, I want you here, at my side."

"I'm here," he said. "You know, all you had to do was ask."

"No, you don't understand," she continued, "I want you here, at the Palace, all the time. I'd like you to move in, there's a room just down the hall from mine. It's yours if you want it."

A tear came to Gerald's eye. "I'd like that, very much," he admitted.

"Good," added Alric. "Now that's settled, let's get on with other matters, shall we?"

"What about all my stuff?" asked Gerald.

"Stuff?" said Jack.

"Yes, you know, clothes, armour and such?"

"Don't worry about that, Gerald," said Anna. "I'll have it all brought back here, to the Palace."

"But what about the manor? Is it just going to remain empty?"

"I have a better idea," said Anna, "we'll turn it into the Weldwyn Embassy. Alric can move in with his own people."

"A capital idea!" added Jack. "Now we can host parties."

Alric turned to the cavalier with a surprised look. "I should have known," the prince said, "only Jack would think of such things first."

"Good," said Anna, "then it's all settled. Now, we need to plan my coronation."

"And then?" asked Gerald.

"Once I'm queen, I'll amend the succession laws and marry Alric."

"That's the old Anna I fell in love with," said the prince.

The Coronation

Anna sat looking over her advisors, her gaze finally settling on her oldest friend. "Gerald, where would you like to start?"

"The coronation is in three weeks," he said, "and I'm concerned we have too few troops to guard you during the procession. Are you sure I can't convince you to hold it here, at the Palace?"

"The Sovereigns of Merceria have always been crowned in a cathedral," said Anna. "I can't go against tradition on this, or my rule will be seen as illegitimate."

"Then what if we take you directly there," he suggested, "without the entire procession marching through the streets of Wincaster?"

"And have people say I skulked?" declared Anna. "No, I must be seen by the commoners. I shall not show weakness."

"I'm more concerned with keeping you alive, Anna. These are still dangerous times."

"We simply need more troops," said Anna.

"Yes," agreed Gerald, "but from where? We have little in the way of funds."

It was Hayley that supplied the answer. "What about the Orcs?" she asked.

"What about them?" said Gerald. "They're mostly up in Hawksburg."

"That's not quite true," corrected Hayley, "I've had a large number of them training new rangers."

"You have?" Gerald asked in surprise. "Why wasn't I informed?"

"They come under the command of the Queen's Rangers," defended Hayley, "and, as such, they only fall under your command during times of war."

"Or special occasions," corrected Gerald. "Just how many of these Orcs are there?"

The ranger smiled before answering, "Close to one hundred. I've had them staying just north of the city."

"I don't understand," added Aubrey, "I thought we were short on funds."

"We are," said Anna.

"Then why are we training rangers?"

"I had to dismiss quite a few," said Hayley. "They proved to be... difficult."

"Then who's been patrolling the king's roads?" asked Aubrey.

"The queen's roads," corrected Hayley, "and they've been patrolled by Orcs and Elves."

"I thought all the Elves went home?" said Aubrey.

"They did," answered Anna, "but Telethial returned with her archers. They've been helping out with Hayley's duties."

"Does that mean we can call on them for help with the coronation?" asked Beverly. "I'm a little hesitant to use the Knights of the Sword to guard Her Highness, and with the Guard Cavalry up north, we have little left."

"Might I suggest," offered Prince Alric, "that the men of Weldwyn be allowed to assist?"

"Putting Weldwyn troops in the parade might be seen as a foreign influence at court, Highness," warned Arnim.

"They could be used for crowd control," suggested Alric. "They wouldn't necessarily be accompanying the princess."

"I think it a grand idea," said Anna, "and I'd also like Prince Alric to be riding with me, along with Gerald, of course."

"Do you think that wise?" asked Arnim. "Your political enemies may see it as a challenge. They'll use it against you."

"Soon, it won't matter," said Anna. "They can make of it what they will. Once I put through my reforms, we'll announce our engagement, and it'll be out in the open."

"So you've decided to take control of the Nobles Council?" asked Hayley.

"I have," said Anna. "With the goodwill that comes from the celebration of my crowning, I'll appoint new nobles and hold a vote. I expect to have these matters settled by the end of the week."

"That soon?" said Alric. "Are you sure that's not moving too fast?"

"Yes, I'm sure," said Anna. "Once the Royal Engagement is announced, we can start moving towards a permanent alliance with Weldwyn. That will help immensely."

"And when is the wedding to be?" asked Beverly.

"A year after the engagement is announced," said Anna.

"It's a Weldwyn custom," explained Alric, "and both my parents will want to be here for the wedding."

"A Royal Visit?" said Jack in surprise. "Has that ever been done before?"

"Not from a reigning monarch," said Anna. "In fact, until I visited Weldwyn, no royal from either country had visited the other."

"A truly monumental occasion to be sure," said Jack.

"Yes," agreed Gerald, "and one that will require a lot of planning."

"Let's get through the coronation first, shall we?" said Anna.

"Yes," agreed Gerald, "then we'll all have to refer to you as Your Majesty."

"I'll always be Anna to you, Gerald," said the princess.

Gerald laughed.

"What's so funny?" asked Anna.

"You always said you'd be a mighty warrior queen, do you remember?"

She smiled. "I seem to remember warrior princess, but then again, I said I'd make Tempus a duke." She petted the great mastiff's head, and Tempus let out a giant yawn then lay back down.

"I'll leave the final arrangements to Gerald and Beverly," said Anna, "but make sure Aubrey is close by, in case of any trouble."

"What about Revi," asked Gerald, "where is he?"

"Studying the flame at Uxley again," said Hayley. "He says he's close to unlocking something."

"Again?" said Gerald. "I thought he'd finished with all of that?"

"No," said Hayley. "He's convinced there's more to these portals than ever before."

"Why would he say that?" asked Anna.

"The runes," added Aubrey. "He says there are too many runes at the site of the flames."

"Too many?" said Gerald.

"Yes," continued the Life Mage. "There are runes that we don't use to open the gates, indicating the others may serve a purpose we don't, as yet, understand."

"As fascinating as that is," said Anna, "we have more important things to see to. Now, I have to get back to Sophie for the final fitting of my coronation dress."

"Very well," said Gerald, "I'll let you know when we have everything settled here."

Alric climbed into the carriage. As a royal, he was second only to Princess Anna, though technically he was third if you included Tempus. The great dog lay at Anna's feet, and Alric had to step over him before sitting to face the princess. Gerald climbed in next and sat beside Alric, while Sophie took her place next to Anna.

The young prince gazed across at Anna, taking her in. "You look stunning today," he said.

"Thank you, Alric," she said, blushing slightly, "and may I say you cut a fine figure this day as well?"

"I'm surprised to see you wearing your sword," added Alric.

"Wouldn't you expect a king to wear a sword?" asked Gerald.

"Yes, of course," the young man replied.

"Then why not a queen? We are a warrior culture, after all."

"Yes, I suppose you are," agreed Alric. "I hadn't thought of it that way. Where did you get that sword from, anyway?"

"It was a gift," said Anna, "from Herdwin to Gerald's daughter."

"Gerald's daughter?" said Alric in surprise.

"Yes, me, silly," she continued. "When I was much younger, Gerald and I travelled to Wincaster and went out on the town incognito. I was posing as his daughter, it was great fun."

"I'm afraid we couldn't do that now," said Gerald, "you're too well known."

"And well-liked," added Alric. "From what I've heard, the commoners love you. You truly are the people's princess."

"Not after today," said Anna. "Now, I'll be the people's queen."

A group of horsemen took up their station around the carriage. Anna looked at them in surprise, for they were wearing the livery of Merceria, and yet she didn't recognize any of them.

"How do you like your guard?" asked Gerald, a grin breaking across his features.

"Who are they?" she asked. "I don't think I've seen them before."

"You have," said Alric, "but usually they're wearing the blue of Weldwyn."

Anna turned to Gerald in surprise, "You put Weldwyn troops around us?"

"Relax," said Gerald, "they're actually Alric's personal guard. It was his idea to dress them in Mercerian colours. The crowd won't know the difference, and they're likely to be more trustworthy than Knights of the Sword."

"I suppose that means we're breaking with tradition today," mused Anna.

"Let's just say we're making some adjustments," said Gerald. "Our current situation is very different than it was back in your ancestors' time."

"I'm excited for you, Anna," said Alric. "I've never seen a coronation before. My father was crowned long before I was born."

"I expect it'll be quite dull," said Anna, "with lots of speeches and droning on by the Holy Father."

"It'll be anything but dull with you," said Alric, reaching forward and gently squeezing her hand. "Are you nervous?"

"Not really nervous," she confessed, "but eager to be on with it. Where's Beverly?"

"She'll be along shortly," said Gerald. "She's commanding the escort, aside from the prince's group, that is. They'll be under the command of Jack."

"And the rest of my family?" she asked.

"Hayley's up on the rooftops with the Orcs, she'll join us at the Cathedral after we've arrived. Aubrey will be in the carriage just behind us, along with Arnim and Nikki."

"What about Revi," she said, "or is he too busy with his studies?"

"He's waiting at the cathedral," said Gerald. "Unfortunately, given the troubles in the north, Baron Fitzwilliam couldn't make it, but he sends his regards and best wishes. He promises to hold a celebration in Bodden in recognition of your crowning."

"We've also arranged a little surprise for you," added Alric, peering towards the Palace.

They all turned their heads to see Beverly emerge from the building. She made her way to Lightning and mounted in one smooth action. Trotting forward, she saluted the princess and her entourage with her sword, and then took her place at the head of the column, nodding to a nearby herald.

Horns blared, announcing the beginning of the procession. Anna watched as troops took up positions by the gates to the Palace. The gates were opened wide to reveal a small army formed up beyond. At the head of the procession were a dozen Trolls, led by their leader, Tog.

Behind them, Elves lined up under the command of Telethial, each archer with their Elven bows strung and in hand. Next, stood two dozen Dwarves, their chainmail dark despite the morning sun.

Just beyond the gate, following the Dwarves, were a dozen Kurathian horsemen, carrying the standard of Merceria.

"An impressive sight," said Anna, "and a wonderful surprise. You've outdone yourself, Gerald."

"It wasn't all me," the marshal replied, "everyone wanted to be a part of this day. We might not have a full complement of troops in Wincaster, but we can still put on a good show."

The troops began moving at a sedate pace. Anna watched the procession head down the street, and then the Royal Carriage rolled forward, taking up its position.

Anna gripped Sophie's hand, "Isn't this exciting?"

"It is, Highness," said the maid, "but I still don't understand why I'm here?"

"You're my friend, Sophie, and you helped put me here."

"I did?" she said in surprise.

"Of course," Anna continued, "you all did. It was your devotion and support that made me what I am today. Without you, I wouldn't be here."

"Yes," agreed Gerald, "and if it hadn't been for you, Sophie, I might not be alive."

"Why would you say that?" the maid asked.

"Do you remember when I was badly injured by bandits?"

"I do," she said, "what of it?"

"I seem to recall the other servants not heeding Anna's instructions. It was you that took matters into hand. That was the day you endeared yourself to the princess."

"I was just doing my job," Sophie defended.

"You did more than that," said Anna, "and you're part of my family now!"

The carriage passed through the gate and onto the promenade. The streets were lined by crowds, held back by guards at regular intervals.

A sound erupted as they made their way south, starting as one or two people calling out, then soon become a deafening roar. Anna looked about in surprise to see hundreds of commoners waving and cheering them as they passed.

"What do you think, Gerald?" asked Alric. "Do the people of Merceria love their princess?"

Gerald grinned, "They do indeed, Your Highness."

"I wonder how they'll feel when I start making changes?" pondered Anna.

"I somehow doubt they'll change their minds," the prince replied. "People want someone to believe in. Someone who'll make a difference, and you've promised them that."

"I know," she said, "but now I have to follow through with my promises."

"You will," said Alric.

"I know," she agreed, "and I should have known better all along."

"What do you mean?" asked the prince.

"I've always known things will be all right when Gerald and I are together. I lost sight of that when I made him Duke of Wincaster. I should have kept him close."

"I'm here now, Anna," offered Gerald.

The procession rounded the corner, heading west. They were nearing the location where, years before, an attempt had been made on Princess Margaret's life.

Gerald looked instinctively to the rooftops to see a pair of Orcs watching the events below.

"We're safe," assured Alric. "Dame Hayley has things under control."

"Lady Hayley now," corrected Anna.

"It's strange to think how different things have become," mused Gerald. "When I first met you, you were a little girl with dirty feet and matted hair, do you remember?"

"I do," said Anna, with a grin. "I wash my feet every day now, and Sophie makes sure my hair is kept nicely brushed."

"Not an easy task," added Sophie, "it tangles so quickly."

Alric turned to look towards the head of the column. "How long is this route we're taking?" he asked.

"A while yet," said Gerald, "though we'll be turning north soon, then you'll see the cathedral."

"You said you've never witnessed a coronation," said Anna, "but surely, you must be familiar with traditions in Weldwyn regarding it?"

"I am," Alric admitted, "though they're much less a spectacle than what you have here."

"We're a warrior culture," said Anna, "and a coronation is a chance to project that strength."

"I can see why you worship Saxnor," said Alric. "The God of strength suits you, as a people. I'm glad you're on our side."

"So am I," Anna replied, blushing slightly.

Sitting in the carriage, they watched the crowds erupt into cheers as they rolled by. Anna even waved at one point, sending the commoners into a frenzy of activity. The noise grew even louder, causing the young princess to break out in a broad smile.

Soon enough, the procession turned north, and the cathedral loomed into sight, its pure white stone and large dome dominating the buildings around it.

Soldiers were lined up in front, keeping the crowds at bay. When the carriage rolled to a stop, a servant rushed forward to place a stool. As they had agreed, Gerald exited first, taking up station to the right side while Alric, following, moved left.

Anna descended next, stepping forward to be flanked by the other two, and then paused while Tempus and Sophie brought up the rear.

By this time, Dame Beverly had appeared, and presented herself before the princess, saluting with her sword, then turned to lead the group towards the great doors of the cathedral. These stood open, the sunlight streaming into the room beyond.

They entered the atrium, pausing a moment as Sophie made a final check of the princess's dress. The maid took up her position behind Anna once more, nodding to Beverly, who knocked on the inner door with the hilt of her sword.

The door opened to reveal a Holy Father.

"Who wishes to enter the Holy Sanctuary of Saxnor?" he formally asked.

"Princess Anna, rightful heir and ruler of Merceria," answered Beverly.

The Holy Father bowed deeply, stepping to the side. "We are honoured and blessed by your presence," he said.

They began moving once more, but as they crossed the threshold, Alric fell back to join Sophie. These two would not be participating any further in the ceremony and would soon take their seats.

Anna held onto Gerald's arm as they made their way down the nave. The place was packed to the left and right with the well-to-do. Above them, looking down on the procession, was a balcony full of well-wishers, mostly commoners with a smattering of guards to keep things orderly.

Before them stood the Bishop-Supreme of Saxnor, who would conduct the ceremony. He waited by the warrior's throne, the same seat that had been used to take the oath of office. As they approached the front, Gerald halted, and Anna released his arm, moving to stand in front of the officiant. Tempus moved up beside her, causing a stir amongst the crowd, but he seemed to realize the solemnity of the occasion, and merely stayed by her side. The Bishop-Supreme gave a blessing, and then Anna moved towards the throne, turning to stand with it behind her so that she faced the crowd.

Alric and Sophie had taken their seats up front, and Gerald quickly joined them. No sooner had he sat than the Bishop-Supreme called everyone to their feet. Once more words flowed from his mouth, this time extolling the virtues of honesty, integrity and strength, the prime characteristics of Saxnor himself.

Gerald stood in mute silence as a hymn was sung. It was not that he had any objection to it, but his life experience had never prepared him for such an act. To him, religion was a private thing between a man and his God, not this strange public display of devotion.

The song completed, the audience held their breath as a choir of children began to sing, the sound drifting through the halls of the cathedral, to echo back and forth, filling the room with its resonance.

Afterwards, a small mat was placed before Anna, and she knelt upon it, waiting. Two Holy Brothers carried out pillows that bore a ceremonial sword and shield, symbols of the power and might of the Royal Line.

Anna took these, holding them easily and with skill, no doubt mentally thanking Gerald for his training all those years ago. She looked every bit the warrior queen as she knelt there, staring out into the crowd, her face a mask of calmness.

Finally came the last item of all, the warrior's crown. It was fashioned long ago, a simple iron ring, unadorned with gold or jewels and yet somehow projecting great power. This was no flight of fancy, but a crown to be worn in battle.

The Bishop-Supreme held it over Anna's head, reciting the ancient words that had been uttered down through the centuries.

"We do, by Holy Right, charge you to uphold the laws and protect the people that inhabit this kingdom of Merceria, and to keep this land free from all enemies. Do you accept this sacred responsibility?"

"I do," uttered Anna, in a clear and commanding voice.

"Then I do, by these acts, make thee sovereign ruler of Merceria," he added, placing the crown upon her head. He moved to the side, turning to the crowd.

"I present to you, Her Majesty, Queen Anna of Merceria. Long may she reign."

Horns sounded, and then a great cheer went up from the crowd. It reverberated throughout the entire room until Gerald thought he might go deaf.

Anna bowed her head, the last act of supplication a new Mercerian monarch would ever make. It was said that a king, or in this case a queen, was bowing to Saxnor, but Gerald thought the real reason for the bow was to acknowledge the commoners, for, without them, there would be no crown. She stood up and stepped back, taking her rightful seat upon the throne of Merceria.

The choir began anew, calling on Saxnor himself to shower their new monarch with his blessing. When they finished, Anna rose, and the room fell back into silence as horns sounded, announcing her departure. She proceeded back down the nave, pausing only long enough for Gerald to make his way to her. He bowed deeply, then took up a position behind her, along with Alric. Only Tempus remained at her side, barking loudly as the trumpets reached their crescendo. When they finally entered the atrium, Anna handed over the sword and shield to a servant.

She turned briefly to Sophie, who rushed forward to adjust the crown, which had started to drop down over her eyes. Her task complete, the maid fell in behind, and they all exited the cathedral, Anna once again leading.

Another blare of horns sounded, filling the open air with their sound. Those assembled outside cheered yet again, and Anna halted, waving at her subjects before continuing to the waiting carriage. The queen climbed in first, with Tempus hot on her heels, taking up his customary position at her feet. Alric entered next, and then Gerald invited Sophie to take her seat, before joining them. He sat back, letting the padded chair engulf him, a far cry from the wooden benches of the cathedral.

"Congratulations, Your Majesty," said Gerald.

"Thank you," Anna replied, "but in private, I'd still like you to just call me Anna." She turned to Alric, "What did you think?"

"A strange ceremony, to be sure," said the young prince, "although I had expected it to take longer."

"The first such coronation took place on the field of battle," said Anna, "and the king was in a hurry to defeat his enemies. They've been short ever since."

"I wish Weldwyn had the same idea," mused Alric. "All of our ceremonies seem to take forever. I remember when my brother, Alstan, was married, the ceremony took the better part of an entire day. I can tell you I was exhausted by the end."

"Luckily, my coronation was short and sweet," said Anna. "Though I suppose we'll have to start thinking about a Royal Wedding soon enough."

"I suppose we will," grinned Alric, "but that's some time off yet."

The carriage rolled forward, starting the long procession back to the Palace.

"Do you feel any different, Your Majesty?" asked Alric.

"Yes, and no," replied Anna. "It certainly feels good to have it over and done with. I suppose it will take some getting used to being called Majesty all the time, but I don't feel any different."

"That's because you're not," offered Gerald. "You're the same old Anna inside, that's the important thing."

"Yes," agreed Alric, "and don't let it get to you this time. Remember, you and Gerald are a team."

"And you," added Anna.

"Eventually," agreed Alric, "but there's still been no official announcement."

"I'm sure people realize it by now," said Anna. "You were, after all, travelling in my carriage."

"Yes," Alric agreed, "but you need to push through your reforms before we announce anything. You don't want to risk losing any votes in the Nobles Council."

Anna removed the crown, rubbing her head slightly. "This thing's heavier than it looks."

Gerald laughed, "You know, you don't have to wear it, other than today."

"I don't mind wearing it," said Anna. "It will remind me of the weight of responsibility that I bear, but I wouldn't mind having it sized properly."

"Perhaps a cap could be inserted, Your Majesty?" suggested Sophie. "It would lessen the burden."

"A marvellous idea, Sophie," Anna agreed, "and one we'll have to look at in future. I'll just have to tough it out for today."

"I suppose I understand the need for the long procession on the way to the cathedral," mused Alric, "but do we have to repeat the same journey in reverse? Surely, there's a shorter route we could take?"

"There is," said Gerald, "but the throne needs to be moved back to the Palace, so it's there upon our return. It wouldn't do to get back and have nowhere for the sovereign to sit."

"I hadn't thought of that," said Alric.

"That's all right," said Anna, "that's what we have Gerald here for."

Lord Montrose watched as the queen's carriage pulled away.

"It appears," offered Lord Barrington, "that our plans have come to naught."

"Be patient," offered Montrose, "there are yet things we can do. We might have failed to pry the old man away from her, but more direct action may be successful where guile has failed."

"Meaning?" said Barrington.

"Meaning that we can lose a battle, but still win the war."

"What about the north?" asked Barrington. "I thought that Fitzwilliam woman was supposed to go there, and yet I saw her leading the procession today."

"That was unforeseen," said Montrose defensively. "It seems they sent someone else to command the northern frontier."

"Who?"

"A traitorous dog named Heward," spat out Montrose.

"He was one of yours, wasn't he?" asked his companion.

"He was," growled out the earl.

"What are we to do now?" asked Barrington.

"Why, enjoy the festivities. The queen is hosting us at the Palace. Eat, drink, enjoy yourself. We need to be seen as gracious and happy with the way things have turned out."

"And then?"

"Then we will let the situation develop naturally," said Montrose.

FOURTEEN

The Council

Anna peered out from behind the curtain to watch the nobles milling about the great hall. Tempus, eager to see what interested his mistress, sniffed the air, then moved closer, the better to spot the object of her attention.

"Are they all present?" she asked.

"They are," said Gerald, "and waiting for you."

"Very well," she said. "Let's begin, shall we?"

Gerald stepped out and waited a moment as the Master of Heralds, who acted as the host of these meetings, met his gaze and then rapped the floor with his staff, drawing everyone's attention.

"Her Majesty, Queen Anna," he announced.

They all turned as one, giving her their full attention when she entered. She made her way directly to the throne and sat, with Gerald taking up his customary position to her right while Tempus lay to the left. Wearing the warrior's crown, the very symbol of her power, along with her Dwarven short sword, she looked every part a queen.

"You have all received notice of my intent to change the laws of succession," she said, without preamble. "We meet here today to carry out the vote."

"Your Majesty," soothed Lord Montrose, "surely you must realize you lack the votes to pass such an act."

"Do I?" said Anna. "I think you are mistaken, Lord Montrose."

Montrose looked unsettled, giving Gerald a sense of satisfaction, a feeling no doubt shared by the new queen.

"Before we vote," she continued, "it has long been a tradition that the title of Viscount Haverston is held by a member of the Royal Family. As it falls to me, the sole remaining member of my line, I have decided to award it to a deserving individual. I, therefore, appoint Sir Arnim Caster as Viscount of Haverston."

The Earl of Shrewesdale stared back in disbelief.

Arnim stepped forward, kneeling before his sovereign. "I pledge my sword to your service, Majesty," he said.

"Arise, Lord Arnim Caster, Viscount of Haverston, and take your place on the Nobles Council."

Gerald watched the face of Lord Montrose turn red.

"On the matter of succession, how vote you, lords and ladies?" the queen asked.

"All those in favour, say aye," said the Master of Heralds, in his role of impartial executor. He then counted the votes.

"All those opposed?"

Once more the vote was counted, though much smaller in number.

"What say you, Master Herald?" asked Anna.

"The vote is passed, Your Majesty," the man replied, "by a clear majority. Henceforth, the next in line to the throne shall be the firstborn child of the monarch, regardless of gender."

"And now," said Anna, "I call upon you all to recognize that I shall reign, regardless of marriage. You have all read the proposal. Will any speak against it?"

Montrose wanted to speak up, Gerald saw it in his face, but the earl decided, in the end, to hold his tongue.

"The vote, Master Herald," she called out again.

"All those in favour?"

Once more, the votes were tallied, and again a clear victory for Anna. Surprisingly, even the Duke of Colbridge voted in favour, startling Gerald by his choice. Was this some sort of ruse on his part, or was young Markham Anglesley now content with his lot in life?

"All those opposed," droned on the Master of Heralds.

"What say you?" asked Anna once more.

"The motion is carried, Your Majesty," he replied.

Anna sat back, a smile of satisfaction on her face. "Lord Matheson," she called out.

Gerald was startled out of his musings by the use of his name. "Yes, Majesty?" he replied.

"Send in the Weldwyn Ambassador," she commanded.

Gerald turned to the door, nodding to the guards. Moments later, Prince

Alric entered, preceded by Jack. The young cavalier took up a position beside Beverly as Alric made his way to stand before Anna.

"Lord Marlowe," she announced, "will you address the Nobles Council?"

"I will, Your Majesty," said Jack. He turned to face the assembled nobles, rolling open a parchment. "It is with the greatest respect and honour that King Leofric of Weldwyn offers his blessings to the union of his son, Prince Alric of Weldwyn, to Queen Anna of Merceria."

Anna turned her attention to Alric, who stood, waiting. "Prince Alric, what have you to say about this proposal?"

"I humbly accept this honour," he replied, "and understand it means I will not rule as king."

"I, too, will accept this offer," said Anna. "Let it be known to all that the wedding shall take place one year from today."

"It is so noted," said the Master of Heralds. "Word shall be sent to all corners of the realm to bring news of this joyous event."

Gerald smiled, knowing full well that word had previously been sent. It was likely already posted in Uxley and Burrstoke, the closest towns, and it wouldn't take much longer to reach the far borders of Kingsford and Bodden.

"Now, ladies and gentlemen," announced Anna, "it is time I retire, the better to learn more about my prospective husband."

"This is most improper," called out Lord Stanton. "To be unchaperoned in the company of this... this prince of Weldwyn, cannot be tolerated!"

"Fear not, Lord," said Anna, "for I shall be chaperoned by none other than Lord Matheson."

Stanton backed down, but to Gerald's mind, he looked utterly incensed.

Anna rose, holding out her hand for Gerald. He offered his arm, which she gladly took, then moved towards the door.

Montrose stepped forward, perhaps a little too eagerly and Tempus, ever alert, growled deeply, causing the earl to back up.

Anna turned at the noise. "Is there a problem, Lord Montrose?" she asked.

Once more, he backed down. "No, Majesty," he said.

"Very well," she replied. "Prince Alric, will you accompany us?"

"Very well," said Alric, falling in behind.

They exited the room, Jack and Beverly following. The door closed, and Anna took a deep breath. Turning to face Alric and catching him off guard, she wrapped her arms around his neck, kissing him deeply. He responded in kind.

"Perhaps we should give them some privacy," suggested Jack.

"They're only kissing, Jack," said Beverly.

"They're not kissing me," said Jack, "though you're welcome to give it a try, Dame Beverly."

"I think not," said the red-headed knight.

Hayley turned to Aubrey, "You know what this means, don't you?"

"Of course," replied the young mage, "it means that Anna will still be queen after she marries."

"No, it's more than that," the ranger said. "It means I'll still be a baroness when I marry Revi."

"You're going to marry Revi?" said Aubrey in surprise.

"Eventually," replied the ranger, "but I haven't asked him."

"Isn't he supposed to ask you?"

"If I waited for our mage to propose, I'd be an old maid," said Hayley.

"How's he doing?"

"Who, Revi? He's doing just fine, though he does tend to ramble on a bit about the runes."

"I suppose it's only natural," said Aubrey. "After all, he's the one that learned to unlock their secrets."

"Well, not all of them," added Hayley, "he still thinks there's more to it."

"And what are you up to, now that the queen's settled in?"

"I have to return to Queenston," she mused, "there's lots of work to be done there. You?"

"Hawksburg," replied Aubrey, "though I still have some things to do here in Wincaster before I go. How's my cousin doing?"

"She's a little sad," confessed Hayley. "She's been lonely ever since Aldwin returned to Bodden."

"I can't say I blame her," said Aubrey. "The war's over, but she still hasn't had time to marry him."

"I know," Hayley commiserated, "it's heartbreaking."

"They'll have their moment," said Aubrey, "though if I know my cousin, it won't be a public spectacle."

"No?" said Hayley. "That surprises me. I thought she'd be the type for an all-out wedding. She could have half the kingdom present if she wanted, her father's a popular man."

"She's public in her devotion to the queen," said Aubrey, "but Aldwin is close to her heart. There's very few she'll share that with."

"I suppose that's true," mused Hayley. "Are we likely to see you getting married anytime soon?"

"Me?" the mage replied in exaggerated shock. "Why would you ask that?"

"You're a baroness, and likely the most eligible woman in the realm, now that the queen's spoken for."

"I'm in no hurry to wed," said Aubrey. "I have too much work to do. Between my duties to the queen and rebuilding Hawksburg, I have little time left for my magical studies, let alone a suitor."

"Speaking of your studies," asked the ranger, "how are those going?"

"Surprising well, actually. When I return home, Kraloch is going to help me understand the spirit realm. I'm afraid my great grandmother's notes on the topic are sparse."

"The spirit realm? You mean the dead?"

"Yes and no," the mage answered cryptically. "Kraloch says it's much more complicated than that."

"How so?"

"I have no idea, but I'll let you know once I find out. In the meantime, we'd best start mingling with these other nobles."

"It won't do any good," said Hayley. "They don't like having women on the Nobles Council."

"Well," said Aubrey, "they'd better get used to it. From now on we're here, whether they like it or not."

"I'll let you take the lead," said Hayley, "I'm just a country girl, remember? I'm not used to this life of rank and privilege."

Aubrey laughed, "That's all right, my father was a baron. I'll teach you all you need to know. Now, come along, we mustn't appear rude."

The Earl of Tewsbury made his way over to Lord Montrose.

"It appears our new queen has found her voice," he mused.

Montrose, still red in the face, seethed, "This is outrageous. It's become quite clear she will not see reason."

"You forget your history," offered Lord Stanton. "King Andred wouldn't have even called for a vote. He simply would have threatened imprisonment for any dissenters."

"That was different," said Montrose, "we were the influencers."

"And now you are out of favour," offered Stanton, "there is really little difference. The real question is how we will respond. If we sit back and allow her to proceed unopposed, we will be doing ourselves a great disservice. I fear the time for more direct action is upon us."

"I would have to agree," said Montrose, "but perhaps the better question would be when?"

"It will have to be soon. The longer we delay, the weaker we will appear."

"A valid point," Montrose agreed, "but I think we shall have to abandon the northern option. The situation at the Norland court is becoming too volatile."

"How bad is it?"

"It may yet come to war," said Montrose, "and I fear, that being the case, it will undoubtedly cross the border to involve us."

"Yes," agreed Stanton, "and then we'll be forced to pick sides, something we must resist for as long as possible."

"I think we are in complete agreement on that," said Montrose.

"And this other plan?"

"I have men standing by, Lord Stanton. Say the word, and they shall proceed."

"Let our new queen think she has won, for a few days at least. Strike when the moon is full once more. Can you do that?"

"I can," said Montrose, "and will, I promise you."

"Good," said Lord Stanton. "Then, once the queen is out of the way we'll deal with the old man, then the crown shall be ours to do with as we see fit."

FIFTEEN

Summersgate

SUMMER 963 MC

Aegryth Malthunen, Earth Mage and adviser to King Leofric of Weldwyn, lifted a book from the shelf.

"Think this might be what you're looking for?" she said, passing it to her guest.

"Thank you," said Albreda. "It's been wonderful having the library at my disposal, but I fear there are far too many books to peruse in a timely manner."

"Not at all," Aegryth continued, "it's nice to be able to help a fellow druid."

"I must say it's refreshing to see a library run by mages," Albreda continued. "In Merceria, we have a great library in Shrewesdale, but there are no mages to look after it."

"Tell me again what it is you seek, perhaps I can assist further?"

"That would be nice, thank you," said Albreda. "Are you familiar with the spell of recall?"

"No," Aegryth responded, "I can't say I am. What does it do?"

"It allows instantaneous transport to a circle of magic."

"A teleport?"

"Precisely."

"And this is an Earth Spell?"

"No," said Albreda, "it is a universal spell, able to be mastered by all mages, regardless of their specialization."

"And you have knowledge of this spell?"

"I do," said Albreda. "In fact, I've already taught it to Lady Aubrey Brandon, one of our Life Mages."

"Oh, yes," said Aegryth, "she accompanied the princess when they came to Weldwyn, didn't she?"

"She did," Albreda continued, "though at that time she was still just an apprentice. Her powers have far exceeded those she demonstrated in her short time here."

"It's always nice to learn of new mages," confessed Aegryth. "We hear of them so infrequently these days. I envy you Mercerians."

"You do?"

"Yes," Aegryth confessed, "you are at the dawn of a resurgence of magic. Everything is fresh and exciting for you."

"Fresh, I'll grant you," said Albreda, "but I could do without all the excitement, I had enough of that in my youth."

"So, if you can already use this spell of recall, what is it you need to research?"

"The magic circles themselves. We have some that are legacy sites, left behind by our ancestors, but no knowledge of how to produce new ones."

"Sadly, we are in the same situation," said Aegryth. "Though there is a powerful magic circle here, in the Dome."

"Someone must have created it," said Albreda. "Perhaps, if we can discover when it was made, we can then uncover who created it."

"An excellent idea," said Aegryth. "Would you be willing to show us how this spell of recall works?"

"I'd be delighted," agreed Albreda. "Then the mages of our two realms could work together to better the arcane arts."

"What a marvellous idea," agreed the Weldwyn druid. "Let us begin with the construction of the Dome. My understanding is that the circle was part of its original plan."

"When was it built?" asked Albreda.

"I'm not entirely sure," admitted Aegryth, "but Tyrell would know."

"Tyrell? I'm not sure I've met him."

"You'll like him," said Aegryth. "He's a grand mage, but he's rather subdued and quiet. He's possibly the most powerful mage in the kingdom, and the unofficial leader of the mages."

"Unofficial leader?"

"Yes," Aegryth explained, "we don't recognize any one mage as a leader, but he was chosen as the chief administrator, and tends to run things around here. He has a real gift for administration. I believe he's even corresponded with your princess on occasion."

"Then let's go and find him," said Albreda.

Aegryth led Albreda through the great structure. The Grand Edifice of the Arcane Wizards Council, known more commonly as 'The Dome', was organized into circular corridors that ran around the outside of the impressive chamber that gave the place its name. They made their way to the upper floor, passing many young apprentices as they went.

"You appear to have a lot of mages here," Albreda commented.

"Not as many as you might think," said Aegryth. "We take on new apprentices all the time, but very few of them develop magical ability. Unfortunately, there's no way to tell if someone has that inner ability to cast magic. It's a very hit and miss way of finding mages."

"A curious situation," agreed Albreda.

"What about you?" asked the Weldwyn druid. "How were you discovered?"

"Me?" said Albreda. "I wasn't discovered at all. I learned magic all by myself."

Aegryth halted, surprised at the remark. "You're a wild mage?"

"I am," said Albreda. "Does that shock you?"

"It surprises me," confessed Aegryth, resuming her walk. "I don't think I've ever met a wild mage before. There's certainly none in Weldwyn, as far as I know."

"That doesn't surprise me," said Albreda, "for I've never encountered another."

"Then how did you learn your magic?"

"I discovered a stone circle built by someone known as the Meghara, though I didn't know that at the time. Have you heard of her?"

"I can't say I have," said Aegryth, "though I suppose she must have been an Earth Mage."

"Yes," said Albreda, "and an Orc. We owe them a lot when it comes to magic."

"Really?" mused Aegryth. "I was led to believe we learned our magic from the Elves. I've never heard of Orcs using magic."

"You surprise me," said Albreda. "For a culture so well educated, you have very firm beliefs."

"I meant no disrespect," apologized Aegryth, "but we don't really interact with the green folk here in Weldwyn. I couldn't even begin to tell you about them. As far as I know, they only exist in the Greatwood, which lies to the north of our kingdom."

"They are practical people, from what I can tell," offered Albreda, "and they were very helpful allies during the war for the crown."

"We heard all about the war, of course, but the news here was lacking in details."

"Suffice it to say we were successful," said Albreda, "due in no small part to the use of magic, amongst other things. The princess wants magic to be more prevalent under her rule, though I suppose I should start calling her the queen as she has surely had her coronation by now."

"Here is Tyrell's office," said Aegryth, "though perhaps study might be a better term for it. I should warn you, he's somewhat fussy when it comes to his research, so please don't touch anything."

"Of course," agreed Albreda, "I wouldn't dream of such a thing."

Aegryth knocked on the door, then opened it slightly.

"Tyrell? Are you in there?"

"One moment," called out a deep voice. There was a shuffling noise as papers were rearranged, then a thin man with slightly greying hair pulled the door open the rest of the way.

"What is it?" he asked.

"This is Albreda," said Aegryth. "She's come from Merceria seeking knowledge."

"Has she now?" said the Water Mage, looking at Albreda.

"Yes," said Albreda, "I seek information about your casting circle, the one in the middle of the Dome?"

"Then you've come to the right place," said Tyrell. He stepped from the room, offering his hand in friendship. Albreda shook it.

"And so we finally meet," he said.

"You know of me?" she asked.

"Of course, I've been in correspondence with your princess for years. She's quite the letter writer. She tells me you were instrumental during the recent war."

"I did my part," said Albreda, "but now I need your help."

"Yes, of course," he replied. "Come with me, and we'll see what I can dig up."

"Where are we going?" asked Albreda.

"To the circle of magic," said Tyrell. "I don't know who constructed it, but his mark should be easy enough to identify. Once I know that, we can look up his writings."

"Tyrell knows all about the ancient mages," explained Aegryth, "it's one of his passions."

"Yes," agreed the Water Mage, "they lived in such interesting times, before mages became old and stodgy."

"Is that how you see yourself?" said Albreda. "I've always thought of myself as energetic."

"And so you would," offered Tyrell, "but our training is what makes us the way we are. We are raised on the rote study of magic, while you, on the other hand, are a wild mage, are you not?"

"How did you know that?" asked Aegryth. "I only just found that out myself."

"As I said, I've been in correspondence with Princess Anna. Now come, let us examine this circle."

They entered the impressive chamber, its domed ceiling stretching overhead.

"We don't usually allow outsiders to see the circle, of course, but you come with the highest recommendation."

"It's quite immense," said Albreda, "far larger than what I've seen in Merceria."

"It's the largest one that we know of," confessed Tyrell. "You'll notice there are multiple rows of runes within concentric rings. You can use that to judge a circle's power. The more runes, the greater the power."

"Fascinating," offered Albreda, "and, I assume, very expensive to make. It looks like gold was used to inlay the circle."

"Very observant," noted Tyrell. "In fact, if memory serves, half of the original budget for the building went into the circle. It truly is a king's ransom."

"How did you afford the cost?" asked Albreda. "A circle such as this would surely bankrupt Merceria."

"I have no doubt," said Tyrell, "but Weldwyn was named for the greatest mage of his time and King Loran's closest friend."

"King Loran, he was the founder of Weldwyn?"

"He was," said Tyrell, "and a man with great foresight."

He started walking around the perimeter of the circle, staring at the floor as he did. "Ah, here it is, the maker's mark," he said, pointing at a rune.

"I've seen similar marks before," said Albreda, "though not this particular one. Who is it?"

"Halcraft Invaris," said Tyrell. "I should have known."

"I take it you've heard of him?"

"I have," he admitted. "He was one of the founding members of the Dome and its principal architect."

"Would he have kept notes?" asked Aegryth.

"Undoubtedly," he assured her. "Now, we must go to the inner library, that's where personal notes are kept. Follow me."

He led them back into the hallway, the two druids rushing to keep up.

"The inner library is seldom used these days. Its primary purpose is to preserve the legacy of our ancestors, and it is only available to full mages. We can't have clumsy apprentices damaging priceless writings, after all."

He stopped at a door, pulling forth a key from around his neck. "Only a few of us have the key," he explained, opening the door.

The room was much smaller than Albreda had expected. Shelves lined the walls, and a glowing sphere hanging from the ceiling lit the room with a bright light. In the centre sat a single table surrounded by six chairs.

Tyrell Caracticus led them inside, then began scanning the bookshelves. He paused, reading the spine of one such tome, then pulled it forth. "Here it is," he said, moving to the table.

He opened the book, flipping through its pages. "This is the journal of Halcraft," he announced. "I imagine the information you seek is in here."

"May I?" asked Albreda.

"By all means," he replied.

Albreda sat and began scanning through the book. It was old, pages yellowed with age, and the ink faded in parts, but still quite readable.

"He has a steady hand," she said, "not like some I've seen."

"Halcraft was originally the apprentice to Weldwyn himself," said Tyrell. "It must have been a great burden to take his master's place after his death."

"I can only imagine," said Albreda. She stopped flipping pages, lingering on an illustration. "I think I have it," she announced.

Tyrell leaned over her shoulder. "I would have to agree," he added. "Though the notes describe the construction, not the spell that enchanted it."

"It's a start," said Albreda. "I shall have to take notes."

"Do you want the assistance of an apprentice?" asked Aegryth.

"No," said Albreda, "my satchel contains everything I might need, though I wonder if you'd care to assist, Aegryth. This research would prove beneficial to both our kingdoms."

"I would be delighted," said the Weldwyn druid.

"Good," said Tyrell, "then I'll leave you two ladies to it. Feel free to find me if you need further assistance."

"We shall," said Albreda, "and thank you, once more."

"Not at all," the grand mage replied. "It is we that must thank you. Without your visit, we never would have considered such research."

Albreda popped a hazelnut into her mouth, chewing it absently.

"I think I've found something," said Aegryth, "a description of a spell."

Albreda shifted her chair slightly, the better to see the page. "That's it," she exclaimed, "the secret to creating the circles!"

"Yes," agreed Aegryth, "but it describes an enchanter's circle. It won't work for other schools."

"Nonsense," said Albreda, "it merely requires some adjustment."

"Pardon me?" said the Weldwyn druid in surprise. "What do you mean, some adjustment? Magic isn't a simple recipe you can alter at will."

"It most certainly is," said Albreda. "If there's one thing I've learned over the years, it's that magic is precisely that."

"That goes against all our teachings," argued Aegryth.

"It's not against mine," Albreda responded. "I've been adapting magic my entire life, once I started casting, that is. I believe you'll find it's not as hard as you might think."

"It seems you've found what you've been looking for," said Aegryth. "I suppose that means you'll be returning to Merceria soon."

"I will," Albreda admitted, "though not before I teach you recall, as promised."

"How long will that take?"

"Not long, I assure you. Most likely a morning or so to learn the circle and then the spell."

"Learn the circle?" asked Aegryth.

"Yes," said Albreda, "didn't I mention that? You have to commit it to memory if you hope to use it for a spell of recall."

"When shall we start?"

"We'll need undisturbed access to the circle while we study it," said Albreda. "Can such a thing be arranged?"

"Of course," said Aegryth, "though I'll have to get permission from Tyrell, of course."

"Then I suggest that's our next step," said Albreda. "Once we've studied it in detail, it won't take long to learn the spell. Lady Aubrey managed to perfect it quite quickly, I don't imagine one of your skill will have any issues."

Tyrell watched as Albreda showed Aegryth how to study the circle, then the Weldwyn druid attempted her first casting. Standing outside the circle, she called forth arcane powers as she had been instructed. A wall of force enveloped her, then she appeared, quite suddenly, within the casting circle.

"It worked!" exclaimed Aegryth.

"Indeed it did," agreed Tyrell. "You have brought new magic to an old institution, Albreda. We are very thankful."

"I'm glad we could work together so effectively," said Albreda.

"How far can I travel?" asked Aegryth.

"That depends on your individual power. The more power you can call forth, the greater the distance you can travel. You'll have to experiment to find your own limitations."

"I take it you'll be leaving us now?" she asked.

"I will," agreed Albreda. "In fact, I'll use the spell to return home almost immediately."

"To Wincaster?" asked Tyrell.

"No, to the Whitewood," said Albreda, "that's my home. I honestly don't know if I have the power to recall directly to Wincaster from here. Even if there was a magic circle, it's a significant distance from Summersgate. But I will get to the capital soon after. Would you like me to take any letters?"

"If you would be so kind," said Tyrell. "Once we perfect this spell of yours, perhaps we could come and visit your kingdom."

"I would like that," said Albreda, "but it would be the queen's decision as to whether or not you'd be allowed to use the circles we build."

"Understood," said Tyrell. "As I suspected you'd be leaving soon, I have a letter here for your queen, and one for Revi Bloom."

Albreda took them, placing them into her satchel. "Farewell, mages of Weldwyn," she said. "I look forward to seeing you again in the future."

She raised hands into the air, calling on her arcane knowledge. There was a surge of energy as the spell took effect, boosted by the magic circle. A brilliant cylinder of light erupted from the floor, obscuring the room around her as the magic took hold. She concentrated on the Whitewood, conjuring a vision to her mind of her home. Moments later, the stale air of the Dome was replaced by the fresh scent of the woods.

She lowered her hands as the magic left her. A howl echoed in the distance, welcoming her home.

SIXTEEN

Midnight

SUMMER 963 MC

A dark figure made its way across the grass, keeping to the shadows. Reaching the wall, it turned back, beckoning its companions to follow. Five more shapes raced forward, each clothed in black.

Their leader waited until they were all together, then started climbing the wall, gripping the ornate stone decorations as he ascended. After making his way to the second floor, he pulled tools from a leather arm-guard and began working away at the window latch. Moments later, he pushed it open, casting his eyes about one more time before crossing the sill.

Looking around the room, he let his eyes adjust to the darkness before moving forward. The room was unused, as he knew it would be, offering an excellent place from which to mount their attack. Gazing out the window, he signalled those below to advance. One by one, they followed his path up the wall and silently entered the room.

The leader drew his short sword, its blade covered in a dark oil to mask the steel. Putting a finger to his lips to indicate silence, he pressed his ear against the door. Beyond, lay the corridors of the Palace, and hearing nothing, he quietly opened the door. Candles flickered in the sconces on the wall, only dimly lighting the hallway for it was the middle of the night. He exited the room, making his way down the hall while staying close to the wall.

They had entered the Palace on the east side, the queen's suite directly above them. Now, all they had to do was find the staircase and silence the guards, a task for which they were eminently well suited.

The leader halted at the bottom of the stairs, peering into the stairwell.

At the top, he knew, stood two soldiers, restricting access to the rooms above. Once past these, there would be two more, directly outside the queen's chambers. He turned to his companions, signalling using only his hands. Two removed crossbows from their back while the leader and another man crept silently up the stairs, their swords at the ready.

As he neared the top, he began crawling, lifting his head just high enough to see over the last step. One guard leaned against the door frame, looking away from the stairs, while the other stood within the hallway itself, his back facing their undetected visitors.

The leader moved forward quietly, taking a position to the left of the doorway, while his companion did likewise to the right. He held his hand in front of his face and counted off three fingers as his companion watched. When he reached the last one, they both launched themselves forward.

The leader's blade slid effortlessly into the first guard's throat, his victim failing to make any sound at all. As the body crumpled, the leader caught him, dragging him back into the stairwell.

While this was happening, his companion struck out quickly, driving his blade into the other man's chest. It made a thudding noise as it drove deep, then the second guard collapsed silently. The attacker paused, staring down the hallway, but no sign of detection was forthcoming, and so he dragged the body into the stairwell to join his dead companion.

The leader returned to the stairs, waving the rest forward. Once assembled, they moved into the hallway, breaking into a run, ignoring all doors but the one where the guards stood. Their footfalls drew the attention of the two soldiers guarding the queen's suite. While one turned, drawing his sword and moved to intercept, the other yelled out in alarm.

The leader lunged forward, but his blade failed to penetrate the sturdy mail of the soldier. In answer, the warrior struck back, but the assassin deftly jumped out of reach. From the darkness, a crossbow quarrel flew down the hall, burying itself into the guard's shoulder, sending him staggering back in pain.

One of the other invaders struck out at the second guard in an attempt to silence him, but the blade, blocked by an armguard, merely bounced off, ringing out with the sound of metal on metal.

Shouts of alarm erupted from the nearby rooms, and the leader knew their chance of success was quickly coming to an end unless they could gain entrance immediately! He struck out in desperation, slicing his blade across the guard's face, sending the man to the ground clutching his wound, his voice choked off by the explosion of blood that poured forth.

The second guard retaliated, slicing deeply through one of the attackers.

The man in black stumbled backwards, gripping his forearm, the blood dripping onto the carpet.

A door flew open, and a woman appeared. The leader thought to take her hostage, but as he moved towards her, she produced a warhammer with lightning speed. Driving it into his right shoulder, she shattered the joint, forcing him to the floor in pain.

One of the assassins drove his blade into the second guard's leg, piercing through to the floor. Realizing their target was now within their reach, the two crossbowmen moved up, letting loose their quarrels to keep the unknown woman at bay. She ducked behind her door as the missiles dug into the frame, then launched herself at them as they struggled to reload.

The last two assassins rushed the queen's door, kicking it open to reveal a young woman and a massive dog. The great mastiff launched itself forward in a blur of movement. The lead man fell back, his head caught in the mighty beast's mouth. A sickening crunch ended his life as blood and brains splattered his companion, who fell back in fear. He flailed wildly with his sword, desperate to keep the beast at bay. Finally, he felt the blade sink in, but the massive creature continued his attack, the mighty jaws digging into the assassin's leg, crushing bone with their strength.

In the hallway, the woman swung the hammer again, this time striking an invader on the arm. The force of the blow knocked him off his feet, and he flew across the hall, hitting the opposite wall and then sinking to the floor, unconscious.

The leader, now down to half his men, bellowed an order. Those remaining launched themselves at the hammer-wielder while their leader, ignoring the pain of his destroyed shoulder, raced towards the ultimate prize, the queen herself.

He rushed past the dog, a look of triumph on his face, but then the queen struck out, her blade easily penetrating the man's armour. A moment later, he collapsed, his severed hand lying on the floor beside him as he watched blood pulse forth, just before the world went black.

Beverly struck a final blow, a solid hit to the chest that knocked the intruder to the floor. He lay still, his breathing ragged and thin.

"Majesty," she called out, "are you all right?"

"I'm fine, Beverly," the queen yelled back. "They're all down."

Another door opened, revealing Gerald. He was only half-dressed and carried his sword.

"Anna!" he called out.

"It's all right," replied Anna, "I'm fine. We need Aubrey, we have men down."

"I'll get her," said Gerald.

Beverly knelt by the two guardsmen. One was holding his face, blood flowing freely, while the other lay still, his leg bleeding profusely. She ripped the hem of her nightdress, binding the wounds as best she could.

Anna rushed back inside, emerging a moment later with bed linens, which she started cutting up into bandages.

"What about the invaders?" asked Beverly.

"Never mind them," said Anna, "save our own first, and don't forget Tempus. We'll deal with the others afterwards."

Beverly worked quickly, tying off the wounded leg as fast as she could. She was relieved by Aubrey, who, bidden by Gerald, had finally arrived.

Soon, the words of magic poured forth from the Life Mage's mouth, and the wounds were mended. With the two guards now healed, along with Tempus, she turned her attention to the invaders. Gerald had been securing them while Aubrey dealt with the injured guards, but now, as the Life Mage turned to examine them, it was clear they would not all survive this night.

"These two are dead," said Gerald, "and this one won't last much longer. I'm afraid Nature's Fury collapsed his chest."

Even as he spoke, the attacker gurgled his last breath, and then lay still.

"These three, however, are still alive," announced Beverly.

"Keep them that way," ordered Anna, "we'll need them for interrogation. We must know who ordered this attack. Where are my other guards? There should have been two more at the top of the stairs.

"Dead, I'm afraid," said Gerald. "I noticed their bodies when I fetched Aubrey."

"Thank Saxnor for your training, Beverly," said Anna, "or we'd all be dead."

"We'll get to the bottom of this, Your Majesty," said Beverly, "I promise you."

Aubrey continued her ministrations. Finally, she looked up. "I've healed them, and kept them unconscious by a sleep spell, just in case."

More guards entered the hallway now, trusted men of the queen's personal guard, accompanied by a half-asleep Arnim and Nikki.

"Take these men to the dungeons," Anna ordered.

The soldiers bent to the task of removing the invaders.

"This is Shrewesdale's work," said Beverly, "I know it."

"Likely so," said Gerald, "but we need proof."

"Someone will talk," offered Anna.

"No," said Nikki, surprising everyone, "they won't."

"How can you be so sure?" asked Gerald.

"These are Shadowblades, killers for hire."

"How do you know?" asked Anna.

"This one," said Nikki, indicating a corpse, "I recognize."

"You know him?" asked Gerald.

"I know of him, he has rather distinctive features, note the small scar on his cheek?"

"What of it?" said Gerald.

"His name's Corsun, though I doubt that's his real name. Someone spent a lot to hire him and his people."

"I'll get answers out of the survivors," said Arnim, "don't you worry, Your Majesty."

"These men won't talk," repeated Nikki. "They have a reputation for such things."

"Then how do we break them?" asked Gerald.

"I have an idea," said Aubrey, "but it's a little unorthodox."

"I'm listening," said Anna.

"I propose that we keep them in good health and lock them up together."

"To what purpose?" asked Arnim. "Nikki already said they wouldn't talk."

"Not to us, no," said Aubrey, "but they might talk amongst themselves, especially if they think no one is listening."

"The cells don't provide much privacy," said Arnim, "you can always tell when someone is nearby."

"Not if they're in spirit form," suggested Aubrey.

"Can that be detected?" asked Gerald.

"Perhaps by a mage," said Aubrey, "but if any of them were mages, why would they attack with weapons?"

"She has a good point," said Anna.

"This spirit form you're talking about," said Gerald, "this is what you used during the siege, isn't it?"

"It is," said Aubrey.

"Can you take others into the spirit realm with you?" asked Anna.

"I've never done so before," said Aubrey, "but there's no reason I shouldn't be able to, why?"

"I'd like to see how it works before we commit to it."

"Very well," said Aubrey, "when would you like to try."

"How about right now?" asked Anna.

"I think we should all get dressed first, Anna," said Gerald.

"Very well," the queen continued, "get your clothes on and meet me in my rooms."

. . .

They were soon assembled, with Revi and Hayley joining them after being alerted to the invasion of the Palace. They now stood in the queen's bedchamber, for it, alone, had enough room to fit them all comfortably.

"I'm not so sure of this," said Gerald. "What if we get stuck in the spirit realm?"

"We won't," said Anna, "and we've done this before."

"We have?"

"Yes, back in the Greatwood, remember? The Orc shaman took us on a journey in spirit form."

"And this is the same thing?" he asked.

"From your description," said Aubrey, "I would say yes. I know the Orcs use this spell, but of course, I wasn't there when you travelled the last time."

"What do you need us to do, cousin?" asked Beverly.

"You'll need to stand watch over our bodies. We'll look like we're sleeping as our spirits travel."

"Perhaps you should lie down?" suggested Revi.

"A good idea," said Aubrey, "but we'll have to be close together for the spell to affect us. Who's going to join me?"

"I will," said Anna, "and so will Gerald."

"I will?" Gerald added.

"Of course," said Anna, "who else would I take?"

In answer, Tempus barked.

"What do you think, Aubrey?" asked Anna.

"I'd rather not take Tempus," she replied. "Moving around in spirit form is tricky, and I don't know if he could get used to it."

"Fair enough," said Anna. "Then just the three of us, for now."

"I would suggest you lie down on the bed," said Revi. "It'll be much more comfortable."

"A sound idea," said Anna. "You go in the middle, Aubrey, then Gerald and I will lie on either side."

"Should we draw weapons?" asked Gerald. "What if there's something there?"

"There shouldn't be anything other than us," soothed Aubrey, "and your sword won't be present in the spirit realm."

Gerald climbed onto the bed, lying down with his hands crossed over his chest. "I feel completely ridiculous doing this," he admitted.

Aubrey climbed onto the bed from the other side, lying beside him. "I hope you don't snore," she said, then giggled.

"Very funny," he said. "You're as bad as our queen."

Anna climbed on last, leaving Aubrey between them. "Whenever you're ready, Aubrey."

The mage began gesticulating while the words of power issued from her mouth. Small glowing runes appeared, hovering in front of her as she traced their patterns. Those going into the spirit realm heard an audible snap, and then their spirits drifted free.

"What was that?" asked Gerald, floating beside her. Aubrey looked at the old warrior, his image grey and colourless. A brilliant light made her turn to the right, where the queen hovered in a similar state, but all around her was a bright aura, almost blinding in its intensity.

"I don't see anything," came a muffled voice.

Aubrey turned to look at the rest of their companions. The room appeared as though seen through gauze, the colours washed out and subtle.

It was Beverly that was talking, "Did the spell work?"

"We hear you, Beverly," said Gerald.

"She can't hear you," said Aubrey, "though we can hear them."

"I feel like I've got water in my ears," Gerald complained.

"You get used to it," said Aubrey.

"Anna," said Gerald, "you're glowing brightly."

"Yes," the queen agreed, "and Aubrey has a subtle aura about her."

"Do I?" said Aubrey. "It must be my magic. How interesting."

Gerald cast his eyes about, "The only aura I can see is Anna's."

"Strange," said Aubrey, "I would have thought you'd be able to see mine as well."

"What now?" asked Gerald.

"Now comes the fun part," continued Aubrey, "learning to walk."

"I don't understand," said Gerald. "When we were in the Greatwood, we had no problem."

"Yes," said Aubrey, "but I doubt there were stairs to navigate. It's not too hard, but you have to visualize your actions. You won't be able to feel the ground beneath you, so it can be a bit disorienting at first." She moved across the room, standing amongst the others, who took no notice.

Anna was next to master the action, moving slowly at first, but speeding up as she grew accustomed to the feeling. This time Tempus sat up, sniffing the air.

"He can detect you," said Gerald. "How is that possible?"

"I don't know," said Aubrey, "perhaps he can sense spirits?"

"He was with me when I saw the grey wolf the first time," said Anna, "and he saw it too, even though no one else did."

"Interesting," said Aubrey. "I wonder what another mage would look like in spirit form. Perhaps one's aura can be used to determine magical ability."

"Are you saying Anna has the potential for magic?" asked Gerald.

"Not necessarily," replied the Life Mage, "but I can't explain her aura, it's so bright."

"Because she's younger, perhaps?" offered Gerald.

"I'm only slightly younger than Aubrey," said Anna, "so that can't be it."

"Something to consider for another day, then," said Aubrey. "Now, let's get you moving around. Come on, Gerald, you have to move some time."

Gerald took a step forward, a strange sensation as his feet floated above the ground.

"Close your eyes," urged Aubrey, "and imagine yourself on the floor."

Gerald did as he was bid and then began gently floating downward until his feet looked like they were touching the floor. He opened his eyes, a look of relief flooding his face.

"Now you have it," said Aubrey. "Next, we'll exit the room."

"But the door's closed," objected Gerald.

"That's no obstacle," said Aubrey, "we'll simply walk right through the wall."

"Through it?" said Gerald.

"Yes, it doesn't exist in the spirit realm. You'll probably want to close your eyes as you do, it can be a strange sensation seeing the inside of a wall. I'll go first."

Aubrey stepped through the wall, her ghostly form disappearing from view.

"This is fun," said Anna, quickly following.

Gerald hesitated a moment. He walked to the wall, closing his eyes, but his mind kept trying to tell him that he was going to hit something solid. He finally took a deep breath and plunged through, only to emerge on the other side.

"That wasn't so bad, was it?" asked Anna.

"It's very strange," said Gerald. "I don't know if I could get used to it."

"Nonsense," said Anna, "you've done it before, though last time you were a wolf."

Aubrey turned in surprise. "A grey wolf?" she asked.

"Yes," said Anna. "Why, does that mean something?"

"I'm not sure," replied the mage, "but I seem to remember a reference to it somewhere in my studies."

"I think I'm ready to return to my body," said Gerald.

"Yes," agreed Anna, "we don't want to use up all your energy, Aubrey."

"The spell is already cast," explained Aubrey, "but I can return us if you wish."

"Then do so," said Anna. "Do we have to move back into the room?"

"No," the young mage replied, "as long as we're within range, it will work. You'll feel a bit of a pulling sensation as if a rope is drawing you back, then you may hear another snapping sound. You'll be slightly disoriented once you awaken. Are you ready?"

"Yes," said Gerald, "most emphatically so."

"Go ahead," said Anna.

Aubrey dismissed the spell, feeling the familiar tug as her spirit was pulled back to her body. She heard the snap, this time echoing two more times as Gerald and Anna returned. Opening her eyes, she let her brain become accustomed to the flood of normal colours. It was almost like letting one's eyes adjust to a dim room after being out in the bright sun.

She sat up, "Everything all right, Your Majesty?"

"I'm fine," she answered. "How about you, Gerald?"

Gerald sat up, his hand going to his forehead. "I've a bit of a headache," he confessed. "I almost felt like something was struggling to get out."

"I wonder," said Anna, "perhaps the wolf was trying to be released?"

"I have no idea," said Aubrey, "but it certainly bears investigation."

"How was it?" asked Revi.

"It was terrific," said Anna, her enthusiasm evident to all. "You should have a go."

"Shall I cast again, Master Revi?" asked Aubrey.

"If that's all right with Her Majesty," Revi replied.

Aubrey turned to Anna, who simply nodded.

"Very well," said Aubrey, "then climb aboard the bed. You too, Hayley."

Gerald watched as they took up their positions. Aubrey cast her spell, and then the three bodies went still as if they were sleeping.

Anna moved towards the lifeless form of Hayley, placing her fingers upon her neck. "It's like she's dead," the queen announced. "I don't even think she's breathing."

"Fascinating," mused Gerald, "but I can see some obvious disadvantages to this spell."

"Like what?" asked Beverly.

"Well, for one thing, their bodies are completely vulnerable."

"We'd need to have guards to keep watch," said Arnim, "that's all. Shouldn't be too difficult."

"If she's to do this to listen in on the prisoners, she's going to need a room nearby where her body can rest."

"Easy enough to arrange," said Arnim. "We'll move a comfortable bed down there and keep it nearby."

"It can't be too close," warned Gerald, "we want them to think there's no one else about."

"Don't worry," soothed Arnim, "there are plenty of rooms we can use, all within walking distance of the cells."

"You don't suppose someone could use this spell to infiltrate, do you?" asked Nikki.

"I hadn't thought of that," mused Anna. "I suppose it could be used to listen in, but my understanding is that you can only return to the material world through your own body."

"So we don't have to worry about spirit assassins," said Arnim, "but spying is a distinct possibility."

"I doubt many others can use the spell," said Anna, "but, just to be on the safe side, we'll have Aubrey check for the presence of other spirits before any important meeting."

"I think it's a wise precaution, Majesty," said Arnim.

Aubrey suddenly sat up on the bed, her eyes blinking in adjustment.

"How was it?" asked Anna.

"Much as before," said Aubrey, "and Revi did have an aura to him, very similar to mine."

"And Hayley?" asked Beverly.

"None that I could see," the mage confessed. "I'm guessing that means that Hayley could never cast spells."

"That's fine with me," said the ranger. "One spellcaster in the family is enough."

"You have a spellcaster in your family?" said Revi in surprise.

"Not yet," said Hayley, blushing slightly, "but perhaps, someday."

"How about you, Arnim," asked Aubrey, "do you and Nikki want to give it a go?"

"No, thank you," the warrior replied. "I'll keep my feet on solid ground. How about you, Nikki?"

"I'm with you on this one," the woman responded. "I think we'll leave the spirit realm to the more adventurous members of our little group."

"I noticed Tempus didn't react this time," observed Gerald.

"Yes," said Anna, "I thought that strange."

"Perhaps he only reacts to you, Majesty," suggested Beverly.

"And Gerald," added Anna. "Tempus definitely reacted to the grey wolf, remember."

"I wonder if that has anything to do with your auras," said Aubrey.

"Why?" said Beverly. "Was there something strange about them?"

"The queen had a brilliant white aura," said Aubrey, "while Gerald's was a grey colour."

"And the mages?" asked Beverly.

"Mine was a pale white," said Aubrey, "much more muted than the queen's, while Revi's was white tinged with green."

"Perhaps white represents Life Magic," suggested Revi, "since we both have it."

"But why did yours have green?" asked Aubrey.

"Enchantments," said Anna, "don't you see? Revi's been learning a new school of magic."

"I wonder if an untrained mage would have an aura," said Aubrey, "or if it would only show up after training."

"It would be interesting to see Albreda's aura," said Revi. "She was self-taught."

"Yes," added Aubrey, "and she's an Earth Mage. I wonder what colour we'd see?"

"A very interesting development," agreed Anna, "but perhaps best investigated at a later date. We need to arrange for Aubrey to watch over the prisoners in spirit form."

"I doubt there's much of a hurry," said Arnim, "it'll be a few days before they'll feel much like talking anyway. With the blood loss most of them sustained, they won't feel much like doing anything."

"Very well," said Anna, "then we'd all best get back to bed, we've had an eventful night."

"I'll double the guards," said Beverly.

"Yes," agreed Arnim, "and I'll take a team and investigate how these Shadowblades made it into the Palace. We don't want them trying again."

"I don't know about the rest of you," said Aubrey, "but I can't sleep after learning about all these auras. What about you, Revi?"

"It's interesting," replied the mage, "but not as compelling as the flames. I'll leave it to you to follow up with more research, I'm far too busy to add it to my plate."

"Well, I, for one," said Gerald, "will welcome the warm embrace of sleep."

SEVENTEEN

The Streets

SUMMER 963 MC

Albreda made her way through the Palace, her footsteps echoing on the stone floor. She paused before the queen's office, the two guards nodding their heads in recognition.

Her knock was answered by a single word. "Enter."

The door opened to reveal the queen, sitting behind a desk. Tempus, on the floor in front of her, raised his head, then lowered it again upon seeing the druid.

"Your Majesty," Albreda started, "I have returned from Weldwyn with news."

"You discovered how to create the circles?" Anna said.

"I have, though I'm afraid it's not all good news."

"Oh? You must tell me more."

"There are two elements to these circles," Albreda continued, "the first is the physical construction. Which is, perhaps, the more difficult of the two."

"And the second?" asked Anna.

"The spell to enable it to work," said Albreda, "which should prove less troublesome."

"So you have the spell already?"

"Not quite, Majesty, but I'm working on it."

"Working on it? That doesn't sound promising. Do you have the spell or not?"

"It appears," said the druid, "that the spell is an enchantment, but I am confident we can adapt it to different schools. Of course, that means we shall have to decide what type of circle to create in each city."

"I hadn't thought of that," noted Anna. "I suppose it's another decision that will have to be made. What would you suggest?"

"It will depend on who casts the spell to empower it," Albreda explained. "The spell is called 'create magic circle', not the most original name, to be sure."

"Does that mean if you created it," asked Anna, "that it would be a circle of stones?"

"Not necessarily," the druid replied, "it's entirely up to the physical construction to determine that."

"You mentioned that's the hard part," urged Anna.

"Yes," Albreda said, "the construction will be quite expensive, as it needs gold and silver to hold its magic. It will also require the work of a master smith."

"A smith? Not a stoneworker?"

"The stonework required is not great, but the working of metal must be precise."

"I would suggest Herdwin," said Anna, "but he's away in Stonecastle, working with the Dwarves there. I don't expect him back for some time."

"We already have a smith that will fit the bill, Majesty."

"Really? Who?"

"Aldwin," said Albreda.

"And you think he'd be willing to come back here to do the work?"

"I'm quite sure he would, Majesty," said Albreda.

"How can you be so sure?"

"Beverly's here," Albreda replied.

"And the cost?"

"There's the rub," said the druid. "It will cost thousands."

"Can you be more precise?" asked Anna.

"It literally depends on the power level required."

"And how do these power levels work?" asked Anna. "You have me intrigued."

"The circle in the Dome is a level six magic circle. The creator, a man named Halcraft Invaris, postulated that there was, theoretically at least, no limit to the power of a circle. The only limitation was that of the caster that originally empowered it."

"And what do these power levels represent?"

"When a mage uses a magic circle, they gain additional power, that is to say, the circle boosts their casting. It would be like running on the deck of a ship. The ship's speed would be added to your own."

"That makes sense," said Anna, "but I assume that means you'd need a powerful caster to create a more powerful circle."

"Exactly," said the druid. "It also requires the permanent expenditure of magical energy."

"Meaning?"

"Meaning the caster would no longer have the same level of power. It could be built up again with further study, of course, but that would take months, if not years. It's similar to what happened when I imbued Nature's Fury, a part of me was diminished."

"So we'd have to limit the circles, in terms of strength. How powerful would we need?"

"Ideally, at least level three," said Albreda.

"How can you be so sure?" asked Anna.

"Halcraft's notes were quite precise on this point. We know that each circle is aligned to a particular type of magic."

"The schools," says Anna. "Yes, I'm familiar with the concept."

"He speculated that anyone from another school would operate a circle at a lower power."

"We've known that for some time, haven't we?"

"We have," agreed Albreda, "but now, thanks to his research, we know exactly how much lower."

"Two levels," interjected Anna, "that's why you'd need at least a level three."

"Yes, Your Majesty, but the bigger restriction is likely to be the funds. I know the coffers are low. Surely now is not the time to spend coins on such things?"

"It's interesting you say that," said Anna, "for I've just been considering something that might alleviate the problem, at least for the short term."

"Which is?"

"I'm going to sell off the Royal Estates," proclaimed the queen. "Well, some of them anyway."

"How many are there?"

"Seven in total," said Anna. "Far too many, if you ask me. Selling them off will save us a lot in expenses, not to mention their sale value."

"And how many do you intend to sell?"

"All but two," Anna replied. "I'll keep Uxley, that's my home, and I thought to give the estate at Hawksburg over to the Mages Council. They can use it to start their magic school."

"A wonderful idea, Majesty," said Albreda. "I'm sure Aubrey will be pleased."

A knock at the door interrupted their conversation.

"Who is it?" called out Anna.

"Lady Aubrey Brandon," the guard answered back.

"Well, that's a welcome coincidence," said Anna. "Let her in."

The door opened to reveal Aubrey, who bowed her head as she entered, then broke into a smile when she saw Albreda.

"You're back," she said. "I hope things went well?"

"They did," said Albreda. "I was just informing the queen of my discoveries."

"How are things with the prisoners?" asked Anna.

"Prisoners?" said Albreda.

"We captured some men attempting to assassinate me," said Anna. "They infiltrated the Palace, and we placed the three survivors in the dungeons. Aubrey's been listening to them while in spirit form."

"Very clever," said Albreda. "I assume you've discovered something?"

"I did," said Aubrey. "It appears they were hired by a man with a scar over his left eye. He found them at a place called the Black Dagger. Do you know of it?"

"No," admitted the queen, "but I'm sure Nikki would. Do we have anything else?"

"No," admitted Aubrey, "the men didn't know his name, but speculated on who he might be. Looks like one of the dead men conducted all the negotiations."

"At least it's a place to start," said Anna. "I'll get Nikki on it right away."

"Is there anything else we can do?" asked Aubrey.

"Yes," added Anna, "you work with Albreda and the other mages. We're going to construct a magic circle, here in the Palace. You'll have to figure out the best place to do that and then hire the appropriate people."

"When will construction start?" asked Aubrey.

"Soon," the queen promised. "All I have to do is sell off some estates first."

Nikki sat in the Three Rings, nursing a drink while Arnim sat beside her.

"Where is he?" complained Arnim. "He was supposed to meet us at noon."

"Be patient," said Nikki. "Harry will be here soon, he probably just got busy."

As if on cue, the man in question entered, moving to the bar. He ordered an ale, and once served, grabbed the tankard, carrying it to their table.

"Good to see you, Nik," he said, "and you, too, I suppose."

Arnim grunted a greeting.

"How are things, Harry?" asked Nikki. "Still keeping out of trouble?"

"Oh, you know how it is," replied the man. "So what is it you wanted to see me about?"

"We have a little job to do," Nikki continued, "and you're just the man to help."

"Really? You have me intrigued. What's the pay?"

"Is it always about payment with you?" asked Arnim.

"Of course," said Harry, "a man has to make a living, after all."

"Don't worry, Harry," said Nikki, "you'll be well paid."

"So what's the job?" he asked.

"We're trying to find a man that hired some Shadowblades," said Nikki.

Harry pursed his lips, "That's not something I'd care to get involved with."

"Relax, you don't have to," said Nikki, "we just need some help getting me inside."

"Inside the Shadowblades?"

"No, inside the Black Dagger. I need to get a job there. I thought you might be able to pull a few strings."

"That shouldn't be too difficult," said Harry, "but why the Black Dagger, of all places?"

"It's where the Shadowblades were hired. We're looking to find the man that hired them, and we think someone might remember seeing him."

"It's worth a try," said Harry, "but I doubt the patrons will talk to you."

"That's why I thought I'd get a job there. Servers don't miss much, I'm hoping one of the staff can help."

"Oh, I see now," said Harry, "you want to make friends with the servers."

"Precisely," Nikki confirmed.

"What about it, Harry?" asked Arnim. "Can you do it?"

"Give me a couple of days, and I'll make some enquiries," he responded.

Nikki grabbed his hand, holding it to the table, "This is important, Harry."

"How important?" he asked.

"Let's just say that if this pays off, you could find yourself permanently on the payroll."

Harry smiled, "I like the sound of that. I suppose that means we'll be in business together."

"Yes," agreed Arnim, "but no one must ever know."

"Of course," he agreed, "my lips are sealed."

"Good," said Nikki, "we'll meet back here at the end of the week."

Harry downed his ale, wiping his mouth with his sleeve. "Until then," he said, then left.

· · ·

Three days later, Nikki was working the tables, dropping off drinks and collecting tankards. It was an easy enough job, all she had to do was occasionally flirt with the customers, but she was careful to remain safe.

Soon, she learned the regulars, who were mostly harmless, and began to recognize troublemakers when she saw them. It wasn't until she'd been there a week that she made any progress that would help their investigation.

She was standing behind the bar while the barkeep went outside to relieve himself. One of the other servers, a girl named Marlee, dumped a table full of empty tankards on the counter.

"Well, that was interesting," the girl said.

"Customers giving you trouble again?" asked Nikki.

"Just one," said Marlee, looking back at the table. "The one with the red tunic can't keep his hands to himself."

"I don't think I've seen him before."

"I have," the girl added, "but not for some weeks. It's a shame, really, he's quite good looking, aside from the scar. Too bad he doesn't have manners to match."

"He's scarred?" said Nikki.

"Yes," Marlee added, "but you can't see it from here. Somewhere along the line, he got a cut over his eye."

"His left?"

"Yes, why, do you know him?"

"I know of him," said Nikki. "Do you know his name?"

"No," said Marlee, "and I don't think I want to. I wouldn't trust him not to hurt me, he seems the type."

"What type is that?"

"I think he gets women for someone else," she continued.

"What makes you say that?" Nikki asked.

"He was in here a few weeks ago, along with a rich gentleman. They were talking business over in the corner with a third man, but he didn't arrive with them."

"How do you know?"

"He left early, then just the two of them sat and talked all night. They didn't say anything while I was around, mind you, but they were generous tippers."

"This well-dressed man, can you describe him? I might have seen him before."

"Not much to say, he was rather average looking as far as I could tell."

"As far as you could tell?"

"Yes," said Marlee, "he wore a brimmed hat that hid his face most of the time. Very fancy clothes though, that much was obvious, but he tried to hide them under a cloak."

"So he obviously had wealth," mused Nikki.

"He did," admitted the girl, "and he spent it freely. He gave a bag of coins to that other fellow, the one that left, and then spent all night drinking."

"And was he free with his hands, like the other patrons?"

"No," said Marlee, "in fact, he was quite the opposite. Maybe he preferred the company of men?"

"What makes you say that?" asked Nikki.

"He had embroidery on his sleeves," she replied.

"I'm told that's common amongst the nobility," said Nikki.

"Yes, but it looked like ivy. That's not something I've seen before. What kind of a man uses ivy on his sleeve?"

"I don't know," offered Nikki, "but perhaps it had some sort of special meaning to him."

"I suppose," Marlee continued, "but he seemed to resist my charms when I tried to flirt with him."

"Why would you flirt with him if you thought he was procuring women?"

"Hey now, a little flirting helps with the tips. You can't expect me to make a living based on my wages, now can you?"

"No," said Nikki, "I suppose not."

"Anyway, it doesn't matter," said Marlee, "he hasn't come back since."

The barkeep re-entered the building, freeing up Nikki. She moved back around the front of the bar, into the common area, then turned to the barkeep. "I think I'm going to leave now, Lucan, I don't feel very well, and the place isn't busy."

"Very well," the barkeep said, "but you'll lose the day's pay."

"Agreed," she said, making her way towards the door. She soon exited, heading down the street, farther into the slums.

She had gone two blocks when she cut down an alley, pausing halfway to make sure she wasn't being followed. She exited onto the back street, then turned west until she saw the familiar sight of the run-down boarding house she temporarily called home.

She entered, then climbed the stairs, making her way to her room, where she paused and knocked three times. Someone replied with two, and then the door opened, revealing Arnim Caster.

"Did anyone follow you?" he asked.

"No one," she declared.

"You're back early."

"I think I may have discovered something, but I don't know how valuable it is."

Arnim sat on the bed. "Go ahead," he prompted.

She sat in the flimsy chair, pulling off her shoes and letting out an audible sigh.

Arnim reached over and lifted her feet towards him, then started massaging them. "What did you find?"

"A barmaid remembers seeing our man. He was in the company of someone of means."

"That doesn't help us much," said Arnim. "There are far too many wealthy people in Wincaster."

"Yes," said Nikki, "but she mentioned embroidery on his sleeves."

"Once again, not enough. We're not familiar with everybody's wardrobe, Nikki. Was there anything distinctive about it?"

"She said it looked like ivy."

Arnim stopped rubbing her feet, "Are you sure?"

"Yes, why? Is that significant?"

"It is," said Arnim, rising to his feet and dropping Nikki's to the floor.

"Can't it wait?" she begged. "I've been on my feet all day."

"I promise you a full foot rub later, Nikki, but we have to get to the queen."

"Why, what is it?"

"There's only one man I can think of that would have ivy on his clothes, it's part of his coat of arms."

"Who is it, Arnim?"

"The Earl of Shrewesdale!"

Arnim finished his report.

"Is that everything, Arnim?" asked Anna.

"It is, Your Majesty. There's no doubt in my mind that Lord Montrose is responsible."

"Yes," agreed Gerald, "but there's a far cry between knowing and proving. We have only the flimsiest of evidence. We know he was in Wincaster on the day in question, but we can't prove it was him in the Black Dagger. None of this would stand up in court."

"Then let us not use the courts," said Arnim. "A knife can kill, regardless of the victim's social status."

"No," said Anna, "we will not stoop to their level. I want Shrewesdale punished publicly. If we can't get him on this, we need something else."

"But what?" asked Arnim. "We've looked into it. The man covers his tracks."

"I've given this some thought," said the queen, "and I think I know how we can proceed. Arnim, you used to be on the town watch, correct?"

"I was, Your Majesty," Arnim responded.

"Good, I'm sending you north to get a written statement from Heward."

"Sir Heward? Why?"

"He was party to the death of a knight," said Anna.

"It was war," said Arnim, "lots of knights were killed."

"No, not in the war," said Anna, "before the war. I'd like you to get his statement about a knight named Olivia, back when he was in service to the Earl of Shrewesdale."

"You think the case has merit, Majesty?" said Arnim.

"I don't know yet," said Anna, "we'll know more once I see his statement."

"Very well, Majesty," said Arnim, "I shall leave directly."

"And when you return," Anna continued, "I'll likely be sending you to Shrewesdale to find some witnesses. If my plan works, we'll have Lord Montrose where we want him, and a trial can commence."

"Are you sure that's a good idea, Anna?" asked Gerald.

"We have to stop the man," the queen replied. "He's too dangerous to remain on the loose."

Arnim bowed, then left the room, leaving Anna and Gerald remaining.

"What are you thinking, Anna?" asked Gerald.

"If we can't get him for hiring those Shadowblades, perhaps we can accuse him of treason."

"But you gave amnesty to those nobles that swore an oath," objected Gerald.

"Yes," said Anna, "but before the war, he ordered the death of a Knight of the Sword, and I might remind you that the amnesty only relates to their military opposition, nothing more."

"I'll go and find Beverly," said Gerald, "she'll need to be apprised. I don't think she's going to like it becoming public, though."

"I can't say I blame her, but it may be the only way to stop him. Bring Beverly here, Gerald, it's probably better if I talk to her."

"Very well," said Gerald, "but remember, it was a traumatic experience for her. You'll need to have patience."

"I will, Gerald. I promise."

EIGHTEEN

Shrewesdale

SUMMER 963 MC

Arnim halted his horse, staring off at the distant city of Shrewesdale.

Nikki pulled up beside him. "Well," she asked, "how do you want to proceed?"

"I think it best if we split up," he replied. "We'll enter together, but I'll spread the men out throughout the city while you make some discreet enquiries."

"You think they might try to flee?" she asked.

"I wouldn't put it past them. Heward said there were a total of twelve witnesses to the orders, not including himself. Eight of those died either before or during the war. That leaves only four. I imagine they're a pretty tight bunch. If they get wind we're after them, we might lose them. All you have to do is identify them. We know their names, but we need faces, or they'll slip through the gates."

"I'll do what I can," she promised, "though I don't imagine it will take very long."

Arnim turned to the man behind him, "Captain Newbury?"

"Yes, my lord?"

"Keep the men close. When we enter the city, I want you to detail four of them to watch the gate. The rest will come with me."

"Yes, sir," the captain responded.

Arnim worried that his presence might too easily be noticed. He was, after all, a viscount now, but his fears seemed to be for naught, for when he entered the gate, no one gave him any special attention, even with the men of the Wincaster Light Horse following behind.

Nikki soon peeled off, making her way towards the estate of the earl and the knight's barracks. Arnim, meanwhile, led the men farther into the city, posting them at key intersections.

His mission complete, he rode within sight of the barracks but kept his distance. He waited for some time until finally he saw Nikki emerge, carrying some empty bottles on a tray. As soon as she spotted him, she dumped them in an alleyway, then ran across to join him.

"Any luck?" he asked.

"They're all there," said Nikki. "In fact, they're all drinking in the same room."

"I didn't think it would be so easy," said Arnim.

"It's not done yet," Nikki warned. "There's more in there than just the ones we're looking for. They might put up a fight."

"A good point, I suppose," said Arnim.

"What do you want to do now?" she asked.

"You keep an eye on them from here," he said. "I'll go and collect the light horse. We'll cut off their retreat and then move in to take their statements."

"And if they resist?" she asked.

"Then they'll be arrested for obstructing justice," declared Arnim.

Sir Gavin laid down his last card, "There, you see? The king of swords." He reached forward to pull the coins towards him but was stopped by Sir Albert.

"Wait a moment," the man said, "I believe two mages trumps a king."

"Don't be ridiculous," Gavin objected, "you can't have two mages, they've all been played."

"You forget," said Albert, "we re-dealt the deck. You really should pay more attention, my friend."

Their two companions tossed their hands onto the table.

"It appears you win again, Sir Albert," said Sir Peter. "You have the luck of an Elf."

"More like the luck of a cheater," accused Sir Tristram. "I can't believe he's won the last four rounds."

"What can I say," defended Sir Albert, "you're just not very hard to fool."

Sir Gavin was about to say more when the barracks door swung open. A stranger stood in the doorway, with more men behind.

"I'm looking for some men," he announced.

"Oh, yes?" said Sir Gavin. "Then perhaps you should try the Red Hen, I hear they cater to all sorts?"

"Are you Sir Gavin?" asked the stranger.

"I am," he admitted, "what of it?"

"My name is Lord Arnim Caster, Viscount of Haverston. I'm here seeking statements."

Sir Gavin rose, "I'm sorry, my lord, I had no idea who you were. You say you're seeking a statement, may I enquire as to what it concerns?"

"Yes," said Arnim, "it concerns the death of a fellow knight, back in '56."

"A fellow knight, you say?" asked Sir Gavin. "I don't recall such an event, do you, lads?" He looked around the room.

"Let me jog your memory," said Arnim. "It was a woman by the name of Dame Olivia Jacobson."

The room suddenly went quiet.

"I'm not sure we have much to tell you," said Sir Gavin.

"I already have a sworn statement from Sir Heward," Arnim announced, "so you can either give your version of the events or share in the punishment." He stepped inside, allowing Captain Newbury to enter as well. Six more men waited outside.

Arnim looked down at the table, "This game is over, gentlemen. Put aside your winnings."

He waited as they cleared the table, then placed a stack of papers down. Captain Newbury stepped forward, giving each an inkpot and quill.

"I expect a full account, gentlemen, and they'd better match. I might also remind you I have been granted permission from the crown to take whatever means are necessary to ensure your cooperation."

Sir Gavin glanced at Sir Albert with a worried look on his face.

Arnim slammed his fist down on the table. "There will be no talking while you write. If I see any of you coaching the others, it will result in a charge of treason. Am I understood?"

They all nodded, then bent to the task of writing.

Arnim watched as they worked. Sir Gavin's penmanship was at least legible, while that of Sir Tristram was nothing but scratches. He grabbed the knight's notes, crumpling them.

"Captain Newbury?" Arnim said.

"Yes, sir?"

"Take Sir Tristram outside, and write his statement for him as he dictates it. He can sign the declaration once he's done."

"Very well, my lord."

The captain escorted the errant knight out while Arnim looked around, daring the witnesses to object, but they all sat silently as the three remaining knights wrote their statements.

Finally, the last man, Sir Albert, looked up. "Is that all?" he asked.

"No," said Arnim. "Pack your things."

"My things, Lord?" the man responded.

"Yes," said Arnim, "are you deaf?"

"No, my lord, but why?"

"You're coming back to Wincaster, all four of you."

"But I'm in service to the earl," he objected.

"Not anymore, you're not," declared Arnim.

"You can't do that!" said Sir Albert.

Arnim fished a folded paper out of his tunic. "This says I can," he stated.

"What is that?" asked Sir Gavin.

"Orders for your reassignment, signed by the queen herself. Of course, you're more than welcome to take it up directly with her, once we're in Wincaster. Any objections?"

"No," said Sir Gavin.

"No, what?" yelled Arnim.

"No, my lord," the man replied in a subdued tone.

Sir Peter raised his hand, "A question, if I may, my lord?"

Arnim rounded on the man, then took a breath, calming himself. "Yes?"

"May we gather our things, my lord?"

"Of course," said Arnim, as if talking to a child. "Captain Newbury will have some of his men come and help you pack." Arnim gathered up the statements, tucking them into his tunic. "We'll meet in the courtyard when you're ready."

He nodded his head at the rest of the knights. "Gentlemen," he said, "a good morning to you all," then strode from the room.

Nikki saw him exit the barracks and let out a deep breath. "I trust everything went well?"

"Yes," said Arnim, "much better than I had anticipated. It appears the Knights of Shrewesdale were not as loyal to the earl as I had thought."

Nikki smiled, "Good to hear, let's just hope the trial goes as easily."

The winds had turned cold, and the first snow of the year threatened in the sky by the time Wincaster came into view. Arnim halted, staring at the far off city, his thoughts elsewhere.

Nikki rode up beside him. "Problem, my love?" she asked.

Arnim turned, looking at the men who had halted behind him. The Wincaster Light Horse encircled the knights, though truth be told, their prisoners looked relieved to be nearing the capital.

"This isn't going to work," he stated.

"What isn't?" asked Nikki.

"This trial that the queen is engineering."

"Why would you say that?"

"Shrewesdale is too clever," Arnim continued, "he'll have a contingency plan."

"What can he do?" she asked. "We have all the witnesses we need. You worry too much."

"I disagree," he said, smiling to lessen the argument. "We tried digging up dirt on him before. The man's made himself immune to prosecution."

"It's the queen's right to charge him with treason."

"Yes, but her insistence on a trial may be the end of it."

"You think he'll be found innocent?" she asked.

"Maybe," he mused, "but even if he's found guilty, he'll leverage his power to damage us."

"How? He's charged with treason. How could he possibly turn that on us?"

"I don't know," he admitted, "but just thinking about it gives me an uneasy feeling."

"It's the only way, Arnim."

"Is it? I sometimes wonder if a dagger in the back would be preferred, at least then we'd be rid of the man."

"Queen Anna wants the rule of law," Nikki reminded him "She won't rely on murder to achieve her objectives."

"No," he admitted, "I suppose not, but perhaps someone will do us a favour and save the crown the cost of a trial."

"Arnim, no!" she reached out to touch his arm. "Don't do anything of the sort, promise me. I can't bear the thought of losing you again."

He looked at her a moment, indecision wracking his features. He finally nodded, "I won't, I promise."

"Good," she replied, "you have too much to live for."

"What's that supposed to mean?" he asked.

She looked back at him, love in her eyes. "I was going to wait to tell you the news," she said, "but I think now is the best time."

"Tell me what?"

"I'm with child," she said.

His forehead wrinkled up in thought for just a moment, then his whole face lit up. "That's wonderful news!" he exclaimed. "Saxnor's beard, Nikki, I thought you were going to tell me there was something wrong with you!"

"So you're happy?" she asked.

"Happy? No, I'm ecstatic!" He grabbed her hand, crushing it to his lips. "How long have you known?"

"Only a few days," she admitted, "but I was hoping to wait till we were back in Wincaster before telling you."

"Why would you wait?" he asked.

"I don't know," she admitted, "I suppose I wanted a more romantic setting. I never imagined that when I told you I was pregnant, we'd be on the road like this." She looked over at the horsemen behind them. "You have to admit, it does stink of horses."

"Does it?" he said. "I hadn't noticed. All I can see right now is you, my love."

"I suppose this means I'll have to meet your family," said Nikki.

"Of course," he replied, "and we shall have a great celebration! Is it a boy or a girl?"

She looked at him in surprise, "There's no way to tell until it's born. You should know that, you come from a large family. Why? Does it matter? Are you that determined to have a son?"

"No," he said, "I suppose not. We live in a new age, Nikki, our child can rise to great heights."

"And if they don't want to?"

"Then we shall love them anyway," he promised.

"Now that's the Arnim I fell in love with."

Arnim turned to face the riders. "I am happy to announce," he called out, "that we are to have a child."

"Congratulations," yelled back Captain Newbury. The horseman then turned in his saddle, to face his men. "A cheer for Lord and Lady Caster! Hip, hip."

"Hooray," the men bellowed back, their voices filled with gusto.

"Of course," the captain continued, "you realize, my lord, that it is customary to buy a round of drinks at such an announcement."

"And so I shall," replied Arnim, "but I will wait until we are within the city and have safely discharged our duty to the crown." He looked back at Nikki, who was watching him through tears of happiness. He nodded in the direction of Wincaster, "Shall we, Lady Caster?"

"We shall, my lord," she replied.

NINETEEN

The Rose of Bodden

WINTER 963/964 MC

Gerald stared down at his troop roster once more, determined to sort things out. He was interrupted by someone opening the door and looked up in annoyance at the unannounced visitor. His attitude was replaced by a smile when he saw the queen and Tempus.

"Anna," he said, "I'm surprised to see you down here. I'd have thought you'd have other things to look after."

She smiled back as Tempus trotted over for a pet. "We thought we'd come and visit," she said, "and Tempus was missing you."

Gerald rubbed the great dog's ears. "He looks in fine form," he remarked, "I don't remember him being so soft."

"It's Aubrey's doing," said Anna, "her regeneration spell has made a marked improvement. I'm thinking of having her give you regular treatments."

"I'm too old for that," he replied.

"Nonsense," she said, "it would make you feel better, and I must admit to a little self-interest in the matter."

"Oh," he said, "and what would that be?"

"Why, keeping you around longer," she said. "I want you here when my children are born. They'll need their grandfather, after all."

He smiled at the thought. "In that case, I'd be honoured," he said, "but I don't know that I'd have the time, just yet."

"Not to worry," said Anna, "it doesn't take long to cast. I expect Aubrey would like you to receive a spell once a month, perhaps a little more as you grow older."

"Older? I'm already old, Anna. How much older do I have to be?"

"As old as you can," she said, smiling. She moved closer to look at his desk. "What's this you're working on?"

"I've been going over the muster lists for the army," he said. "Since the war ended, I've had a hard time deciding who we keep and who to discharge. It's easy enough for the common soldiers, but good officers are hard to find. I'd hate to lose them."

"Why not create a reserve," she suggested, "and then we can keep track of them? If war breaks out, we'll have a core of decent officers to rapidly expand the army."

"That's an excellent idea," said Gerald, "but how can we afford it?"

"Interesting you should ask that," she said, "for I've been going over the realm's finances."

"You have?" he said in reply. "Wasn't that a lot of work?"

"It was," she admitted, "but one that was well worth my time."

"I take it you found something," he said.

"I have," she said. "It appears the Master of Finance has been skimming from the treasury."

"Has he now?"

"He has," replied the queen, "and would you like to guess who it is?"

"I don't know," admitted Gerald, "such things are far too complex for me. I'm just a simple soldier."

"No, you're not," said Anna, "and I might remind you that you're the one that taught me to read ledgers, or don't you remember the finances at Uxley Hall?"

"Yes," he said, "and you were a quick study if memory serves."

"I was," she admitted, "but I couldn't have done it without you, Gerald."

"All right then, I'll bite. Who's the Master of Finance?"

"A man named Lord Barrington, do you know him?"

"No," said Gerald, "why? Should I?"

"I suppose not," continued Anna, "but Beverly knew the name."

"She did? I never took her for an expert on finance."

"She's not," said Anna. "In fact, she'll tell you that herself, but Lord Barrington, along with Lord Montrose, are the two men that pressed for your execution after what happened on Walpole Street, all those years ago."

"Walpole street? You mean the riot? Why would they do that?"

"They met with Baron Fitzwilliam," said Anna. "Beverly told me all about it."

"She was there, too?" he asked.

"She was, at her father's insistence. He wanted her to witness the exchange."

"So what, exactly, transpired?" he asked.

"Lord Barrington was pressing for a scapegoat in the death of Lord Walters. You remember him?"

"I could hardly forget him," admitted Gerald, "the man completely lost his head. It led to a slaughter."

"He wanted your death," Anna continued, "and Shrewesdale agreed, but Baron Fitzwilliam talked them out of it."

"And that's why I was sent to Uxley," said Gerald, "I should have known. All these years I thought it was a reward, but I suppose they just wanted me out of the way."

"Fitz did his best to protect you," said Anna. "He only had your best interests in mind."

"I know that, Anna, and I'll still thank the man. If he hadn't sent me to Uxley, I wouldn't have met you."

"There, you see?" she said. "It all worked out for the best."

"So this Lord Barrington, how did he become the Master of Finance?"

"He held the position under King Andred. When my brother, Henry, took over, he simply remained in place."

"And he's still there?" said Gerald. "How much do you think he's pilfered over the years?"

"Thousands," said Anna. "I've put him under arrest pending a full investigation."

"Then who's going to look after the finances?" he asked. "You can't do it, you're too busy."

"For now, Aubrey's agreed."

"Her plate's pretty full already," said Gerald.

"I know," said Anna, "it's just temporary until I can find someone else."

"And Lord Barrington, what will happen to him?"

"I'm of two minds. On the one hand, I'd like to see him punished, but on the other, a deal might enable me to recover some of what he stole. What do you think I should do?"

"I would give him an option. Perhaps if he were to plead guilty to a lesser charge and paid back as much as he could, you might spare his life?"

"An excellent idea," she said, "and it would save me the cost of a trial. See, this is precisely why I like having you around."

"So THIS is why you came to visit me," he said in a satisfied tone.

"Not exactly," said Anna, "there's more."

"Do tell," he encouraged her.

"I've decided to go ahead with the charge of treason against Lord Montrose."

"The Earl of Shrewesdale? Are you sure? He's the most powerful person in the kingdom."

"No," said Anna, "I am, and I intend to keep it that way. He must be seen to be punished for his crimes."

"What do you mean, 'must be seen'?"

"I mean to make the trial public," she said.

"Is that wise?" he asked. "What if you lose?"

"I won't," she replied.

"Are you saying it's a show trial?" he asked. "That could backfire."

"No, not a show trial, the charges are real as is the evidence."

"What evidence do you have?" he asked.

"Lots of witnesses, all of reputable character. In addition, Arnim brought back logbooks and order books chock-full of interesting tidbits. I believe the evidence to be quite convincing."

"I see," said Gerald. "It appears you have everything well in hand."

"I do," said Anna, "but I need your help."

"I'll do whatever you want," said Gerald, "but I'm not an expert in law."

"And you don't have to be," said Anna. "I need someone to serve the warrant for his arrest."

"You want me to arrest Shrewesdale?"

"Not personally," said Anna, "but I'm in a bit of a dilemma."

"Which is?"

"I can't trust the Knights of the Sword to make the arrest, too many of them served the earl in the past."

"Then send Beverly," said Gerald, "she wouldn't flinch."

"I can't, don't you see?" said Anna. "If I send someone close to me, they'll say it's been trumped up. I have to give it legitimacy. I need someone unbiased to place him under arrest."

"Who do you suggest then?" he asked.

"I was hoping you might have an idea," she said.

"It's quite a dilemma," he mused. "We need someone that's known to be neutral." He sat for a moment in silence, thinking things over. "It has to be Baron Fitzwilliam," he finally said.

"But he's our ally," said Anna.

"Yes," said Gerald, "but he's universally acknowledged to be a fair and honest person. He's even worked with Montrose before, you said so yourself."

"You're right," said Anna, "I should have seen it."

"Of course, we'll need to bring him to Wincaster to make the arrest. Is Albreda here?"

"She is," said Anna. "She's been helping Aubrey plan out our magic circle. Why?"

"She can get to Bodden quickly and return with Fitz."

"You called him Fitz!" said Anna with a chuckle.

"Of course," Gerald admitted, "he's not here."

"What about the north?" asked Anna. "The Norlanders have been hopping about a bit of late."

"I'll dispatch Beverly to take his place while the baron is here, that is if you can spare her?"

"Very well," Anna said. "You'll also need some men to accompany Fitz when he makes the arrest."

"Montrose is a noble," said Gerald, "you'll have to allow him house arrest. I'll arrange some soldiers to keep an eye on him."

"It'll have to be someone we can trust," warned Anna. "I wouldn't put it past Shrewesdale to try to bribe them."

"Don't worry," said Gerald, "I have just the men, though I'm hesitant to use the term."

"Why? What have you got in mind?"

"I thought I might use the Queen's Rangers," he said with a grin.

"Do we have enough of them?" she asked. "I thought they were still in training."

"They are," Gerald confirmed, "but some of them are Orcs. I have a hard time believing they'd take a bribe."

"All right," she said, "but we'll have to be careful, we don't want to give him any cause for getting the charges thrown out. This must be done according to the law, I insist on it."

"Very well," Gerald agreed. "I'll make the arrangements. How soon can you get Fitz here?"

"I'll talk to Albreda and Beverly. I'll let you know by dinner time. And don't be late," Anna warned, "last time the gravy got cold."

"I won't," he promised.

Albreda looked to Beverly, "All set?"

"Ready when you are," the red-headed knight replied.

Albreda began the incantation, calling upon arcane forces to activate the spell of recall.

Lightning shifted nervously as the area around them began to whip up dirt and leaves. Soon, the entire yard was obscured, then the air changed, releasing the scent of the woods. The dust swirl dropped, and the forest of the Whitewood surrounded them.

Lightning snorted, causing Beverly to laugh, "He doesn't seem to like the experience."

"He'll get used to it," offered Albreda. "I remember the first time I took Snarl through a recall spell, he wasn't too impressed either."

Beverly extended her hand. "Come on," she said, "Lightning can easily carry us the rest of the way, it'll be much faster than walking."

A moment of indecision crossed the druid's face before she nodded her head. "Very well, we are in a hurry, after all."

Albreda took the proffered hand and settled in behind the knight, who then urged the great Mercerian Charger forward. They were in the western end of the Whitewood, only a short ride from the Keep at Bodden, and once they cleared the forest, Beverly could see the place she had always called home.

The inner Keep rose above the other fortifications, providing a clear view of the surroundings. Beverly could almost imagine her father, staring out the windows of his beloved map room, watching them as they rode across the countryside.

"I hear you're building a magic circle in the Palace," called out Beverly.

"Yes," confirmed Albreda, "though the actual construction hasn't started yet. We're still in the planning stages."

"When do you expect to begin?"

"Soon," replied the druid, "I should like to have it well underway by mid-winter."

"You might consider putting one in at Bodden," suggested Beverly. "It would certainly see its fair share of use."

"Yes," agreed Albreda, "but the stone circle in the Whitewood will have to do for now. Unfortunately, each time we create a permanent structure of that type, we lose a little of our magic."

"Like you did when you created Nature's Fury?" she asked.

"Exactly the same," said the druid. "In a sense, they're both magical artifacts, imbued with part of our power."

"I must thank you for doing so with the hammer," Beverly continued, "it certainly saved us at Redridge. I don't think anything else could have hurt those blights."

"I knew it had to be empowered when I first saw it," said Albreda. "Aldwin has exceptional skill. In fact, we're going to need him to come to Wincaster to create the circle."

"Aldwin? Create a circle?"

"Yes, for the actual construction," said Albreda.

"But he's a smith, not a stonemason."

"The circle calls for worked metal. Do you think he can work with gold and silver?"

Beverly laughed, "I suppose so, they're just metal. He'd probably find it easy after dealing with sky metal."

"Yes, I was hoping you'd say that," said Albreda.

They rode on in silence until the walls loomed closer. Soon, they passed through the gate into the village itself, the guards welcoming them. Not long after, they rode into the inner courtyard of the keep itself.

Albreda chuckled as they did. "I see they've finally managed to repair the gate I destroyed."

"About time," said Beverly, "it had been that way for more than a year."

"Well," added Albreda, "there was a war on, after all. We can't expect every repair to be carried out immediately."

They halted, and the druid dropped from the back of Lightning. Beverly soon followed and began leading the great warhorse towards the stables.

"Dame Beverly," called out a familiar voice. "Good to see you, my lady."

Beverly looked to see Sergeant Blackwood. He was just mounting, no doubt ready to head out on a patrol. "And you," she responded.

"Are you joining us?" he asked.

"I'm here to take my father's place while he's needed in Wincaster."

"Anything you need me here for? I can delay the patrol if you want."

"No, Sergeant. That won't be necessary. Is my father in the map room?"

"Of course," the man replied, "where else would he be?"

"A valid point, I suppose," said Beverly.

"Your father always did like the view," added Albreda.

Blackwood dismounted, "Let me take your mount, my lady, it'll free you up to go and see your father."

Beverly hesitated, her duty to Lightning warring with her duty to her father. "Very well," she said at last, "but he needs a good brushing."

"I remember, my lady," said Blackwood.

"Now that's settled," said Albreda, "shall we find your father?"

"By all means," agreed Beverly.

They made their way into the Keep and through the great hall. While they were climbing the steps to the map room, Beverly remembered her youth. As a little girl, she always found the steps intimidating, but now, as a full-grown woman, they weren't as steep as she recalled. She rushed up the last few to find Baron Fitzwilliam standing by the window. He turned at her entrance. "Beverly, so good to see you," he said with a smile.

She moved closer, embracing him, "So good to see you too, Father."

It was then she noticed the other occupant of the room.

"Aldwin? What are you doing here?"

"I er..." the smith mumbled.

"He was consulting with me," said Fitz quickly.

"About what?" asked Beverly, suspicion colouring her words.

"About this," said Aldwin. He stepped forward, something held in his hand.

"What is it?" asked Beverly.

"A ring," answered the smith. "I made it for you."

She moved closer, looking down at the silvery-grey ring.

"It's sky metal," she said, "like Nature's Fury."

"It is," Aldwin admitted. "There was a little left over."

"And you made this for me?" she asked. "What is it? Is it magical?"

Her father chuckled. "In a sense, yes," said Fitz. "It's meant to join you in holy matrimony."

"A wedding ring?" she said, peering closer. "It's beautiful!"

"Yes," agreed Fitz, "and we've been talking. I think it's time we settled this matter, once and for all."

"Whatever do you mean, Father?"

"I mean that it's time you two were married."

"Of course," said Beverly, "I've been saying that for years."

"I mean right now!" the baron persisted.

"Now?" she said in surprise.

"Yes," added Aldwin, "that is if you want to?"

"Nothing would make me happier," Beverly admitted, "but surely there are plans to be made?"

"Nonsense," said Fitz. "All it really needs is the Holy Father. I can have him up here in no time unless you can think of a better place to get married."

"The great hall, perhaps?" suggested Albreda.

"No," said Beverly, "this room would be perfect."

"Good," said Fitz, "because I called for the Holy Father when I saw you coming across the fields."

"How did you know I'd agree?" she protested.

"Come now, my dear, isn't it obvious? You're my daughter, I think I know your mind by now."

"I haven't a wedding dress," said the knight.

"I don't care," said Aldwin, "and perhaps it's fitting that you get married in your armour."

"I should have to agree," came a voice from the door. Father Baldrim entered the room. "I understand my services are needed?"

"They are," said Fitz.

"I assume you shall present the bride?"

"I shall," confirmed the baron.

"And what about the groom?" asked Father Baldrim.

"I shall have that honour," said Albreda, "assuming it's all right with him?"

Beverly looked to Aldwin, "Well?"

"Of course," said the smith, "I would be honoured."

"Very well," said the Holy Father, "then let us proceed."

They lined up in front of him, Beverly and her father to one side, Albreda and Aldwin to the other.

"Do you, Dame Beverly Fitzwilliam, take Aldwin Strongarm-"

"Just Aldwin," interrupted the smith.

"My apologies," said Father Baldrim. "Do you, Dame Beverly Fitzwilliam, take Aldwin as your husband. To love and honour all your days?"

"I do," she said.

"And do you, Aldwin, take Beverly as your wife, to love and honour all your days?"

"I do," the smith said.

"Then take the ring and place it upon her finger," the Holy Father said.

Aldwin tried to slide the ring on her finger, but there was a brief moment of panic as it didn't seem to fit. Once Beverly bent her finger slightly, it slipped on quite easily.

"I don't have a ring for you," she said.

"You can sort that out later," said the baron.

"Very well," Father Baldrim continued, "then with the blessing of Saxnor, I pronounce you husband and wife."

"Is that it?" asked Albreda. "Somehow, I was expecting more."

"This is a warrior's wedding," defended Fitz, "short and sweet. After all, it's not the wedding, but the life together that's most important."

"As it should be," agreed the druid.

Beverly and Aldwin were both staring at the Holy Father, waiting for something.

"Oh, yes," Father Baldrim resumed, "you may now kiss."

Beverly stepped forward, her lips meeting those of Aldwin. All her worries faded to nothingness in that moment, and she held on, not wanting it to stop. She could sense Aldwin's strong arms wrapping about her waist and felt almost weak at the knees, and perhaps, just a little giddy. They finished the kiss but kept their embrace, staring into each other's eyes.

"I think it's time we give them some privacy, Richard, don't you?"

"Of course," said the baron. "Beverly, your old room has been prepared for you and your new husband."

"Thank you, Father," said Beverly, choked up with emotion. "You too, Albreda."

"You're quite welcome, my dear," said Fitz. "Now, you two hurry off, there'll be plenty of time for a celebration dinner later. We'll have a huge feast set up for you in the great hall."

When they broke their embrace, Beverly took Aldwin's hand in hers. "Come on," she said, rushing from the room in glee, "I've waited a long time for this!"

They disappeared down the stairs, their footfalls echoing behind them.

"They make such a happy couple," observed Albreda.

"So they do," agreed Fitz. "Tell me, would you ever consider marriage?"

Albreda looked at him with a stern look, "Richard, I'm flattered, but it's not necessary."

"But it's not proper to be together if we aren't married," he objected.

"Marriage is not necessary for a loving relationship," said Albreda. "Now come, let me show you."

She led him down the stairs towards his bedchamber.

"I present to you, Lady Beverly Fitzwilliam and Lord Aldwin Fitzwilliam," said Fitz, as he raised a cup. They sat at the head table, a great feast laid out before them.

"I'm not a lord, my lord," objected the smith, "nor am I a Fitzwilliam."

"Nonsense, my boy, I'm the Baron of Bodden, I can call you whatever I like."

"I'm just a simple smith," he insisted.

"So you are," agreed the baron, "and a damned fine one, but as husband to Beverly, you rank as a noble. In Merceria, it's customary for the wife of a noble to become a lady, I see no reason why the reverse should not be true."

Beverly smiled at her husband. "Lord Aldwin Fitzwilliam," she mused, "I like that."

"Yes," agreed the baron, "and it ensures that future generations shall continue the family name. Though I must admit, Beverly, I gave you bad advice all those years ago."

"What advice was that, Father?"

"I once told you to marry a weak-minded man, then you'd control the barony, but you've fooled me. You married a strong man and still managed to find a way to rule Bodden when I'm gone. I couldn't be happier for you!"

"Thank you, Father," Beverly replied, "though I'm in no hurry to assume the position."

The baron chuckled, "And glad I am to hear it. Now, it's time you two received the blessings of the hall."

As if in answer, the guests started banging their tankards on the table. Beverly dutifully kissed Aldwin, causing a cheer to erupt.

Sir Gareth rose, and the room fell silent. "Ladies and gentlemen," he began, "we are gathered here today to celebrate the union of our noble Lady Beverly, to Aldwin, Master of the Forge. I would like to wish the bride and groom the best of health, wealth and future happiness. For many years men have sung of the Rose of Bodden, and now, it seems, her heart has been captured by the man with the arms of steel and a pureness of heart."

"He captured my heart years ago," called out Beverly, to be met with hoots and hollers.

"I stand corrected," said Sir Gareth, slurring his words slightly. "However, it falls to me to remind her ladyship of the honour and obligation that falls to one who will eventually inherit the barony."

"Which is?" called out Beverly.

"Children!" yelled back the knight.

The guests all started pounding the table again, prompting yet another kiss from the happy couple.

"Let us allow them some time," said Fitz. "After all, she's not the Mistress of Bodden, yet."

Everybody laughed, prompting Sir Gareth to take his seat. Then started the song. Beverly couldn't tell who began it, but soon, the whole room was singing, a marching song that brought a smile to her face.

T'was the mistress of Bodden, a knight of renown.
She fought many battles and rescued the town.
She fought with great bravery which set her apart,
And the great smith of Bodden did capture her heart!

TWENTY

The Arrest

WINTER 963/964 MC

"Baroness," said Fitz, "are your men ready?"

"They are," replied Hayley, "though they're not all men."

"Sorry," the baron said. "You have men, women and Orcs. I'm not sure which form of address would be appropriate.

"They're all rangers," she suggested.

"Of course," he said. "In that case, are your rangers ready?"

"They are, my lord," Hayley replied.

"Good," said Fitz, "then let us delay no longer."

He turned, looking directly at the impressive structure that stood before him. The Earl of Shrewesdale was a rich man, thanks to his marriage to his late wife, the daughter of the previous earl. Fitz strode up the walkway to the door, the rangers following. Halting, he rapped the door three times with the hilt of his sword.

"Open up, in the name of the queen," he called out.

People on the street stopped to stare as a servant opened the door. The colour drained from the man's face at the sight of the rangers.

"In the name of Queen Anna, I am here to arrest Lord George Montrose, Earl of Shrewesdale. Stand aside!"

Fitz pushed his way in, followed by Hayley and two rangers. The rest waited at the door, taking the servant into custody, lest he try to warn his master.

They found Montrose in his library. He had risen at the sound of the knock on the front door and now stood, waiting, his face a mask of calm.

Fitz halted as he entered the room. "You are under arrest," he announced, "on the charge of treason."

"I see," said the earl. "I suppose I should have expected as much from our young queen. Am I to be hauled off to the dungeon?"

"You are hereby placed under house arrest," said Fitz, "and are forbidden to leave Wincaster, under penalty of death."

"And how long is this punishment to remain in place?" asked the earl.

"Until such time as a trial can determine your guilt or innocence."

"Guilt or innocence?" said Montrose. "I should have thought my guilt would have been a foregone conclusion. Why else would the queen arrest me, if not to see me executed?"

"The queen believes in the law," said Fitz, "and promises a fair and just trial. You are allowed to seek counsel. The rangers will guard your estate. You are not to leave it, do I make myself clear?"

"You do," said the earl, "very clear indeed. May I ask who is to be my jailer?"

"Baroness Hayley Chambers of Queenston," said the baron. "Though you will likely not see her in person."

"I see," said the earl. "In that case, who is to be my intermediary?"

In answer, the baron nodded to Hayley. She disappeared into the hallway to reenter a moment later, an Orc in tow.

"This is Graluk," said Hayley. "He will be your jailer."

"An Orc?" said the earl. "This is preposterous. How am I to communicate with him?"

"Graluk is fluent in our language," said Hayley, "and I might add, he's a very gifted hunter."

"Hunter?" said Montrose.

"Yes," said Fitz, "an expert tracker, should the need arise."

"I see," the earl said. "Are there any other restrictions until my trial?"

"Yes," said Fitz. "All communications in or out of the estate are subject to search. Any visitors must be announced to the rangers. Any staff members that leave the estate will be followed. Within those restrictions, you are at liberty to act as you see fit."

"And my defence?" he asked.

"You may choose your own representative, but his name must be forwarded to us so that his passage may be allowed."

"This hardly seems fair," complained the earl.

"I should think it far more comfortable than the dungeons of Wincaster," said the baron, "or would you prefer that?"

"No," said Montrose, "I accept your limitations."

"Very well then," said Fitz, "I bid you a good day, Lord Montrose."

"And a good day to you, Lord Fitzwilliam," the earl replied.

. . .

Gerald made his way through the Palace, plate in hand. He had been to the kitchens only to find that Anna had not eaten. Taking matters into his own hands, he arranged for food to be prepared and resolved to deliver it himself. Now, he wandered the halls, a covered plate in hand, wondering why the damn thing was so heavy.

Finally, he approached the door to her office, nodded at the two guards there, and then opened the doors. Anna was, as usual, behind her desk while Tempus stretched out on the floor in front. The great mastiff immediately sat up on Gerald's arrival, capturing the young queen's attention.

"Gerald!" she said, a smile creasing her lips. "What have you got there?"

"Your dinner," he said, laying his burden on the desk. He pulled the cover from the tray, revealing the tasty meal beneath.

"Sausages," she said, "my favourite. Will you join me?" She pushed the papers aside, then lifted the plate, placing it before her.

"I've already eaten," he said.

"I've never known you to resist an extra sausage," she countered.

He looked at the plate, indecision evident on his face. "Very well," he finally decided, "maybe just one." He reached across the table, plucking a sausage from the plate. Looking around the room, he spotted a chair, so he dragged it to the desk and sat.

"What have you been up to?" he asked.

She tucked a slice of meat into her mouth and chewed it, deep in thought. Gerald could almost see her mind working out the details of something.

"I've been giving this trial some thought," she said at last, then sliced off another piece of sausage.

"And?" he prompted.

"Shrewesdale is proving to be quite... what's the word I'm looking for?"

"Difficult?" he suggested.

"Yes, difficult." She popped another slice into her mouth, chewing it quickly.

"The man's fighting for his life," said Gerald. "I would expect him to resist as much as possible. What is it he's being difficult about?"

"He knows the law well," said Anna, "and he's insisting things be done properly."

"Meaning?"

"Meaning he knows that, by law, he can only be judged by his peers."

"What does that mean?" asked Gerald. "He can only be judged by other nobles?"

"Not just nobles, but peers. The nobles must be equal or greater in rank than him."

"So just the earls and dukes then," said Gerald. "Is that a problem?"

"It might be," said Anna. "You see, there are only four people that can rule on the case at the moment."

"Four? Is that all?" said Gerald. "I would have expected more."

"The only other earl is Tewsbury," said Anna, "and we know he's a friend of Montrose."

"But the dukes, surely we have enough of them?" said Gerald.

"Well," she continued, "there's you, of course, along with the Duke of Kingsford. The only other duke is the Duke of Colbridge, and his father stood against us in the war."

"So you expect a stalemate," said Gerald. "Two votes for either side."

"Yes," confirmed Anna. "We can appoint someone to Eastwood, but that might be seen as interference if we name someone we trust."

"A fact that Montrose is no doubt counting on," mused Gerald. "Now, I see the problem."

"The problem is plain enough, but what I don't see is a solution."

"I think the solution is clear," said Gerald. "Appoint your own person and let him hang."

"I want a fair trial," said Anna, "and the kingdom deserves it. I can't push for new laws and then ignore them to get my own way. The law must be fair to all, even if I don't agree with it on occasion. I don't want the realm returning to an absolute monarchy."

"You have to appoint someone to rule Eastwood," said Gerald. "It's been without a duke since Valmar fled."

"I will," said Anna, "though I'm going to return it to an earldom, as it should be."

"Why was it made a duchy?" asked Gerald.

"King Andred made the decision after the rebellion. He gave it to Valmar and wanted him to be a duke rather than an earl. I suppose it sounded more grandiose. It really doesn't warrant that, though, its population is too small."

"Still, you have to appoint someone to the position."

"I suppose I do, but if I make the wrong decision, it could ruin everything we've worked for."

"You can't keep second-guessing yourself, Anna. During your reign, you'll have to make many decisions. They won't all be easy."

"I know that, Gerald, but this one comes at a pivotal moment."

"Pivotal?" he said. "What makes this any different from the other choices you've had to make?"

"This one will have far-reaching consequences," she explained. "If the trial is considered fair, the people of the realm will see a bright future, but if they think we're just putting on a show, they'll lose their faith in me. It's a heavy burden to bear."

"You're not bearing it alone," said Gerald, "I'm here for you, we all are."

"Thank you," she said. "It's nice to know there are people I can trust. I suppose that's the root of the problem. I'm fine with those I know, but I have a hard time trusting those outside my circle of friends."

"That's only natural, Anna," he said, "but, as queen, you have to learn to accept the things you can't change. There's far too many positions to fill to use only your friends."

"And therein lies my dilemma," she said. "What do I do?"

"You trust your own people to find others," he said. "It's not unlike the army."

"Oh? What do you mean?"

"Well," he continued, "you put me in charge of the army and allowed me to delegate command to others. It's the same way with the rest of the realm, isn't it? You don't tell Aubrey how to run Hawksburg, or Lord Avery how to run Kingsford, do you?"

"No, I suppose not," she admitted.

"Then you must allow your people to make their choices for you. They won't always make the right one, but it's important that you support them, nonetheless. You can't have people second-guessing themselves all the time. King Andred did that, and look what it got him, nothing but fear and loathing."

"You're right," said Anna. "Thank you, Gerald, you've lifted a great weight from my shoulders."

"That's what I'm here for," he said. He took a bite of his sausage, feeling the fat dribble down his beard.

"There's more of them here," said Anna.

"More of what?" he asked.

"The sausages, silly," she giggled. "I'm not going to eat them all."

"You're obviously feeling better," he said.

"I am," she admitted. "You always know how to help me think things through."

"So what are you going to do about Shrewesdale?" he asked.

"I'll arrange a meeting with him," she said, "and we'll come to an agreement as to an acceptable jury. If we're going to lose this trial, let us at least be seen as being fair and just."

. . .

Gerald, in his position as Duke of Wincaster, was the one to meet with Shrewesdale, at least officially, but it was Aubrey who did most of the talking, a fact that was much to the marshal's liking.

They sat at a large table, Gerald, Aubrey, and a clerk on one side while Shrewesdale and his retinue took the other.

"I take it," said the earl, "that you've come to resolve the issue of the jury." He smiled in what Gerald felt was a condescending manner.

"We have," said Gerald, "and we think we may have a solution that will be acceptable to both sides."

"I'm intrigued," said Montrose. "I had expected you'd place one of your own on the jury."

"The queen wants a fair trial," insisted Gerald.

"So you keep saying," said the earl, "and yet here you sit, yourself a commoner elevated to the ranks of the nobility by the queen herself. Fine clothes do not a noble make."

Gerald remained calm, despite the insult.

"If I may," interrupted Aubrey, "we are here to come to an agreement suitable to all. Will you hear us out?"

"I will," said Montrose, "though it pains me to be in the company of one so rustic." He stared at Gerald, daring him to say something.

The marshal merely smiled at the man's attempts. "Please proceed, Baroness Brandon," Gerald said.

"In light of the recent war," said Aubrey, "we maintain that Valmar's claim to the Duchy of Eastwood is null and void, wouldn't you agree?"

"I suppose I would," said Montrose. "After all, the man has fled, has he not?"

"We would further propose," continued the baroness, "that we recognize the claim to the title Earl of Eastwood put forward by Lord Spencer."

"The previous earl's nephew?" said Shrewesdale in surprise. "Now that is an interesting thought, considering his uncle took up arms against his rightful king."

"The sins of the father are not the sins of the line," said Aubrey, "and, truth be told, Eastwood fought against tyranny, not unlike our present queen."

"You realize," said Shrewesdale, "that the Winthrop-Spencer family trace their nobility back for countless generations."

"We are aware of that," said Gerald.

"And that he's unlikely to side with a commoner," Montrose added.

"We are willing to take that chance," said Aubrey. "The queen desires a fair trial, even if we should lose."

"Tell me," said Montrose, "if I should lose, I'll obviously lose my head, but what will happen if I win?"

"You will receive full restitution of your lands and holdings," said Aubrey.

"And your queen is willing to accept that decision, should it be rendered? I would hardly like to be fighting this for years."

"She is," confirmed Gerald.

"Excellent," Montrose replied, "though I would like to consult with my people before I make a decision on this appointment."

"Of course," said Gerald, rising from his seat.

Aubrey followed his lead, along with the clerk. They made their way from the room, walking down the hallway a little before halting, well out of earshot.

"Well," said Gerald, "what do you make of it?"

"I think he might go for it," Aubrey stated. "He didn't offer any real argument to the contrary. It's more of a gamble for us."

"How so?" he asked.

"We don't know much about Lord Spencer," she said, "or how he'd feel about the charges."

"I've met him once," admitted Gerald.

"I didn't know you mingled with the nobility, Gerald. When did you meet him?"

"It was years ago, at Uxley. Henry came to visit, he was only a prince then, of course. He was meeting two of his friends before they continued north to hunt. One of them was a young Lord Spencer."

"What was he like?" she asked.

"He didn't impress me much," Gerald replied, "in fact quite the reverse. He tried to force himself on poor Sophie. At least he would have if we'd have left him alone long enough. I can't abide someone that would do such a thing."

"Does the queen know all this?" Aubrey asked.

"She does, but she has little choice. There's no other legitimate claim to the title."

"Can he be trusted to behave?"

"Anna will warn him when she offers him the title. He's likely smart enough to agree."

"Poor Sophie," said Aubrey. "I imagine it would be quite disturbing to see him at court."

"I'm sure Anna would have talked to Sophie about it. She trusts her maid implicitly. If she thought it hurtful, she'd never suggested it in the first place."

"It gives me the shivers, just thinking about someone like that," said Aubrey, "and to have him at court..."

"Sophie's a different woman now," he said. "She's the queen's confidant and Lady-in-Waiting. She'd stab him if he tried anything like that again."

"Stab him?"

"Yes, and the queen wouldn't argue, that's how much she's trusted."

"How long ago was this?" Aubrey asked.

"Let me think now," he said, looking at the ceiling as he thought back. "Must have been five years ago or so."

"Didn't the Earl of Eastwood have a son?" asked Aubrey.

"He did," said Gerald, "he was a Knight of the Sword, but he died during the war. Beverly told me he was awarded his spurs during the same ceremony as her."

"I assume he fought for the king?" she said.

"He did," agreed Gerald, "and he died at the Battle of the Crossroads."

"Killed by the men of Bodden?"

"Actually, I believe he was killed by the Kurathians," corrected Gerald.

"How do you know all this?" she asked.

"As marshal, it's my job to keep track of such things. With the war over, we had to go through the list of knights and see who was left."

"And out of curiosity," said Aubrey, "how many remain?"

"Not many, I can tell you. The order was decimated, but that's no surprise. They were, after all, the chosen knights of the king."

"The very reason we can't trust them now," mused Aubrey, "with a few exceptions, of course."

"You're thinking of Heward," said Gerald.

"He seems the capable sort," she replied, "and a good man to have around in the north."

Gerald turned to her in surprise. "Are you fond of the Axe?" he asked.

"Not in the way that you think," she said, "I merely respect his ability. Besides, he's far too old for me."

"I suppose you'll have to marry, eventually," suggested Gerald.

"Speak for yourself," said Aubrey, "you're the Duke of Wincaster now, the same could be said of you."

"Well spoken, Aubrey, I'll give the victory to you. Shall we see if the earl has agreed to our proposal?"

"Yes," she said, eager to change the topic. "I think he's had long enough."

They made their way back down the hallway and knocked on the door. One of Shrewesdale's men opened it, admitting them.

"Have you come to a decision?" asked Gerald.

"Yes," said Montrose, "we have decided to agree to your proposal. Please convey to Her Majesty that I find the appointment of Lord Spencer to the rank of Duke of Eastwood to be most acceptable."

"The queen has returned the title to that of an earl," said Aubrey, "as befits the size of the city."

"It makes no difference," said Montrose, "it is still acceptable."

"Thank you, Your Grace," said Aubrey, bowing slightly.

Gerald remained standing tall, refusing to honour the earl.

"I suppose now the trial can move forward," said Montrose.

"It can," said Gerald.

"Good," said Shrewesdale, "I'm looking forward to it."

"You are?" asked Gerald.

"Indeed," confirmed the earl, "once this is over, I can resume the life to which I have become accustomed."

"You're assuming you're going to win," said Gerald.

"What can I say, I'm an optimist," said Montrose, a smile breaking across his face.

TWENTY-ONE

Preparation

WINTER 963/964 MC

Beverly dismounted, her breath frosting in the chill morning air. Beside her, Aldwin squatted, trying to stretch his legs out.

"I don't know how you can sit in the saddle for such a long time," he said.

"I've been riding all my life," she defended, "and Lightning is a much larger mount than yours."

"Perhaps I should have a Mercerian Charger," he suggested.

"I doubt that would help," she said, "unless, of course, you're intending to take up arms."

"No," he replied, "I'll leave that to you, though I must confess I do like these early morning rides."

He let the stable hand take his mount away, then followed his wife as she led Lightning into the stable.

"I love watching you two," he said. "You have such a bond with each other."

Beverly continued removing the saddle, "My father always said that it's a knight's duty to look after their mount."

"I feel guilty," he said, "letting the stable hand do my work."

She smiled, "It's fine, Aldwin. Your place is in the forge, not the stables. It's different for me, I have to rely on Lightning during battle."

Aldwin leaned back against the wall. "Well, I, for one, am grateful that the knights are here. I don't think I could do everything you do."

"And I couldn't do half the things you do," she retorted. "That's what I love about you, you're so creative." She looked at the ring she wore, pausing a moment and smiling. "This ring is so beautiful," she said.

"Yes," he said, "and now I have one to match."

"Just how much of that sky metal did you find?"

"There was only enough left for my ring," he confessed, "though I suppose there's a sliver or two remaining, but not enough to make anything useful."

"The design is so beautiful," Beverly continued, "and you even managed to inscribe a rose."

"Of course," he said, "you are the Rose of Bodden, after all."

"And yours has an anvil," she said, "how very appropriate."

"It sounds like a pub," mused Aldwin, "The Rose and Anvil."

"So it does," agreed Beverly. She produced a brush and began the process of grooming her mount, while the great beast stood still, enjoying the attention.

A soldier poked her head in at the entrance to the stables.

"My lady?" she called out.

"Right here, Samantha," Beverly replied.

The archer entered, moving towards the stall. "Begging your pardon, but we've spotted visitors approaching."

"I suppose you were a bit premature in removing your saddle," suggested Aldwin.

"Nonsense," said Beverly, "we don't need to ride to the wall, we can walk."

"Good," he said, "my legs thank you, as does my backside."

"I'll massage it later," offered Beverly.

Aldwin blushed, and then Beverly remembered they weren't alone.

"We'll be along directly, Sam," she said, "but call out the guard, just in case."

"Very well, my lady," the archer replied, heading out the doorway.

"Shall we?" Beverly asked.

"We shall," Aldwin agreed.

They made their way to the gate tower, looking out over the fields to the north. It didn't take long for Beverly to recognize the visitors.

"It's Albreda," said Aldwin.

"Yes," she agreed, "and Sir Heward. I'm surprised to see him back here. I thought the frontier was having problems."

They waited patiently as the two riders drew closer, then Beverly ordered the gates opened. Soon, the visitors were within the defences.

"We weren't expecting you, is something wrong?" asked Beverly.

"Not at all," said Albreda, "but the queen wants you back in Wincaster. I've brought Sir Heward to take command of Bodden."

"What of the north?" asked the red-headed knight.

"That will fall to Commander Lanaka," said Sir Heward. "The marshal saw fit to promote him on my recommendation."

"What's happening in Wincaster that requires my attention?" asked Beverly.

"The earl's trial is to begin soon," explained Albreda. "The queen wants you there for it. She'll be watching the whole thing from the balcony, and she needs you there to protect her."

Beverly turned to Aldwin. "It looks like I have to go," she said.

"He's going with you," added Albreda.

"He is?" Beverly said in surprise.

"Yes, he is," said the druid. "We're ready to begin construction of the circle, and we need his smithing skills."

Beverly's face lit up, "That's marvellous. We'll be able to stay at the Palace!"

"Yes," agreed Albreda, "and the queen said to tell you they've arranged for a nice big bed for you and your new husband. Oh, and she also sends her congratulations."

"Congratulations from me as well," said Heward. "I'm sorry I missed the celebration."

"Thank you," said Beverly.

"When do we leave?" asked Aldwin. "I would like to pack a few tools."

"First thing in the morning," said Albreda. "I'll recall you to Hawksburg, and then we'll ride for the capital."

"It'll be nice when your circle is finished in Wincaster," mused Beverly.

"Indeed," the druid agreed, "but don't worry, we'll get there soon enough."

"When is the trial set to begin?" asked Aldwin.

"It's still a few weeks away," said Albreda.

"Why the delay?" queried the smith.

"The queen has ordered rows of seats made for the spectators," said Albreda.

"Spectators?" interjected Beverly.

"Yes," the druid continued, "didn't I mention that? The trial is to take place in the cathedral. The queen wants it seen by as many people as possible."

"I didn't think nobles were tried in public?" said Aldwin.

"They're not," explained Beverly, "but it looks like that's going to change from now on."

"Yes," agreed Albreda, "though hopefully they won't all be held at the cathedral."

"We're going to need more troops in the capital," said Beverly, "especially if we're going to keep the cathedral secure."

"Already being taken care of," offered Heward. "We're moving troops south from Hawksburg."

"What of the frontier?" asked a concerned Beverly.

"It's wintertime," explained Heward. "The Norlanders won't make an effort till late spring. Even so, we've plenty to hold them off with, and the marshal has ordered some new defences built for Wickfield and Mattingly."

"What type of defences?" asked Beverly.

"Mostly earthworks for now, though I know there's a plan to eventually build some towers."

"It seems things were well in hand during my absence," Beverly noted.

"Your absence was keenly felt," continued Albreda. "The marshal will be glad to have you back."

"Agreed," said Heward, "and you'll be able to show off your new husband."

Beverly blushed while they all chuckled. "I suppose I can," she said. "I hope they aren't upset that I didn't include them in the ceremony."

"They're fine," said Albreda, "though I do remember someone saying it was 'about time'!"

"Well," said Beverly, "if we're going to return to Wincaster, we'd best make the necessary arrangements. If you'll accompany me to the map room, Sir Heward, I'll fill you in on what's happening here at Bodden."

"Good idea," said Aldwin. "That gives me time to go to my forge and see what tools I think I'll need."

"I'll come with you, Aldwin," said Albreda. "I have some sketches that Aubrey created for the circle. It'll give you some idea of what we have in mind."

"Very well," said Beverly, "we'll meet up again when we're all ready."

Next morning found Aldwin waiting in the inner courtyard. He had a chest with him, full of tools, instruments, and his leather apron. Beverly soon joined him, bringing Lightning from the stables. She walked him over, stopping to look down at the massive chest.

"Are you bringing the entire smithy?" she asked.

He grinned back, "From what Albreda tells me, the measurements will be precise. I've developed a lot of specialized tools."

"They have smithies in Wincaster," the knight objected.

"The same could be said for horses," he replied, looking at Lightning.

"All right, you win," she said.

"It's not a competition," the smith reminded her.

"You're right, of course. I apologize."

"In any case," he continued, "even without the chest, I still have the most valuable thing I need."

"What's that?" Beverly said.

"You," he answered, staring into her eyes.

They were interrupted by Albreda, who exited the Keep, moving towards them. "Sorry for the delay," she said, "but your father wanted me to pick up a few things for him while I was here."

"We're ready whenever you are," said Beverly.

Albreda halted, looking down at the chest, and then to Lightning. She shifted her position, placing herself in the middle. "This looks best," she said, more to herself than anyone in particular.

The druid began casting the recall spell, causing dust and dirt to fly up around them. Soon, it obscured the nearby Keep. The swirling wind continued, and then the sky changed, from a bright winter day to the ceiling of a room.

"I think you'll find the stairs a tad constricting for your horse," explained Albreda. "Aubrey has plans to open up the ceiling and put in a ramp, but I'm afraid we have to make do with what we have for the present."

"I'm glad I wasn't mounted," observed Beverly. "At least there's light down here. Who arranged that?"

"Aubrey had the Orcs put in a small window to let in the light. It's actually in the ceiling."

"Can't you cast a globe of light?" asked Beverly.

"I'm afraid it's not in my repertoire," replied the druid. "Now, let's get out of this cellar and find the rest of us some horses, shall we? You can leave the chest here, Aldwin, we'll have someone retrieve it later."

Albreda led the smith up the stairs, with Beverly following. The knight waited till she was at the top and then called Lightning. The great warhorse squeezed his bulk through the stairwell, emerging, a moment later, into the remains of the library.

"Definitely a tight fit," mused Aldwin.

"He's seen tighter," said Beverly. "Now, let's get a move on, shall we?"

They exited the building and trod through the snow to the main manor house. The group of Orcs on guard noticed their arrival and waved them through. They were soon in front of the manor, where the Orc shaman, Kraloch waited.

"Redblade," the Orc said in greeting, "you surprise us with your arrival, it was not expected."

"I'm afraid I'm not here for long," Beverly explained, "we must be off to the capital. We'll be leaving as soon as these two can arrange mounts. Oh, and we'll need a packhorse for Aldwin's chest, as well."

Kraloch turned, barking out commands. Soldiers rushed off to secure horses for the travellers.

"I hear Lanaka has been placed in command," said Beverly.

"He has," said the shaman, "but he is at Wickfield, setting up constant cavalry patrols to watch the river for any sign of crossings. He left me in charge here."

"I'm sure you'll do a good job," said Beverly. "Have you any dispatches for Wincaster? I'd be happy to take them if you do."

"I anticipated your offer," he said. "My Orcs are gathering my notes as we speak."

"Does that mean they're in Orcish?" asked Aldwin.

"Of course," replied Kraloch, "but the marshal can read and write our language."

"He can?" said Beverly.

"Yes," the Orc continued, "he's been working on it for some time. He felt it offered a secure means of communication."

"Secure, how?" asked Aldwin.

"If a message were to be intercepted, none but an Orc would be able to read it."

"Unless they had magic," cautioned Albreda.

"There is that, I suppose," said Kraloch, "but there are few that can cast that spell."

"Few enough for it to be secure, I'd wager," agreed Aldwin.

Kraloch stared at the group a moment, his eyes flickering between Beverly and Aldwin. "Something is different," he finally said.

"Different?" asked Aldwin.

"You and Redblade wear matching rings," he said. "Does that mean you are bonded?"

"We are," admitted the smith.

Kraloch moved forward, grasping Aldwin in a bear hug and lifting him from his feet. "The best of hunting to you," he said, then lowered the man to the ground. The Orc moved to Beverly, repeating the gesture. "And to you," he added.

"Thank you, Master Kraloch," she replied.

"And when is the blessed union to produce a child?" the shaman asked.

"Why does everyone keep asking that?" responded Beverly.

"It will be a while yet," explained Aldwin. "We're both rather busy to be raising a child."

"This is a great day," said Kraloch. "I shall be happy to tell our brethren of the bonding of Redblade and Steelarm."

An Orc came from the house, holding a satchel. He stood waiting until two men rounded the corner of the building leading horses.

Kraloch took the satchel, handing it to Beverly. She had already mounted Lighting, ready to ride, while Albreda and Aldwin were still settling onto their horses. Soon, they were all ready to depart.

"I'm sorry we didn't have more time to visit, Master Kraloch," said Aldwin, "but our business in Wincaster cannot wait."

"Understandable, Steelarm," said the Orc. "May the ancestors guide you."

They rode off into the distance as a light snow began to fall.

Gerald looked up at the balcony. It was to be the Royal Seat from which Anna would watch the proceedings, but he wondered, once again, if she would be safe enough.

A cough caught his attention, and he turned to see Captain Sanderson. The man had served in the army of Weldwyn and then under Gerald when they came to Merceria's aid. He had been amongst the first of the westerners to volunteer to aid the cause and had risen to become the captain of the Guard Cavalry.

"What is it, Sanderson?" asked Gerald.

"I have word that Dame Beverly is on the way," the captain replied.

"Good," said Gerald, "I'd like her opinion on the balcony."

"It looks strong enough to me," ventured the captain.

"I'm not concerned about its strength, merely its ability to protect the queen. Someone with a crossbow could easily shoot at her."

"We'll be searching all the visitors," advised Captain Sanderson. "I think that doubtful."

"Perhaps," said Gerald, "but I've been mistaken about things before, and I won't take the risk."

"Perchance a higher railing?" the captain suggested.

"That might obstruct her view of the proceedings."

"She only needs to see the one end," Sanderson said, "where the accused will sit, does she not?"

"That's true," Gerald mused. "Why, what do you have in mind?"

"You can block the view of the commoners if you feel the need. That would undoubtedly make her safer."

He was tempted to agree, but then he remembered the purpose of the balcony. "No, it won't work," he finally realized, "the queen wants the commoners to see her. She's their queen as much as the nobles. We'll just have to be extra careful about searching people when they enter the cathedral."

"Who is to be in the other balcony?" asked the captain.

"Some of the higher-ranking nobles," said Gerald, "but I'll want a few of your men over there as well. The footmen will be in charge of securing the lower level, while your men will all be up here until needed to escort the queen back to the Palace. It would be so much safer if that magic circle were finished, then we could just use it to return."

"I doubt the queen would wish that," offered the captain. "You know how she is about seeing the common folk."

"As we both know," said Gerald, "but I swear this trial will be the end of me."

"Sir?"

"It's wearing on me, that's all," said Gerald. "I'm getting too old for this sort of thing."

The captain grinned, "That's why you want Dame Beverly here, isn't it?"

"I see I appointed the right man to the job," said Gerald. "Any news on when she'll arrive?"

"My understanding is they'll be here as soon as she's finished reporting to the queen. They arrived early this morning."

"They?" said Gerald.

"I was told that she arrived with Lord Fitzwilliam."

"You mean Baron Fitzwilliam," Gerald corrected.

"No," insisted the captain, "I mean her husband, Lord Aldwin Fitzwilliam."

Gerald looked at the man in surprise, "You might have mentioned that."

"I believe I just did, sir."

"Very well," Gerald continued, "when the happy couple arrives, send them directly here, to me. I still have to organize the seating on the main floor."

"Very well, sir," said the captain, turning to leave.

"Oh, and one more thing, Captain!"

"Yes, sir?"

"Next time you have news like that, bring it up first."

"Yes, sir!"

Beverly and Aldwin made their way through the imposing doors of the cathedral. The smith looked up, awed at the sight of the magnificent edifice.

"Is this where you were awarded your spurs?" he asked.

Beverly halted, turning to see the joy in his face. "It was," she said, "though technically, I won my spurs at Bodden. This is where the official ceremony was held, though."

"Incredible," said Aldwin. "I've never seen its like."

"You've been in Wincaster before," she teased.

"Yes," he admitted, "but I've only seen this place from a distance." He examined a section of wall, "The stonework here is astounding."

"Some of the best in the realm," agreed Beverly.

"I don't know how I'm going to compete with the likes of this," he mused.

"Compete?" she said.

"With the circle, I mean," he clarified. "My understanding is it requires a high degree of skill."

"You made Nature's Fury," said Beverly, "not to mention our rings. I'm sure some gold and silver runes won't be a problem for you. Don't let this place intimidate you."

Footsteps drew closer, echoing throughout the structure.

"What's the meaning of this, Dame Beverly?" called out Gerald.

Aldwin wheeled about at the marshal's approach.

"You should have told us you were getting married," continued Gerald, "we would have had a celebration."

"It was a quick decision," said Beverly. "I didn't know anything about it until I got to Bodden."

"I'm just teasing you both," said Gerald, breaking into a grin. "Congratulations, though I must say it took you long enough."

"Hey now," said Beverly, "it wasn't my fault."

"Good to see you, Aldwin," said Gerald, "or should I say, Lord Aldwin?"

"Aldwin will do fine, Marshal."

"Gerald, please, let's keep this informal."

"Very well," said the smith, "Gerald it is."

"Now," continued Gerald, "if I can tear you two apart for a while, I need your opinion on a few things, Beverly. You can tag along if you like, Aldwin, but I'm afraid you likely won't find it very interesting."

"You two go ahead," said the smith. "I'll just look around the cathedral some more, I find this place quite spectacular."

Aldwin made his way into the structure, his eyes wandering to the ceiling, its expansive mural capturing his imagination. The cathedral was remarkable, the tallest building in the city aside from the towers on the wall, but it was more than just its size, for the interior held no single spot that was devoid of carvings or paintings.

His wanderings led him down the nave and into the back of the building to the offices of the Holy Father himself, as well as those of the church hierarchy.

Soon, Aldwin was lost to the world, totally absorbed by all he saw. Finally, he found himself in front of an ornamental door frame, decorated with creatures from the Afterlife. Catching the attention of a passing guard, he enquired, "What's this?"

"It leads to the crypts," the soldier responded.

"Shouldn't it be guarded?" asked Aldwin.

"There's no other exit," explained the guard, halting. "It's a dead end."

"Fascinating," Aldwin observed. "What's it like down there?"

"It's just a collection of tombs," the soldier explained, "and it goes on forever."

"What do you mean, 'forever'?"

"It's like a maze down there," the man corrected, "but we've searched it thoroughly, there's no other way out than through this door."

"Thank you," said Aldwin.

"My pleasure," the guard replied. "Might I ask who you are and why you're here?"

"I'm Aldwin… Lord Aldwin Fitzwilliam," said the smith, struggling with the new title.

"Sorry, my lord," the guard bowed, "I didn't realize."

"Don't worry," said Aldwin, "I'm not quite used to it myself."

"Is there anything else I can do for you, Lord?"

"No, thank you, you've been quite helpful."

The soldier bowed once more, then resumed his journey, leaving Aldwin to examine the crypt entrance.

Anna looked around the table, the meal complete.

"How are things looking for tomorrow?" she asked. "Is everything ready?"

"It is," said Gerald. "The troops all know their assignments, and we have soldiers stationed around the cathedral tonight to prevent anyone from sneaking in."

"I'll do a walkthrough in spirit form first thing in the morning," said Aubrey.

"And the escort will be ready at first light to take you there," added Beverly.

"And Arnim," the queen continued, "are you ready to prosecute?"

"I am, Your Majesty," Arnim replied. "I've gone over all the testimonies and statements. I'm confident we'll win."

"Good," said Anna, "but remember, Lord Montrose can be a tricky opponent. He'll likely have something up his sleeve. You must be wary of traps."

"He's ready," offered Nikki, "believe me. He's done nothing but review the testimony for days."

"Revi, your thoughts?" said Anna.

The mage looked up, and Gerald was shocked; his eyes had dark circles under them, and his entire face looked sunken.

"Are you feeling all right?" Gerald asked.

"I'm fine," replied Revi. "I've just been up late, studying. I wouldn't expect you to understand."

Gerald was taken aback by the mage's response, but before he could say anything, Revi continued.

"The preparations seem adequate, though I cannot speak for the prosecution of this case."

"You think we missed something?" asked Arnim.

"Perhaps," said Revi.

"Care to elaborate?" pressed Nikki.

"Much as Her Majesty has indicated, I fear a ploy of some sort will be forthcoming from the earl. He has shown himself to be a careful player, from all I know of him."

"You think there might be an attempt to free him?" asked Gerald.

"No," said Revi, "I think his play might be legal in nature. That is to say, he'll try to use the law to his advantage, though not being learned in legalities myself, I cannot say what this ploy might be."

"We'll have to be extra careful," said Nikki.

"Agreed," said Anna. "Now, it's time we were done here. We have an early start in the morning, and I expect the trial will drag out for days." She stood, prompting the others to do likewise.

"A good rest to you all," she said.

TWENTY-TWO

The Trial Begins

WINTER 963/964 MC

Gerald looked down from the balcony. The cathedral was packed with commoners, all eager to see the display of the queen's justice. He looked across at the balcony on the other side, noticing the nobles of the realm watching the events below with eager anticipation.

To his side sat Anna, along with Aubrey, Sophie, and of course, Tempus. Revi had declined the offer to join them, while Beverly and Hayley's duties kept them busy elsewhere, securing the cathedral.

The trial began with introductions, a suggestion that Anna had made, along with the reading of the charges. Gerald knew his time here, with Anna would be limited, for he was to form part of the jury that would decide the earl's fate.

He saw Fitz moving along the balcony towards them and stood.

"It's time," said the baron.

"Thank you," said Gerald, freeing his seat.

Baron Fitzwilliam bowed to Anna. "Your Majesty," he said, "you do me a great honour."

"Please be seated," said the queen, "the trial will soon start in earnest."

Gerald made his way along, exiting by the far stairs. He passed several guards as he went, members of the Guard Cavalry and each a face he recognized. He reached the floor where Hayley waited to guide him to his place at the table where the jury would sit in judgement.

He nodded to the Duke of Kingsford as he joined them, while the others mostly ignored him.

Arnim was just beginning his opening speech, though Gerald had already heard it. Lord George Montrose, the Earl of Shrewesdale, was charged with treason. He had ordered the death of a Knight of the Sword, an act that was only permitted by the reigning monarch. Arnim was well-spoken, his opening speech rehearsed, and once done, he sat down with confidence.

It was now the turn of Lord Montgomery Harwood to stand, he being the chosen defender of the earl. Lord Harwood was a distant cousin of Montrose's, though Gerald couldn't remember exactly how they were related. He was said to be an eloquent speaker, no doubt the reason he was chosen for this task.

Lord Harwood stood, waiting for the booing of the commoners to subside before speaking.

"My lords," he said, addressing the panel of jurors, "before we begin, I should like to bring up a point of order."

"Which is?" asked the Duke of Kingsford, Lord Somerset.

"I propose that since the alleged offence took part under the rule of King Andred the Fourth, our present queen cannot bring these charges forward. It simply wasn't during her reign."

"I object," said Arnim, standing. "The queen is of the Royal Line and can act on behalf of any previous monarch."

"And by what right do you claim such a thing?" enquired Harwood.

"Down through the centuries there have been examples of such behaviour," defended Arnim.

"Have there, now?" said the defence. "Then I think it necessary to provide evidence of such examples."

"This is outrageous," complained Arnim. "His lordship is merely trying to delay the inevitable."

Lord Stanton, the Earl of Tewsbury, turned to his fellow jury members, "He may have a point."

"What are you saying?" asked Lord Somerset.

"I'm saying," the old man continued, "that as a point of law, we must establish if this is true. Ruling hastily in this manner could have long-lasting repercussions."

"You can't be serious!" accused Gerald.

"I'm afraid I must agree," added Lord Anglesley, the young Duke of Colbridge. "If we are to do this properly, we must address the earl's concerns." He turned to Lord Somerset. "You're the head of this jury," he continued, "if we are to reach a consensus on innocence or guilt, we must allow the earl to use all possible methods in his defence. To do otherwise would not be considered a fair trial."

"Very well," said Lord Somerset. He rose, waiting as the murmurings of the crowd quieted. "It is the decision of this jury that this line of enquiry is allowed. We, therefore, call on the court to recess until tomorrow. Will that be enough time for the crown to gather the information it requires?"

"Yes, your lordship," said Arnim.

"Then, the court is adjourned. We shall gather again tomorrow morning."

The Master of Heralds, the host of the proceedings, called on the visitors to stand as the jury exited the chamber.

Anna watched with interest, still seated.

"That was a surprise," said Fitz.

"We should have anticipated it," said Anna.

"What do we do now?" asked Aubrey.

"We return to the Palace. Aubrey, I want you to give Arnim a hand. He'll need all the information you can find on historical precedents. I'll give you full access to my office. I think you'll find what you need there."

"What will you do, Majesty?" asked the Life Mage.

"I'm going to look into something else," Anna said. "I have a feeling this won't be the only obstacle he's going to throw up."

"Shall we announce you're leaving?" asked the baron.

"No," said Anna, "we'll let the commoners file out without interruption. I want to talk to Arnim before I leave."

"Shall I fetch him?" asked Aubrey.

Anna was looking down at Arnim even as the mage spoke. The Viscount of Haverston was talking to Nikki, collecting his notes as he did so. When he briefly looked up towards the balcony, the queen beckoned him. He nodded his head, passing his notes to his wife, then made his way to the stairs.

A short while later, Arnim stood before the queen.

"Your Majesty," he said, bowing.

"He caught you off guard today," said Anna, "you should have expected that."

"I apologize, Your Majesty, if I failed in my duty."

"This is not a game, Lord Caster," said Anna, her voice tight. "If we lose this, the crown will lose face. I need you at your best. If you cannot perform satisfactorily, then I will have to relieve you of your duties."

Arnim's stance grew more rigid, "Understood, Your Majesty."

"Good," said Anna. "Now, you'd best get to work, you've a lot to do before this trial continues, and very little time in which to do it. I'm sending Aubrey to help you."

"Thank you, Majesty," the Viscount uttered. He backed away from the queen, bowing again, then turned, fleeing the encounter.

"He's trying his best," offered Fitz.

"I know he is," said Anna, "but he must anticipate the earl's tactics."

"This is not a battlefield," protested the baron.

"Isn't it?" she replied. "It may not involve armies, but don't believe for a moment that this isn't a test of resolve. We must win this, or all our future plans will be in doubt."

"Time to go, Your Majesty," Sophie interjected quietly.

Anna turned to her servant. "You're right, of course," she said. "Thank you, Sophie."

The queen rose, moving towards the stairs, Tempus following. The baron watched her leave the balcony, and then looked to Aubrey.

"She's under a lot of pressure," the Life Mage explained.

"So I see," said Fitz, "but she must learn to control her temper if she is to continue to rule."

"She will, Uncle," said Aubrey, "but she doesn't have Gerald here as a calming influence. I don't expect it will lessen until the trial is over."

"I hope you're wrong, Aubrey, for both our sakes."

Gerald's eyes struggled to remain open. Arnim was presenting documents to the court, a seemingly endless stream of examples wherein choices made by previous rulers were upheld by their successors.

He felt a nudge and turned to see Lord Somerset looking at him.

"I think we've seen enough," the Duke of Kingsford said, "don't you?"

"I would agree," said Gerald.

Somerset turned to the others, "Are we in agreement, gentlemen?"

They all nodded, prompting Sommerset to stand. "The jury finds that the crown has presented enough evidence on this matter. It is the opinion of the court that the queen is quite within her rights to carry out this prosecution. We entreat the representatives of both sides to continue on with more pressing matters and let the trial resume."

Lord Harwood stood, bowing, as did Arnim, but when the viscount made to speak, he was cut off.

"If I may," Lord Harwood began, "there is another matter which has come to my attention that deserves the consideration of the jury."

"And what might that be?" asked Lord Stanton.

"That Her Majesty, Queen Anna, is not the legitimate ruler of Merceria."

The audience erupted in a furor, causing the Master of Heralds to call for silence. He even had to threaten to empty the room before the noise finally subsided.

"I do not make this accusation lightly," Harwood continued, "but recent information has come to my attention that casts our sovereign in a new light."

"This is preposterous," burst out Gerald, "of course she's the queen."

"I beg to differ," said Lord Harwood. "To be the rightful ruler of Merceria, she would have to be the offspring of King Andred IV."

Gerald's blood ran cold, and he sat in stunned silence as Lord Harwood continued.

"I have here," he said, producing some documents, "a journal of the king's activities in the time prior to Queen Anna's birth." He placed the papers on the juror's table. "I think you'll see it plainly shows that not only was he not present at the birth, but didn't in fact, spend any time with Queen Elenor for the entire year before. There is no way that King Andred could be Queen Anna's father."

Once again, noise erupted, and the Master of Heralds struck his staff repeatedly to calm things down.

"In addition," Harwood continued, "I have affidavits here that detail significant, some would even say controversial matters about Queen Elenor."

He placed another piece of paper on the table. "This document details those present at the birth of our sovereign, at the Royal Estate outside of Hawksburg. You'll notice that only one man of significance was present, that of the queen's confessor. This same man," he dropped another page, "had been in the company of the queen for a significant amount of time, almost three years, to be exact."

He waited for the crowd, using their shouts of indignation to his advantage. "And this," Harwood produced another page, "is a description we have compiled of all the rulers of Merceria. You'll note they all had black hair, a trait which, I believe, is dominant amongst the men of the Royal Line, daughters, as well. I need not mention the blonde hair that adorns our queen, but also, let me read the description of the queen's confessor, shall I?"

Gerald heard the words flow from the Lord's mouth, condemning the heritage of Anna. He wanted to lash out at the man and strike the sense of victory he wore but knew it would do no good. He felt the public revelation of Anna's past like a crushing weight and looked to the balcony. She sat, stone-faced, her eyes boring into Lord Harwood.

Finished, Shrewesdale's defender sat down in triumph, the crowd afire with indignation. Did they hate the queen, wondered Gerald, or were they outraged with Harwood's actions? He couldn't tell.

Arnim stood, taking a moment to gather his thoughts. "If it pleases you, my lords," he started, "it is not our place here to answer such scurrilous accusations but to address the matter of the legitimacy of Queen Anna's rule. We are a warrior culture. Many generations ago, our ancestors fought for this land, establishing a dynasty that continues to this day. While it's true that there has always been an unbroken line of succession, I might remind you that our own history has multiple examples of illegitimate children that were accepted as heirs, and even, in at least two cases, kings."

He paused, taking a deep breath, "But let's say, for the sake of argument, that you find this accusation of interest, are we to believe that the entire rule of our young queen is illegal? No, of course not."

"Then how do you counter it?" said Lord Harwood, still wearing a smile.

"I don't have to," said Arnim, keeping his tone even. "For you see, we have always had laws that do so for us."

"Nonsense," said Harwood, "what are these laws?"

"It's called Force of Arms," explained Arnim. "An ancient law, to be sure, and one that was formulated in the days of our mercenary ancestors. It allows that a sufficient force of arms will determine the rule of the country in times of strife. Or perhaps his lordship will try to tell us the recent civil war was not a time of strife?"

"A ridiculous law," said Harwood, in his defence, "and too old to be of consequence."

"In that you are wrong," said Arnim, "for it has been used twice in our history, though public accounts only talk of one."

He moved to his own desk, where Nikki handed him a sheaf of papers. These he deposited before the jury.

Somerset glanced over the writings, "I think the jury will require time to examine these in detail. We shall adjourn to do so."

The room was called to attention, and once again, the jurors left, making their way to more private offices while the crowd burst into conversation.

Gerald sat while a servant handed him a cup of wine.

"What do you make of it?" asked Somerset.

Lord Stanton, who was examining the documents, looked up from a page. "The queen's case is solid," he said, a note of defeat to his voice. "We shall have to acknowledge that her rule is legitimate."

"You sound disappointed," accused Gerald.

"Nonsense," said the earl, "I'm merely disappointed at all the documents we've had to read, my eyesight's not what it used to be."

"And what of you, Lord Anglesley, do you concur?"

The young duke looked back at him, blushing slightly, "Yes, I suppose I must."

"Good," said Lord Spencer, the new Earl of Eastwood, "then we can put this behind us and move on."

"How much more of these ridiculous arguments must Shrewesdale present?" asked Somerset.

"As many as he likes," said Stanton, "or do you not wish a fair trial?"

"A fair trial is one thing," said Somerset, "but this is getting carried away. All he's doing is delaying the inevitable."

"Then you're saying it's inevitable that the earl will be found guilty?" remarked Stanton. "And here I was, thinking it a fair trial."

"That's not what I meant," argued Somerset, "and well you know it. We need to get to the crux of the matter and weigh the trial on the merits of the case, not waste our time on matters of the court."

"It's all of consequence!" defended Lord Stanton.

"Yes," said Gerald, "but perhaps now that the games are over, we'll get back to the meat of it."

"Well said," offered Anglesley, "this trial has been wearing on me."

Stanton looked at him in surprise. "Wearing? Saxnor's sake man, you're the youngest one here!"

"Shall we resume the court?" asked Lord Spencer.

"No," surrendered Somerset, "it's too late now, we'll resume tomorrow morning."

"How long is this going to go on?" asked Anglesley.

"As long as it needs," said Stanton.

Somerset moved to the door, sending a message to the Master of Heralds.

"Very well then, gentlemen," he said, "I suggest you all get a good rest. If today was any indication, it'll be a long one tomorrow, and we must be at our best."

They began filtering out of the room, one by one. Somerset lingered until just he and Gerald remained.

"Lord Matheson," the duke began, "if I may have a word?"

"Of course," said Gerald. "What is it?"

"The evidence presented today was likely quite distressing to Her Majesty. Please convey my deepest apologies to her on behalf of the jurors."

"I will," Gerald promised, "though I doubt all the members of the jury would be in agreement on that note."

"Even so," said Somerset, "it wounds my heart to see her so callously mistreated. Regardless of her ancestry, I have the deepest respect for Her Majesty."

"I'll make sure she knows," said Gerald.

The crowd watched eagerly as Sir Arnim rose, beginning this day's activities.

"The crown contends," he started, "that Lord George Montrose, the Earl of Shrewesdale, ordered the death of Dame Olivia Jacobson, a Knight of the Sword."

"I must object," said Lord Harwood, "the Earl is within his rights to administer justice throughout his earldom."

"On the contrary," injected Arnim, "his powers have limits, and he overstepped his authority by ordering the death of a representative of the crown."

"I would argue," said Harwood, "that he was quite within his rights, since they were due, in no small part, to his position, which was granted by the then King of Merceria."

"So you contend that there are no limits to the earl's powers?"

"In this case," said Lord Harwood, "it is precisely what we are saying. What do you offer in the way of proof?"

"I should like to call an expert in such matters," said Arnim, "if the court would permit?"

"Of course," said Lord Somerset.

"I call Lord Richard Fitzwilliam, Baron of Bodden," said Arnim.

Fitz made his way forward, having been warned ahead of time that his presence might be required. He took a seat, then recited the oath that he would tell the truth. Finished, he waited while Arnim organized his thoughts.

"Lord Fitzwilliam," the viscount began, "can you tell us your responsibilities as they pertain to Bodden?"

"I am lord of the land, responsible for keeping the people safe and guarding the northwest frontier of the realm."

"And in that capacity, what limitations do you operate under?"

"I am not allowed to cross the border into Norland," Fitz replied, "nor am I to take offensive action of any kind outside of the borders of Bodden."

"Are you allowed to make a declaration of war?" asked Arnim.

"No, I am not," the baron replied.

"And are you allowed to execute prisoners in the queen's name?"

"Only if they are commoners," Fitz replied, "though we have not executed anyone in my time as baron."

"And if a noble were, shall we say, caught in the act of a crime?"

"Then he would be remanded into the custody of Royal Troops, to face the queen's justice."

"And, if I may ask, where did you get this information from?"

"I beg your pardon?" asked the baron.

"How do you know the limitations of your position?"

"They are laid out in the laws of the land or by Royal Proclamation when there is a change," explained Fitz. "During King Andred's reign, each noble presented themselves at court once a year for the sole purpose of receiving the king's orders."

"And was the Earl of Shrewesdale present on any of those occasions?"

"He was," said the baron. "In fact, all the nobles were present."

"Thank you," said Arnim, "I just have one more question. Please take your time before answering."

"Of course."

"Who is allowed to create a knight?"

"Only the king or a member of the Royal Family. Though in truth, it's been only the king until Queen Anna created the Knights of the Hound, back when she was still a princess."

"So, the Order of the Sword is a Royal Appointment?"

"It is, exclusively," said Fitz.

"And as such, the power of life and death is the exclusive domain of the sovereign?"

"Yes," said Fitz, "on that, there can be no doubt."

"Thank you," said Arnim, "I believe that's all we need you for."

"Not so fast," called out Lord Harwood, "I have a few questions of my own."

"By all means," said Arnim, relinquishing the floor.

Lord Harwood moved slowly towards the baron, carefully considering his words before he spoke.

"Baron, are you familiar with the rules governing female knights?"

"Of course," said Fitz.

"And would you explain to the court how you gained that knowledge?"

"My daughter is Dame Beverly Fitzwilliam," he replied, "Knight Commander of the Order of the Hound."

"But not a Knight of the Sword?" asked Harwood.

"No," said Fitz, looking rather uncomfortable.

"Can you tell us why?"

"She was dismissed from the order by King Andred after the Battle of Eastwood," the baron confessed.

"Did the king give a reason?"

The baron's face turned red, "The king felt she let the Orcs escape, and he wanted them destroyed. But I was there-"

"I'm not concerned with your experience at Eastwood," interrupted Lord Harwood, "but if not for the fact that she is a Knight of the Hound-"

"Knight Commander," clarified Fitz.

"Yes, I stand corrected, Knight Commander of the Hound. If not for her position with this new order, she would no longer be considered a knight, is that not true?"

"She was dismissed from the order," said Fitz, "so no, she would no longer be a knight."

"And therefore no longer under the king's protection," said Lord Harwood, his face smiling in triumph."

"No, but-"

"That is all for now, Lord Fitzwilliam."

"One moment," objected Arnim, "there are still some unanswered questions." He rose, making his way back to the baron.

"Lord Fitzwilliam," Arnim began, "can you explain the differences between knights and dames for us? Aside from the obvious that is. How are the rules different?"

"A knighthood is an honour granted for life," said Fitz. "Female knights trace their history back to the founding of the kingdom. A few of the mercenaries that came here originally were women. When the Knightly Order of the Sword was first created, it was decided that men and women could both receive that honour. The principal difference is merely title, dame being used for women instead of sir, but there are a few other differences, chief amongst them the ability of women to leave the order to bear children."

"And are they allowed to return to the order in the future, say after their children are grown?"

"They are," said Fitz, "though it is seldom done."

"Can a male knight leave the order?"

"He can," said Fitz, "though once again, it's rare."

"And what are the repercussions of such an act?" asked Arnim.

"He would not be liable for military service except in times of war."

"So you're saying that if a war broke out, the knight could be called on to serve again?"

"Exactly," said Fitz.

"And what of the women? Do they have the same obligation?"

"They do," said Fitz, "unless they have children, in which case the obligation is waived."

"So, just to be clear, if a woman leaves the order and has no children, she can be recalled in times of war. Is that correct?"

"It is," said Fitz.

"So that would mean," continued Arnim, "that Dame Olivia, even though she left the order, could still be called to service?"

"As long as she had no children, yes," the baron agreed.

"I would like to inform your lordships," said Arnim, turning to the jury, "that it is on record that Dame Olivia bore no children, nor was responsible for any child. In other words, she was subject to service at the king's discretion, making her a Royal Representative."

Lord Montrose whispered something to Lord Harwood, who then rose. "We agree to this interpretation," he said, "but the fact is that the earl did not order the death of Dame Olivia."

"I beg your pardon?" said Lord Somerset. "If that's true, why are we here?"

"Would you care to clarify?" asked Lord Spencer.

"Gladly," Lord Stanton replied. "You see, Lord Montague ordered the woman to be locked up, nothing more. Her death was caused by others."

"That's not true!" yelled out Beverly from the audience.

The entire cathedral was suddenly flooded with shouts of angry commoners. The Master of Heralds tried to calm them to little effect. It was finally Anna that succeeded by standing in the balcony, drawing everyone's attention. She waited till they quieted, then sat back down.

"You claim that he ordered her locked up," said Arnim, "but we have multiple sworn statements that he ordered her placed in a cage, suspended outside of the city."

"What of it?" said Harwood. "The cage is a typical punishment for her crime, it need not be a death sentence. In fact, it was Dame Beverly that killed her, using a sword."

The audience gasped, then went so silent you could hear a pin drop.

Lord Somerset looked to Gerald, "Is this true?"

"I have no knowledge of this," Gerald replied. "I had heard of some difficulties that she faced, but this is the first time I've heard this accusation."

Somerset whispered briefly to the other jurors and then stood. "The court shall recess until tomorrow. When the day commences, we expect Dame Beverly Fitzwilliam here to be questioned over this matter."

The Master of Heralds brought the room to attention as the jurors filed out.

The Truth

WINTER 963/964 MC

Beverly waited in the back offices, pacing nervously.

"It'll be all right, Bev," said Hayley.

"I don't know if I can do this," the knight replied.

"All you have to do is tell the truth," the ranger implored.

"No, don't you see?" said Beverly. "Aldwin will hear of my disgrace, I can't bear it."

Hayley steadied her by holding her shoulders and then looked into her eyes. "He loves you, Bev. Nothing in your past will change that. What happened to you was terrible, everyone will see that. You're the victim here, not the criminal. Just tell the truth and unburden yourself."

"You're right," she said, shaking her arms to release the tension.

A servant at the door turned to face them, "They just called for you, Dame Beverly."

"Good luck," said Hayley, giving her friend a hug.

"Thank you," the knight replied.

Beverly entered the chamber, moving in front of the seat provided to take the oath. She had elected to wear her armour, and so she sat in the proffered chair and closed her eyes, trying to calm herself, remembering Aldwin's words.

"I will make your armour, and when you wear it, it will be as if my arms are holding you."

. . .

She opened her eyes, finally feeling at peace.

"Dame Beverly," began Lord Harwood, "did you, or did you not kill Dame Olivia?"

"She was suffering from terrible wounds," said Beverly.

"Answer the question," ordered the lord.

"Left in the cage, she would have died a painful death."

Lord Harwood's voice grew angry, "I must insist you answer the question. Did you kill Dame Olivia?"

"I did," admitted Beverly, "she begged me. It was an act of mercy."

The room sat in stunned silence until Lord Stanton finally spoke. "There, you see? The earl is innocent, though I do think the crown should charge Dame Beverly with treason. That's what you get for killing a knight, isn't it? After all, you can't have two sets of rules!"

He returned to his seat, a smug look on his face. Lord Montrose was smiling and patting him on the back.

Arnim rose, making his way towards Beverly. He paused, gathering his thoughts. "Dame Beverly," he began, "you have had a distinguished career in the service of the princess, and then the queen, have you not?"

"I have," she replied, her voice dull and devoid of emotion.

"As a knight, we often hold the power of life and death, at least on the battlefield, wouldn't you say?"

"I suppose so," she said.

"Life Mages aside, if you found a wounded comrade on the battlefield that had no hope of recovery, wouldn't it be charitable to end their life to prevent suffering?"

"It would," she said, energy beginning to return to her voice.

"I would maintain that, given the same circumstances, any knight would have dealt the same mercy to Dame Olivia, wouldn't you?"

"I would hope so," Beverly replied.

"I must object," said Lord Harwood, "we've already established that she killed the woman, what else is there to tell?"

"If the honourable lords would permit," continued Arnim, unfazed by the remark, "I would like to delve into the events that led to the actual arrest and sentencing of Dame Olivia."

"You think it relevant?" asked Lord Somerset.

"I do," said Arnim. "In fact, I believe it will explain a great number of things, including the culpability of the earl in Dame Olivia's death."

"Very well," said Lord Somerset, "you may continue."

"When did you first meet Dame Olivia?" asked Arnim, his voice softening.

"When I first arrived in Shrewesdale," said Beverly. "I was in service to the Countess."

"The earl's wife? Not the earl?" asked Arnim.

"That's correct. Lady Catherine wanted me to stop the predations of the earl's men."

"Can you clarify that for the court?" asked Arnim.

"Yes. The Knights of Shrewesdale preyed on young women, taking advantage of them."

"Was this all of the knights?"

"No, just some of them, those closest to the earl."

"I must object," said Lord Harwood. "Dame Beverly is in no position to know who was or wasn't closest to the earl."

Arnim stood waiting as Nikki moved across the room, handing him a paper. "I have here the sworn statement of Sir Heward, Knight of the Sword. It addresses that very fact." He dropped it on the table in front of the jurors, then returned to face Beverly.

"Can you relate the sequence of events that took place on the night you were arrested?"

Beverly took a deep breath, avoiding the eyes of the onlookers. "The countess had just died, and I was ordered to take up residence in the barracks."

"This was," said Arnim, "the barracks of the earl's knights, I assume?"

"Yes," she admitted, "though I was given my own room."

"And what happened?"

"I drank quite a lot. I was upset over the countess's death, and then I went to sleep."

"And then?" he prompted.

"I was awoken by the sound of wood splintering. Someone had kicked in the door," she paused, looking nervous.

"Go on," he prompted, "take your time if you need to."

"A hand was pressed over my mouth, while others pinned my arms and legs." She took a deep breath, "They pulled me from the bed and tore my clothes off."

"Do you remember how many there were?"

"I can't be sure of the exact number, but there were at least four, maybe five."

"What happened next?"

Tears came to Beverly's eyes, "They tried to rape me."

"You say they tried?"

"Yes," she continued, "Olivia showed up. Her brother was a smith, and he'd made a dagger for me, it was to be a gift. She was bringing it to me. If she hadn't arrived at that precise moment, I'm sure I'd be dead."

"Objection," said Lord Harwood, standing, "the woman was merely being raped, not murdered."

The crowd suddenly turned angry, yelling obscenities at the man. He sat back down, cowed by the hostility.

Aldwin, watching from the balcony, gripped the arm of his chair, his fingers turning white with the force. He wanted to get up and hurl his seat at the earl. Only the presence of Beverly on the stand prevented his actions.

"Olivia saved me," Beverly choked out, her tears coming freely now, "and it cost her her life."

"I know this is difficult," said Arnim, "but the truth must be known. Please continue when you can."

"I, I don't quite know the full details," she stammered, "but during the fight, she stabbed one of the knights, Sir Remington, I believe. The rest of the knights fled."

"And that was it?"

"No," said Beverly, "they came back later with the earl. Olivia had wrapped something around me, a blanket, I think. She was just holding me. I was shaking and couldn't do a thing. They accused us of consorting in an unholy manner and ordered our arrest. That's the last I saw of her."

"I see," said Arnim.

Baron Fitzwilliam, sitting beside the queen, was no longer able to contain his outrage. He stood, ready to challenge the earl for his behaviour. It was Aldwin that calmed Fitz, a firm grip pulling the baron back to his seat.

Arnim walked across the room and then back again, once more thinking things through. He resumed his questioning, "From your point of view, what happened after you were arrested?"

"I was held in a cell all night. In the morning, I was hauled before the earl. They took all my possessions, and then forced me to walk out of the city under guard."

"Naked?" asked Arnim in shock.

"No, they gave me a ragged dress. When I reached the city gates, I saw Olivia. They had beaten and tortured her-"

"Objection," yelled Lord Harwood, "there's no proof that the earl was responsible for her treatment."

Once more, the crowd turned ugly, yelling obscenities.

Arnim waited until the noise abated. "When you were held before the earl, do you remember what he said, precisely?"

"I do," she said, "it is burned into my memory. He said I was led astray by the wicked acts of a woman of loose and questionable morals. He also said she would pay for her crimes with her life."

"You understood that as a death sentence for Olivia, I take it?"

"Of course," said Beverly, "wouldn't you?"

"I most certainly would," Arnim agreed. "Now, when you left the city, is that the next time you saw Olivia?"

"It was," she continued. "She was hanging in a cage, as I said, bloody and bruised. Someone had broken her ribs and... degraded her."

"How did you know that?" Arnim asked softly.

"She told me," said Beverly, "just before she asked me to put her out of her misery."

"And so you killed her, ending her suffering," said Arnim.

"I did," said Beverly breaking down into great sobs. They echoed throughout the cathedral as the spectators sat in stunned silence.

Up in the balcony, Aldwin rose quietly. Baron Fitzwilliam looked at him in surprise.

"There's something I must do," said the smith.

Fitz nodded as Aldwin made his way towards the stairs.

"My lords," said Arnim, turning to face the jury, "I have here the written testimony of several knights that bore witness to this exchange between Dame Beverly and the Earl of Shrewesdale." Nikki rose, depositing the documents before the jury, then returned to her seat.

"As to her death," continued Arnim, "there can be no doubt that the intent was to kill her. I have an extensive collection of information for you, but the gist of it is this: No one who is sent to the cage has ever survived. To think that the earl did not desire her death is not believable."

"Dame Beverly," said Lord Somerset, "you may leave the court."

Beverly rose, feeling the weight of the world on her shoulders. Hayley rushed out from the back of the room, guiding her to some privacy where Aldwin was waiting for her, a look of concern on his face.

Beverly stood in the doorway, despair in her features. Aldwin's heart broke, and he moved towards her, enveloping her in his arms. "It's all right," he soothed, "it's over now."

"There can be no doubt of the earl's guilt," said Lord Somerset.

They were in the private offices once more, discussing the verdict.

"I beg to differ," said Lord Stanton, "I think the crown was weak."

"Oh, give it up," called out Lord Spencer. "The man's as guilty as a boy with his hand in the pie. You can't possibly still think of him as innocent. Have you bothered to read the statements?"

"I disagree," Lord Stanton insisted.

"What about the rest of you?" asked Somerset. "Lord Matheson?"

"Guilty," Gerald spat out in disgust.

"Lord Anglesley?"

"Guilty," the young man announced.

"Lord Spencer?"

"Is the sky blue? Guilty, of course."

"I suppose I don't need to ask what you say, Lord Stanton? Perhaps you're content to let the mob club you to death."

"Innocent," Lord Stanton replied, "though it matters little. You have the majority of votes, therefore you must pronounce the man guilty."

"Have you no shame, Alexander?" asked Lord Somerset.

"None at all," replied Lord Stanton.

"Then let's get back inside and get this over with," said Gerald. They all rose, making their way into the chamber.

The court was quiet as they took their places. Beverly had taken a seat near the queen, but Aldwin was nowhere to be seen. Instead, Lady Aubrey held her cousin's hand in a reassuring grip.

The Master of Heralds rapped his staff and called out in a strong voice, "Have you reached a decision, my lords?"

"We have," replied Lord Somerset.

"And what say you? Is the prisoner guilty or innocent?"

"Guilty."

"And the sentence?"

"Death, but we await the queen's pleasure as to the method of execution."

"The normal punishment is to be hanged, drawn and quartered for such an offence," announced the Master of Heralds. He turned to face the balcony, "What say you, Majesty?"

Anna turned to Aubrey, giving her a letter. The young baroness rose, disappearing from sight as she descended the stairs to emerge a moment later. She walked to the Master of Heralds, delivering the queen's decision. The man looked to Lord Montrose, who stood, awaiting the sentence.

"George Montrose," the Master of Heralds intoned, "it is the decision of this court that you are found guilty of the charge of treason and are sentenced to death. In accordance with the wishes of Her Majesty, Queen Anna, you are to be stripped of all your wealth and titles and held in the dungeon until you are taken from your cell to a place of execution. The queen, in her mercy, has sentenced you to death by decapitation."

The commoners broke into a great cheer at the news. Two soldiers, members of the Guard Cavalry, moved forward to take Montrose by the arms. They led him away towards the back of the building with Lord Harwood following closely behind.

The small entourage was just stepping through the doorway when Lord Harwood tripped on the tile flooring, causing him to lurch forward. He grabbed a guard, trying to stop himself from falling, taking both he, and the soldier to the ground. As he struck, he called out, "Montrose!" At that precise moment, whether by plan or by luck of circumstance, the earl struck, pulling forth a concealed dagger and plunging it into the neck of the second guard. The man fell quickly, freeing up the prisoner to make a bid for freedom.

Montrose ran, grabbing the guard's sword as he moved, a plan firmly in mind. There was no chance of escape, but if he could make it to the crypt, he need only remain hidden until reinforcements arrived. As he turned down the corridor, the ornate doorway of the crypt was before him. He pushed it open, rushing inside, only to stop abruptly when he noticed someone waiting for him. At first, he thought it was an ally, but then, as he drew closer, he saw the look of resolve on the unknown man's face.

"Who are you?" called out Montrose.

"My name's Aldwin," the stranger replied, his voice barely concealing his anger.

"Get out of my way!"

"No," Aldwin replied stubbornly.

Montrose struck out with the sword, a jab aimed at the unarmoured man's chest. In reply, Aldwin blocked the blade with his left arm, letting it dig deeply into his flesh.

The smith stepped closer, years of working the forge having made him strong, and swung with his right fist. He felt the nose break beneath his onslaught and saw the earl beginning to fall, but Aldwin punched again, this time with his left fist, ignoring the pain racing up his arm. Teeth embedded themselves in his knuckles as he smashed the man's face. George Montrose fell to the floor, a bloody mess, crying out in pain, while Aldwin glared down at him.

Before the smith could do any more damage, guards appeared, calling for help. They had lifted Montrose securely by the arms just as Aubrey arrived, summoned by all the noise.

Montrose stared at Aldwin with loathing. "This man assaulted me," he said as he spat out a mouthful of blood. "I'm a noble. I want him arrested."

Aubrey walked up to Aldwin and used a spell to heal his wounds, then turned on Montrose, who was struggling in the grasp of his guards.

"You were a noble, but you're not anymore," she corrected. "When you were found guilty, you were stripped of your title. This, on the other hand," she indicated Aldwin, "is Lord Aldwin Fitzwilliam, and as such, he may have you arrested and charged. What do you say, Lord Aldwin? Do you wish to add charges?"

"No," said the smith, "he's already sentenced to death. I don't want anything to delay his punishment."

"Then take him away," ordered Aubrey.

"But my face!" objected Montrose. "I need healing!"

"You ordered the assault on my cousin, you'll get no healing from me. Broken teeth and a broken nose are a just reward for your actions," Aubrey announced. "As for the pain, your execution will cure that." She nodded at the guards, and they hauled him off.

The wagon trundled through the city at a walking pace. George Montrose, the former Earl of Shrewesdale, glared at the crowd from his cage. A cabbage struck the bars, covering him in its decaying leaves.

Baron Fitzwilliam, who was walking behind the wagon, smiled at the prisoner's discomfort. "You should feel lucky, the queen has seen fit to grant you a merciful death. If it were up to me, you'd suffer a far worse fate."

Montrose simply glared, "She's a whore, that queen of yours. I hope she gets the pox!"

Fitz ignored the jibe, smiling instead as a tomato navigated its way through the bars, striking the prisoner on the side of the head. Montrose let out a curse.

Ahead walked a procession of soldiers, while behind rode the Guard Cavalry, followed by the Royal Carriage and escort. They turned, making their way towards the west gate, drawing ever nearer to the open square where the execution would take place.

Soon, the platform came into view; it was raised four feet into the air to better enable the crowd to see. At the top was a mighty Troll, his hands gripping an equally impressive axe.

The wagon halted, and the soldiers came forward to unlock the door. They dragged Montrose from his cage and pushed him towards the platform, his feet dragging the heavy chains around them.

Fitz followed. He was the official prisoner escort, a position he had asked, nay insisted, he should be allowed to perform.

The prisoner mounted the steps as Fitz watched closely. He quickly scanned the crowd, noting the presence of the rangers amongst the throng. Gerald had been concerned there might be a rescue attempt, and so had taken extra precautions, but it appeared there would be no such reprieve this day.

Fitz cleared the stairs and watched as Montrose was led to the wooden block. The guards pushed him into position, holding his arms out to either side to restrain him.

The Troll lifted the axe, placing it over the prisoner's neck to line up the swing. Montrose was muttering something, though Fitz couldn't hear the words clearly. Suddenly, the smell of urine came to his nose, then the axe was raised, and the crowd held its collective breath.

"Saxnor give me strength!" called out Montrose.

The baron had no doubt that Montrose would spend an eternity in the Underworld but held his tongue. The Troll waited, arms raised while his eyes shifted to the Baron of Bodden.

Fitz looked to the Royal Carriage to witness the queen nod her approval. He returned his gaze to the Troll and nodded solemnly.

The axe came down in a blur, slicing through the prisoner's neck with little effort. It dug into the block, striking with such force that the wood split. The crowd roared its approval.

A soldier stepped forward, lifting the corpse's head by the hair to display it for all to see. Two more removed the headless body, tossing it to a wagon that lay behind the platform, where men stood ready to take it away. Montrose would be buried in an unmarked grave, in a location unknown to his family, the ultimate penalty for betraying the crown.

When the crowd finally began dispersing, the soldier tossed the head into a wicker basket to join the rest of the corpse.

Baron Fitzwilliam, his job finished, left the platform, making his way to the wagon for one final view of the prisoner. Montrose's eyes stared back at him, a look of terror permanently etched on them, but Fitz felt no sympathy.

"It's done," declared Gerald, tearing his eyes from the carriage window. "He can trouble us no more."

"I should have been more visible," said Anna. "Perhaps in an open-topped carriage?"

"No," said Gerald. "Shrewesdale still has supporters that might have tried to take their vengeance."

She turned on him in a sudden burst of anger, but before the words could come out, she calmed herself. "You're right, of course. I can't continue with my changes if I'm dead."

"There'll be plenty of time for people to see you in the future, Anna. Let's get this behind us, we still have work to do."

"Very well," she agreed.

Gerald knocked on the carriage ceiling. Moments later, it rumbled forward, heading back towards the Palace.

TWENTY-FOUR

Spring

SPRING 964 MC

Aldwin sat cross-legged on the floor, smoothing the gold rune he had created. He had poured it into a mould to form the letter, and now it sat on the floor, a perfect fit for the stone indentation that held it. Satisfied with the work, he rose, stretching his back as he did.

"That's the last one," he announced. "What do you think?"

"Marvellous," declared Albreda. She wandered around the room, looking at each rune in turn. "You've done an outstanding job here. I daresay your skills will keep you in work for the next few months."

"How many of these are we to make?" he asked.

"One in each city, eventually," replied the druid, "but that won't be for years. It takes too much of a mage's strength to empower them to go any faster."

"Are YOU going to empower this circle?" asked Aldwin.

"No," replied Albreda, "that honour will fall to Aubrey, though I'll doubtless be here to witness it. We all will, actually."

"We will?" asked Aldwin in surprise.

"Well, all of the mages, at least. I'm afraid the rest wouldn't find it of very much interest."

"How long does it take?" he asked.

"The casting time to empower a circle depends on its strength. This one is quite strong, it'll likely take the better part of a morning to do it."

"Will all the circles look the same?" he asked.

"No," said Albreda. "This one is a life circle. The next construction will likely be in Bodden. I'll be empowering that one, so it will be a circle of stones."

"But others can use it?"

"Of course, just not at the same power level."

"And that will allow instant travel?"

"You've gone with me before, Aldwin, you know how they work. With circles here and in Bodden, you could travel to the Keep for breakfast and be back before your toast gets cold."

"I like the sounds of that," he mused, "but I doubt it'll be used as often as you think. It still needs a mage to operate it, doesn't it?"

"It does," she agreed, "and the power of the caster will determine how many people can travel with a single casting of the spell."

"And how far they can go."

"Very good, Aldwin, you're learning."

The smith smiled at the compliment, then began gathering his tools.

"How's Beverly doing?" Albreda asked.

He stopped his actions, turning to look at the druid. "She's getting better. I don't think she ever really grieved for Olivia, not to mention what the earl's men did to her." He balled his fists at the thought.

"He's dead now, Aldwin," Albreda soothed, "he can't hurt her anymore."

"I know that," he replied, "and yet I can't help feeling for her. It's like she lost a part of herself when she testified at the trial."

"She'll recover, you'll see, it just takes time. The important thing is that you're here for her. On the plus side, the kingdom has been quiet these last few months."

"I hadn't noticed," mused Aldwin, resuming the collection of tools. "I've been rather busy. How's the north?"

"Quiet, which is rather unexpected. The kingdom is also in funds again, that's why we were able to carry on with this circle."

"I'd very much like to see Aubrey enchant this circle," he said.

"It's called empowering," corrected the druid, "not enchanting."

"What's the difference?"

"Empowering is done once, and permanently makes the circle usable. Enchantments are performed by a mage that has learned the school of Enchantments, the two are really quite different. Of course, those who are uninitiated into the ways of arcane power often use the term enchantment for anything that holds magic."

Aldwin made an exaggerated bow, "I stand corrected. So what's next?"

"Well," mused Albreda, "I have things to discuss with Aubrey, but I would suggest you go and find Beverly and maybe take her riding. I think she'd like that."

· · ·

It was late afternoon by the time Aubrey and the other mages came to visit the completed circle. Revi took an intense interest in the workmanship, examining each rune in great detail before declaring it acceptable. Aldus Hearn also spent a lot of time going over every single marking, muttering the whole time about how fascinating it all was.

Aubrey was simply delighted, a quick scan being all that was needed for her to accept it as ready.

"When can I begin?" she asked.

"I thought tomorrow morning might be best," said Albreda. "You'll want to rest up ahead of time and make sure you have a good breakfast, you won't be able to eat once you start casting. The ritual will take some time, and it'll also drain a lot of your power."

"I remember," said Aubrey. "I'll expend all my energy in the casting, and a small portion of it I won't be able to recover."

"That's correct," confirmed the druid, "though, in time, you'll be able to build your power level back up."

"How much power will I lose?" she asked.

"This is a strong circle," said Albreda, "the biggest one we have planned for Merceria, so I'm afraid it will take quite a bit. It will feel strange for a few days, almost like losing a tooth, but you'll get used to it."

"I'm honoured to have the opportunity," said Aubrey.

"You've earned it," said Albreda, then switched to a quieter voice. "You're likely the most powerful mage after me."

"I am?" she said in surprise.

"Not so much in experience," corrected the druid, "but in terms of potential, I'd say you're one of the most powerful mages I've met. I rather suspect that's because of your great grandmother. That reminds me, how are things going in Hawksburg?"

"Quite well, thank you."

"And the circle there?"

"Easier to use now," said Aubrey, "thanks to the efforts of the Orcs. Kraloch was a great help. We cleared out the ground floor and opened up the cellar. There's even a ramp now, which makes getting horses in and out much easier."

"And the guards we discussed?" asked Albreda.

"In place," said Aubrey, "and the building can be locked if desired, though the guards are always on duty to keep outsiders away."

"And the guards are?"

"Orcs," said Aubrey, "that was my idea. They won't take bribes to let people in. Don't worry, they all have to speak our language."

"Well, that's a relief," said Albreda. "I could just imagine trying to ask an Orc to let me out when they couldn't understand me."

Aubrey laughed, "It does paint a rather funny picture, doesn't it."

Kiren-Jool made his way towards them, his examination of the circle complete. "What's so funny?"

"Just a private joke," said Albreda. "What do you think of the circle?"

"Truly a work of art," the Enchanter replied. "Is the queen to allow all of us to use it?"

"Yes," said Albreda, "but there are a few conditions."

"Such as?" he asked.

"We are to let no other mages have access without Royal Approval, and we must always have someone available here, in Wincaster, to carry important dispatches and such."

"In other words," he clarified, "we serve the crown. That's quite reasonable. Who is to be the first?"

"That honour will fall to me," said Albreda.

"You?" he said in surprise. "I thought Aubrey would be the first."

"She'll be empowering it," the druid replied, "but she'll be tired from her casting. I'll take her through, along with some others."

"And what will be the first destination of our new circle?"

"Hawksburg," said Albreda. "We intend to have a small family get-together."

"Oh?" said the Enchanter.

"Yes, the Fitzwilliams will be joining us. They're related, you know. Aubrey is the baron's niece."

"Oh yes," said Kiren-Jool, "I remember, now that you mention it."

The door opened, revealing Beverly and a group of guards.

"What's this, now?" asked Revi, irritation evident in his voice.

"These are the new guards," answered Beverly. "They've been hand-picked to guard the circle. I thought it best to let them see what it is they'll be protecting."

"A grand idea," said Albreda.

"Nonsense," said Revi in annoyance, "they should remain outside, this room is for mages only."

Beverly stared at the mage, surprised by his hostility. "The queen agreed with my intent," she said, a hard edge to her voice.

Revi threw up his arms in surrender, "Well, the queen knows best!"

Aubrey moved to intercept her cousin before the situation got away from her.

"Beverly," she soothed, "aren't you excited to go to Hawksburg?"

Her features calmed, returning her to the Beverly of old. "Yes," the red-headed knight said, "though obviously not as much as you."

Aubrey laughed, "Well, you can't blame me, can you? I haven't had family in Hawksburg since... well, you know."

"I hear you've decided to finally build some defences," Beverly added.

"Yes," Aubrey agreed, "but it'll be years before they take shape. We're going to start with a wall around the town."

"And a keep?" asked Beverly.

"Eventually, I suppose, but a wall to begin with. I had thought to begin with a wooden palisade, but Gerald insisted it be done with stone."

"I'd have to say I agree with him," mused Beverly. "If you're going to build defences, best you do it properly. Anyways, I should be going, I just wanted to show off our newest circle."

She left the room, leaving the mages in sole possession of the chamber.

The morning came far too soon for Aubrey's liking. With the excitement of the day looming in her future, it had been difficult to sleep and now, keyed up as she was, she found breakfast almost distracting.

"Nervous?" asked Beverly from across the table.

"Terribly," replied Aubrey. "What if I mess up?"

"You won't," added Aldwin, "you've been studying it for weeks."

"Agreed," said Beverly, "but you really should eat something. You're going to be casting for quite some time, aren't you?"

"I am," Aubrey confessed, "but I'm worrying about everything."

"Why?" asked Beverly. "It's not as though you haven't cast spells before."

"Yes," Aubrey continued, "but everyone will be watching."

"Put that out of your mind," suggested Aldwin. "Just concentrate on the here and now."

The Life Mage closed her eyes and took a deep breath. She dug down deep inside herself, searching for her inner strength. Instead, her stomach gurgled, sending the three of them into fits of laughter.

"Well," Aubrey mused, "I suppose that answers my question. Food it is."

"I'm surprised the queen isn't here," said Aldwin.

"She doesn't want to overshadow Aubrey's achievement," said Beverly, "but she sends her best regards. She's looking forward to trying it sometime."

"Of course," said Aubrey, "but I have to empower it first." She dug into her food.

Some time later, she sat back, her stomach full. Looking over to Aldwin, she noticed he had two plates empty before him.

"How can you eat so much?" she asked.

"He works hard to keep those muscles of his," answered Beverly. "It takes a lot of strength to work the forge all day. He even finished off my plate as well as his!"

They all chuckled, and Aubrey thought it nice to see Beverly returning to her old self.

"Shall we?" the Life Mage said, rising.

"Of course," said Beverly, "lead on, master mage."

"Or would that be mistress mage?" asked Aldwin.

"We're family," said the young spell caster, "how about you just call me Aubrey."

"Very well," the smith replied, "shall I get the door?"

Aubrey paused as Aldwin opened the door, and looked at her cousin, "He's pretty handy to have around."

"He certainly is," Beverly agreed with a smile.

They made their way through the Palace to the casting room where Baron Fitzwilliam and Albreda stood waiting at the entrance, guards to either side.

"Good morning," said the baron. He stepped forward, giving them each a hug. Albreda watched, smiling the whole time.

"Father," said Beverly, "you look in fine form today. Is Albreda letting you get some sleep?"

The baron blushed slightly. "I could ask you the same," he said, eyeing Aldwin, who, like him, turned crimson.

The guards opened the door, revealing the magic circle within, where the other mages of the kingdom stood around it in anticipation.

"I must say it looks rather impressive," said Fitz.

"Thank you," said Aubrey. "Albreda and I designed it, but it took Aldwin to help us build it, along with Master Brullin."

"Brullin?" said Fitz. "What kind of a name is that?"

"That was our Dwarven stonecutter," added Aldwin.

Beverly laughed.

"What's so funny?" asked Fitz.

"Nothing," she defended, "it's just that any feat of engineering always seems to be done by Dwarves."

Aldwin smiled, for it was good to see Beverly laughing again. "Shall we step into the middle?" he suggested.

"Not yet," said Aubrey, "I still have to empower it. You can watch from over there if you like, but it will take some time. Are you sure you wouldn't prefer to just come back later when we're ready to travel?"

"Of course not," said Fitz, "this is your big moment. I wouldn't miss it for all the gold in the kingdom."

"There are seats over here," said Albreda, "if you'd care to sit. It will, as Aubrey indicated, take a while to perform the ritual."

They sat down as Aubrey walked about the room, clearing her mind. While this was happening, a servant carried in a small table, placing it at the dead centre of the circle. Kiren-Jool followed, placing a book upon it and opening it to a page filled with magical runes. Satisfied that all was ready, he joined the observers, taking a seat.

Aubrey moved to the book, examining its contents. Torches were set about the room, filling it with light, but Revi stood to cast a glowing orb. He floated it over to Aubrey where it hung, illuminating the book clearly.

She began the casting, reading the runes as they appeared before her. The words spilled forth, echoing throughout the room, filling it with a sense of power. Aldwin could feel the hair on his arms stand on end and watched in wonder.

Albreda rose, crossing to stand opposite Aubrey. Words of power continued to pour forth, and then the druid turned the page, revealing even more. This continued for some time, the sound growing monotonous to the observers, and yet their anticipation increased with each turn of a page.

Aldwin sensed a taste of metal in his mouth and then there was an audible sound, a sort of thudding noise that a person might make when stomping their foot. He watched in amazement as one of the runes that he had poured came to life, pulsating with glowing energy and giving off a bright white light. He looked over at his companions to see their attention riveted on the ritual before them.

Aubrey's words continued to flow as more pages were turned, and then a second rune lit up. The air began to buzz as if a swarm of bees was filling the room, and soon the entire area was bathed in bright light as more and more runes began to glow, the Life Mage's energy filling them.

Finally, the last rune illuminated, and although Aldwin couldn't say how much time had gone by, he expected the spell was now complete, but still, the ritual continued.

Within the circle, the air about Aubrey began to turn hazy, as if moisture was being sucked from her body. The cloud spread out from her, and then he realized it wasn't a cloud, but a ring of mist, expanding until it covered all the runes. The magical symbols began to pulse with light and Aldwin was struck by the idea that they were somehow absorbing the strange mist. All he could do was watch, immobilized with fascination.

Aubrey's voice grew louder, its pitch rising higher even as her voice became hoarse, but she kept up the ritual, letting the words erupt from her mouth.

As she called out the final rune, a clap of thunder shook the very walls, and then the runes faded, returning to their natural gold colour.

Aubrey lowered her arms, swaying slightly. Albreda stepped around the small table, steadying the Life Mage while guiding her to a seat. Beverly brought her cousin some water, and the mage drank thirstily.

"It worked!" declared Albreda. "You've done it, Aubrey. How do you feel?"

"Tired," said the Life Mage, "as if I'd run for days."

"That's the power drain," replied the druid, gazing into the young woman's face. "Your eyes look fine, you didn't overdo it."

"Her eyes tell you that?" asked Aldwin.

"Yes," the druid replied, "one of the first signs your energy is almost depleted is bloodshot eyes, but Aubrey's look clear. She has more reserves than I thought."

"I'm hungry," Aubrey complained. "It feels as though I haven't eaten in weeks."

"Let's get you to Hawksburg then," declared Albreda. "After all, there's a feast waiting there."

The druid nodded to Aldwin and Beverly, who each took one of Aubrey's arms and guided her into the circle. A servant had cleared away the table, giving them ample room to assemble. Fitz joined them as Albreda placed herself in the centre.

"All set?" the druid asked.

Once everyone had nodded, Albreda began the spell of recall. The runes lit up once again, and then a circle of light leaped up from the floor, blinding in its intensity. Moments later, the light vanished, and the room around them was replaced with that of Hawksburg.

Beverly looked around in surprise. There had, indeed, been changes in the circle here. Now, instead of a narrow stairway, there was a gentle ramp. It headed north, then turned east and south again, forming a 'U' shape, the upper end even with the ground floor.

The ceiling above had been removed, creating a balcony of sorts that oversaw the casting room below. Beverly noticed a trio of Orcs watching them. Moments later, they descended the ramp, eager to help carry Aubrey.

"I love what they've done with the place," commented Beverly. "The last time I was here, it was quite crowded."

"Yes," agreed Albreda, "it's nice, isn't it."

"Where's the food?" asked Aldwin.

Beverly laughed, "Is that all you ever think about?"

Aldwin looked at Beverly with a wicked grin, and the knight blushed.

"Apparently not," said Fitz, a chortle escaping.

"Now, now," chided Albreda, "let the children have their fun."

"They're not children anymore," said Fitz.

"Let's find the food," said Aubrey, bringing the discussion to a close.

Back in Wincaster, things were busy at the Weldwyn embassy. Servants were scurrying back and forth as guests were seated.

"You've laid on quite the spread," said Gerald as a servant filled his goblet.

"We've spared no expense," said Alric. "After all, it's not every day the Queen of Merceria comes to dinner."

Anna smiled, "Thank you, Alric. I must say it's a nice change to not eat in the Palace. What do you have planned for us this evening?"

"Some Weldwyn favourites," the prince answered. "How do you feel about mutton pie?"

"I remember it well," said Gerald, rubbing his hands together. "A particular favourite at the Summersgate Palace, if I recall."

"Yes," Alric agreed, "it was always one of my favourites."

"And you found someone here that could make it?" asked Anna.

"Of course," replied the prince. "When my father sent the new troops, he insisted on sending some servants. I suppose he was afraid I'd starve on a Mercerian diet."

"I see you have the fancy forks," noted Gerald, still fascinated with the things. "I take it you brought your own silverware."

"Yes," admitted Alric, blushing slightly. "You don't want to know how many wagons my mother sent. I think she must believe you don't have blankets here, she quite literally sent everything she could think of."

"You're lucky to have a mother that cares," said Anna. "Mine stopped visiting when I was just a young girl."

"That's terrible," Jack commiserated, holding his goblet up for a refill.

"That's not the only thing," she continued, "before she stopped, she only visited Uxley Hall once a year."

"How did you ever survive?" asked Alric.

"The servants looked after me," she answered, "and then Gerald came into my life. After that, it was just like having a real family."

"And how are you finding the experience of being a queen?" asked Jack.

"Nothing like I thought it was going to be," Anna replied. "I suppose I pictured there'd be more celebrations and parties. It's such a lot of work running a kingdom."

Jack took a deep draught of his wine. "Is it a kingdom?" he mused. "I should think it'd be called a queendom now."

Gerald chuckled, "I'd never thought of that. You're far too quick on your feet for me, Jack."

"I'll take that as a compliment," replied the cavalier.

A servant entered, carrying a large metal bowl aloft.

"What have we here?" asked Gerald. "Something smells tasty."

"That's for Tempus," announced Alric, "our meal will be along shortly."

The servant placed the bowl before the great mastiff. He sniffed it gingerly, then started eating.

"What is it?" asked Anna.

"It's a special recipe my father told me about," said Alric.

"Your father had dogs?"

"Years ago," said Alric. "He used them for hunting, but as he grew older, he hunted less and less."

"What happened to the dogs?" asked Anna, her curiosity peaked.

"They were sent down to Hillsworth. We have an estate down there."

"Sounds interesting," said Anna. "We didn't make it there on our visit, what's it like?"

"It's a rugged area," explained Alric. "The estate is up on the edge of the hills, giving a nice view of the countryside."

"Does anything interesting live in the hills?" asked Anna, eager for more information.

"Nothing too interesting," said Alric.

"Unless you like Ogres," offered Jack.

"Ogres?" said Gerald. "What are they like?"

"Yes," added Anna, "do tell."

"They're large creatures," explained Alric, "close in height to a Troll, but much more massive and their skin is soft. They always remind me of an old fat man who never sees the sun."

"Do they give you trouble?" asked Gerald.

"I wouldn't say so, would you, Jack?" said the prince.

"No," responded the cavalier, "definitely not. I don't think they're capable of causing trouble."

"Why is that?" asked Anna.

Jack brandished a utensil, "They're about as smart as this spoon."

"Still," mused Anna, "it would be interesting to see one, don't you think, Gerald?"

"I suppose," said Gerald, as plates were brought in that set his mouth to watering. "Now that's more like it."

"Yes," agreed Alric, "Weldwyn pie!"

Gerald looked at the meal before him. "It looks like Mercerian pudding," he mused.

"That's because it is," said Anna, "they just have a different name for it."

"How are the preparations going for the wedding?" asked Jack.

"Quite well," answered Anna, "but that reminds me, I had a question for you, Alric."

"Go ahead," the young prince insisted.

"I need a guest list," she continued. "You already told me your parents are coming, but I have no idea how many others."

"No other nobles," Alric replied, "unless you count my sisters."

"Edwina and Althea are coming?" she said. "How wonderful!"

"Alstan has to remain behind to look after things."

"I was thinking there might be a way to make it even easier," suggested Anna.

"Oh? How?" asked the prince.

"Our magic circle is complete, and Albreda's been to Summersgate before. We could bring them here using a spell of recall."

"I'm not sure my father would trust a foreign mage," said Alric.

"We can have Albreda bring one of your mages here, to learn our circle," said Anna.

"Are you sure?" asked Alric in surprise. "I know you want to keep them secure."

"We'll soon be married," said Anna, "and our two kingdoms need to become closer. I meant it when I said we'd be allies. I see no reason why we shouldn't start by trusting your mages."

"That's a marvellous idea," said Alric, "much better than a lengthy trip. I'll send word to Summersgate."

"I'll have Albreda carry it for you, she can have it there by tomorrow night."

"So soon?" said Alric in surprise.

"Of course, it's magic," said Anna.

"I suppose this really will bring our kingdoms closer together, won't it."

"I hope so," observed Gerald. "It would be of great use if either one of us was attacked."

"You can move troops that way?" asked Jack.

"Not many," replied Gerald, "the distance is too great. A mage would use up most of their reserves making the journey, or so I'm told."

"Just how many soldiers could you carry?" asked Jack, his interest peaked.

"I talked to Aubrey about it at some length," said Gerald, "and she seems to think she could take about a dozen, but bear in mind she's one of the more powerful mages. Very few others have that kind of ability."

"Still," said Jack, "over a week or so, some substantial numbers could be moved, especially if all the mages worked together."

"You should come and visit me at my office," said Gerald. "I'd love to pick your brain about how our two kingdoms could work together."

"I'd be delighted," said Jack, "as long as his highness has no objection."

"No objection at all," offered Alric. "I'm all for it, you should know that by now. It's more likely to be my brother, Alstan, that objects."

"Not your father?" said Anna.

"No," the prince replied, "he's quite taken with the idea of having allies."

"And why not Alstan?" asked Gerald. "He's the crown prince, I'd have thought he'd want to follow in your father's footsteps."

"I don't think he trusts mages," said Alric.

"Why is that?" asked Anna. "He always struck me as quite reasonable."

"My brother never really took the time to learn about them. I think he's fearful of their intelligence, or perhaps he's concerned that his own mind is not as quick as theirs."

"Mages aren't smarter," said Gerald, "they just know different things than we do."

"I'd have to agree," said Anna, "though Aubrey appears to know more than most."

"She's just more educated than most," defended Gerald.

"I'm not complaining," said Anna. "I like Aubrey, but at the same time, I can see how she might intimidate others."

"Nonsense," said Gerald, "everyone likes her."

"How's Dame Beverly doing?" asked Jack. "I heard she had a rough time of it at the trial."

"She did," said Anna, "but she's getting better. Aldwin's been very supportive."

"Aldwin?" said Jack. "Who's that?"

"Her husband," said Gerald.

Jack looked at him with a stunned expression. "Beverly's married? Why wasn't I told?"

"She was married just this last winter," said Anna. "It was a private ceremony, in Bodden, her home."

"Who is this Aldwin fellow?" asked Jack. "Is he a noble?"

Gerald looked at Anna, who simply smiled. "Sort of," he answered.

"What do you mean, 'sort of'? Is he a noble or not?" Jack pressed.

"He is now," explained Gerald. "He became a lord when he married Beverly."

"Then who is he?" begged Jack. "I must know who tamed her wild heart."

"He's a smith," said Gerald.

"A master smith," corrected Anna.

"Yes," Gerald agreed, "the same smith that created Nature's Fury."

"I must meet this man!" Jack announced.

"Why?" asked Alric.

"I must see what type of man stole her heart. I find it astounding that it wasn't me!"

TWENTY-FIVE

The Meeting

SPRING 964 MC

Lord Markham Anglesley, Duke of Colbridge, stared out the window of his carriage at the large manor that took up half a city block, its stately architecture much grander than that of his own home.

He wondered, briefly, at the cost of such a building, but then put all thoughts from his head. A servant scurried forward, placing a step upon the ground, then hurried to open the carriage door.

Lord Anglesley exited his confined space, taking a deep breath of the cool evening air. It was still early spring, and the land had not yet wholly shaken off winter's icy grip. He watched his breath drift away on a slight breeze, then dissipate quickly.

The door to the manor stood open, the soft light from within beckoning him, and so he moved with purpose, his cane clicking on the stone as he went. He fancied himself a proper lord now, bristling with wealth and newfound influence. The cane was just an affectation, a mark of his power that he held in a determined grip.

"Welcome," said the servant, his voice soft and melodic. "Lord Stanton is inside with the others. May I take your cane?"

"I'll keep it," said the young duke, pushing his way into the house. The elegant trappings of the Earl of Tewsbury were renowned throughout the kingdom. Anglesley had visited the Tewsbury Estate but had never before seen the earl's Wincaster mansion. It came as a surprise to observe precisely how much wealth was on display here. He gazed at the walls, which were painted in swirls of gold.

"Is that young Anglesley?" came a familiar voice.

Lord Alexander Stanton, his host, entered the hallway, drink in hand.

"Ah, there you are. Come in, my dear fellow, the rest are already present."

Markham followed the man into a much larger room, filled with familiar faces.

"You know the rest, of course, though our numbers are somewhat diminished," said Lord Stanton.

"I don't see Barrington," commented Lord Anglesley.

"He's no longer one of us," offered Lord Stanton. "It appears he'd been dipping his fingers into the Royal Treasury and was caught."

"He was executed?" asked Anglesley.

"No," the earl replied, "but his funds have been severely curtailed, and thus he is no longer of any use to us. You've met Lord Pearson and Lord Webster, of course."

"Naturally," said Anglesley, "as well as Captain Eldridge and Lord..."

"Walters," the last man responded, "Lord Montgomery Walters."

"Ah, yes," agreed Anglesley, "it's so good to see you again. I take it things are going well?"

"As well as can be expected," Lord Walters responded. "Though, with the death of Lord Montrose, I daresay our plans have been crushed."

"Nonsense," interjected Lord Webster, "my cousin would have wanted us to carry on."

"I'm afraid we wield little power these days," offered Lord Pearson.

"We can still offer opposition to the crown's reckless disregard of tradition," fumed Webster. "Surely we must do something!"

"I still say we should punish that peasant they call the marshal," said Lord Walters, full of venom. "The man's a very affront to our way of life."

"Oh, I don't know," said Lord Anglesley. "The man's proven himself on the battlefield. He's not all bad."

"I'm not disparaging his military ability," said Walters, "but we can't have commoners in such positions of authority."

"I agree," added Captain Eldridge, "and he has such a grip on the queen. Perhaps, with him out of the picture, she would be more reasonable."

"What are you saying, man?" asked Pearson. "That we should just murder him?"

"No," admitted the captain, "though it would serve our purposes just as well."

"We need some way to disgrace him," suggested Walters, "to pry him away from the queen, if you will."

"Yes," agreed Pearson, "we need to drive a wedge between him and his precious queen."

"I think you'd find it a difficult task," offered Anglesley. "I hear the two of them are firm friends."

"Nonsense," said Webster, "a queen doesn't have friends, only advisers."

"What is this grip he has over her?" asked Lord Walters. "I don't understand it."

"She is young, nothing more," said Lord Stanton. "I think she is merely inexperienced, though perhaps she is held in check through fear?"

"I doubt that," offered Anglesley. "He's been protecting her for years. I remember meeting him back in Uxley."

"You met him before?" asked Stanton. "I didn't know that."

"Yes," continued the young duke, "back in '59. King Andred held a hunt at his country estate."

"And you say this Matheson fellow was there?" asked Stanton.

"He was," confirmed Anglesley.

"My cousin," offered Webster, "before his untimely demise, told me as much. It appears he was sent there after the disgrace at Walpole Street."

"I was promised he'd be executed," barked out Walters. "I still say the man deserves death for what he did to my nephew!"

"The exile was arranged by Lord Fitzwilliam," continued Lord Webster.

"Hah!" exclaimed Lord Walters. "I should have known."

"If my cousin thought it necessary, you would have been informed," said Webster.

Lord Walters exploded, "Now, see here-"

"Gentlemen," interjected their host, Lord Stanton, "let us not quibble over what is done. Let us, instead, focus on the future."

"I see little to focus on," offered Pearson.

"Quite the contrary," said Stanton. "You see, there is another individual that has been active in our cause for some time."

"Oh?" said Webster. "Do tell!"

"A man not without resources," the elderly earl continued, "who had been working, behind the scenes, with Lord Montrose."

"I was not aware of this," said Webster in irritation.

"Your cousin didn't tell you everything," explained Stanton. "In fact, I, myself, didn't know of this man until he approached me."

"And who is this person?" asked Lord Webster.

"He'll be here shortly," Lord Stanton replied, "and then you can see for yourself."

"Why all this secrecy?" asked Lord Pearson. "Surely you can tell us his name!"

"He would not want it bandied about," Stanton explained, "and I'm sure, once he arrives, he'll explain everything."

"What's to explain?" asked Captain Eldridge. "Our cause is lost."

"That's a very maudlin statement," said Stanton. "Though we have suffered a setback, we are not down and out, gentlemen. I would like you to listen carefully to our visitor once he arrives. He will, I think, impress you with his vision."

"I'm skeptical," admitted Webster, "but willing to give him a chance."

"I suppose it's worth a try," added Walters.

"When is he due?" asked Anglesley.

Lord Stanton paused before answering, "Any time now, I should think." He took a sip of his wine, relishing the taste.

As if by magic, a servant opened the door, making his way to the elderly earl. He whispered in his lord's ear and then exited the room.

"Gentlemen," announced Lord Stanton, "it appears our guest has arrived."

They all turned in anticipation, watching the door for their mysterious guest to make his appearance. They were not disappointed, for moments later, he stood in the doorway, eliciting a gasp of recognition from the guests.

"Lord Valmar!" said Webster in surprise. "We thought you had fled."

"Never!" the villain replied. "I have merely been biding my time here, in the capital."

"But they are looking for you!" exclaimed Lord Walters. "How did you evade capture?"

Valmar smiled, "I still have friends. They shan't be rid of me that easily."

"Montrose," said Lord Webster, "you and he were always close. I take it he kept you safe?"

"He did," said Valmar, "and for that, I shall be eternally grateful. He kept me informed of your plans as well, gentlemen, though I was a little disappointed to see they didn't bear fruit."

"As are we all," added Lord Pearson, "but Lord Stanton tells us you have a new plan."

"I do," Valmar continued, "and I have already taken steps to ensure its success."

"You have us enthralled, Roland," said Stanton. "Would you care to explain it to us?"

"I would," said Valmar, "but it is, perhaps, a mite lengthy to talk of on a dry throat."

"Pardon my manners," offered Lord Stanton. "Captain Eldridge, fetch the duke a drink, will you?" He turned to Valmar as the drink was poured. "I keep the servants away from these meetings," he explained.

"A wise precaution," said Valmar. Taking the proffered drink from

Captain Eldridge, he drained it in one long draught, holding his hand out for more. The cup was dutifully refilled, and Valmar swirled it as he looked around at the faces of those assembled, gauging their character.

"It occurs to me," he said at last, "that the unfortunate fate of our dear colleague, Lord Montrose, has provided us with an opportunity to destroy the queen's adviser."

"How so?" asked Lord Anglesley.

Valmar ignored the question, turning instead to stare at their newest member. "Lord Walters, I believe you have a claim against our new marshal."

"I've been saying that for years," offered Walters. "Why an interest now?"

Valmar smiled, "If the queen wants her laws, let her have them. We shall use them against her."

"How, exactly?" pressed Anglesley.

"Lord Walters will make an accusation of murder against Marshal Matheson."

"That carries the death sentence," said Anglesley.

"If it's proven, yes it does," agreed Valmar.

"Do we have enough proof?" asked Lord Stanton.

"I think you'll find plenty of witnesses that can paint a picture."

"The man is popular," warned Lord Anglesley. "Surely they will find witnesses to defend his honour."

Valmar smiled, a look which the young lord found intimidating. "I think you'll find scant witnesses for his defence."

"What's that supposed to mean?" asked Webster.

"I have it on good authority," said Valmar, "that many of those witnesses perished during the war, and those that didn't may not have lived long afterwards. It's such a harsh world we live in these days, wouldn't you agree?"

Markham Anglesley felt a cold shiver go down his spine. This man's very presence unnerved him. He swallowed down his fear before speaking, "How sure of this are you?"

Valmar turned his gaze on the young lord. "As sure as I'm speaking to you. It only waits on Lord Walters to make the accusation."

"What if they ignore it?" asked Anglesley, finding his voice.

"They won't," assured Valmar. "The queen is too dedicated to the rule of law. To ignore it would set her back considerably."

"Can you guarantee we'll win the case?" asked Lord Stanton.

"No," confessed Valmar, "but the trial alone will discredit the man. A guilty verdict would be better, of course, but we must take what victories we can. We need to sow distrust between the marshal and his queen. We can do that by painting a picture of him as a brute and a tyrant, leaving her no choice but to separate herself from the man."

"Much as I'd like to see this proceed," said Walters, "are you sure it'll work?"

"I have had months to work on this," mused Valmar. "Months during which I studied the laws of the realm, including these so-called changes the queen has been making. I will advise you on how to proceed, don't you worry."

"And who will press the case?" asked Lord Webster. "Someone has to bring it to the attention of the crown."

"I'll do it," volunteered Lord Stanton.

"No," said Valmar, "it must be someone else. If you were to lay the charges, you could not sit in judgement, something I'm counting on."

"Explain yourself," said Stanton.

"Matheson is the Duke of Wincaster now," said Valmar. "That means he must be judged by his peers. With Montrose out of the picture, that leaves only four jury members to decide the case."

"I see," said Stanton, "and I'd be one of them, along with Anglesley here."

"Yes," agreed Valmar, "along with Lord Spencer and Lord Somerset."

"Somerset could be a problem," warned Webster.

"Yes," agreed Valmar, "but you only need three votes. I believe we can sway Lord Spencer to our cause."

"And if the queen appoints a new Earl of Shrewesdale?" asked Pearson.

"It still works to our advantage," said Valmar. "The next in line to the earl would be you, Lord Webster, would it not?"

Webster's face lit up in surprise. "Yes," he admitted, "I suppose it would."

"And if we had Lord Webster here," said Walters, "we'd have a clear majority, even without Lord Spencer!"

"Precisely," said Valmar. He took another drink, this time sipping it lightly.

"How does one go about making these accusations?" asked Captain Eldridge.

"I would suggest," said Valmar, "that Lord Walters, as the offended party, present the case to the High Ranger."

"The rangers?" said Eldridge. "Why would we do that?"

"It's tradition," said Valmar. "The head of the rangers is responsible for keeping peace in the kingdom."

"I thought the rangers just kept the roads safe," said Anglesley.

"They do," explained Valmar, "but if you research things, you'll find they do so much more. Under Andred, they were the king's muscle, but if you dig into history, you'll find they were originally created to enforce the laws. They predate even the town watch."

"Interesting," mused Lord Walters. "I'm warming to this plan of yours."

"Good," said Valmar, "now I want everyone to play their part in this. Lord Walters should wait a few days to make his accusations. I'll provide all the documentary proof he'll need to make his case."

"Isn't the leader of the queen's rangers that jumped-up baroness?" asked Lord Walters.

"Yes," confirmed Lord Stanton, "Lady Hayley Chambers."

"What do we know of her?" asked Webster.

"She joined the Knights of the Hound just before the battle of Eastwood," said Valmar, "and she's served the queen ever since."

"Is she close to the queen?" asked Webster.

"Not as close as some," offered Valmar, "but my sources tell me she has a sense of justice. She'll see it as her duty to carry out her charge, whether she likes it or not."

"Even if the queen objects?" asked Anglesley.

"Yes," said Valmar, "even then."

"Very well," said Stanton. "You have given us a way forward. What is the next step?"

"I have a series of instructions for each of you," Valmar explained. "I want you to read the notes I give you and commit them to memory. When you are confident in your role, the letter must be burnt, here, tonight. At no time should you discuss your role with the rest of this group. It is imperative that only I know the full plan if it is to come to fruition. Do you understand?"

They all nodded their heads in agreement.

"Good, then let us begin, gentlemen."

Valmar reached into his tunic to withdraw a set of small folded papers, each with a single name inscribed upon it. He handed them out, watching as every member of the group spread out, keeping their letters private as they read.

Pearson was the first to burn his. He lay it gently on the coals, watching as flames burst forth, eating away at the parchment. Webster soon followed, crumpling his up and tossing it onto the growing flames.

One by one, the letters were added until only Walters remained. His was the longest, his instructions more detailed, and he took his time, scanning over it several times. Finally satisfied, he bent down to the fire, waiting as it touched the corner of the note. It flamed to life, and he held it upright, allowing the flame to grow along its edge. Once fully alight, he dropped it on top of the now smouldering ashes, his sight captivated by the light.

"It is done, gentlemen," said Valmar. "I shall now take my leave of you."

"Wait!" called out Lord Pearson. "How should we contact you, if needed?"

"You cannot," said Valmar, "it is better that way. While you are pursuing these charges, I shall be busy adding fuel to the fire. Fear not, gentlemen, we shall meet again, but it will be a place and time of my own choosing."

He turned and left, leaving the others in stunned silence.

TWENTY-SIX

The Spirit Realm

SPRING 964 MC

Albreda stood in the centre of the circle, with only Fitz standing beside her. "Are you sure you won't change your mind?"

"I need to talk to Kraloch," explained Aubrey. "I have some questions about Life Magic that I'm hoping he can answer."

"And you two?" Albreda asked, turning to the younger Fitzwilliams.

"We're going to stay a few days," said Aldwin. "It's been a stressful few months in the capital, and we've decided we need some rest."

"Very well," said the druid. "In that case, I'll see you when you return to Wincaster."

She cast the recall spell, bringing up a circle of light. From Aldwin's point of view, the entire room was bathed in brilliant white, almost painful to the eyes. It lingered for a moment then dropped, revealing an empty circle.

"I don't know if I can ever get used to that," admitted Aldwin.

"It beats the flame," said Beverly. "At least the recall doesn't make you dizzy."

"What are you two up to today?" asked Aubrey.

"The weather's nice," said Aldwin, turning to his wife, "what do you say we go riding?"

"I'd like that," Beverly replied. "I can show you where Aubrey and I used to race."

"We can't race," objected Aldwin. "Lightning would far outpace any horse I'm likely to find."

"Don't worry," she chuckled, "I have no intention of racing today. I'm looking forward to a nice leisurely pace."

Aubrey smiled at her cousin. Without her armour, you would never know she was a warrior. She corrected herself as she noticed the hammer hanging from Lightning's saddle, no other lady of the realm would carry such a weapon on a leisurely ride.

"You two enjoy yourselves," said Aubrey. "Will I see you at dinner time?"

"Of course," answered Beverly, "we could hardly miss the legendary hospitality of the Brandon estate."

"Not to mention the food," added Aldwin.

Aubrey laughed as they turned and strode off towards the stables. It was good to see her cousin enjoying herself, free from the responsibilities of court. She waited till they were out of sight, then made off to find Kraloch.

The Orc shaman sat on a tree stump, watching a group of men put up the frame of a house. After bracing the upright timbers, they were ready to start the process of threading the thin branches between them, prior to the liberal application of mud and straw.

"Such strange methods of construction you have," he said as Aubrey approached.

"How did you know it was me?" she asked. "I thought I was being quiet."

"And so you were," Kraloch replied, "but I could sense your power."

"You can feel my magic?" she said. "I've never heard of that before."

"It is rare," the shaman revealed. "A gift from my ancestors."

"Can others sense magic?" she asked, intrigued.

"None that I know of," he said.

"Does that mean you could detect the power within an untrained mage?" she asked.

"Alas, no," he confessed. "Though I wish it were so. It would be so much easier to pick an apprentice if it were true."

"I didn't know your people had apprentices," said Aubrey.

"I merely use the term because it is familiar to you," he replied. "We train all those that show potential."

"And how do you know if someone has potential?"

"It can be difficult," he said, "but for the elemental schools, it is simpler. A potential mage would reveal their affinity in different ways. An Earth Mage might find it easy to get along with animals, let's say, or a Water Mage might be able to calm small waves."

"And a Life Mage?" she asked.

"Much more difficult. They don't show signs of healing, so it's hard to gauge."

"So how do you pick someone to train?"

"Trial and error," said Kraloch.

"I suppose that would make for a lengthy process," said Aubrey.

"Not as long as Humans," he replied.

"Why is that?"

"You have the habit of teaching everything about magic that you can before teaching spells."

"Of course," defended Aubrey, "we have to prepare the candidate for the use of magic. How else would you train them?"

"We have a more practical method," he continued. "Instead of teaching a student the entire magical alphabet, we start with only the runes needed to cast the first spell. In this way, we are optimizing our training while limiting the time spent in failure."

"That makes a lot of sense," said Aubrey, "though I can't help but think it would be easier if a person's affinity for magic could be discovered before training began."

"I would have to agree," said Kraloch, "and yet it is an option we do not possess."

"That's why I wanted to talk to you," said Aubrey.

"Oh?" said the Orc. "I find that a remarkable coincidence, for there is something I wanted to talk to YOU about."

"Me?" said Aubrey. "Now it's my time to be surprised. What is it?"

"You have learned the spell of spirit walk, have you not?"

"I have," she confirmed. "It was in my great grandmother's book of spells. Why?"

"The spirit world can be a dangerous place. I should know, I have travelled there many times. Most spiritualists summon a guide."

"I didn't know I could do such a thing," said Aubrey, "but it sounds fascinating. Who acts as a guide?"

"An animal spirit," Kraloch revealed. "We refer to them as 'Spirit Companions'."

"And you can communicate with them?"

"Not in the physical sense," said the Orc, "but they can understand you as much as a regular animal can. They form a bond with you when you first call them, so they can sense that they are to guide you and protect you as you travel the spirit world."

"Although I've been to that realm, I know little about it," confessed Aubrey. "What can you tell me?"

"It is home to the spirits of our ancestors," explained Kraloch, "but so much more, for it is also home to those that would feed off of your energy."

"If the spirit realm is where dead people go, why is it not full?" she asked.

"Your own beliefs explain that, I suspect. Do all men and women go to your Afterlife?"

"Not if they show lack of strength," she answered.

"Then, that being the case, where do they go?"

"The Underworld," said Aubrey, "at least that's the belief. I rather suspect the truth is much more complex."

The Orc grinned, "You are clever to have such suspicions. Our own knowledge of the spirit world is not complete, but we know that not all who die will travel there. It is our belief that only those who linger remain there."

"Meaning it is a conscious act?" she asked.

"Perhaps," he continued, "but we really don't know for sure. What we do know is that distance is a foreign concept there."

"I'm not sure I understand," said Aubrey. "I still have to move about in spirit form. Surely it is in parallel to the material world?"

"One would think so," said Kraloch, "and yet our experience shows us otherwise."

"I'm afraid you've lost me," admitted Aubrey.

"Think of your spell of recall," started the Orc. "When you cast that spell, you travel a set distance. The farther the distance travelled, the greater the strain on your magical power, correct?"

"Yes, I suppose so," she confirmed.

"In the spirit realm, distance has little effect on such things."

"So if I cast recall in the spirit realm, I can travel any distance?" she asked.

He chuckled, "No, not precisely. That particular spell would likely not work there. Let me put it this way, you've heard of us communicating over long distances, yes?"

"I have," she replied, "though I've never understood how."

"We contact other shamans using the spirit realm. For us, it is not the distance that limits our ability, rather it is our familiarity with those we attempt to contact."

"So someone you know is easier to contact than someone you don't!" she said excitedly.

"Exactly!" the Orc replied. "It has allowed us to stay in touch with many tribes spread throughout the world, from the Netherwood to the continent."

"The Netherwood? Where's that?"

"Your pardon," said Kraloch, "I believe you Humans call it the Great Wood, that which forms the northern border of Weldwyn. Your race picks such simple names for things."

"That's how the Orcs near Norwatch had heard of Redblade," mused Aubrey. "Beverly told me all about it."

"It is," the shaman confirmed.

"Tell me, Master Kraloch, when you're in spirit form, have you ever noticed an aura around others?"

"Yes, sometimes," he confirmed, "what of it?"

"I believe it can be used to determine magical potential. Have you seen any pattern to these auras, colour, for instance?"

"No," said Kraloch, "but then again, perhaps Orcs don't see the same as you do. Our eyes are more sensitive to light, so we see better in dim conditions, like night time."

"Is it possible to see into the spirit realm without entering it?" she asked.

"Yes," he said. "I, for example, can call ancient warriors to this world to fight for me."

"I understand that," said Aubrey, "but I was thinking there might be a way to see someone's aura without having to enter the spirit realm."

"An interesting prospect," said Kraloch, "and one that hadn't occurred to me. If that were true, you would be able to spot someone with magical potential before they begin their training."

"Precisely," said Aubrey, "but I have yet to learn how to read these auras."

"I'm not sure I understand," said the shaman.

"In the few trips I've made, I discovered that mages give off different hues around them. Life Mages give off a pale white aura, for example, while Enchanters show a pale green."

"Fascinating," he said, "we must explore this in more detail."

"I was hoping you'd say that," she said. "I'd like you to accompany me into the spirit realm."

"An excellent idea," said Kraloch, "and then I can show you how to call your spirit companion."

"When would you like to start?" asked Aubrey.

"I see no reason for a delay," said Kraloch. "Are you recovered from yesterday's ritual?"

"I am," she said.

"Then let us begin," he said, rising from the stump.

They moved to a clear spot, and then the Orc beckoned to two of his companions. "We will need them to guard our bodies," he explained.

He waited until the Orc hunters were in place, then started his spell. Moments later, Aubrey heard a snap and then the familiar feel of the spirit realm.

"Am I glowing?" asked Kraloch.

"You are," she replied, "the same pale white light that I exhibit. If my suspicions are correct, it's due to your Life Magic."

The Orc looked at her carefully, "It is difficult to see, but if I stare, I can just make out your aura."

"As you said earlier, it's likely because your vision is different."

They both took a moment to cast their eyes about, letting them adjust to the muted colours of this strange world.

"I take it there are many different spells that will work in the spirit realm?" she pondered.

"There are," he explained, "and some that will work in the material world as well, though with strange, secondary effects."

"Such as?" she asked.

"In the material world, spells are powered by your magical energy, but here, in the spirit world, it is your body that powers it."

"I'm not sure I understand," she said.

"Have you ever cast a spell and spent so much energy that your nose bleeds?" he asked.

"Yes, that happens when your magical energy is depleted, why?"

"In this realm, everything is reversed. Here, you would consume your physical body first, before your energy."

"Does that mean my body would take damage as I cast?"

"To a certain extent, yes. Those observing would see no physical change, no bruises or cuts, for example, but when you return, you will feel tired, even though you might have a full charge of magical energy."

"I assume my body would take longer to recover than my energy would," she said.

"Yes," he agreed, "I can see you understand. You are a quick study."

"Thank you," she said. "This is most interesting. How long ago did you learn to do this?"

"Many years," he revealed. "I was taught by the great shamaness Tarloch, who no longer walks this mortal land. Now, let me show you how to call your spirit companion."

He began speaking the words of power. They were much like those in the mortal realm, but the sound here was different, reminding Aubrey of having her ears covered.

Moments later, Kraloch stood, his arms held out in front of him, palms upward.

Aubrey felt the movement before she spotted it, a form that glided through the strange colours of this realm. It took shape as it drew closer, revealing a white wolf with piercing green eyes.

"This is Greylig," he explained, "she has been my companion for many years."

"Are all companions wolves?" she asked.

"I cannot say for sure," he replied, "I can only tell you that I have always had Greylig."

"Have you heard of other companions?" she asked.

"I have heard tell of unusual ones. It is said that Kragon, one of my ancestors, called a bear for a spirit companion, but I have no proof."

"And it's always the same creature?"

"Yes," he answered, "and much like an animal companion in the material world, you will learn their likes and dislikes, though there are some advantages to the spirit world."

"Such as?" she asked, intrigued.

"You don't need to feed them," he half-laughed, "and, of course, if they don't eat, they don't leave spoor."

"So they can't be tracked," said Aubrey.

"One would think so," continued Kraloch, "and yet, they are somehow able to sense things. No doubt you hardly noticed Greylig's approach, but she can sense others coming long before I see them."

"This is all so fascinating," said Aubrey. "Can you show me how you cast the spell?"

"Of course," he replied, "let us go through the incantation."

It only took a short while for Aubrey to learn the litany, though time here appeared to have little meaning. Soon, she was ready, confident the spell would work. She wondered what type of creature she might call, then put the matter aside, focusing instead on the task before her.

She stood still, her eyes closed, concentrating on calling out the magical letters. The words of power spilled from her lips in a cascade of sound, filling the immediate area with a slight echo.

Her spell complete, she waited, her hands held before her as she had seen Kraloch do. She sensed something approach before she saw it. The creature drawing near took the form of a wolf, softly padding towards her, its grey fur looking sharp and focused compared to the strange hues of this world.

"It's a wolf," she announced as it came closer. Halting just before her, it sat on its hind legs, its blue eyes staring at her. She moved forward, her hand outstretched. The wolf sniffed, then licked her fingers.

"He seems friendly," she said.

The wolf stood, circling them. Aubrey took it all in. "He has a scar on his flank," she said, "as if something attacked him."

"Indeed," said Kraloch, "though I doubt it was anything here. Bodies in this world do not behave like that."

"So he bore these scars in life?" she asked.

"It would appear so, though I have never seen its like before, nor have I heard of such a thing."

"He looks as though he was injured by some sort of claw," she remarked.

"Quite possibly," he agreed.

"Why is it he appears so clear to me? When I look at Greylig, she looks much like the background here, as if the colours had been washed out."

"It is the bond you share," explained the shaman. "To me, he appears 'washed out' as you describe it, though my own companion is clear to see."

"What else can we do in the spirit realm?" asked Aubrey.

"There is much," said Kraloch, "but you have learned sufficient for one day. It is time we returned."

"What will happen to our companions?" she asked.

"They will remain here, of course, to be called on another trip if need be."

"And if we cast a long way from here?"

"You need to release your preconceptions," he said. "As I told you, distance has little meaning here. If you cast the spell again, he will be waiting, regardless of where you are."

"So he follows me around?" she asked.

"No, but your spirits are linked. Call, and he will come."

"And by call, you mean cast the spell, of course."

"Naturally," he agreed.

"One more thing, Master Kraloch. Since you brought us to this realm, are you the only one that can return us?"

"No, anyone who knows spirit walk can do so. You, yourself, could cast it here, sending you back to the physical world, but I will save you the effort. Are you ready to return?"

"Yes, I am," she stated.

"Good, then I shall dispel my incantation."

He called forth his magic powers once more, and Aubrey felt the familiar tugging sensation. Moments later, she opened her eyes to stare up at the sky.

"That was fascinating," she remarked. "We'll have to try this again sometime."

"I am ever at your disposal," said Kraloch, getting to his feet.

Aubrey followed suit, then blinked as her brain tried to adjust to the riot of colours. "I always find myself a little disoriented after leaving the spirit realm, don't you?"

"I do," said Kraloch, "though you'd think I'd be used to it by now."

"You said you can talk to distant shamans?" she asked.

"I can," he replied. "It's a skill that I can show you at some point in the future. Of course, to work properly, you must communicate with someone you know well, but perhaps we can talk to each other that way. It would save having to travel to Hawksburg all the time."

"Is that only a Life Magic spell?" she asked.

"Alas, yes," he said, "Life and none other."

"Pity," she said, "it would have had huge ramifications for the defence of our borders."

"Indeed it would," the shaman replied.

Beverly picked up a small loaf, dropping it onto her plate. She moved along to the next table and waited as Aldwin put yet more meat on his own platter.

"What did you call this style of eating?" she asked.

"I don't know that it has a name," said Aubrey, "but it's efficient when you're feeding a large number of workers."

"I quite like it," said Aldwin, "you take as much as you like."

"He would say that," said Beverly, smiling. "Sometimes I think that's all he ever does."

"Hey, now," he said, "I have to keep my strength up. I work hard, you know." He placed some meat on Beverly's plate. "More?"

"No, that's plenty, thank you." They moved farther down the line.

"I'll take some of that cheese," she said, "as long as it's not Hawksburg gold."

Aldwin dutifully cut a chunk, placing it gingerly on her plate. "Is that enough?"

"Perfect, thank you," the knight replied.

It was now Aubrey's turn to examine the cheese, "Did you two get much riding in?"

"We did," said Beverly, "but I think it's time we were getting back to Wincaster."

"You're sure?" asked Aubrey. "You're more than welcome to stay as long as you like."

"She feels she needs to get back to work," offered Aldwin, "thinks the army's going to fall apart without her."

"It IS good to have a purpose," said Beverly.

They reached the end of the line, then started moving towards the bench seats.

Aubrey looked around the hall. "Over there," she called out, "by Kraloch."

Aldwin threaded his way through the room, finally arriving at the Orc's location. "May we?" he asked, indicating the table.

"Of course," replied the shaman.

They all sat down, arranging their plates.

"I hear you've been busy with my cousin," said Beverly, looking at Kraloch.

"I have," he admitted. "I've been educating her on the spirit world."

"I thought it was spirit realm?" said Aldwin.

"Orcs prefer the term world," said Kraloch, "but it is merely a turn of phrase. It matters little whether we call it a world or a realm; it is what it is."

"That's very profound," said Beverly with a grin. "You should become a philosopher."

"I already am," admitted the Orc. "It is one of the shaman's responsibilities for the tribe."

"Do you miss your home?" asked Aldwin.

The Orc looked around at the gathered people before answering. "A little, I suppose, but it is exciting to be here as we rebuild the town. There's a very real sense of accomplishment I've not felt in years."

"I'll agree with that," added Aubrey. "What happened to Hawksburg during the war was terrible, but rebuilding it has certainly brought people together."

"There's a lot of Orcs here now," mused Aldwin. "Do you think they'll settle here once they are finished rebuilding?"

"They're certainly welcome to," said Aubrey. "What do you think, Kraloch? Will your people stay?"

"No doubt some of them will," the Orc replied, "but as we are a race of hunters, I rather expect most will want to move on."

"Is there going to be a permanent garrison here, then?" asked Aldwin.

This time it was Beverly that answered, "There is. Gerald wants units stationed here, farther back from the border. It allows us more flexibility to reinforce Wickfield or Mattingly if they're attacked."

"Any word on which units?" asked Aubrey.

"Not yet," said Beverly, "but if I know our marshal, you can bet there'll be a company or two of cavalry in addition to the foot."

"They should post the Orc spears here," mused Aldwin.

Beverly looked at him in surprise, "I didn't take you for a strategist. I'm surprised you take an interest in such things."

"Why wouldn't I?" he said. "After all, you're my wife, and you're part of the army."

"He's got you there, cousin," said Aubrey. "You can't argue with logic like that."

"Nor would I want to," said Beverly. "But tell me, Aldwin, why Orcs? I'm curious as to the reason you'd suggest it."

"They're fast at marching," answered Aldwin, warming to the task, "and disciplined fighters. They'd be able to reinforce the frontier quickly."

"I'm impressed," said Kraloch. "The smith shows great foresight."

"I get it from my wife," said Aldwin, grinning.

"What else should we put here, husband?"

"I suppose that would depend on what was available. I would think some archers would be preferable."

"What about Orc archers?" asked Aubrey.

"Yes," said Aldwin, "they're good, but you need a Human contingent so that the villagers don't feel overwhelmed. I'd leave them here, in Hawksburg. Eventually, they could man the walls, but they have to finish building them first."

"Very astute of you," said Beverly. "Tell me, who do you think should command this group of soldiers?"

"It would have to be someone experienced," he said. "I'd say you, Beverly, but you're needed in Wincaster. That being the case, you'd have to delegate someone. I know Lanaka is in charge at the moment, but you'd likely need to pick someone born a Mercerian, if only for political reasons. Sir Heward is likely the best man for the job."

"You should stay in Wincaster more often," said Beverly, "you can take over my job if you like."

Aldwin shook his head, "No, I'd much rather spend my time at the smithy. I was thinking of setting one up in Wincaster."

"Why would you do that?" asked Aubrey.

"To be closer to Beverly," he replied. "We can't keep travelling back and forth to Bodden all the time."

"What part of the city would you set up in?" asked Aubrey.

"Likely in Artisan's Alley, with the Dwarves."

"There is no Artisan's Alley," corrected Beverly, "it's called Gareth Street."

"The smiths call it Artisan's Alley," defended Aldwin, "but you're right, that's not the real name."

"Why with the Dwarves?" asked Aubrey.

"I still have much to learn about smithing," said Aldwin. "I can learn a lot by working around them."

"You made Nature's Fury," said Beverly, "not to mention my armour. What else is there to learn?"

"Lots," he continued. "I'd like to learn how to fold steel. I've seen the blade on the queen's sword, that's the type of thing I'd like to make."

"But you don't need to sell things in Wincaster," said Beverly, "you're a lord now."

"I know," he replied, "but I enjoy the work. As I'm not worried about making a living anymore, it frees me up to try so many other things. I've even heard Elves have their own secrets when it comes to the forge."

"I didn't know that," said Aubrey, "but I suppose it makes sense. Someone has to make their weapons, after all."

"They are not as skilled as you might think," offered Kraloch.

"Why would you say that?" asked Beverly.

"Elves are a long-lived race. While it's true they can make fine armour and weapons, it takes them years to do so. You would die of old age long before they had you complete anything."

"I suppose I'll take that off my list then," said Aldwin. "What about your tribe, Kraloch? Do you have smiths?"

"We do," the Orc replied, "though none as skilled as you. We make basic weapons, favouring spears and axes."

"Doesn't your chieftain, Urgon, use a sword?" asked Beverly.

Kraloch smiled, "He does indeed, but it was forged by Dwarves."

"Is it magic?" asked Aubrey.

"Yes," answered Beverly, "I've seen it in battle. It was enchanted by shamans, wasn't it?"

"It was," said Kraloch, "though the weapon predates my own time. It was handed down to Urgon from his ancestors, as is often the way with such things."

"One day soon," said Aubrey, "the queen will officially recognize the Artisan Hills as the domain of the Orcs."

"How do you know that?" asked Beverly.

"She told me," Aubrey revealed. "Of course, she's been busy with other things right now, but I think it likely to happen just after her wedding this summer."

"That would be nice," said Beverly. "With the Artisan Hills as one of our provinces, we can officially integrate the Orcs into our army."

"Yes," added Aubrey, "along with the Dwarves and possibly even a few Elves."

"I'm surprised," said Aldwin, "I thought the Elves kept to themselves."

"They generally do," said Aubrey, "but some of the younger ones wish to change that. They want to be a part of this realm, and it promises a bright future for everyone."

"And we'll all be the richer for it," said Aldwin. "Think of all the knowledge that could be shared between the races! It'll be a new age of cooperation."

"Yes," said Beverly, "and a lasting peace, especially once the queen marries Alric."

Aubrey looked at her cousin, "Do you remember when you first visited Hawksburg, all those years ago?"

"I do," said Beverly. "I seem to remember a young cousin who kept pestering me."

"That's what I'm here for," said Aubrey, "but did you ever think things would end up like this?"

"Not in my wildest dreams," said Beverly, touching Aldwin's hand, "but I'm so glad they did. You?"

"I wish my family had lived to see it," said Aubrey, "but I know, in my heart, that this," she spread her arms out to encompass the area, "all of this, is something they would have appreciated. They always were about serving the people."

"My father is very big on that, too," said Beverly. "He feels it is the obligation of the nobles to look after the commoners."

"Exactly," said Aubrey, "though I wonder who thought of it first, my father or yours?"

Beverly laughed, "I doubt it really matters anymore. The important thing is that we carry on the tradition."

"Hear, hear," said Aldwin, raising his goblet. He tapped Beverly's cup, spilling a little wine. "Sorry about that."

"You're so unlike the other nobles, Aldwin," said Aubrey. "I've never seen one apologize for spilling their wine."

"Oh, shouldn't I?" the smith asked.

"You keep doing what you're doing," insisted Beverly.

"Agreed," said Aubrey. "It's what I love about you. You and Beverly are my family now, and your father, of course."

"I think you should include Albreda along with him," said Aldwin, "they seem to spend a lot of time together."

"Do you think your father will ever marry her?" asked Aubrey.

"I'm sure he wants to," said Beverly, "but I don't think Albreda is the marrying type."

"You'll have to be careful, cousin," said Aubrey with a grin, "if Albreda has a child, you might find yourself out of a barony."

"There's no danger there," said Beverly, "the queen has already changed the law, and I'm the oldest child. You couldn't pry Bodden away from me with anything."

"Glad to hear it," said Aubrey.

"Hear, hear!" said Aldwin, once again holding his cup aloft. "To the next Baron of Bodden, or should I say Baroness?"

They all raised their arms, the Orc joining in.

"To Bodden!" they all cried, then downed their drinks.

"I quite like this wine," said Kraloch. "What did you say it was called?"

"A Hawksburg Red," said Aubrey.

"I shall have to trade for some," the Orc replied.

"I shall be honoured to gift it to you," said Aubrey.

"I couldn't," the Orc protested.

"Nonsense," said Aubrey, "think of it as a reward for all the knowledge you've given me."

"In that case, I would be pleased to accept the offer."

Aubrey turned once more to Beverly, "When did you two wish to return to Wincaster?"

"Soon," said Beverly, "I've still much work to do reorganizing the cavalry."

"How about tomorrow morning?" Aubrey offered. "It gives us one more night at the manor house."

"That would be wonderful," said Beverly.

TWENTY-SEVEN

Charges

SPRING 964 MC

The Palace in Wincaster, aside from being the official residence of the monarch, also contained the Royal Bureaucracy. As such, it was home to the marshal's office, as well as that of the High Ranger. It was to the latter that Lady Hayley Chambers, Baroness of Queenston, made her way.

The rangers were far more informal than the army, and so, as she approached the door to her office, the two rangers standing there merely nodded, leaving the High Ranger to open the door for herself.

Inside, was a modest office, replete with a desk. As Hayley sat, rifling through the papers, she knew that her aide would soon arrive. She was not to be disappointed, for moments later, the door opened, revealing the countenance of the Orc ranger, Gorath.

The aide placed a hot drink before her, then proceeded to consult a page held in his hand.

"What have we today, Gorath?" Hayley asked.

"Reports from training are encouraging," he replied, using the common tongue of Humans. "We have more recruits signed on, and they should start training within the week."

"And the graduates?" she asked.

"On their way to their first postings," he replied.

She took a sip of her drink, a nicely warmed rum, then cast a glance at her own notes. "I'd say that still leaves us short."

"It does," Gorath agreed, "but the numbers are steadily increasing. If we continue at the current rate, we should have a full complement by the end of the year."

"Good to hear," she agreed. "I suppose we'll just have to keep relying on the army to make up the shortfall in the meantime. Anything else?"

"Yes," he continued, "I have a request here for warbows."

"You mean longbows," Hayley corrected.

"No," he repeated, "I mean warbows."

She looked up from her seat to see if he was joking, but the seriousness of his face told her otherwise. "What's a warbow?" she asked. "I've never heard of it."

"It is a bow said to be used by my people," he explained. "It's similar to a longbow, but with greater pull and balanced for an Orc's physique."

"How long have they been around?"

"Not long," he said. "They originated with a tribe of Orcs known as the Red Hand."

"Never heard of them," she confessed. "Are they near here?"

"No," the Orc replied, "they live on the continent."

"Then how are we to get these warbows?"

"They need to be manufactured by a master bowmaker," explained Gorath.

"How do we make a bow we've never seen?" she asked.

"Kraloch will communicate with our brethren on the continent. Once he has done this, he will explain how to do it."

"What's so special about these warbows?" she asked.

"They can penetrate the strongest of armours," he explained.

"Even better than an Elven bow?" she asked.

"I don't know," he replied. "I have never seen them compared, but I think it likely."

"You have me intrigued," said Hayley. "Get in contact with Kraloch and ask him to move forward on this. We'll see if we can get a few made for testing. If they're as good as you say, we'll start equipping as many as we can."

The Orc grimaced, an expression that Hayley had learned to recognize as one of happiness, similar to a Human smile.

"Anything else?" she asked.

"Yes," he said, "there's someone here to see you."

"There is?" she said in surprise. "That's rather unusual. Who is it, Gerald?"

"No," Gorath replied, "I would have told you if the marshal were here. It is someone else, someone I don't believe you've met before."

"What's his name?" asked Hayley.

"Lord Walters," the Orc responded.

"Did he say what he wants?"

"No," said Gorath, "though he did indicate it was a matter of great importance."

"Very well, send him in."

"Yes, Blackbow."

"What did I say about making up names for me?" asked Hayley.

"It is our way," said Gorath. "Do you not like it?"

"No," she replied.

"What of Oakenbow?"

"My bow is made of yew," she explained.

"Yewbow sounds strange," the Orc mused.

"Just call me Hayley," she insisted.

"But you need a hunter's name," he protested.

"Hayley means 'one who shoots well'," she lied.

He looked at her in surprise, "It does?"

"Yes," she lied again.

"Very well, Hayley, I shall show him in."

He left the office, returning shortly thereafter to allow entry to a well-dressed man.

"Good day," said Hayley, "I'm Lady Hayley Chambers, Baroness of Queenston. How may I help you."

"You are the High Ranger?" he asked.

"Yes," she said, "I have that honour."

"I wish you to lay charges," he demanded.

"I see," she said, careful with her words. "May I ask what kind of charges?"

"Murder," he stated.

"That's a rather serious accusation," she said. "Are you sure?"

"It is your job to do so, is it not?" the man asked.

"It is," she agreed. "What did you say your name was?"

"I didn't," he retorted, "but it's Walters. Lord Montgomery Walters."

"I'm afraid I don't know the name," she said.

"I wouldn't expect you to," he said. "My family is lesser nobility, but we are distantly related to the Chestertons of Stilldale."

"I see," Hayley replied. She was aware of the lesser nobility but had seldom encountered it. They consisted of relatives of those titled nobles that everyone knew. As relatives, they were allowed the honorific of Lord or Lady, but little else. She stared at him a moment, trying to judge his sincerity.

"Might I enquire as to who was murdered?" she asked at last.

"My nephew," he stated.

"And his name?" she pressed, dipping a quill to write.

"Lord Efram Walters," the man said. "He was the commander of the Wincaster Foot."

"All of them?" asked Hayley.

"No, just one company."

"So he was a captain," she made a notation on her paper. "And when did this alleged murder occur?"

"Back in '53, in the spring," Lord Walters said.

She wrote it down without thinking, and then the date sank in. "'53? And you're only just reporting it now?"

"It was reported at the time," the man said, "but nothing could be done about it. Now the murderer has returned to Wincaster, and I want him charged."

"That's your prerogative," she said, making a further note. "What's this murderer's name?"

The man looked at her and smiled slightly. His delay caused her to look up from her notes.

"Gerald Matheson," he said, meeting her gaze.

"The marshal?"

"The very same," said Walters.

"He's the leader of the army, and the Duke of Wincaster," she said in disbelief.

"I know who he is," he barked back, "but the law is the law. Or is the law only for those who aren't the queen's favourites?"

"The law applies to all," Hayley said, "regardless of their position or influence."

"Then I insist that you lay the charges."

"Are you sure you wouldn't like to reconsider?" she said.

"You cannot persuade me otherwise," he insisted, "and it is the duty of the crown to carry out the prosecution, is it not?"

"It is," she agreed.

"Then do your duty," he demanded.

"One moment," she said, "what proof have you? To say your nephew was killed is one thing, but to accuse an individual is quite another."

The man reached into a satchel, pulling forth some notes.

"These are eyewitness accounts," he said, handing them over.

"Where did you get these?" Hayley asked.

"I have been collecting evidence for some time," he explained.

She glanced over the pages. "I shall give this my attention," she promised.

"I expect more than that!" he roared.

Hayley turned to stare at the lord. "I can't very well charge a man with murder without an investigation. I need to verify these witnesses, not to mention account for the accused's whereabouts when the incident took place."

"It's not an incident," Walters insisted, "it's a murder."

"And I promised you I will look into it!"

"How long will that take?" demanded Lord Walters.

"I can't say for sure," the ranger answered, "but I would suspect no more than a week."

"Very well," the visitor said, "then I will come back in one week's time for an update."

"And I shall endeavour to have one for you," she replied.

Lord Walters nodded his head, "Good day to you, High Ranger."

"And to you, Lord," Hayley replied.

He turned and left, closing the door behind him. Moments later, Gorath opened it again.

"What was that all about?" he asked.

"He wants me to investigate a murder," said Hayley.

"Who died?" the Orc asked.

"His nephew, but that wasn't half as surprising as the man he accused of the crime."

"Who does he feel is responsible?" asked Gorath.

"Gerald Matheson," she said, still in disbelief.

"Perhaps he has mistaken him for another?" the Orc offered.

"It doesn't sound like it," said Hayley. "He made it very clear that he was referring to the marshal. He even provided me with some written accounts by witnesses."

"What do we do about it?"

"We investigate," she replied, "and if there's any merit to it, we must charge Gerald with murder."

Anna sat before the fire, warming her toes. The chill of the morning was still on them, even though the day promised to warm up.

"I don't want to work today," she announced.

"You're the queen," said Gerald, "you don't have to work if you don't want to."

"I do, and I don't," she said, a very model of contradiction.

"What's that supposed to mean?" he asked.

"It means I want things to happen, but I can't bear to sit in that office all day."

"Then take your work outside," he suggested. "Who says you can't spend time in the gardens?"

"A good idea," she said, "and we could make a picnic out of it."

"It's sounding less and less like work," he warned.

"I suppose it does," she agreed. "Perhaps I'll just take the morning off. I can always work this evening if I want to."

"All right," he said, "what do you want to do instead?"

"If we were at Uxley, I'd say let's walk the estate, but the Palace grounds are far too small for my liking. What do you say we go into the city?"

"You'd have to be protected, Anna. That means a bodyguard."

"I'm sure it's perfectly safe by now," she argued.

"May I remind you we never caught any co-conspirators," he warned.

"I suppose you're right," she grumbled.

The door opened, revealing Sophie. "I'm sorry, Your Majesty, but Lady Chambers wants to see you on a matter of some importance. She's brought guards with her!"

"Odd," said Anna. "Send her in, let's see what she wants."

Sophie disappeared from sight, closing the door behind her.

"What's that all about?" asked Gerald.

"I don't know," Anna confessed, "but I think we're about to find out."

The door finally opened, revealing Hayley and two rangers, a man and a woman. The baroness walked over to the queen, bowing formally.

"Your Majesty," she said, "you once told me that we must uphold the law, regardless of the cost. Do you still believe that?"

"Of course," said Anna, "why?"

"I must inform Your Majesty that a charge of murder has been laid against Lord Gerald Matheson."

"Is this some kind of joke?" asked Gerald.

"No," said Hayley, "unfortunately, it is not."

"And who has made this accusation?" asked Anna.

"Lord Montgomery Walters," said Hayley.

"Walters!" said Gerald, recognizing the name.

"You know him?" asked Anna.

"I did," he confirmed. "I served under him when the riot broke out at Walpole street."

"That was his nephew," corrected Hayley, "and he claims to have proof of your guilt."

"What kind of proof?" asked Anna.

"Sworn statements from eyewitnesses," said Hayley.

"And you've investigated these claims?"

"I have," the ranger responded, "in person. If this were any other case, I'd have no doubt about an arrest."

"Then you must do your duty," said Anna, her voice breaking slightly.

Hayley moved to stand in front of Gerald, the two rangers taking up flanking positions.

"Lord Gerald Matheson, Duke of Wincaster," announced Hayley officially, "you are hereby arrested on the charge of murder. You must surrender your weapon and face incarceration until such time as you are proven guilty or innocent in a court convened for such an occasion."

Gerald unbuckled his sword, passing it to one of the rangers.

Hayley turned to the queen. "Will house arrest be sufficient?" she asked.

Anna, grateful for the offer, simply nodded, too upset to speak.

"I will leave a ranger posted to keep watch over you, Gerald," said Hayley, "but you must surrender your position as marshal until you are judged. Do you understand the charge laid against you?"

"I do," said Gerald, his voice sounding defeated.

"I'm sorry, Gerald," said Hayley, "but I must do my duty."

"I understand," he said.

Hayley returned her attention to the queen. "You will have to recall Baron Fitzwilliam to Wincaster, Your Majesty, to take command of the army."

"I will," said Anna.

"And it must be made clear," insisted the ranger, "that Gerald is no longer in command, otherwise the troops might try something foolish. You know how much they like their marshal."

"I know," said Anna, "and I promise it will be done."

"Thank you, Majesty," said Hayley. She bowed once more, backing away, then turned and left with her two rangers, ordering one to remain outside the door. Hayley knew it was all so unnecessary, but she must be seen to be doing her job. Gerald would stay put, of that she was certain!

Gerald avoided Anna's gaze, too ashamed of his actions.

"What happened that day, Gerald?" she asked at last.

"It was chaotic," her oldest friend explained. "The troops went wild and started slaughtering innocents. Lord Walters lost his head and died."

"And his family blames you?" she asked.

"Yes," he confirmed, "they want to clear their nephew's name, but he was the one that let them loose."

"What have you to do with any of that?" she asked.

"I was his sergeant in the Wincaster Foot."

"Go on," she urged, "I'm trying to understand things."

"We were the fifth company," he continued, "deployed to block Walpole Street. Our job was to stop the rioters from reaching the richer area of the city."

"And these people were rioting because of starvation, weren't they?" she asked.

"That's right," he confirmed. "The harvest had been poor the year before, and there was nothing in the granaries. The people were starving, and to make matters worse, it was one of the hottest summers ever. Anyway, we formed a thin line across the street, ready to halt the mob."

"And did it? Halt the mob, I mean?"

"It did," he said, "and I can remember them getting ready to flee when they realized the futility of it, but then Lord Walters panicked."

"What did he do?" she asked.

"He ordered us to attack them, even though they were backing off."

"What did you do?" she asked.

"There was little I COULD do," he defended. "I had to take the place of a man named Henderson, standing in the line at the last moment."

"Why, what happened to this Henderson fellow?" asked Anna.

"He was hit in the head by a bottle," said Gerald, "and as he'd recently lost his helmet, he went down like a dropped sword."

"What happened then?" she prodded.

"I was using numbleaf back then," he explained, "and someone had cut my leg, likely just a broken bottle, but I didn't feel it. When Walters gave the command to advance, my leg collapsed on me, and I fell to the ground, bleeding out."

"I remember the numbleaf," she said. "You were using it when you first came to Uxley."

"I was," he confirmed. "I don't know how long I was out, but I woke some time later to find that the men had already scattered, and I had to scramble to find them."

"And so you were blamed for this," said Anna. "I think I understand now. They simply want a scapegoat."

"They did," confessed Gerald, "though I thought it was over years ago."

"That's why they sent you to Uxley," said Anna, "to get you away from the capital."

"Yes," he admitted, "that was the baron's idea. He was trying to protect me."

"And then you met me," she said, smiling.

"I did," he said, "and you changed my life."

"As you changed mine," she said, "and I'll do whatever I can to protect you, Gerald. You have my word."

"What do I do in the meantime?" he asked. "If I'm not to be allowed my duties as the marshal, I'm useless to you."

"Of course you're not useless," said Anna, "and quite frankly, you're still in charge of the army."

"But Hayley said-"

"It doesn't matter what Hayley said," Anna continued, "she's just doing her duty. I'll make it clear to Baron Fitzwilliam that you are still in command, but he will carry out any public appearances on your behalf. It'll be a secret amongst the three of us."

"And the soldiers that serve under me?"

"You know who you can trust," she said, "but we'll make a show of you not doing anything, just to coddle the Walters family."

"And if I go to trial and lose?" he said.

"You won't," she replied.

"You don't know that," he argued. "You wanted the rule of law, Anna. You can't make exceptions, you know that. It's the basis for your entire reign."

"I know," she replied, "and that is what makes this so much more difficult. We'll investigate this thoroughly. There has to be a way to win against these charges."

"I'm sorry I put you in this situation," said Gerald.

"I know," she replied. "Tell me the truth, Gerald, did you kill Lord Walters?"

He stared back at her for a moment, considering his words carefully before answering, "I never killed a man that didn't deserve it."

She nodded in understanding and pressed him no further.

Gerald tried to be positive, but he could feel the weight of the world descending on him. He had done things in his past that he wasn't proud of, and he had always thought they might catch up to him. Was this to be his punishment? Was Saxnor upset at his choices? He remembered back to the death of his wife and child. If only he hadn't gone out looking for the escaped pig, he told himself, they'd be alive today. Was this his punishment before being sent to the Underworld to spend an eternity in torment?

TWENTY-EIGHT

Investigation

SPRING 964 MC

Nikki passed by the dusty shelves, making her way to the table where Arnim sat, his eyes scrutinizing even more documents.

"Any luck?" she asked.

He grunted in annoyance and looked up. "The records here are badly kept," he griped. "It's a miracle I can read any of them."

"Who entered them?" she asked.

"An illiterate, by the looks of it. I'd have an easier time trying to talk to a dead man."

"What is it you're trying to read?"

"The records for the Wincaster Foot," Arnim replied, "specifically, the fifth company."

"That was the one Gerald was attached to?" she asked.

"Yes," he replied. He looked at her a moment, considering his words. "I'm sorry I barked," he finally said, "but I'm finding the lack of progress distressing."

"I understand," Nikki said, "perhaps I can help?"

"How?"

"When I ran with the gangs, they often needed assistance with their records."

"Criminals keep records?" Arnim said in surprise.

"Of course," she retorted. "It's the only way they could make sure they weren't being cheated."

"How does that help us?"

"They were all from the slums. I'm sure if I could read their sloppy writing, this should be a breeze."

"Very well," he stated, "at this point, I'm willing to try anything."

He turned the book to lay it in front of her.

Nikki sat, flipping through and scanning the pages. "It's a tough read," she admitted, "but not as bad as some I've seen. What's the date of the riot?"

"Late summer of '53," said Arnim.

"And we need the names of all the soldiers, correct?"

"Yes," he admitted, "at least all the men that were at the riot. A company is fifty men strong on paper."

"On paper?" she asked. "What's that supposed to mean?"

"It means," he explained, "that in real life the numbers are often considerably less. There'll be minor injuries or deaths that haven't been replaced."

"But these are pay records," said Nikki.

"Precisely," he said. "We'll be able to compile a list of all the soldiers that were paid for that month. It won't tell us who was there, but it's a start."

"What about Gerald?" asked Nikki. "Can't he give us a list of names?"

"I've already spoken to him," said Arnim. "He offered up a few, but has a hard time remembering the rest."

"I find that unusual," she said. "He tends to know his soldiers very well, it's what makes him a good leader."

"It's the leaf," explained Arnim.

"Numbleaf?" she asked.

"Yes," her husband continued, "he suffered from a debilitating leg wound and was taking it to manage his pain. Quite frankly, I'm surprised he remembered as much as he did."

"Perhaps you can use that in his defence?" suggested Nikki.

"I work for the crown," he reminded her, "there's a very good chance I'll have to prosecute him."

"Arnim, you can't!"

"It's my job, Nikki. I don't have to like it, but I must do my duty."

"And what of your duty to the queen? Would you break her heart by going after her father?"

"He's not her father!"

"He is," said Nikki, "in all the ways that matter. If you prove him guilty, he'll be sentenced to death. It'll devastate her."

"If he's innocent, the evidence will prove it," countered Arnim.

"My poor, sweet husband, is that what you think? These men that are lined up against us are ruthless, and they'll stop at nothing to achieve their objectives."

"Oh, you know them, do you?" Arnim exploded.

"No," she soothed, "but I've met enough like them. They might wear fancy clothes, but underneath they're just as filthy as those gang leaders in the slums."

Arnim took a deep breath, forcing himself to relax. "I'm sorry," he said at last, "I find this whole investigation to be quite taxing." He glanced back over at the book, "Found anything useful?"

"I have," she responded. "If we remove the captain and Gerald, we're left with thirty names."

"Gerald said there were only twenty at the riot," offered Arnim, "so we'll still have to whittle the list down a bit."

Nikki began copying the names to a paper.

"There," she said, putting checkmarks next to two of the names, "now we only have to identify the other eighteen. What's the next step?"

"We have to check the order books," said Arnim. "If we're lucky, they'll mention the deployment to Walpole Street."

"Why didn't we start there?" she asked.

"It's a long shot," he replied. "The riots erupted rather quickly, and it's likely there's no record of the company orders."

"And if that fails to yield the information we need?"

"Then we'll move on to the next step," he said. "That will involve a visit to army records."

"Isn't this the army records?" she asked.

"No, these records are the property of the treasury. The army records should detail deaths, at least those that died in the army. I know the Wincaster Foot fought against us in the siege and they likely took some casualties, so that will make the list shorter."

"But it won't tell us who was present at the riot," said Nikki.

"No, but at least we won't be wasting time looking for dead men. If we can find survivors, perhaps they'll be able to give us the names of others who were there?"

"A good idea," she agreed, "but shouldn't we visit the fifth company directly?"

"We can't," said Arnim. "I already checked, it was disbanded when the army was reduced. Whoever was left was either transferred to another company or dismissed."

"If they were transferred, the army would have records!" declared Nikki.

"Precisely," Arnim agreed, "but once a soldier is dismissed, we lose track of him."

"You give me names, and I'll find them," promised Nikki.

Arnim smiled, "I was hoping you'd say that."

. . .

That afternoon found them in the bowels of the Palace, walking down long corridors in the gloom of Arnim's lantern.

"It's got to be here somewhere," mused Nikki.

"Here it is," said Arnim, pausing by a door. He tried to open it, only to discover it was locked. "Saxnor's balls! Now we have to go all the way back upstairs to get the key."

"Or not," said Nikki, lifting her skirt to pull a small packet from her garter, opening it to reveal her lock picking tools."

"You're still carrying those?" he asked.

"Of course," she replied, "I never go anywhere without them."

"But we live in the richer section of town now, and spend most of our time at court."

"And yet here we are," she said, "in need of a lock pick!"

She was about to insert her pick when she paused.

"Arnim," she said, "I think someone's been here before us."

"Why?" he asked. "Did you hear something?"

"No," she replied, "but there's signs that someone's tried to pick the lock."

He moved closer, holding the light to the door handle. Sure enough, rough scratches were visible.

"It was a poor lock pick that tried this," he stated.

"Yes," she agreed. "No one worth their salt would leave marks like this. It was clumsy."

"The big question is, were they successful?"

"There's no way to tell," she replied.

"If they were, it jeopardizes the entire investigation."

"How so?" she asked.

"They could have compromised evidence," he said. "There's no telling what they might have removed from here."

"Or," suggested Nikki, "they simply came to find information, just as we did."

"Let's hope that's all it is," he said. "Go ahead and get us in, Nikki. If they did gain access to the records, we might have to speed up our search."

She inserted the tools, twisting them slightly until she felt what she was searching for. "Here we are," she said, pushing slightly. There was a loud click, and then the door swung open, revealing rows of shelves beyond.

Arnim stepped forward, illuminating the room with his lantern. Dusty tomes filled the shelves, each a leather-bound book with rough numbers etched on their spines.

"These archives record all those soldiers who died while in service to the crown," he told her.

"Where do we start?" she asked.

"The books are all dated," he said. "You start on the day of the riot and work your way forward, and I'll look at the most recent first, then work my way back. We're searching for any recorded deaths that are on the list of names we made. Of course, not all records are completely accurate, so we may find that a few deaths are not listed, but I'm hoping we can at least reduce the number of names."

"Surely more witnesses is better for Gerald," Nikki pointed out.

"Yes, but they'd require more time to track down. I'm hoping we can eventually find one or two that can corroborate Gerald's version of things." He paused at the end of a bookshelf. "I've found my first book, you?"

"I have it here," she said, pulling a dusty tome from the shelf before her.

They both moved to the table where Arnim set the lantern before them, illuminating both books as they began to peruse the pages.

"I wish we had a mage with us," commented Nikki, "an orb of light would be useful right about now."

"So it would," agreed Arnim, "so it would."

Beverly knocked on the door, watched by the guards that stood on either side of it.

"Enter," came the queen's voice.

The knight pushed the door open to reveal the opulent room within where Queen Anna sat before a mirror while Sophie brushed her hair.

"You wanted to see me, Majesty?" said Beverly.

Anna raised her hand, halting her maid's ministrations.

"Would you give us some privacy, Sophie?" she asked.

"Certainly, Your Majesty," the young woman replied.

Sophie walked past Beverly, exiting the room and closing the door softly behind her.

Anna rose from her chair, moving across to where more comfortable seating awaited.

"Have a seat, Beverly," she requested, "there are things we need to discuss."

Beverly followed the queen's lead and sat, waiting for further enquiries.

"I take it you've heard of the charges against Gerald?" Anna asked.

"I have," said Beverly, "though I have a hard time believing them."

"What do you know of the events surrounding the massacre?"

"Only what I was told at the time," Beverly revealed. "From my under-standing, Lord Walters ordered a full-scale slaughter."

"Yes," agreed Anna, "and died as a result."

"A fitting end for him, if you ask me."

"Gerald has been accused of murdering Lord Walters. His family claims to have proof."

"And?" asked Beverly.

"And, at first glance, the evidence appears substantial. Tell me, do you think Gerald would kill a man to save others?"

Beverly thought long and hard before making up her mind, "I would say it's quite possible, under the right circumstances."

"Yes," agreed Anna, "and, I would add, not just possible, but likely."

"So you think him guilty?" asked Beverly in surprise.

"Yes, though I can't blame him, and therein lies the problem."

"I'm afraid I don't understand."

"I've always believed that a kingdom must be ruled by laws, laws which I've spent a lifetime learning. Now, I find myself at a crossroads. On the one hand, I desperately want the rule of law, but on the other, my dearest friend may pay the price for that belief."

"It's a dilemma," Beverly commiserated. "Given a reversal of our roles, I'm not sure what I would do."

"Tell me, Beverly, what would you do to ensure the safety of Gerald."

"Whatever it takes," said the knight, looking straight into Anna's eyes. The queen's own eyes stared back, unblinking.

"I was hoping you'd say that," Anna finally responded.

"What is it you wish me to do?" asked Beverly.

"For the moment, nothing, but at some point in the future, I may ask you to take action. If that happens, I'll need you to carry out my orders without questions."

"I stand ready to serve, Your Majesty."

"Good," said Anna. "In the meantime, say nothing of this to anyone, do you understand?"

"I do," the red-headed knight responded. "I shall speak to no one, on my honour."

"What time is it?" asked Arnim.

Nikki looked up to see his face bathed in the soft glow of the lantern. "I don't know, evening perhaps? We've been down here for quite a while."

"We're almost done," he said. "This book is the last to check. How does our list look?"

"We've eliminated ten names," she said, "but there's no telling if they were all at the riot or not."

"Ten out of thirty," he said, "at least we're making progress."

"Perhaps we'll find one or two more in that book you're reading."

"We can hope," said Arnim, "but we'll have to decide how to move forward."

"Have we exhausted all our options with the army records?" asked Nikki.

"Maybe not, there's still the chance that some transferred to other units."

"Would that be here, in the archives?"

"No," he replied, "the disbanding of the companies is more recent. We'll have to check the current records. We'll need access to the marshal's office for that."

"I can't see that as being a problem," commented Nikki. "The queen assured us of her full cooperation. She wants to get to the bottom of this as much as anyone else."

A look of worry crossed Nikki's face, causing Arnim to look on in concern.

"What's the matter?" he asked.

"I hate even to suggest this," said Nikki, "but could Gerald be trying to bury his past?"

"What would give you that idea?"

"He's the marshal. He could post witnesses to the far end of the kingdom to keep them from answering questions."

"Isn't that a little unlikely? After all, it's Gerald we're talking about here."

"Think about it," she continued. "What do we know about him prior to his service with the princess?"

"I met him in Uxley," said Arnim.

"Under what conditions?" she pressed.

"I was captain of her bodyguard. You know that."

"Yes, but what was his position at the time?"

"He had fallen out of favour at court," said Arnim, "and been banished from the capital. They also removed him from his position at Uxley Hall."

"So, he defied orders to return to Uxley?"

"I suppose he did," said Arnim. "What are you getting at?"

"Just that we know so little of his life before Uxley."

"Beverly knows him well," defended Arnim, "as does Baron Fitzwilliam. They both think the world of Gerald."

"Yes," said Nikki, "but he was lost to them. Think about it, Arnim. Everything he held dear was ripped away from him. First, his family, then his very life as a warrior. That's a heavy burden to bear."

"And your point?" he pressed.

"People will go to great lengths to recover that which has been taken. Perhaps he seized an opportunity to vent his frustrations on Lord Walters?"

"Isn't that a little far fetched?" he accused.

"He lost everything," she insisted, "and he likely blamed the king's court. He was wounded, saving the king, wasn't he?"

"He was," confirmed Arnim, "and now that you mention it, I see what you mean. He never received any recognition for his part in the king's rescue, even though it cost him his livelihood. That's a bitter brew to drink, and then, on top of that, he's put under the command of a man that represents all that's wrong with the nobility."

"I think he snapped," said Nikki. "He was on numbleaf, which doesn't lead to rational thinking in the first place, and he stumbled across Lord Walters, yelling his head off and urging more death and destruction. I think Gerald took the only action he felt he could."

"So he killed the lord to save everyone?" asked Arnim.

"Possibly, or perhaps he saw the chance to give back some hate to the nobility in the form of his commanding officer. Think of all the rage he must have built up, being sent to the dregs of the army."

"That still doesn't mean he did it," said Arnim.

"Agreed," added Nikki, "but it does give him the motive to kill Walters."

"I hope you're wrong," said Arnim.

"So do I," she replied.

Beverly made her way to Gerald's quarters, the queen's words still fresh in her mind. The knight had thought to send an aide to ask him some questions, but the queen's insistence on keeping things between them made it imperative that she do this herself.

Upon reaching the third floor, she stepped from the stairwell into the long corridor that led to the marshal's room, but something was wrong. There should have been a guard on his door, but instead, all she saw was an empty hallway. Perhaps, she thought, he had merely decided to visit the queen, his guard following along, then she scolded herself, for if this were the case, they would have surely passed by her.

Senses alert, Beverly unslung Nature's Fury from her belt, gripping it tightly. As she drew closer, she spotted a mark on the floor and quickly identified it as blood. The door to Gerald's room sat partially open, and she moved forward, using her left arm to swing it wide.

A dead body lay on the floor, a ranger by the look of it, while a trail of blood angled off to the right. The knight crept forward, ready to fight, her pulse quickening.

Instead, she found Gerald lying face down, a large pool of blood beneath him. She rushed to him and felt for a pulse. It was weak, but he lived, though how much longer Beverly had no idea. Casting her eyes about, she looked for the intruder, but whoever had perpetrated this assault had fled, leaving little behind to follow.

She rushed to the door, calling for the guards at the top of her lungs. Hearing the distant echo of replying voices, she returned to Gerald in an effort to stem the flow of blood. Pulling a sheet from the bed, Beverly used her dagger to cut it up for bandages and packed the wound as best she could, but still, the blood poured forth, staining her hands.

Three Royal Guards appeared at the doorway.

"Get Lady Aubrey," she called out, "and seal the doors, someone's tried to kill the marshal!" Beverly cursed herself, she should have been here to prevent this.

Another guard approached, pulling a blanket from the bed and using it ineffectually to stop Gerald from bleeding out.

Footsteps out in the corridor announced the arrival of Aubrey. The young mage crouched beside Beverly to examine the marshal's wound.

"Can you save him?" pleaded Beverly.

In answer, Aubrey began casting, pulling forth magical energy until her hands glowed a brilliant yellow. She touched Gerald, and the light bled into him, pooling in an area lower down on his back. Finally, the marshal gave an audible gasp, and then his eyes fluttered open.

"Gerald, can you hear me?" called out Beverly.

"The guard," he stammered.

"He's weak," warned Aubrey, "and he'll need to rest; he's lost a lot of blood."

"Where's his guard?" asked one of the soldiers.

Beverly, content to let her cousin look after Gerald, stood, examining the scene. "Which Royal Guard was on duty in this area?"

"Styles," answered the soldier. "He took over from me a little while ago."

"He must have killed the ranger, then entered the room."

"This wound is from behind," reminded Aubrey.

"So Gerald didn't expect it. I suspect the assassin dragged the ranger's body in here to delay discovery." She turned to the guard, "Search the entire Palace, find Styles and place him under arrest."

"Gerald will survive," announced Aubrey, "but we need to get him into bed." She looked at the blood on the floor. "We need to move him to a safer location."

"My room," said Beverly, "it's just down the hall, next to the queen's."

"We need more guards," said Aubrey, "but who can we trust?"

Beverly looked around in a mild panic. Who could they trust? Before this, she'd have sworn the Royal Guards, but now she had her doubts.

It was Aubrey who supplied the answer. "We can take him to Hawksburg," she suggested. "The Orcs will keep him safe at the manor."

"Very well," replied Beverly, "but we'll take precautions all the same. I'll watch over him here. Send word to Prince Alric. Tell him we need six men, and Jack, if he's available. Once you return with them, we'll carry Gerald to the circle. Is he sufficiently healed enough to go through?"

"Yes," said Aubrey.

"How did this happen?" wondered Beverly.

"It wasn't your fault," urged Aubrey.

"I should have anticipated it," the knight replied. "What am I going to tell the queen?"

"That we saved Gerald and that we're taking him to safety."

"We have another problem," said Beverly, "if a guard could get to Gerald, there's a very real possibility they could get to the queen."

"They've already tried," reminded her cousin.

"Yes," agreed the knight, "but we're stretched to the limit. We need people here that we can trust. Her safety is at stake."

"Once we get to Hawksburg, I'll bring Kraloch and some Orcs back here. I know it's a temporary measure, but at least it will buy you some time to sort things out with the guards."

Donald Harper had started soldiering at the tender age of fifteen, and now, ten years later, he had earned the coveted position of Royal Guard, a situation that was much to his liking, even if it did include this room to room search of the Palace. He looked to his companion, Evard Brenton, who was walking, sword drawn, beside him.

"What d'you make of it, Ev?" he asked.

"It's crazy," Brenton replied, "to think that a member of our own guard turned on the marshal. What was Styles thinking?"

They turned a corner to see someone kneeling in the hallway, a guard by the look of it, bent over a door handle.

"You, stop!" called out Harper.

In answer, the man looked in their direction and stood up.

"It's all right," he said, "I just lost my key."

"Don't lie, Styles," called out Brenton, "we know it was you that attacked the marshal."

In answer, Styles drew his own weapon and advanced, snarling as he did. He rapidly closed the distance, striking out at Brenton, driving the blade deeply into the man's arm.

Harper, surprised by the sudden attack, struggled to draw his blade, a somewhat worn piece he had used for years.

Brenton struck back, a weakened blow that was easily deflected by his opponent, then Styles replied with a lightning-fast stab, thrusting the sword into Brenton's stomach.

Harper finally slashed out, striking high to avoid any armour. The trusty blade dug deep, slicing into the sinews of the traitor's neck. Styles collapsed in a heap, his breath stopped cold.

What Harper saw next astounded him, for as Styles fell, his face contorted, losing all of its features, to then take the form of a blank face. This was the only way the guard's mind could explain it.

Brenton, who had fallen to the ground, clutched his wound, breathing heavily. "What in the Underworld is that thing?" he asked.

Harper poked it with his toe, ensuring it was dead. "I have no idea."

Alric looked at Anna, who was sitting beside him.

"He's safe in Hawksburg now," he soothed.

"Thank you, Alric," she replied, "but we still need to get to the bottom of this." She turned to the rest of the assembly, "Ideas, anyone?"

"I don't think this attack was the work of our political rivals," announced Hayley.

"Why do you say that?" asked Anna.

"They already have a strong case against Gerald, why kill him?"

"That makes sense," agreed Aubrey, "but if not them, then who?"

"Yes," said Alric, "and what was that creature they found?"

"A bartok," offered Revi.

"I've never heard of them," said Hayley. "Are there many of them?"

"They are a creation of Necromancers," he stated, "though my understanding is that their image must be based on an actual person."

"So the Dark Queen is in play," mused Beverly.

"It would appear so," added Anna. "It makes sense, she did have to flee Merceria. This is her way of telling us she's not done with us yet."

"How long has it been amongst us?" asked Anna.

"I'm afraid there's no way to tell," said Revi. "Months, perhaps even years."

"Is there any way to discover if there are more?" asked Beverly.

"Perhaps," offered Kraloch.

"Care to explain?" said Anna.

"A creature such as this, a construct, if we use that term, would have no representation in the spirit realm."

"And what does that mean?" asked Hayley. "Are you saying they'd be invisible there?"

"No," explained the Orc shaman, "but living creatures look different than the non-living."

"The washed-out colours?" said Aubrey.

"Yes," agreed Kraloch, "their colours would have the same hues as the other non-living things, like furniture."

"We need to check this room," said Hayley. "We have no way of knowing if one of us isn't one of these bartoks."

"I can vouch for myself," offered Alric.

"That's precisely the point, Alric," said Anna. "If you were a shapeshifter, that's exactly the answer you'd give."

"So what's the solution?" asked Alric.

"I shall go into spirit form and examine the room," offered Kraloch.

"No," said Anna, "not alone, you won't. Take Aubrey with you."

"Majesty?" said Beverly.

"He must," explained Anna, "don't you see? If he were one of these creatures, he could lie to us. This way, they'll both be able to view our spirits."

"And if they're both in on it?" asked Revi.

"A risk I'm willing to take," said Anna, "though I suppose we could send Beverly with them. Would that satisfy everyone?"

They all nodded their heads in agreement.

"Very well," said Kraloch, "I shall cast the spell." He moved to an open space and lay down, waiting as Beverly and Aubrey joined him. He began the incantation, the words of power causing the air to buzz. Moments later, there was the familiar snapping sound, and the room changed around them.

Aubrey rose first, her eyes on Beverly. "Your hammer's glowing brightly," she said.

Beverly, the next to rise, held it in her hands in wonder. "Is it? I don't see anything."

"It is magic," said Kraloch, "enchanted with the power of nature."

"It has an aura," remarked Aubrey.

"What colour is it?" asked the Orc.

She examined it in more detail before answering, "It's a light brown colour."

"Appropriate for magic of the earth," said Kraloch.

Aubrey looked about the room. Revi's aura was multicoloured, much as she had seen it before, whereas the queen's aura was still a bright, white light.

"I don't see any sign of a bartok," she said.

"Nor do I," responded Kraloch. "What do you see, Dame Beverly?"

"No auras," said the knight, "and no sign of any of those creatures. Still, I wish Albreda were here."

"She's due back any day now," said Aubrey. "She's been taking some measurements at Bodden."

"Measurements?" asked Beverly.

"For the next magic circle," Aubrey explained, "or rather, a circle of stones."

"I thought the Whitewood was close by," offered Kraloch.

"It is," said Aubrey, "but that wouldn't help us if the Keep were under siege."

"No," said Beverly, "I don't suppose it would."

"Well," said Kraloch, "it appears we're safe from these creatures, at least for the present."

"Yes," agreed Aubrey, "though I'd like to repeat this spell to check over all our guards."

"A good idea," said Beverly, "but we'd best reassure the queen. She'll be worried about us taking so long."

Kraloch cast again, and the familiar tugging pulled at them. Moments later, they were back to lying on the floor.

It was Aubrey that raised her head first. "It's safe," she announced. "There's no sign of any bartoks in the room."

"Yes," agreed Beverly, "but we'll check the guards, just to be sure."

TWENTY-NINE

Members of the Court

SPRING 964 MC

Beverly bowed before the queen, while Tempus, lying nearby, merely raised his head in recognition.

"You sent for me, Majesty?"

"I did," Anna responded. "I am about to meet with Lord Walters about the trial. It appears he's concerned with the fairness of the proceedings. I'd like you here when he visits."

"Very well," Beverly replied. "Is there anything, in particular, you want me to do?"

"For now, I need you to bear witness, but feel free to ask questions if you have any, though let's try not to threaten him."

"Of course," the knight replied.

A knock at the door interrupted them.

"That's probably him," said Anna, turning her attention away from Beverly. "Come in!" she called out.

A Royal Guard opened the door to reveal Lord Montgomery Walters. He bowed deeply, then advanced to stand before the queen. Beverly stood to the side, watching intently, while Tempus, his interest piqued at the arrival of this newcomer, sat up.

"Your Majesty," he started, "I hope this day finds you in good health?"

"It does, Lord Walters. How kind of you to ask."

"I trust the kingdom is running smoothly?" he continued.

"Of course," she replied. "And why would it not? Are you in possession of information that would be of interest to the crown?"

"No, Majesty," the man blushed, "I merely wish to engage in friendly conversation before we get to the subject at hand."

"I see," said Anna, "so you expect to have a friendly chat while you drag my oldest friend before the courts?"

"I merely ask that a wrong be righted," defended Lord Walters. "My nephew's name was maligned, his family's honour impugned. Surely you would take action if the situation were reversed?"

"It appears your interpretation of your nephew's actions at Walpole Street differs from mine," said Anna.

"No doubt," he conceded, "but I seek only the truth of the matter. If the court finds that my nephew was to blame, then so be it, but my family has been subjected to rumour and innuendo for years."

"Something for which I am truly sorry," said Anna, "but at the time, people did what they thought necessary to keep the kingdom secure."

"And I can accept that," Lord Walters continued, "but you offer an enlightened rule, one that uses laws to govern men's actions. Surely it's time that the truth of the matter saw the light of day."

"Your words are wise, my lord," said Anna, "but it was you that came to see me. Tell me, pleasantries aside, what is the purpose of your visit today?"

Lord Walters fidgeted a little before continuing. "I would ask that you recuse Lord Arnim Caster from the trial," he said at last.

"He represents the crown in this," said Anna. "He is needed to carry out the prosecution."

"That is precisely the matter I'd like to address," Walters continued, "for it is my opinion that he cannot be objective."

"Explain yourself," demanded the queen.

"Lord Caster and Lord Matheson have known each other for some time," said Lord Walters. "One might even call them friends. I cannot, in good conscience, believe that such a man would carry out a just prosecution of his friend."

"Are you here, Lord Walters, just to criticize the crown, or are you offering an alternative?"

"I'm sorry if I've caused offence, Majesty, but I believe I have a solution that may serve both our purposes."

"Go on," urged the queen, "I'm listening."

"I would propose that you name another individual to the prosecution, one that won't be seen as favourable to your people."

"My people?" she asked.

"Everyone knows, Majesty, that you have surrounded yourself with trusted advisers. No one denies you that right, but when one of your own is on trial, you must be seen to remain objective. It was you, was it not, that promised the kingdom would have laws applicable to all?"

"It was," she replied. "So tell me, what name would you put forward to represent the crown in this?"

"It must be someone who is seen to have no affiliation to yourself," urged Lord Walters. "I would, therefore, suggest you use Lord Harwood."

"Lord Harwood?" burst out Beverly. "Surely, you jest? He represented Lord Montrose and may even have tried to help in his escape."

"Precisely why he would be ideal," said Walters. "What better way to show that you want the truth than selecting someone who has worked against you."

"An interesting choice," said Anna, "though I'm not fully convinced."

"Your Majesty," continued Walters, "Montrose is dead, and surely you cannot blame Harwood for the earl's attempted escape when it was so clearly an accident. Choosing him would show the people of the realm that you bear no grudge towards the man."

"You make a convincing argument," said Anna. "I shall give it some thought."

"That is all I ask, Majesty," the lord said, bowing deeply. He began backing up until he was in front of the door. A guard opened it, allowing him to exit after one more bow.

Anna waited until the door closed before speaking, "I must admit I wasn't expecting that."

"Quite the surprise," agreed Beverly.

"What do you make of his suggestion?" asked Anna.

"I can't say I relish the thought of Lord Harwood picking apart Gerald's life, yet the man has a point."

"I'd have to agree," said the queen, "but we have bigger problems. In order to prevent a stalemate, I have to appoint a new Earl of Shrewesdale, and that means his cousin, Lord Webster. I don't suppose we have to put much thought into how he'd vote."

"No," said Beverly, "I suppose not, but aren't we still investigating Olivia's death."

"Yes," said Anna, "although Lord Montrose was found guilty, he likely had accomplices. We have people digging into his family connections even as we speak."

"Then perhaps there's another option," suggested the knight.

"You have me intrigued," said Anna, "go on."

"We cannot appoint a successor to the earldom until the investigation into the rest of the family is complete, but at the same time, we need the earl's vacancy on the jury to be filled, correct?"

"Yes," said Anna, "you've summed it up nicely. What is it you were going to suggest?"

"I believe there's a precedent for appointing a temporary governor, isn't there?"

Anna smiled, "Yes, I suppose there is. In the early days of the kingdom, the cities were all ruled by governors. There's still a law that allows the temporary appointment of a military officer in times of emergency."

"I thought as much," said Beverly.

"I will announce an edict. Until such time as the investigation is complete, I shall appoint your father as temporary governor of Shrewesdale."

"That would also make him a member of the jury for Gerald's trial," added Beverly.

"So it would," said Anna, "and a welcome addition he would make, I should think."

"It still won't give us a majority," warned Beverly.

"Agreed," said the queen, "but it will be a closer vote, and with any luck, the evidence will convince at least one more person to change their mind."

"It's still a risk," said Beverly.

"Yes," said Anna, "but it's better than nothing. Have a scribe write up the edict, and I'll sign it as soon as it's ready."

"Yes, Your Majesty," said Beverly.

"And have someone send me Aubrey," said Anna, "there's a matter I'd like to discuss with her."

"Of course," said Beverly, bowing slightly. She strode from the room, leaving Queen Anna to her thoughts.

Aubrey arrived to find the room much as Beverly had left it. The only exception being the presence of Sophie, who was sitting on the floor, brushing Tempus. The great dog lay on his side, enjoying the attention, while the thick brush pulled away stray hairs.

"Aubrey," said Anna, "so glad you could make it."

"I'm always at your disposal, Majesty," said the mage. "How may I be of service?"

"I've been giving some thought to those creatures," said Anna.

"The bartoks?"

"Yes," said Anna, "I'd like to know more."

"I had thought them the stuff of legend," admitted Aubrey, "bedtime stories meant to scare children, but now that we've seen them in person, I realize they're much worse than expected."

"We need to know as much about them as possible," continued Anna, "if we are to defeat them in the future."

"You think there may be more?"

"Don't you?" asked the queen.

"I must admit I've given it some thought. From the little we know, it takes a Necromancer to create them."

"So we discussed earlier," said Anna, "but we need to know more. How difficult are they to create? Can Penelope call up more as she sees fit, or are there limitations?"

"I wish I knew," said Aubrey, "but I don't have that information available to me."

"I think you do," said the queen.

"I do?"

"Yes," Anna continued, "in Revi's house. I'm led to believe he has an extensive library on topics related to magic, much more so than the Palace is likely to contain."

"I would have to agree," said Aubrey, "but surely Revi is in a better position to investigate such things?"

"Revi has grown more erratic of late," replied Anna. "I want you to search out his library and see what you can find regarding these creatures."

"What type of information are we looking for?"

"Anything you think might be of use. I'm curious about the forms they take."

"Meaning?"

"Do they take the shape of existing people, or are they created in a certain image? We still don't know if the guardsman, Styles, was always one of these creatures, or if he was replaced somehow."

Aubrey thought it over a moment, before continuing, "I can look into it, but I can't guarantee an answer. My understanding is that the real library lies in the Tower of Andronicus."

"Yes," said Anna, "but we don't know where that is. Revi's been searching for it and still has no clues as to its whereabouts. You shall have to make do with what books are available."

"I suppose," mused Aubrey, "I could look into the old stories, that would give me a place to start."

"Use whatever resources you must," said Anna. "Go to Shrewesdale if it is needed. I understand the Library of Kendros holds much knowledge."

"Kendros will have to wait for now," said Aubrey. "I'm needed here to search the spirit realm."

"A valid point," agreed the queen. "Is there anything I can do to help?"

"Not that I can think of," said Aubrey. "I'll visit Revi's house this very afternoon, but it will likely be several days before I can find any answers.

His books are scattered throughout the house, with no thought given to their organization."

"Do your best, Aubrey," said Anna, "that's all I can ask."

"Might I enquire what's happening with Gerald's trial?"

"I'm afraid it will be starting soon," said Anna. "I can't put it off any longer."

"You're the queen," said Aubrey, "surely you have the choice as to when it will begin?"

"Up to a point," confessed Anna, "but the longer I put it off, the more it looks like I'm trying to protect Gerald. At some point, it will have to begin, or I risk losing control of the Nobles Council."

"The perils of decentralizing control," said Aubrey. "Perhaps your father had the right of it, pulling all the power back to the crown."

"King Andred wasn't my father," reminded Anna calmly, "and it's taken a lot of work to give some of the power back to the people."

"You mean the nobles," suggested Aubrey.

"Yes," the queen agreed, "at least to a certain extent. I want the Nobles Council to take on more responsibility in the future, freeing me up for the more important tasks."

"They'll like that," observed Aubrey, "most of them are hungry for power."

"I might remind you that you're a noble too," said Anna.

"Yes," the mage agreed, "but the only power I'm interested in is the magical variety."

"You've been to Weldwyn," said Anna. "Tell me, what do you think of the way they run their kingdom?"

"They appear to have a firm grip on things. Why? Is that what we're moving towards?"

"Not precisely, but something along similar lines. You know the mages there can't rule."

"I was aware of that," said Aubrey, "and given a choice between being baroness and being a mage, I'd take magic, every time."

"I'm not suggesting you have to give up your position," mused Anna, "but I was thinking of making it impossible for a king or queen to be a mage."

"To what end?" Aubrey asked.

"Mages are far removed from the common people," explained Anna. "Perhaps a little too removed, though I suppose you could say the same thing of the nobility. The difference, I suppose, is that nobles are bred to rule, whereas mages are bred to, well, do magic."

"I can't argue with that," said Aubrey, "even running Hawksburg is proving to be a drain on my time. If it weren't for Kraloch, I'd be too busy to do anything else."

"That's another promise I haven't kept," lamented Anna. "I promised the other races that I'd give them representation on the Nobles Council."

"You will," said Aubrey, "but you must give it some time. You've only been in power for a short period, and already you've made sweeping changes. You'll get to where you want to be eventually."

"But we could lose their support," said Anna, "and now is such a crucial time."

"They trust you," soothed Aubrey, "and they know you have their best interests at heart. They were here long before Humans came along. I would think they're willing to wait a little longer."

"I suppose you're right," said Anna. "It just feels like the war never ended. I thought once we defeated Henry's forces that things would get better. Instead, they just keep getting worse."

"Change is difficult," said Aubrey, "and great change never came without some form of opposition."

"Do you think I've tried to do too much?" asked Anna.

Aubrey thought it over carefully. The young queen had already enacted some significant changes to the kingdom, chief amongst them the laws of succession and inheritance, but was it too much? She didn't think it was, and yet who was she to judge?

"I think," she finally responded, "that some people will always object to change, but without it, we wouldn't have a kingdom to call home. After all, if the Mercenaries that originally came here didn't favour change, we would still be meandering about in small warbands, fighting each other."

"Well spoken, Aubrey, you're becoming quite the philosopher."

"I do my best," the mage replied.

"As will I," the queen promised, "though I will try to slow things down a little. I don't want to push everyone away."

The queen fell into silence, her knitted brow indicating she was deep in thought.

"I'd best be going if I'm to dig up information on those creatures," said Aubrey.

"Very well," said Anna, "let me know when you find anything."

"You mean IF I find anything," Aubrey corrected.

"No, I mean WHEN," said Anna, "I have faith in you, Aubrey."

Aubrey bowed. "Then I shall do my best to reward that faith," she said.

"As I knew you would," said Anna.

THIRTY

Lost

SPRING 964 MC

"This place never changes," observed Nikki as she nursed a cider, "and to think I used to frequent it."

They were sitting in the Three Rings, a tavern that was showing its age. The floors were well worn, the tables scratched and cut, and the patrons that frequented it, equally as haggard.

"Things are always nicer in our memories," observed Arnim. "It's like when you're a child, and you love visiting some place. You go back as an adult and discover how terribly wrong you were about it."

"Thinking of your own childhood," she asked, "or our child's future?"

"Perhaps a little of both," he revealed.

"I do believe you're getting sentimental on me," she said.

"Nonsense," said Arnim, "I'm just looking to the future."

"Now there's the gruff Arnim I'm used to," said Nikki. "You've let him loose again."

"I suppose," he mused. "Now tell me, this fellow we're looking for, Madson, you say he was killed here?"

"According to the town watch, he was," said Nikki, "but there's something a little fishy going on. They said he died in a fight."

"I was in the watch for years," said Arnim, "and lots of people die in tavern brawls."

"Yes," Nikki agreed, "but from what I've learned, Madson wasn't the type to get into fights."

"So the fight came looking for him?" he asked.

"I think so," she confirmed. "Unfortunately, the body's already been disposed of."

"That's convenient," said Arnim, "but maybe someone here can fill in some details."

"The barkeep would be a good place to start," suggested Nikki.

Arnim was looking over the patrons. "I have a better idea," he said, rising from his chair.

He made his way over to three men that sat in the corner, nursing their ales. They looked up at him in surprise as he called out, "Barkeep, another round of whatever these men are having."

He turned his attention to the table, "May I join you gentlemen?"

"Suit yourself," replied the oldest member of the trio. He had long grey hair and a wispy beard, and appeared to be the spokesman of the group.

"Do you come here often?" asked Arnim.

"As often as we can," chimed in a red-headed man.

"Then you must have heard about the death last week," Arnim prompted.

"We sure did," said the oldest. "In fact, we saw the whole thing."

"Can you tell me what happened?" Arnim asked.

"He were murdered," chimed in his dark-haired companion, "murdered, I say."

"Why would you say that?" asked Arnim. "I heard it was a brawl, and someone drew a knife."

"It weren't no reg'lar brawl," the dark-haired man persisted, "on account of the fact that the man that stabbed 'im 'as done it before."

"I'm not sure I understand," said Arnim. "Are you saying the man responsible for the stabbing has killed people before?"

"'Ats exactly what I'm saying."

"Was any of this reported to the watch?" asked Arnim.

He noticed the look of utter contempt on the face of the redhead. "Ain't no way the watch cares," he said, "all they want to do is keep things quiet."

"How did all this start?"

"The bastard baited him," the dark-haired man revealed. "The poor sod tried to resist, but he kept up at him until he couldn't take it no more. Soon as he took a swing, 'e were a dead man."

"This fellow that stabbed him," asked Arnim, "can you describe him?"

"Tall fellow 'e was, with light brown 'air," the man offered.

"I know him," said the white-haired man. "He stabbed another one down at the Stag just last night."

"Last night?" asked Arnim. "Are you sure?"

"As sure as I'm staring at you," the man replied.

"You don't recall the victim's name, do you?"

"That's easy," the grey-haired man recalled, "Delmar Franklin. I served with him years ago."

"In the Wincaster Foot?" asked Arnim.

"Yes," the old man replied, "how did you know?"

"Were you on duty the night the riots broke out in '53?"

"No," he replied, "I'd fallen sick with a bit of a fever and was confined to barracks."

"So you heard all about Walpole Street?" asked Arnim.

"Aye, I did. I didn't see it with my own eyes, mind you, but I heard all about it."

"And your friends in the company, do you still keep in touch with them?"

"Not really. I hadn't seen Delmar in years, but he told me about the curse, last time I saw him."

"What curse?" asked Arnim, intrigued.

"He said everyone that was there was doomed to die. Said four of them were dead already and it was only a matter of time before the rest were killed."

"Killed? Were those his exact words?" asked Arnim.

"They were," the man confirmed.

Several days later found Arnim standing before the queen.

"Your report?" she snapped at him.

"We have completed our investigation into the men of the fifth company, Your Majesty."

"And?" she prompted, eyeing him with a steely glare.

"There are two survivors that we know of, but they are witnesses for the prosecution, we can find no other living members of that company that were at the Walpole Street riot."

"How can that be?" she demanded. "There were twenty men present. Are you trying to tell me they're all dead?"

"As far as we can tell," explained Arnim, "they either died during the war or were killed in the last nine months."

"Killed?" she asked. "Are you suggesting foul play?"

"Almost certainly," said Arnim. "To expect a death or two in that time would be reasonable, but to discover that almost all of them are dead is far too much of a coincidence."

"Do we know who is responsible for these deaths?" she asked.

"No," said Arnim, "though I've managed to link at least two of them to one individual. The others appear to have been killed by someone else, likely hired for the job."

"That's a mite too coincidental for my taste," said Anna. "Where does that leave us?"

"We have no credible witnesses that can exonerate Gerald, Your Majesty, but we know the accusers have two. As far as we can ascertain, there are no other living witnesses."

"I'm very concerned," said Anna. "Our enemies wouldn't press for a trial if they didn't have some kind of damning evidence."

"Perhaps they coerced statements from the other witnesses before they died?" suggested Arnim.

"Or," said Anna, "they just made up false witness reports."

"Either way," said Arnim, "we'll have no idea until the trial begins. If they do present false testimony, it'll be my job to tear it apart."

"Has Gerald been of any help?" she asked.

"I'm afraid not," Arnim responded. "He told me what he could recall, but there are gaps in his memory. Then again, he was in significant pain and under the effects of numbleaf. I'm surprised he could remember anything."

"You must win this case!" admonished Anna. "Gerald's future depends on it."

"On that, we couldn't be more in agreement," said Arnim. "I give you my word that I will do all I can in his defence."

"Let's hope that's enough," said Anna. "Now, you'd best be on your way, you've a defence to plan."

"Yes, Majesty," said Arnim, bowing. He turned to leave, ushered out the door by Beverly, who stood guard.

The knight returned a moment later, to resume her position by the door.

"Beverly," called out Anna, "come here a moment."

The redhead did as she was bid, then stood, waiting.

"Yes, Majesty?"

"Have you gathered men you trust?" she asked.

"Some," confirmed Beverly, "and I have faith they'll all follow orders without question."

"Good," said Anna. "When the trial nears completion, they are to take up strategic points in the cathedral. If it goes against Gerald, I will seize power, dissolving the court and the Nobles Council."

"You'd be throwing away everything you've worked for," warned Beverly.

"I'm willing to do that if it means I can save Gerald. Are you with me, or not?"

In answer, Beverly took Nature's Fury from her belt, planting it, head down, on the floor and knelt before it. "You are my queen," she solemnly swore, "and I pledged my life and my sword to your service. I shall not abandon you now, even at peril to my own life."

"Thank you," said Anna, "that means a lot to me. I know I have many friends, but few that are as loyal as you."

"If we are to seize the cathedral, I shall need others," said Beverly. "I would like permission to seek them out."

"Of course," said the queen, "but who would you recruit? Your cousin, perhaps, or Aldwin?"

"No, Majesty, for though I love them both, I would not have them involved in this. I mean to recruit other knights, trustworthy men that can take command of soldiers."

"Then do whatever you need to carry out our plan," said Anna, "and may Saxnor have mercy on us all."

Sir Preston waited in the hallway, shifting nervously in place, his armour suddenly feeling constricting and tight. The door opened to reveal a cavalryman.

"The commander will see you now," he said.

The Knight of the Sword rose, making his way forward, hitting the edge of the door frame as he entered and silently cursing himself.

Inside, sat Dame Beverly Fitzwilliam, Commander of Horse.

"Come in, Sir Preston," she beckoned, "and have a seat."

Sir Preston sat awkwardly, his poorly fitted armour pinching the back of his calves.

"You wanted to see me, Commander?" he asked.

"Yes," she replied, "I remember you helping us when we escaped the dungeons of Wincaster."

"I live to serve," the knight responded, then frowned at his own words. He felt so intimidated. The Knights of the Sword had been the epitome of knighthood, but now, after the recent war, they were relegated to little more than guard duty.

"I've come to offer you a chance to distinguish yourself," said Beverly.

This was new, he thought, and completely unexpected. "In what way?" he asked.

"I'm looking for loyal men," she said, "men willing to fight and die for the queen, if needed."

"Then I'm your man," he said, wishing he sounded more confident. "What is it I'm to do?"

"I shall be giving you a special duty," Beverly said, "and you are to speak to no one of it, save for me. Do you understand?"

"I do," he vowed, feeling a kind of elation. For years, he had been the laughing stock of the order. He had fallen from his horse during his investiture, and the other knights had never let him forget the shame he brought to their order. Now, years later, with the entire order in disgrace, he knew it didn't matter anymore, but this was a chance for a fresh start, and he wasn't about to throw it away.

"Good," said Beverly, "here's what I'll need you to do..."

Sometime later, Sir Preston left the commander's office, a new spring in his step. This would, no doubt, be difficult, but he had secured the patronage of the queen, and for that, he would be eternally grateful.

Aubrey knocked on the door of the old, dilapidated house. It was an eyesore, this two-storey building with a single tower built onto the front corner, looking as if it would collapse at any time, and yet somehow, it still looked charming.

There was no answer, and so Aubrey turned the handle. She half expected Revi to be waiting on the other side, but instead, all she saw was a brief entryway, with stairs to the right leading up to the tower, and a doorway opposite which, she knew, led to his library.

"Revi?" Aubrey called out. "Are you home?"

Her voice echoed throughout the house, and then she detected a distant sound, maybe shuffling feet? Perhaps, she thought, he was deeply engrossed in research? She entered the house, treading softly lest she disturb Revi's studies.

She headed for the library then heard the sound again, this time upstairs. Backtracking to the steps, she began her ascent, walking as quietly as she could. The floor above contained several rooms, but she kept moving to the top level, where she knew his casting room lay. Though it didn't hold a magic circle, it did have a large, cleared area, the better for one to practice their skills in the arcane arts.

Aubrey paused at the top step, the sound she heard before now clearly audible behind the door. She put her ear to it, listening carefully. Beyond, she heard a voice muttering and instantly recognized it as that of Revi Bloom. Opening the door quietly, she peered inside to see the Royal Life Mage standing in the middle of the room, examining a full-length mirror. It had a wooden border that was attached to a frame, allowing it to flip on its centre axis. He was staring at his reflection, speaking out loud, not a spell, but in conversation with himself.

Satisfied that no intruder lurked here, Aubrey quietly closed the door, making her way downstairs to return to the library.

In actual fact, the library was simply a room, like any other. It lacked bookshelves, yet books were piled high on the floor, in a haphazard manner. Aubrey looked around in dismay; it would likely take ages to find the book she was looking for. She had once recommended that Revi get some more shelves and organize his books, but the stubborn man had simply stated that he had more important things to do. Now, his obstinacy might prove their undoing, for if she couldn't find the information she sought in a timely manner, another bartok might strike.

Her eyes scanned the room, and then she moved into the next, finding shelves stacked high with yet more books. She was near the back of the house now, with a kitchen off to one side. Doing a quick calculation, she estimated the number of books she could see to be in the hundreds, and not one of them was placed with any rhyme or reason.

She knew of Revi's fascination with the Saurian Temples. It was more than likely that the books lining the floor were ones which he, himself, had been reading, and thus less apt to contain the information she was seeking. Resolving to begin her search in the back room, she reached for the top shelf, picking the book closest to the back door. The best strategy, in her mind, was to skim over each book, one shelf at a time.

Pulling forth the first tome, she opened it, perusing its contents. It was a study of runes, a fundamental text on the magical alphabet, and she quickly put it aside. The next book proved slightly more interesting, a study of the anatomy of the various races. A fascinating book, but likely of no use to her current needs. She continued her search until the light from the windows began to wane.

She cast a globe of light to illuminate the room and continued looking. Finishing one entire shelf, she moved to the next, pulling forth an illustrated volume about animals. She scanned over it, looking for any sign of the bartoks, but still no success.

It was getting quite dark outside, but she kept working, recasting her orb of light several times. Briefly, she considered why Revi hadn't appeared and wondered if she should check on him, but soon thought better of it. The man had likely left already, too engrossed in his own studies to notice her.

Placing a book back on the shelf, she rotated her shoulders to ease the tension in them. For most of the day, she had remained standing, and now her back was sore along with her feet. She grabbed the next three books, carrying them, one atop the other, into the library and took a seat.

Opening the first, she saw handwriting that she recognized as Revi's. The book was full of his scratchy words, written in some haste, by the look of it. Aubrey was tempted to read more but knew her main objective was the bartoks.

She closed the tome, placing it to the side and looked down at the next.

It had a plain cover, a not unexpected thing in itself, but the material that bound this book looked strange, feeling a little like leather. Flipping open the book, she saw a pentagram staring back at her; this was a book of Necromancy! Finally, she thought, something that might prove useful. She began reading.

THIRTY-ONE

Gerald

SPRING 964 MC

Gerald stood in silence as the charge against him was read. Murder, the prosecution said, a word that rang in his head. He felt a tug on his arm and looked down at Arnim who indicated he should take his seat.

Once again, the cathedral was packed, the observers sitting enraptured as the trial began. This was the airing of dirty laundry, and the commoners loved hearing all the sordid details.

The crown's first witness, Henderson, took the stand late in the afternoon to tell his story. Poor Henderson recounted how he had sold his helmet to buy ale, then had taken a bottle to the head early in the battle, knocking him senseless. It was this action that necessitated Gerald taking up a position in the line, an act that led to the series of events that would have a profound impact on them all.

There was little to fault in the man's testimony, and Gerald wondered why he was even up on the stand. All he did was confirm the events leading up to the engagement with the mob. There was no accusation of bad behaviour on the part of Gerald, nor any other word of him trying to kill the captain. It was when the subject turned to the captain himself, that Gerald began to see why Henderson had been chosen to testify.

Lord Harwood paced back and forth, forming his questions carefully. "What can you tell us about Captain Walters?" he asked.

"I'm not sure what you mean?" the soldier replied.

"What was he like? Was he a fair man?"

"He insisted on maintaining discipline," said Henderson.

Arnim rose, "I must object. The witness wasn't conscious during the resulting riot. I fail to see the relevance of this testimony."

"I mean to establish the competency of the captain," said Lord Harwood. "Particularly important, considering that he's not here to defend himself."

"Very well," called out Lord Somerset, "we'll allow it, but get a move on man, we haven't got all day."

"Thank you, my lord," said Harwood. He turned his attention back to Henderson. "On the day in question," he continued, "did Lord Walters give the command to form the line across the road?"

"He did," confirmed Henderson, "then he adjusted it later."

"What do you mean, 'he adjusted it'?" asked Harwood.

Henderson appeared to take a deep breath before continuing, "He told us to move closer together."

"And what happened then?" the lord pressed.

"That's when the sergeant told us to widen out the line."

"So he countermanded the order?" clarified Harwood, the sound of shock evident in his voice.

"He did," said Henderson.

"Is this normal behaviour? For a sergeant to countermand the orders of a superior?"

"No," said Henderson, "but-"

"But nothing," interrupted Harwood. "Just answer the questions, nothing more."

"Yes, my lord."

"What did you do when Sergeant Matheson here," he pointed to Gerald, "made this illegal order?"

"The men did as they were told," said Henderson.

"And when you say that, do you mean they followed the lawful orders of their captain or the illegal orders of the sergeant?"

"We did as the sergeant told us," said Henderson in a low voice.

"And this action led to the massacre," said Harwood. Arnim was about to object, but Harwood kept talking, "Or rather, it led to a sequence of events that resulted in the massacre. Tell me, Henderson, was Captain Walters very strict?"

"No more so than any other," the soldier replied.

"Were you happy serving in the fifth company?"

"Happy?" asked Henderson. "I never thought about it much, at the time, but I suppose I was."

"And what is there to not like?" offered Harwood. "After all, you got paid and were provided with free meals at the king's expense, what's not to love about that?"

"You make it sound like we did nothing," complained Henderson.

"Oh, I'm sorry," said Lord Harwood, "tell the court what you did on a regular day."

"We trained," Henderson said, proudly.

"I see," Harwood continued, "and this training you did, who conducted it?"

"Sergeant Matheson," said Henderson.

"And was the captain ever present at these training sessions?"

"Not that I can recall."

"Get to the point!" called out Fitz from the jury.

Harwood bowed to the nobles. "I am endeavouring to show the level of control that the sergeant held over the men," he said.

"That's a sergeant's job," added Fitz.

"Precisely," said Harwood, "and a fact that allowed the accused to order the men forward to attack the commoners."

"That's a lie," yelled Gerald, rising to his feet. "It was the captain that gave that order."

"Was it?" asked Harwood. "I think you'll find the evidence indicates otherwise."

"So you're saying," asked Fitz, "that the accused ordered the soldiers to slaughter innocents?"

"Yes," said Harwood, "and, if the court allows, I will present evidence to support such claims."

Fitz was about to argue again, but Lord Somerset placed his arm on the baron, forestalling him.

"You may continue," Lord Somerset said.

"Thank you, Your Grace," said Harwood. "I have here two more written statements from soldiers of the fifth company attesting to the sergeant's total, and some might say brutal, control over the men."

He walked across to the jurors, dropping the papers on the desk. Baron Fitzwilliam picked one up. "Utter nonsense if you ask me," he said. "And nothing that would indicate he was trying to take over."

"If I may," said Harwood, "I have a few questions for Baron Fitzwilliam."

"You can't ask questions of a juror," said Fitz.

"I'll allow it," said Somerset. "We need to get to the bottom of this."

Harwood smiled, then looked to Fitz. "Baron Fitzwilliam, can you tell us what position was held by Marshal Matheson during his time with your forces?"

"He was my Sergeant-At-Arms," replied Fitz.

"I see," said Harwood, "and what were his responsibilities in that position?"

"He oversaw the disposition of troops and planned patrols."

"So, in essence," said Harwood, "he was the most senior military official at Bodden?"

"Other than myself," said Fitz, "yes, he was."

"And so he was used to giving orders?"

"He was," said Fitz, "and did a good job of it."

"Indeed?" said Harwood. "Tell me, Baron, how many people have held that position in Bodden?"

"Only one," said Fitz.

"I fail to see the point of all this," said Lord Somerset. "The jury recognizes the fine career of Lord Matheson. Now, move on!"

"Sorry, Your Grace," soothed Harwood. He turned to face the observers, who filled the cathedral to capacity. "So we have an old soldier who is, perhaps, past his prime. He is used to giving orders, so much so that he gave orders to knights, did he not?" He turned again to face Fitz.

"He did, what of it?" the baron replied.

"And I assume the knights followed those commands?"

"Yes, of course," said Fitz.

"So here's a man that's used to getting his way, placed under the command of an inexperienced captain. A man who, by the way, would rank under a knight in terms of his position. I find it hard to believe that this seasoned veteran would defer to such a man, don't you?"

He left the question unanswered, moving instead back to Henderson. "That's all, for now, Henderson," he said.

"One moment," called out Arnim, "I'd like to ask the witness some questions."

"Very well," said Lord Somerset, "I'll allow it."

Arnim rose, making his way to where Henderson sat, his face a mask of calm.

"How long were you under Sergeant Matheson's command?"

"A few months," said Henderson.

"And how long had you been a soldier? Up until the events at Walpole Street, I mean."

"Two years," the man responded.

"And did you respect Sergeant Matheson?"

"Yes," Henderson replied.

"Why?" asked Arnim.

"He was firm, but he treated us fairly. He also had experience."

"So you followed him due to his experience?"

"Yes," confirmed Henderson.

"My lords," Arnim said, turning to the jury, "it is clear from this man's testimony that Sergeant Matheson was doing his duty. I submit to you that when he extended the line, it was not out of a desire to take command, but rather a desire to avoid bloodshed and form a proper defence."

Content with his statement, Arnim took his seat.

Gerald looked at him. "What happens now?" he asked.

"We wait for them to bring the next witness," said Arnim.

"And who will that be?"

"I'm told they only have one more," confessed Arnim, "but under Mercerian law, they're not required to tell us who it is."

Lord Harwood soon introduced the next witness, a soldier by the name of Howard Smith. Gerald immediately recognized him, for he had always been a bit of a troublemaker. Memories started flooding back, and then he remembered seeing Smith in an alley, bending over a woman, fumbling with his belt.

"Do you know him?" asked Arnim.

"Yes," said Gerald, "though I must admit the details are a little hazy."

Smith sat, while Lord Harwood paced yet again. He paused close to the observers, staring out over their heads, perhaps trying to gauge their interest before continuing.

"You were assigned to the fifth company of the Wincaster Foot, is that correct?"

"Yes," Smith replied.

"Can you relate the events that took place on and around Walpole street all those years ago?"

"I can," said Smith. "We were marched into position and then deployed in a two-man deep line. That's where the mob found us."

"And what happened then?" asked Harwood.

"The crowd surged forward, throwing bottles and rocks at us, but we kept our formation."

"And then?"

"We were ordered to attack," said Smith.

"And who gave that order?" asked Harwood.

"I can't be certain," said Smith, looking around nervously, "but I believe it was the sergeant."

"He's lying," Gerald said to Arnim.

"I know," Arnim replied, "let him finish, then we'll take him to task."

Harwood, disturbed by the interruption, waited for silence, then continued, "What happened next?"

"We ran forward," related Smith, "hunting from building to building, killing the rioters, as ordered."

"Did you feel any guilt, killing innocent commoners?"

"No," said Smith, "we were following orders, and the rioters weren't innocent. Are we supposed to just stand by and let them get away with attacking us?"

"Did you witness the attack on Captain Walters?" asked Harwood.

"I did," said Smith, "as plain as day, I did."

"Can you describe what happened?"

"Of course," Smith said. "I saw the sergeant stagger out the alleyway, sword in hand, along with a broom that he was using to steady himself. He'd taken a wound to the leg. Anyways, I saw him standing over the captain. He was yelling at everyone to kill the stinking peasants. His words, not mine."

"And what was the captain doing at this time?" asked Harwood.

"He was begging the sergeant to stop and end the madness. That's when the sergeant stepped forward and killed him."

A collective gasp emanated from the crowd and then silence.

Lord Harwood turned towards Arnim, "I'd be happy to allow you to ask questions, my lord."

Arnim rose, but Gerald caught his arm, "Ask about the girl," he whispered.

"What girl?" asked Arnim.

"The one he was trying to rape in the alleyway."

"You saw this?"

"It's all coming back to me now," confessed Gerald. "I was in a lot of pain, and the numbleaf was still in me, but yes, I remember. I think her name was Marcy."

Arnim turned to look at the first row of observers. Nikki was there, watching intently, and he waved her over.

"What is it?" she asked.

"You need to find a woman near Walpole Street. She goes by the name Marcy."

"Any last name?" she asked.

In answer, Arnim looked to Gerald, who shrugged his shoulders.

"How am I supposed to do that?" she asked. "I don't even have a description."

"I'll see if I can pry one out of him," said Arnim. "Don't go just yet."

Nikki nodded her head and returned to her seat.

Now it was Arnim's turn to question the witness. He moved closer to Smith, staring at the man as he collected his thoughts.

"When you formed up," Arnim began, "you were on Walpole Street, is that correct?"

"Yes, that's right."

"And yet the captain's body was found on Tolpuddle Lane, wasn't it?"

"I believe so," offered Smith.

"Then how do you account for your whereabouts there?"

"I moved there after searching some buildings, of course," Smith said smugly.

"I see," said Arnim. "Now, just for the record, can you tell us how you got from Walpole Street to Tolpuddle Lane?"

"There's an alleyway that leads between the two," offered Smith, "down by the bakery."

"So you moved down the alley beside the bakery that led to Tolpuddle Lane?"

"That's what I just said, wasn't it?"

"It was," said Arnim, "but I wanted to make sure there was no mistake."

Smith sat back, looking relaxed and comfortable.

"Tell us about the girl," Arnim prompted.

Smith's eyes darted about nervously, and he wore a look that said he wanted to run. "I don't know what you're talking about," he said.

"I think you do," said Arnim. "There was a girl in the alley."

"What girl?" the man said, his voice growing more desperate.

"The one you tried to rape," proclaimed Arnim, an edge to his voice.

"It wasn't rape," the man blustered.

"Oh?" said Arnim. "What else can you call it when you try to force your-self on a woman?"

Lord Hardwood stood, "My lords, is this really relevant? What does it matter if there was a woman there or not?"

"It matters," replied Lord Somerset. "If he can't be trusted to leave women alone, his whole testimony is questionable."

"Ridiculous!" shouted Lord Stanton.

Moments later, the entire cathedral erupted into shouts and accusations. The Master of Heralds had to bang his staff on the ground to get everyone's attention.

Arnim waited for silence, then pressed Smith further, "So was a woman in the alley, yes or no?"

"Yes," Smith finally admitted.

"And when you saw the sergeant kill the officer, where were you standing?"

"In the alleyway, my lord."

Arnim nodded his head, "Are you sure?"

"Yes," Smith replied, "as Saxnor looks over me."

"A pretty solid affirmation," said Arnim, "if only it were true."

"Are you calling me a liar?" demanded Smith.

"My lords," said Arnim, "as part of my investigation into this matter, I visited the scene of the massacre. I can tell you, without any doubt, that there was no way for Smith to see the captain's body from the alley. His view would have been blocked."

"Are you sure?" asked Lord Anglesley.

"Positive," said Arnim, "though your lordships are welcome to go and see for yourselves."

After a moment of discussion between the lords that formed the jury, Lord Somerset spoke, "It is the consensus of this body that we shall take Captain Caster's word for it."

"Lord Caster," corrected Arnim, "I'm Viscount Haverston."

"I stand corrected," said Somerset. "You may proceed with your line of enquiry."

"Just one more thing," said Arnim, turning to face the witness again. "Did anything else of consequence take place in the alleyway?"

Smith's eyes shifted to Lord Harwood, who watched impassively from his table. Gerald looked to the lord, seeing only the briefest of head shakes.

"No," said Smith.

"And you're absolutely sure of that?"

"Positive," said Smith.

"Can you describe this woman?" asked Arnim.

"What woman?"

"The one you say you didn't rape," said Arnim in disgust.

"She was of average height, with brown hair, cut short, shoulder-length if I recall. She had an ample bosom and was nice and curvy." Smith's face betrayed his emotions as he thought of her.

"That's quite a description for someone you couldn't remember a few moments ago," said Arnim.

"My lords," called a voice from the jury. Everyone turned to see Lord Spencer, the new Earl of Eastwood. "Perhaps it serves our best interest if this woman were to be located."

"A good idea," said Anglesley. "Maybe she can shed some light on what really happened."

"Very well," added Lord Somerset, standing. "We call on the court to produce this woman. We shall reconvene as soon as she can be found, or at the expiration of sufficient time if she should prove impossible to locate."

The Master of Heralds banged his staff, calling on all to rise while the jury left the room. As soon as that was complete, Arnim turned to Nikki. "Go," he said, "and be careful, you've got our child to look after."

"I will," she promised.

THIRTY-TWO

Searching

SPRING 964 MC

Daylight was once more streaming through the window when Aubrey found what she was looking for, a tome written more than five hundred years ago by the then Witch Hunter General. Witches, or more accurately, Necromancers, were far more common in those days, leading to a concerted effort by the crown to eradicate them. She wondered how many innocent lives had been destroyed by the purge, and whether or not it was worth it.

The history of Merceria was a bloody affair, not only in its military conquests but also in its history of oppression. First, it had been the native Humans, subjugated by the conquerors, then the bloody wars with Weldwyn. It seemed war was the natural order of things, and when times became peaceful, the monarchy turned on their people, purging witches and undesirables. Even without Necromancers, they found enemies within, including rebellions and uprisings.

Aubrey chided herself for letting her mind wander. It had been a long night, but that was no excuse. With her attention now refocused, she kept reading. At the height of the purge, they had broken the will of a Necromancer named Purvis. It was mostly his confession that had led to the knowledge in this book. He spoke of vile deeds and terrifying spells of retribution, but these Aubrey skimmed over until finally, before her very eyes, was the information she sought.

Purvis was believed to have been a powerful Death Mage, and yet even he was loath to use the spell of creation. This spell must be cast on two bodies simultaneously, one male and one female. Aubrey stopped, in shock. If this were true, there was another such creature on the loose somewhere in Wincaster, possibly in the Palace itself! She was torn between her desire to warn the others and her quest for knowledge. It was better to read on, she thought, for there might be more information that would be of use.

What she'd just read terrified her, for the ritual described within would bind the spirits of the deceased into a construct built by the Necromancer, who would then act as a power source of sorts; these bound spirits would be controlled by a portion of the mage's own life force.

Aubrey gazed around the room as she tried to absorb the words before her. Did this mean the Necromancer must give up a portion of his own self? She supposed it was much like creating a magic weapon or circle, placing a part of oneself within the construction, but whereas the circle or weapon was inanimate, the Necromancer gave the creatures intelligence and life.

She read on, and, sure enough, the book referred to the mage becoming diminished with each casting. If this were true, then Penelope, or whoever was responsible, would now be weaker, surely a good thing. As to the creatures themselves, their construction was not detailed, but it was clear that they were somehow built by the Death Mage that cast the spell. It was a lengthy ritual, the book explained, requiring the utmost concentration to give the creatures their final appearance. Upon death, it noted, the bartoks would resort to their original image, that which their creator gave them when initially formed.

Aubrey closed the book, looking up through sleepy eyes to see the noonday sun reflecting in the windows. She rose, placing the text on the floor, absently noting how it joined its brethren in the random piles, and then she rushed for the door, intent on reaching the cathedral as fast as possible.

Nikki felt the kick and instinctively placed her hand on her swollen belly.

"There, there, now," she soothed, "this is not the time to start that!"

She paused a moment before entering the shop, the smell of fresh-baked bread wafting towards her as she opened the door. Inside, it was tiny, little more than a counter with a bit of room to stand behind. The ovens were obviously elsewhere, but loaves were lined up in neat rows on display.

"Can I help you?" asked the baker, an elderly, clean-shaven man with thinning black hair draped over his mostly bald head.

"It smells so delicious in here," said Nikki, "you must do a good trade."

"Not as well as you might think," replied the proprietor. "It's not the best location, we're too close to the slums. People there can afford little."

"I'll take a loaf," she said, pointing to one. She dipped into her purse, extracting a few coins.

The baker handed her the loaf as she dropped the coins on the table.

"Tell me," she said, "do you know Marcy?"

"Yes," he replied. "Funny, you should ask that."

"What's so funny about it?"

"It's been years since she worked for me. Keeps to herself mostly, and yet today you're the second person to ask about her."

"Someone else was here?" asked Nikki.

"They were," the baker replied. "A tall man, with a rough-looking beard and blue eyes."

"How long ago was this?" she asked.

"Not long," he responded. "I was just putting these loaves on the table, and see, they're still slightly warm. You likely passed him on the street on your way in here."

"Did you tell him where Marcy lived?" she asked.

"I did," the baker replied. "What's this all about? Is she in trouble or something?"

"She could be," said Nikki. "There are men who are after her, and I fear your visitor was one of them. Where does she live?"

"On Culver street. Do you know where that is?"

"I do," she affirmed. "Which house?"

"It's a rooming house with a green door. She's on the first floor, on the left as you go in."

"Thank you," said Nikki as she ran from the bakery, leaving the loaf behind. The baker shrugged his shoulders then placed it back with the others, content on making a profit with no goods sold.

Nikki exited the shop, turning right and moving down the alley to Tolpuddle Lane. She had spent years in the slums, knew every street and back alley intimately. She thought things through in her mind, finally settling on the best route.

As she entered Tolpuddle, she turned right, jogging south. She watched the left side of the street carefully, and when the carpenter's shop came into view, she turned left, cutting down another alleyway. Weaving her way through back alleys, she finally emerged onto Culver Street.

It was almost noon, the sun directly overhead casting little in the way of shadows. This worked to her advantage, for as she approached the boarding house, she spied a man standing across the street, his eyes glued to the front entrance.

Slowing her pace, Nikki stopped to look in a shop window. The shutters were wide open, revealing a series of boots arranged within. She had spent years in a boarding house and knew they were rarely more than two floors, with each room a separate dwelling. Aside from the front door, there was often one at the rear, so she decided that was her best method of entry.

Sure of her plan, she made her way down the street, pausing as the baby kicked once again. She cursed her luck, swearing at her husband. Now was not the time to be pregnant!

Nikki slipped down another alley, intending to make her way to the back of the boarding house. She moved slowly, trying to avoid making any noise. If someone was watching the front, likely the same could be said of the back. As soon as the rear entrance came into view, she spotted the other observer, leaning against a wall, using a knife to clean under his fingernails. She cursed her luck and backed up. How would she gain entrance without being spotted?

Looking skyward, she noticed the building next door, its roof hanging over the alleyway, providing shade, and only a slight drop to the neighbour's. With new purpose, she backtracked, soon finding the rear entrance to the adjacent structure. The door was locked but soon fell to her ministrations. She entered, moving quietly, seeking out the stairs. Once upstairs, Nikki discovered a balcony, and she climbed out, using it as a foothold to gain access to the rooftop. The clay tiles were old and worn, but sturdy enough, granting her purchase. She moved across the roof, her hands gripping the tiles in a deathlike grip, for the angle was steep.

Soon, she was at the overhang and staring down at the neighbouring rooftop, Marcy's building. Now was the moment of truth. She gathered up her courage, intending to make the leap, but another kick brought her up short. Should she be risking her unborn baby like this?

She started to second guess her actions and then chided herself for letting her pregnancy immobilize her with fear. Taking a deep breath, she jumped, and as she struck the neighbouring rooftop, she felt the thatching partially give way when her legs punched through the straw. Luckily, the frame prevented her from falling through completely. She paused, listening carefully to ensure no one was alerted by her arrival, but all appeared quiet.

She caught her breath and then pulled her dagger, cutting away the thatch until she could peer below. The tenant wasn't home, and so she dropped down into the small area. Nikki crept through the room, finding the door, and moments later, she was in the hallway, making her way down the stairs. Finding Marcy's place was easy. A quick unanswered knock informed her that nobody was home.

Nikki pulled forth her tools, efficiently unlocking the door, which she then pushed open to look within to see a sparsely furnished room, much as she had expected. A quick search confirmed no one was home and so she grabbed a chair and planted herself, facing the door.

It was unlikely that any murder or kidnapping would occur on the street. Anyone worth their salt would want to be out of sight for such a deed. Nikki calculated that the most obvious plan would be to wait until Marcy was in her room, then a forced entry, or perhaps a trick to make her open the door, would be the most likely approach.

She sat back and waited.

It was late afternoon when Nikki heard the front door to the building slam shut. Moments later, a key scraped the lock, and so she moved to stand beside the doorway, knife in hand. A brown-haired woman opened the door just as the front door was thrust open, heavy footsteps rushing forward.

Nikki grabbed the woman's arm, yanking her to the side. The woman screamed in surprise and fear, but Nikki didn't care, she waited just a moment longer, then stabbed out as a man came through the door.

The blade drove into the invader's forearm, striking bone and causing him to cry out in pain. Nikki stabbed again, but her foe reacted quickly, turning to face her and blocking her attack with his own slim dagger.

Behind her, the woman still screamed, and Nikki knew it would soon draw the one from the back door. She jabbed at the assailant's face, causing him to back up, then sliced his weapon hand. Her blade cut across the back of his hand, and he dropped his dagger, clutching at the wound.

Nikki didn't wait. Instead, she plunged forward again, driving the tip of her dagger into the man's chest. She felt it scrape between the ribs, and then it stuck fast.

Her assailant dropped to the floor, forcing Nikki to release her grip on her blade. Suddenly, the back door was kicked open and heavy footsteps echoed down the hallway. Nikki pulled back behind the door frame just as a second man stepped into the room. She put out her foot, and he tripped, falling face-first to strike the floor, the impact echoing in the half-empty room.

Nikki jumped onto the man's back in an attempt to keep him prone, but he rolled, sending her crashing into the wall. He slashed out with his knife, cutting across her stomach but only slicing through the cloth of her dress. In fury, she kicked out with her heel, driving it into his face, his nose exploding in blood. As he lay on the ground screaming, she struck again, and again, kicking until the invader finally lay still.

"Who are you?" the woman screamed.

"I'm Nicole Caster," she replied, "and I'm here to keep you safe."

"Why?" she asked. "What have I done?"

"You were a witness," said Nikki, "many years ago, during the riots in '53."

"Witness to what?" she cried out.

Nikki stood, then advanced towards her, turning the woman so that the bodies were no longer directly in front of her. "All those years ago, did you help someone in the alley, beside the bakery?" she asked.

"I did," the woman confessed. "A soldier was attacking me in the alley when the stranger saved me. Why would someone kill me for that?"

"That person," Nikki explained, "the one that attacked you, he claims to have witnessed a murder."

"That's got nothing to do with me," Marcy pleaded

"True, but if we can prove he tried to attack you, his whole testimony will be thrown out of court. That man that helped you is now the Queen's Marshal, by the way."

"Gerald," she said, "that was his name. He said he was from Bodden."

"That's right," said Nikki, "but a group of the queen's enemies are trying to destroy him. We need you to testify."

"Me? They won't believe me," Marcy said, "I'm nothing but a commoner."

"You're much more than that," said Nikki, "you're the one that will save Gerald's neck."

"Very well," the woman said, "he saved my life, and now I guess it's time I saved his."

"I was hoping you'd say that. Now, let's get out of here."

"What about those two?" she asked.

"I'll get someone to send soldiers," said Nikki, "but I doubt the bodies will still be here. The gangs don't like leaving their own to be discovered. Now, we must hurry to the Cathedral, and hope it's not already too late."

THIRTY-THREE

The Decision

SPRING 964 MC

The Master of Heralds rapped his staff, bringing all in the immense room to their feet. One by one, the jurors filed in, taking their seats, to sit in silence. It was only after they were all seated that Lord Somerset rose to his feet.

"Master of Heralds," he began, "has the woman been located?"

"She has, my lord," the man replied, "and is preparing to give her statement as we speak."

"Good," said Somerset, "then send her in, if you would be so kind."

"Of course, my lord," said the herald. He turned to the doorway that led to the cathedral offices and nodded at the guard stationed there. The guard dutifully opened the door, revealing the witness.

Nikki took Marcy's arm, guiding her out to the floor to sit in the witness's chair before moving to her own seat beside Arnim and Gerald.

Lord Harwood rose, making his way to stand before the woman.

"Can you relate your experiences during the riots of '53?" he asked.

"I can," she began. "I was working at the bakery at the time. When the owner saw the troops lining up, he decided it was better to shutter the shop for the day."

"And so you left the bakery?"

"Not directly, no, we had to put things away. The riot was in sight by the time we left."

"So you saw the rioters hit the troops?"

"I did," she said, "though I was trying to stay out of their way."

"And how, precisely, did you do that?" asked Lord Harwood, sounding bored.

"I hid in the alleyway that leads to Tolpuddle Lane."

"And how long did you remain there?"

"Not long," she replied, "but I saw the troops break their ranks and begin their slaughter."

At this, Arnim rose. "Did you hear anyone give the order to attack?" he asked.

"You'll get your turn," said Harwood in annoyance.

"It's a valid question," said Lord Anglesley, "let her answer."

"Very well," said Harwood, "please tell us what you heard."

"I heard a very loud voice yelling to kill them all," said Marcy. "It was coming from the man on the horse."

"It was quite hectic, that day, was it not?" asked Lord Harwood.

"It was," she agreed.

"Then surely it's possible that you just assumed it was the man on the horse that yelled the command."

"No," she said, "he was pointing his sword at the mob and yelling."

"Come, come," Harwood pressed, "if they were formed up, how did you see him?"

"He was on a horse," said Marcy, "well above the rest."

"And did you witness the subsequent events," asked Lord Harwood, "specifically, the death of the officer?"

"No," she admitted, "I had run to cover by then."

"So you saw nothing that might indicate who killed Lord Walters? Perhaps you saw someone here today, heading in his direction?"

Marcy looked around the room, her eyes settling on Gerald.

"Do you recognize the accused, perhaps?" Harwood asked.

"I do," the woman replied. "He saved me in the alley."

A look of irritation crossed the lord's face.

Arnim rose to the challenge. "Can you explain to the court how he saved you?" he asked.

"A soldier had knocked me to the ground, intent on assaulting me," she said. "That man," she pointed at Gerald, "knocked him off me, even though he could barely walk."

"Come now," said Harwood, "are you a physician?"

"No," she admitted.

"Then how can you say he could barely walk?" Harwood pressed.

"His leg was bleeding," she said, "and he was using some sort of stick to walk, a broom, I think."

"Marcy," said Armin, moving out from behind his table and drawing closer, "do you remember what the accused did after he saved you?"

"Yes," she said, "I'll never forget it. He told the other soldier to go find the others and form them up."

"Anything else?" Arnim pressed.

"Yes," she said, "he said if anyone was found looting, that they should be stabbed."

"What happened next?"

"I saw that his leg was bleeding, so I ripped off the hem of my dress and bandaged him. When I was done, he told me to hide behind a barrel till the coast was clear, then try to get to cover. I did as I was told, crouching down to avoid trouble. The last I saw of him, he was heading to Tolpuddle Lane."

"Thank you," said Arnim, "you've been a great help to the court." He turned to the jury, "Have you any questions, my lords?"

Somerset turned to the others who simply shook their heads, then his lordship spoke, "You may leave us, my dear. The court thanks you for your service this day."

Nikki rose, walking over to Marcy to escort her from the room.

"My Lords," said Lord Harwood, "it is clear from this woman's testimony that Sergeant Matheson was seen heading in the direction of Lord Walters. In addition, the murder was witnessed by the soldier, Smith. We know the accused loathed the nobility and was mad for power. I put it to you that he killed Lord Walters, for if not, who did? There were no others present that could have done the foul deed. I call on this court to render a decision of guilty."

"We shall take your words under advisement," said Lord Somerset. "Lord Caster, have you anything else to say in the accused's defence?"

Arnim rose, taking a moment to gather his thoughts. "My Lords," he began, "Lord Matheson is a distinguished soldier who's spent his entire life defending the realm."

"Irrelevant," interrupted Harwood, "we are judging his actions that day, not his entire career."

"Be that as it may," continued Arnim, "we now have a witness indicating that it was Lord Walters, not his sergeant, that ordered the assault on the mob. In addition, the witness that supposedly saw him murder his captain was, himself, a rapist and a liar, a man who's testimony cannot be considered reliable. I put it to you that Gerald Matheson tried to stop the carnage, as put forth by our witness, who saw him give such an order."

"All the more reason to consider him the murderer," called out Harwood. "If for no other reason than to stop the mayhem."

Lord Somerset rose, bringing the room to silence. "The jury will adjourn," he said, "the better to examine the evidence."

The Master of Heralds called on the room to stand once more, then the jurors filed out. As soon as the door closed, the cathedral broke out into chatter.

"What now?" asked Gerald.

"We wait," said Arnim.

"Did we do enough?"

"I suspect," Arnim replied, "that the jury will be stacked against us, three votes to two."

"I wish I knew what was happening in that back room," said Gerald.

"So do I, Gerald. So do I."

~

Beverly looked across the cathedral to where Sir Preston waited at the base of the steps that led up to the balcony. Six men stood behind him, hand-picked for this occasion.

She nodded and saw him turn, issuing orders. Moments later, they moved towards the table where Gerald sat, unaware of their actions.

Beverly turned to face her own men, just as sure of their loyalty.

"Move into position," she ordered. "You remember your orders?"

"Yes, Commander," said Sergeant Young. "I take two men and secure the western door. When the signal is given, we'll remove the existing guards, then escort the marshal out when he's brought to us."

"Good," said Beverly, "and remember, there's a very real chance that there'll be resistance."

"Aye, Commander," the sergeant replied. "In that case, we are to render the marshal unconscious in order to facilitate his escape."

"Excellent," said Beverly. "Now, get into position and await my command."

They moved off, each taking up their designated stations. Beverly knew it was a gamble, for the regular guards would likely be attentive when the decision was announced. She was gambling that they would be unable to tell friend from foe. Her hands moved to her belt, feeling the comfort of Nature's Fury. She hoped none of her friends would try to intervene, but knew that, if push came to shove, she would carry out the orders of the queen.

~

Aubrey pushed her way through the crowd. The cathedral was drawing closer, but the commoners had gathered around its base, eagerly awaiting news on what was the biggest trial ever. She had thought the proceedings of

Lord Montrose were popular, but whereas the commoners mostly reviled the former Earl of Shrewesdale, they embraced Gerald as one of their own. She didn't want to think about what might happen if he were to be found guilty.

Moving closer, she spied soldiers holding the press of people back from the doors. Finally, she reached them, calling out above the din of the crowd.

"I'm Lady Aubrey Brandon," she shouted, "Baroness of Hawksburg. I need to get inside."

"We have orders to keep everyone back," replied the guard.

"You don't understand," she called back, "the queen's in danger!"

He looked at her for only a moment before making his decision, "Very well, let her through!"

She squeezed past the other onlookers, joining the sergeant. He led her to the great doors which led into the cathedral, but when he tried to open them, he found them barred.

"I was afraid of that," he mused.

"What is it?" she asked.

"The Master of Heralds ordered the doors barred shut to prevent a panic when the decision is announced."

"I have to get in there!" she insisted.

"You can try the west entrance," he said, "it's guarded by rangers."

Aubrey ran as fast as she could, rounding the edge of the cathedral to see the door. It was towards the back of the building, and three rangers, an Orc and two men, stood outside. They noted her approach and drew weapons, but she was soon recognized.

Halting in front of them, she fought to catch her breath. "The queen," she managed to stammer out, "she's in danger."

"How?" asked one of the rangers. "We've got the place locked up tight."

"A shapeshifter," she replied. "Where's Hayley?"

"Just inside," said the Orc. He opened the door, calling for their leader, who soon poked her head out.

"Aubrey," she said, "what's wrong?"

"There's another bartok," the mage replied, "in the form of a woman. She must be after the queen."

Hayley didn't flinch, merely turned to the Orc at the door. "Give me your bow," she commanded.

The ranger gave it over, along with a handful of arrows. Hayley stepped inside, Aubrey following.

"Where is this thing?" Hayley asked.

Aubrey cast her eyes about, taking in the scene. "I think she's after the queen," she said, looking towards the balcony.

Hayley followed her gaze to see the Royal Party, waiting for the jury to return a verdict.

"Can you use your sleep spell?" the ranger asked.

"No, they're too close together."

Hayley notched an arrow, drawing it to her ear. "Give me a target," she pleaded.

Aubrey's eyes flicked from one person to the next.

"The ranger," said the mage finally, "just behind the queen."

"You better be sure about this," said Hayley, as she let fly.

The arrow sped across the distance. Someone in the crowd spotted it in mid-flight, and there was an immediate gasp of recognition. The Royal Party, too intent on watching events below, sat motionless. Just as the ranger behind the queen shifted slightly, moving closer, an arrow struck her right between the eyes.

From Aubrey's location, little more could be seen, but the ranger had disappeared from view, and the balcony exploded into action. The queen was pushed to the floor as soldiers drew their swords.

Moments later, Anna poked her head back up, looking across to where the arrow had come from. She spotted Hayley and Aubrey and waved them towards her.

They pushed their way across the cathedral while guards tried to maintain order. People were trying to rush the door in a panic, only to be meet with guards who stood with drawn weapons.

"Silence!" yelled the strong and steady voice of the queen. The entire cathedral fell into a hush, save for the rushed footfalls of Hayley and Aubrey.

"It is over," said Anna. "The assassin has been slain. There is nothing further to worry about."

Aubrey followed Hayley up the stairs. There, on the balcony, lay the other bartok, its face once more devoid of features.

"How did you know?" asked Anna, looking at Hayley.

"It was Aubrey that discovered it," the ranger said, turning to the Life Mage.

"They're created in pairs," explained Aubrey, "one male and one female. Since we killed the male, it only made sense that the remaining one was in the form of a woman."

"But how did you know it was her?" the queen asked, looking at the floor.

"It was an educated guess, Majesty," Aubrey replied. "Your other guards are men and the only other woman up here is Sophie."

"How did you know it wasn't me?" asked the queen's maid.

"I read a description of the spell," answered the mage. "Bartoks can't impersonate a real person, and I know Sophie's been with you for many years. It had to be the ranger."

"There might not have been one up here at all," the guard captain suggested.

"True," agreed Aubrey, "but only a Necromancer can create them, and the only one of those that we're aware of is Penelope. She'd already tried to kill Gerald; it made sense that the queen would be her next target."

"It's a good thing you're an excellent shot," the captain added, looking at Hayley.

"Indeed," agreed the queen, "a hands-breadth lower, and I'd be dead myself."

"I had lots of room," defended Hayley.

"Your Majesty," said the guard captain, "in light of these events, I suggest we get you to safety until we can secure the cathedral. We shall have to postpone the verdict until tomorrow.

"Very well, Captain," said Anna, "you may lead the way."

She rose from her seat, taking a moment to look down at the people below. Her gaze met Beverly's, and she shook her head ever so slightly. The knight replied with a nod of understanding. There would be no additional action taken this day.

Baron Fitzwilliam fumed, "You can't be serious!"

"I'd say the evidence is quite damning," proclaimed Lord Stanton.

"I'd hardly call it that," offered Somerset. "In fact, I'd say there was very little evidence whatsoever."

"Nonsense," offered Lord Spencer, "what of the witness, Smith?"

"You'd take the word of a rapist?" asked Fitz.

"I'd hardly call him that," defended Stanton, "after all, he was interrupted."

The baron stared at him in disbelief, "And that makes him somehow more reliable?"

"Gentlemen, please," pleaded Lord Anglesley, "can we return to our discussion of the facts?"

"It is precisely the facts that we are attempting to understand," said Somerset.

"Let me ask you this," said Spencer, "who would have reason to kill Lord Walters? In my mind, there can be only one man, and that is Lord Matheson."

"But why would he do such a thing?" asked Somerset

"To save the city," said Anglesley, "don't you see? Lord Walters went on a rampage, killing indiscriminately. If he wasn't stopped, he'd have gone on murdering innocent folk."

"But we can't condemn a man for that!" said Somerset.

"No," agreed Anglesley, surprising everyone, "but our job is to determine guilt first, then assign the punishment we deem appropriate."

"Don't be ridiculous, boy," said Stanton, "the charge is murder. What other penalty can there be, other than death!"

"And if you killed a man in self-defence?" asked Fitz.

"This was no self-defence," argued Stanton.

"Agreed," said Anglesley, "but if you killed a man to save the queen, would that still be murder?"

"You'd be performing your duty," said Lord Spencer.

"Then can you say this is any different?" asked the young Lord. "Surely, by killing Lord Walters, he prevented a great number of deaths."

"Are you suggesting we let him walk free?" asked Spencer.

"No," said Lord Anglesley, "I'm saying the punishment must take into consideration what was at stake."

A knock on the door interrupted their discussion. It opened to reveal Dame Beverly.

"My lords," she said, "I'm afraid the verdict will have to wait until tomorrow. There's been an attempt on the queen."

"Saxnor's sake," said Fitz, "is she safe?"

"She is," replied Beverly, "and the assassin is dead, but we thought it prudent to suspend the verdict until tomorrow. You still have time to discuss the results if you wish, but the rest of the cathedral is being cleared."

"Very well," said Somerset, "it appears we are at an impasse anyway. I suggest we reconvene first thing in the morning. Are the rest of you in agreement?"

They all nodded, then rose from their seats.

Lord Somerset moved to the door, pausing before stepping from the room, "Good day to you, gentlemen.

The rest filed out, leaving Fitz and Beverly.

"Is everything all right, my dear? You look troubled."

"Everything's fine, Father," she replied. "It's just the burden of this trial, it weighs heavily on me."

"As it does to us all," he replied, "but it'll soon be over."

"Have you any sense of the verdict?" asked Beverly.

"My dear," he replied, a sadness in his voice, "you know I can't speak of what goes on in this room, not until the trial is over. At that point, I shall be happy to relate to you the experience. It's not one I'm soon to forget. Now, let us get back to our Wincaster estate. I'm famished!"

He stepped past Beverly, halting in the hallway beyond.

"Albreda!" he called out. "I'm so glad to see you."

"And I, you, Richard," the druid replied.

"Beverly and I were about to return to our city house, would you like to join us?"

"I'd be delighted to," said Albreda, "but you go ahead, I have to speak with Beverly in private for a moment."

"Oh?" he said. "Nothing serious, I hope?"

"Just some womanly advice," the druid replied, "not the sort of thing that would interest a man."

"Very well," he replied, "I've a carriage out back. I'll wait for you there."

"Perfect," said Albreda. "We'll be along shortly."

The baron's footsteps receded down the hallway, soon followed by the sound of a door closing.

"You wanted to speak with me?" prompted Beverly.

Albreda stared at the knight a moment, deep in thought. "The crown is in jeopardy," she said at last.

"You know of a threat?" pressed Beverly.

"The biggest threat to the crown right now is the queen."

"The queen IS the crown!" defended the knight.

"No," said Albreda, "you're wrong. We are standing on a precipice at this very moment. On the one hand is an enlightened land, ruled by law, and on the other is a kingdom descended back into the brutality of absolute rule. You must choose wisely."

Beverly was suddenly struck by the druid's words. Did she know what the queen had planned?

"What makes you think I have anything to do with that?" she finally asked, hoping her voice didn't betray her.

"I didn't say I did," Albreda replied. "I am not here to tell you what to do, Beverly, that is for you, alone, to decide. I am merely here to tell you that at some point, you may have to make a decision. Whatever you decide, I will still be there for you, as I know your father will."

THIRTY-FOUR

Sentencing

SPRING 964 MC

Gerald took his seat beside Arnim and Nikki.

"Do you still feel the same?" he asked.

"I'm afraid so," said Arnim. "I'm sure Fitz is on our side, as is Somerset, but I'm afraid the rest of the jury is against us."

"How so?" asked Gerald.

"Well," Arnim continued, "we know Stanton was on Shrewesdale's side, and we fought against Anglesley during the war. That evens up the score. The big unknown is Lord Spencer, the new Earl of Eastwood. On the one hand, the queen gave him his title, but on the other, he has reason to hate the crown after what they did to his uncle."

"But surely they'll see the lack of evidence?" said Gerald.

"Trials like this aren't about the evidence," said Arnim, "they're about political power. The jury is supposed to be impartial and yet here we are, discussing how we know they're going to vote."

"Maybe it would have been better if the king had killed me after the riot," mused Gerald.

"Don't talk like that," said Nikki. "Without you, the queen would never have come to the throne."

"Yes," added Arnim, "and Weldwyn would be occupied by the clans, not to mention the Kurathian invasion at Riversend."

"I suppose you're right," the old warrior agreed, "and yet none of that seemed to help me today. I've done some terrible things in my life, and Saxnor's finally seen fit to bring his wrath."

"What do you mean?" asked Nikki.

"I failed to protect my parents," said Gerald, starting to tear up, "and then

I failed my wife and child, chasing after a stupid pig while Norlanders killed them. Whatever they decide today, it's a fitting punishment."

"I don't agree," said Arnim. "Yes, you've suffered more than most, but look what you've accomplished. You taught the princess everything she needed to become queen, and then you led the army that put her on the throne. None of that would have happened if not for you. You say that Saxnor is punishing you, but I say that no one has shown more strength!"

"Perhaps," said Gerald, "but it's up to the jury now. My fate rests in their hands."

The Master of Heralds entered the room, rapping his staff to bring everyone to their feet.

Gerald stood with everyone else, feeling his heart pound as the jurors made their way to their seats. Finally in place, they were allowed to sit, to be interrupted once more as the Master of Heralds called out to the jury.

Beverly nodded to Sir Preston and moved into position, her hand close on her belt, ready to draw her hammer if needs be. She watched the knight move behind Gerald's seat and then glanced at her own men as they advanced towards the western door. Leaning there against the wall was Hayley, observing the event with great interest. Beverly cursed her luck. She had hoped that they could move in without interference, but now the ranger posed an obstacle. She knew her friend well, too well, for she knew that Hayley would never condone what must be done, what Beverly must do.

The knight had no choice but to return her attention to the room when the jury entered and took their seats.

Lord Somerset rose. "Your Majesty," he began, "Lords and Ladies, commoners all." He paused to take a breath, "This has been a trying case for everyone involved. Before us, we have Lord Gerald Matheson, Duke of Wincaster and Marshal of the Army, an accomplished leader and champion of Merceria. This man has had a distinguished career, first as a sergeant, then later as a general, and yet, even a man with such accomplishments is not above the law. Laws are what bind us together and separate us from the lesser creatures. It is the very law that is at the heart of this trial." He paused, taking a deep breath, hesitant to continue his statement.

"We have spent much time in deliberation, and the verdict we pass this day was not unanimous, but a decision has been made nonetheless, and we must abide by it, as the law of the land demands."

"Lord Gerald Matheson, Duke of Wincaster, it is the decision of your peers that you be found guilty of the crime of murder."

The courtroom erupted in pandemonium. Commoners started yelling their disgust at the news, jeering the jury, and it looked like they were about to explode into a riot. Soldiers moved forward, weapons brandished, and finally, the crowd calmed.

Gerald kept his eyes forward, locked on the face of Lord Somerset, dreading the words that would soon seal his fate.

~

As Beverly moved towards the door, she counted the rangers.

"Hayley," she said at last, "can you move some of your rangers around to the front entrance? I don't like the look of the crowd. I'll have my men take this door."

The ranger looked at her in surprise, about to protest, but then noticed the look of determination on the knight's face.

"Certainly," Hayley responded, "but you'll have to let me know what they decide on for punishment."

"I will," replied Beverly.

Anna leaned forward in the balcony, her eyes locking on to those of Beverly. The queen nodded, and the knight moved up behind two of the guards, her hand seeking Nature's Fury.

All attention was on Lord Somerset, who stood, waiting to reveal Gerald's punishment.

"It has been made clear to the jury," the lord continued, "that the deplorable acts of cruelty perpetrated by the king's troops on the day in question should never have happened and yet they did, on that there can be no denial. What is equally as important is the knowledge that if Lord Walters had been allowed to continue the attack, the death toll would have been even worse."

He paused again, before continuing, "Though we cannot condone murder, we find that the accused's actions, taken under duress, saved the lives of many, and in recognition of this, we choose, as his punishment, censure and a fine of ten thousand crowns, payable to Lord Walters family in recompense. It now falls to the queen to approve our method of punishment."

Beverly moved forward slightly, but something made her look upward once more to the balcony. Anna was staring at her a moment, as if deep in thought. The knight was preparing to act, muscles tensed, ready to spring into action, but then the queen shook her head. Relief flooded over Beverly. No more would the kingdom be balanced on the precipice of her actions. There would be no rescue needed today, and no blood shed. She felt herself trembling with the release of her pent up energy.

"Ten thousand crowns!" exclaimed Gerald. "Where will I get that amount?"

"Is the Duchy of Wincaster not rich?" asked Arnim.

"No. It's mostly just a title, with a small living allowance. The estate itself belongs to the crown."

"Then you'll be required to work it off," declared Arnim.

"And how would I do that?" he asked.

"Debtor's prison," Arnim explained. "You'll be locked up whenever you aren't working, and all your earnings will go to the Walters family until the debt is paid in full."

"That will take the rest of my life!" Gerald protested. "Isn't there another way?"

"I'm afraid not, and there's still the matter of the censure."

Gerald looked at Arnim in confusion. "Censure? What does that even mean?"

"It means," said Arnim, "that you'll get a stern talking-to from the queen and have to make a public apology."

"That's it?" he said. "That doesn't sound too bad."

Arnim looked back at the jury, who were watching the discussion. "It's not, if you don't mind making a display in front of people."

The Master of Heralds called the room to order while the jury removed themselves from the table. Now, with the trial over, they were free to mingle, and Fitz made straight for Gerald.

"My dear fellow," he said, "I'm so glad you're all right."

"All right?" said Gerald. "I'll live out the rest of my days in prison!"

"Yes," said Fitz, "but at least you're alive. Some of the jury were calling for blood; they wanted your head."

"What happened?" asked Gerald. "My understanding was that the jury was stacked against me. What changed their minds?"

"You saved the city," the baron explained, "and most agreed that the death toll would have been significantly higher if Walters hadn't been stopped."

"Then why the fine?"

"The Walters family demanded restitution," said Fitz, "and the price of that was ten thousand crowns."

"It might as well be a hundred thousand," said Gerald. "Either way, it's life imprisonment."

"True," said Fitz, "but you'll still be able to perform your duty as marshal, and I'm sure that, given enough time, the queen will be able to raise the rest of the coins. I know it's a hollow victory, but it kept you from the headman's axe."

"I suppose I should be thankful for that," said Gerald. "What happens now?"

"You have a few days to prepare for your public apology. After that, you'll be placed under arrest and taken to debtor's prison."

THIRTY-FIVE

Punishment

SPRING 964 MC

Gerald opened the door to peer into the great hall.

"How does it look?" asked Anna.

"I've never seen it so packed," he grumbled, "and all here to see me getting raked over the coals."

"Nervous?" she asked.

"Wouldn't you be?" he responded.

"I remember a time, not so long ago when I was," she said.

He looked back at her, "Yes, you were about to speak to the nobles for the first time."

"Do you remember what you told me?" she asked.

"No," he replied, "I can't say as I do."

She smiled, "You called Tempus to stand beside me."

"I remember now," he said. "He made you feel safe, he always has."

"You do too, Gerald. I may have to tell you off today, but I shall always value your friendship. This whole gathering is all for show."

He closed the door, shutting out the noise of the great hall. "All right," he said at last, "let's get this over with, and then I can go to prison."

He stood back and waited as a servant came forward to open the door. The queen would go first, taking up her position on the throne while Gerald must wait to be summoned.

Horns sounded as she entered the massive chamber, then the door shut, once more cutting off the noise. Gerald waited, nervously fidgeting. The door behind him opened, revealing Sophie.

"Something wrong?" asked Gerald

"Not at all. The queen asked me to make sure you're doing all right and to lend you something."

"Lend me something? Whatever does that mean?"

In answer, Sophie whistled. The hall beyond echoed with the sound of running feet, then a great head peered around the door.

"Tempus!" said Gerald.

"He's to be your guard," said Sophie, "to keep you safe."

The great mastiff trotted over to Gerald, who bent slightly to rub his head. "My old friend," he said, "we've been through so much together."

"And you've so much more to do," added Sophie, "both of you."

Gerald stretched his back, resuming his upright stance. "Thank you, Sophie, this means a lot to me."

"You're welcome, my lord."

"No," he said, "don't call me my lord. Gerald is fine by me."

"Of course, Gerald," the maid responded with a smile.

The door to the great hall opened to reveal Beverly fully armoured, save for her helmet. She stood in the doorway a moment before speaking, the sound of the crowd evident in the background.

"In the name of the queen, I summon Lord Gerald Matheson, Duke of Wincaster and Marshal of the Army, to receive your censure." Then, in a quieter voice, she added, "Are you ready, Gerald?"

"As ready as I'll ever be," he grumbled.

Gerald stepped into the great hall to be met with utter silence. The room was crowded, as he had noticed earlier, but a path had been cleared from the door to the foot of the throne, lined with soldiers, all with their swords drawn.

He started the slow walk, Tempus padding forward to stay at his side. Gerald had only passed the first half dozen or so guards when movement caught his eye. They all raised their swords, holding them upright in a salute. He felt emotion wash over him, tears forming in his eyes, and made no move to hide them.

Beverly's measured steps echoed behind him as he made his way to the throne, where Anna sat. He halted, facing her, and the great beast sat beside him. Beverly drew her sword, the sound of it being unsheathed clearly audible in the chamber.

Queen Anna rose from her seat, taking a step closer. She looked him in the eye and nodded slightly in greeting.

"Lord Gerald Matheson," she started, "Duke of Wincaster and Marshal of the Realm, you have been found guilty in a court of your peers and have been sentenced to receive your punishment this day."

Her words trailed off, the room still in absolute silence. Gerald could see her fighting to get the words out, and knew it was as hard for her to stand there and issue this punishment as it was for him to receive it.

"You have, by your deeds, brought disgrace to the crown," she continued, "and though you have served the realm with distinction, it does not make you immune to the law. Be it known far and wide that you no longer carry the favour of the crown, and that you will serve out your days in imprisonment until such time as you can make recompense."

She paused, her eyes avoiding Gerald's direct gaze. "Dame Beverly," she commanded, "take the prisoner outside that he may make his amends to the people of Merceria."

"Yes, Your Majesty," said the knight, who then turned to face Gerald. "Lord Matheson," she continued, "prepare to speak to the people. About turn."

Gerald turned, his back now to the queen. He marched forward, the length of the hall, where the soldiers had created another path. Beverly walked behind, the point of her sword held at his back as was the custom. Tempus, as eager as ever to protect his friend, trotted alongside, none daring to interfere with the great mastiff.

As Gerald passed them by, more soldiers raised their swords in respect. He could dimly make out the faces of the crowd in his peripheral vision. They were silent for the most part, but he was sure the family of Lord Walters was happy, as was the Duke of Tewsbury for that matter. They would forever be his enemies, of that he was certain.

He was marched to the door, then through the hallway to the large paved area in front of the Palace. Someone had put up a wooden platform, and he walked up the steps to take his place, Tempus sitting as he halted.

Before him was a massive crowd, a sea of humanity that lined up beyond the massive iron gate that held them at bay. They were all talking, creating a rumbling sound that echoed throughout the city. A horn sounded them into silence, the signal for him to make his speech.

"People of Merceria," he began, his voice echoing, "long have I served this realm, first as a common soldier, then as General of her Army." He waited for the echo to die before continuing.

"But even I, the Marshal of all Merceria, am not beyond the reach of the law. My actions, during the riots back in '53, were contrary to the wishes of the crown, and for that, I ask for forgiveness. It is not the place of men such as I to question the will of the monarchy, but rather to carry it out. I live to serve my country, my god, and my queen."

The crowd erupted into cheering, a sound that rolled over him like a torrential rain, washing away his sins.

Beverly appeared beside him, "It's done, Gerald. Let's get you back inside, shall we?"

He let her lead him from the stage, too numb to react. She guided him through the crowd until they were back in the entrance to the Palace, then she turned left, into the private rooms, rather than the great hall.

He looked around to see his friends assembled. They had all come to see him off, for he must report to the debtor's prison to begin the second part of his punishment.

Fitz was the first to greet him, moving directly towards him, Albreda at his side.

"My dear fellow," the baron began, "so good to see you again, I'm only sorry it couldn't have been under better circumstances."

"My lord," said Gerald.

"Now, now," said Fitz, "you're a duke now, you can't call me 'my lord' anymore."

Gerald chuckled, "Very well, Lord Fitzwilliam."

Fitz sighed. "Ah, well," he said, "it was worth a try."

Albreda, who had remained uncharacteristically silent during the exchange, suddenly took a step forward, embracing Gerald. So surprised was he that he didn't know what to do. He waited, patting her back gently as she held him tight. Finally, she released him and returned to the baron's side.

"Richard tells me the jury had trouble," she said, her voice husky with emotion.

"Yes," agreed the baron, "Lord Stanton was pushing for the death sentence, and he had a majority. If it hadn't been for Lord Anglesley, that might have been the end of it."

"Lord Anglesey," said Gerald, "The Duke of Colchester? I would never have picked him as an ally."

"He appears to have come around to the queen's way of doing things," continued Fitz. "It was his idea to pay a fine to the Walters family instead of executing you. The real problem after that was finding an amount that the Walters could agree to. Mind you, Stanton was furious. He was finally persuaded by the others but insisted on the public apology. I think it was his last chance to try and embarrass you and the crown. I'm only sorry that the payment was so high."

"It matters little in the long run," said Gerald. "I'll be dead long before even a portion of it is paid off."

"At least you're alive, my dear friend," said Fitz, "and as long as you live, there is hope."

"What are the conditions of your sentence?" asked Albreda.

"I must reside in the debtor's prison between sun-down and sun-up. During daylight hours, whatever I make is first used to cover the costs of my imprisonment, with the remainder going to pay off the fine."

"I must admit," said Albreda, "that I found the entire trial utterly ridiculous. If any man deserved death, it was this Captain Walters you spoke of."

"I broke the law," said Gerald, "and I must pay the price."

"Nonsense," the druid continued, "you are far more valuable to the realm here, than rotting in prison."

"Nonetheless," said Gerald, "if Merceria is to have the rule of law, we must abide by the court's decision."

"Come, my dear," said Fitz, turning to Albreda, "let us leave him to say his goodbyes. Others are waiting."

Gerald moved past them, spotting Arnim and Nikki talking quietly between themselves.

Upon noticing his approach, Nikki moved forward to give him a hug, then backed up slightly, instinctively grabbing her stomach.

"Sorry," she said, "the young Master Caster kicked again."

Gerald smiled, "It could be a girl, you know."

"If it is," said Nikki, "it's a strong one."

"Congratulations to you both," added Gerald. "I'm afraid I've been too busy of late to say it sooner."

"Understandable," said Arnim, "you've had a lot to worry about."

They stood awkwardly in silence, unsure of what to say.

"You know," said Arnim at last, "I know a few people at the prison. I can put in a good word for you, if you like?"

"I doubt that will be necessary," said Gerald, "I'm still the Duke of Wincaster and Marshal of the Army."

"A good point, I suppose," muttered Arnim.

"Take care, Gerald," said Nikki, "and look after yourself."

"I will," he promised, though he felt his spirits sink deeper as the sentence drew closer.

Hayley was next, with Revi tagging along.

"I'm sorry, Gerald," she said.

"You were only doing your job," said Gerald. "If it hadn't been you, it would have been someone else. I have no complaints about my captivity during the trial."

"You know," interjected Revi, "debtor's prison falls under the purview of the High Ranger. In a sense, Hayley remains your jailer."

"You're not helping, Revi," insisted Hayley.

"Still," the mage persisted, "it is a most curious thing."

Unsure of what to make of the exchange, Gerald pushed past them, excusing himself. He was moving towards Beverly and Aldwin when a hand caught his arm.

"Gerald," said Jack Marlowe, "I wonder if I might have a word?"

"Of course," the marshal replied.

Jack guided him to the side of the room, the better to talk privately.

"What do you know of this Aldwin fellow?" he asked.

"Aldwin? You mean Beverly's husband?"

"Yes," said Jack. "I know he's a master smith, but how in the name of Malin did they meet?"

"Why don't you ask Beverly?" said Gerald.

Jack made a face. "That wouldn't be seemly," he said. "After all, I have my pride."

"But you'll stoop to gossip?" asked Gerald.

"I prefer to use the term 'staying informed'. Tell me, is it serious between these two?"

"They're married, Jack, of course it's serious. They've known each other for years."

"You should have told me, old fellow," said Jack.

"I tried to," defended Gerald, "back in Weldwyn."

"So what's he like, this Aldwin?"

"Why don't you come and see for yourself?" said Gerald. "I'd be happy to introduce you."

"That's awfully decent of you," said Jack. "I believe I'll take you up on that offer."

Gerald led him back towards Beverly and her smith.

"Jack," said Gerald, "may I introduce Lord and Lady Fitzwilliam."

Beverly bowed slightly while Aldwin extended his arm. The cavalier took the proffered hand, shaking it with a firm grip. Gerald saw the look of surprise on Jack's face as Aldwin's firmer grip returned the shake. Was this about to become a test of strength, he wondered?

Aldwin released his grip and Jack looked him up and down. "A most worthy man for Dame Beverly," he announced.

"It's not your place to judge, Jack," said Beverly, a note of irritation in her voice.

"I meant no disrespect," explained the cavalier, "but one of your calibre requires a husband to match."

"I think he means it as a compliment," added Gerald.

"I would hope so," said Beverly.

Aldwin, amused by this discussion, simply smiled.

"I imagine Beverly told you all about me," offered Jack.

"No," said Aldwin, "she's never mentioned you."

"Oh," said Jack, "it wounds my soul to hear you say that. You must ask her sometime about how we fought together to kill the drake of Tivilton."

"I seem to remember Gerald being there as well," said Beverly, "not to mention all the soldiers."

"Perhaps," offered Aldwin, "I can tell you how I forged Nature's Fury?"

Beverly smiled, "He's got you beat there, Jack."

Jack bowed in the old style, an over-exaggerated act, complete with an extended leg. "I resign. There is no shame in admitting defeat by a worthy opponent."

Beverly turned to look at her old mentor. "Gerald," she said, "what are we going to do without you?"

"I'll still see you during the daytime," he defended.

"Yes," said Beverly, "but we'll miss those stories of Bodden."

"You've all grown up now, Beverly," said Gerald. "It's time you start telling your own stories."

Aldwin extended his hand, this time towards the old warrior.

"I shall miss you, Gerald," he said. "Though we haven't spent much time together, I feel as though I really know you. Though I daresay, I won't miss you standing by the doorway, keeping an eye on Beverly."

Gerald chuckled, "That was so long ago. Thanks for reminding me of how old I am."

"Prince Alric awaits," interrupted Jack.

Gerald finished shaking Aldwin's hand, then let Jack guide him towards the Weldwyn Prince.

"Your Highness," the marshal said.

"Gerald, I'm glad to see you safe. I know how much you mean to Anna."

"I thank you for the sentiment," said Gerald, "but I must face up to the error of my ways."

"Tell me," said Alric, "any regrets?"

Gerald thought a moment before answering, "If I were to live my life over, there are things I would change, but we cannot undo the past. We must learn to live with it."

"Truer words were never spoken," the prince replied. "You should become a poet."

"It appears I'll have plenty of time to consider it," said Gerald.

"Let me take you to Anna," said Alric. "I know she'll want to say goodbye."

The prince let Jack clear the way, then guided Gerald through the crowd to where Anna waited.

Gerald could tell the queen was upset, her red eyes betrayed the fact that she had been crying. He felt terrible for placing her in this situation, but could think of nothing to say in his defence.

"We'll get you back," said Anna, through tears, "I promise you." She moved forward, embracing him in a tight hug.

Tears came to his eyes as he held her. She finally released him, and he held her at arm's length, taking her in. He thought back to the little girl with the matted hair he had met so long ago in the hedge maze. How much she had changed. Now, before him, stood a queen, regal and elegant, a woman of power. Words failed him, and he simply looked at her, returning her stare.

Finally, the guards moved forward.

"It's time," he said, and the soldiers escorted him from the room.

THIRTY-SIX

Confinement

Gerald sat in his room, looking around. It was ten paces wide, little more than a dungeon. Three walls were made of stone, while the fourth consisted of iron bars that blocked his entrance, thus ensuring no privacy whatsoever. The bed was naught but a wooden pallet with a thin straw mattress upon it, and the only other furniture was a table and chair at which he could sit for meals. The prison had even provided a candle, which was useful as he was here mainly when it was dark out. The room boasted a single window, but it was high up, out of reach, and was barely big enough to admit sunlight.

Candlelight flickered, throwing shadows about the room as he stared out through the bars and across the hall to a similar cell opposite him. It was empty, but the sounds of snoring could be heard drifting through the prison.

He lay down and tried to sleep, but memories of Walpole Street haunted his thoughts. Things would have turned out far differently if only he hadn't insisted on confronting Lord Walters!

A rattle of keys broke through his thoughts. Light from the open door to the guard room flooded the cells, causing at least one prisoner to groan in protest. Moments later, he heard the heavy footfalls of the head jailer, followed by a second set of feet, these softer.

"You've got a visitor, my lord," the jailer announced.

Gerald wiped away the tears, looking up to see Sophie carrying a basket with great care.

"I've come bearing gifts," announced Sophie as she entered.

"Call me when you're done," the jailer said, then left to give them some privacy.

Sophie placed the basket upon the chair and then removed the top. "Her Majesty wanted you to be comfortable," she said, taking a blanket from the basket and handing it to him. "This should help keep you warm."

Next came a wooden platter, and tankard, which she placed with care on the table. "You'd best come sit down for this," she said. "I've got some nice fresh sausages for you, courtesy of the Palace, along with some decent ale. We all know how much you dislike wine."

"I don't dislike wine," argued Gerald, halfheartedly, "I just prefer ale."

He watched in anticipation as she placed her hands back into the basket.

"Her Majesty also thought you might like something to read," she said, producing a book.

Gerald took the tome, examining its spine. It was a book of poetry, by Califax no less.

"Couldn't she send something with a more martial element?" he asked.

Sophie smiled, "She said you'd complain."

"And?"

"And I'm supposed to tell you the poems are all about war."

Gerald suddenly became acutely interested in the book. He opened it to see Anna's sure hand.

For my father, Gerald Matheson, it read, *with all my love, Anna.*

Gerald wiped his eyes, muttering something about dust.

"Tell the queen," he said, his voice breaking slightly, "that I'm truly honoured by her gifts."

"She also said to tell you," Sophie continued, "that she's already at work raising funds for your release."

"Tell her she has to stop," pleaded Gerald, "the kingdom can't afford it."

"She'll do anything to get you out of here," argued Sophie.

"I know," he said, "but I can't have her throw everything away just to save me."

"She would argue that it would be worth it to have you back, you know she would."

"I do," he admitted, "but she's the queen now. She has bigger things to consider."

Sophie stood, lifting the now-empty basket. "Is there anything else I can get for you?" she asked.

"Thank you, but no," he said. "I'm afraid I'm not in much of a mood for visitors.

"I understand," said Sophie. She moved to the door, calling out for the guard. He appeared in due course, unlocking the cell. The maid paused in the doorway as she was leaving, looking back once more to Gerald.

"I'll bring you more food tomorrow," she promised. "Don't give up on hope, Gerald, it's all we have."

He stared back at her with a dull expression, merely nodding, and then she was gone.

The days became a blur. Each morning, at sun-up, he would be awakened to head out to work. Gerald remained Marshal of the Army, still having to interact with others in the performance of his duties, but it grew harder for him to return to his cell at dusk. The days were bearable, but the nights were intolerable; with no one to talk to, he became increasingly disheartened, withdrawing from life.

He had been serving his sentence for only a few weeks, yet it seemed like a lifetime. Gerald was used to seeing Anna each evening, but now, confined as he was to this cell, all he could do was sit alone with only his thoughts. Sophie would bring a meal each eve, but with other duties to attend to, she could stay but a brief moment and the queen was far too busy these days to spend time with him during the day.

With nothing to do, his thoughts turned to memories of the past. The face of Meredith would come to him, reminding him of how much he'd lost, and then the inevitable sense of anguish as he thought of his daughter Sally, taken at such a young age. Was this his torment, to forever relive the past?

As the days piled on, he grew more despondent, half convinced that he was living in the Underworld; his nights filled with anguish while his daytime became more of a chore to endure than the freedom it was.

They had shown him how much he earned, and how much was owed to the prison. Everything else, he was told, went to the Walters family, the price for the death of the nephew. By Gerald's reckoning, he would have to live another one hundred and twenty years to pay off such a debt.

He was musing on this very topic one night when the jailer appeared rather unexpectedly at his door. Gerald looked up in surprise.

"Gather your things, my lord," the man said.

"Why," asked Gerald, "what's happened?"

"I was told your debt's been paid in full," said the jailer as he unlocked the cell.

Gerald gathered his belongings, meagre as they were.

"I don't understand," he sputtered, "are you telling me the crown paid my debts?"

"I'm not telling you anything," responded the jailer. "All I know is that you're to be released. Now come on, before they change their minds."

Gerald followed him through the prison, emerging into the darkness of night.

"Good luck to you," the jailer said, extending his hand. "I hope there's no hard feelings."

"Not at all," said Gerald, shaking the man's hand. "You've been most gracious, under the circumstances. Can you tell me who paid for my release?"

"Can't say as I can," said the jailer, "though I reckon that carriage over yonder might give you some clue."

Gerald glanced in the indicated direction to see an expensive carriage led by a team of jet black thoroughbreds. A man stood waiting beside them, watching Gerald bid farewell to his imprisonment. Gerald moved closer, soon recognizing the figure as he stepped into the moonlight.

"Jack!" said Gerald in surprise. "What are you doing here?"

"Hop in," the cavalier replied, "there's someone who wants to talk to you."

Jack opened the door, admitting Gerald, then climbed in afterwards. As Gerald took his seat, he noticed his fellow passenger was none other than Prince Alric.

"Your highness," he said in surprise.

"Gerald," said the prince, "so good to see you in such fine health, I'm only sorry it took so long."

"I still don't understand," said Gerald. "What are you doing here?"

"I recently returned from Weldywn," explained Alric.

"I didn't know you'd left," said Gerald.

"You forget the magic circles," the prince continued. "I had Albreda take me to Summersgate and met with my father, the king. When I told him of your predicament, he insisted on paying your debt."

"You did that for me?" asked Gerald.

"You helped our kingdom in our hour of need," explained Alric. "It's the least we could do. I only wish I could have been faster. It took longer than expected to round up the coins."

"But I'm the marshal," argued Gerald, "I cannot be beholden to a foreign power."

"And you won't be, don't you see? We consider this a repayment of our debt to you. We expect nothing in return, other than your devotion to Anna, of course."

"I don't know what to say," said Gerald, feeling overwhelmed.

"I know what you mean," said Alric, misinterpreting the marshal's confusion. "I find it hard to comprehend myself. Travelling from Wincaster to Summersgate now is a matter of a simple recall spell. Of course, you know what this means?"

Gerald looked at him, still in shock. "No, I don't," he confessed.

"It means," continued Alric, a smirk forming on his face, "that you and Anna can visit Summersgate for dinner and be back before bedtime. There's never been anything like this before in the history of our kingdoms!"

Gerald's head was spinning, trying to take it all in.

"Where are we going?" he finally asked.

"To the Palace to meet with Anna. She's hosting a meeting with the Nobles Council. I bet she'll be surprised to see you!"

"It is simply untenable, Your Majesty," said Lord Stanton. "We cannot have a criminal in charge of the army!"

"I might remind you," argued Anna, "that Lord Matheson is only in prison until his debt is paid. It is not your job, nor the responsibility of this council to appoint the Marshal of the Army. That is the sole prerogative of the sovereign.

Lord Stanton leaned back in his chair, wearing a smug look. "But think how it looks, Your Majesty. Is this the image you wish to project to your people."

"The people love their marshal," interrupted Baron Fitzwilliam.

"I don't remember asking you for advice," argued Lord Stanton, "and as a mere baron, you should know better than to interrupt me."

Fitz smiled, "I'm still the acting Governor of Shrewesdale, am I not, Your Majesty?"

"You are," confirmed Anna.

Before Fitz could say more, there was a knock at the door, then a servant appeared, moving to whisper into Anna's ear.

"It appears we have visitors," announced the queen.

"This is a council meeting," declared Stanton, "and as such, should not be interrupted. We have important business to discuss with you, Your Majesty."

"Beverly?" Anna called.

Moments later, the door opened, and the red-headed knight poked her head in.

"Yes, Majesty?"

"Who's here?"

"Prince Alric," announced Beverly, "and two associates of your acquaintance. They say it's important."

Anna's eyebrows furrowed in thought. "I think we can afford a moment for our new allies, don't you?" said Anna. She looked around the table but saw no objections.

"Very well, send them in."

Alric entered first, followed closely by Jack, as was expected.

Tempus suddenly sat up and barked, his tail wagging furiously as Gerald finally entered the room. The great dog even rose from his customary place beside the queen, trotting directly to the old warrior who halted to pet him on the head.

"Gerald!" called out Anna, not even trying to hide her glee. "I didn't expect to see you here."

"I'm free!" he announced.

"I don't understand," said Anna, "we haven't raised the necessary funds yet."

"My father insisted on settling his debt," offered Alric. "The Walters family are now paid in full."

Anna rose, making her way across the room to embrace her oldest friend, tears flowing freely down her cheeks.

"I hardly think this is appropriate for a queen," complained Lord Stanton.

"With all due respect, Alexander," said Fitz, "you can keep your opinions to yourself."

Anna turned to her nobles, "It appears that fate has returned our marshal to us in a timely manner. This meeting is concluded. We shall reconvene tomorrow."

The nobles of the realm stood, bowing respectfully to the queen, then exited the room.

Anna waited till they had left, leaving only herself, Gerald, Alric, Jack and, of course, Tempus.

"It's finally over," she said.

"Not quite," said Gerald, "I need to apologize to you."

"Whatever for?" she asked.

"For being such a burden," he replied.

"You are never a burden," she said. "It was those that conspired against us that were the true burden of the crown."

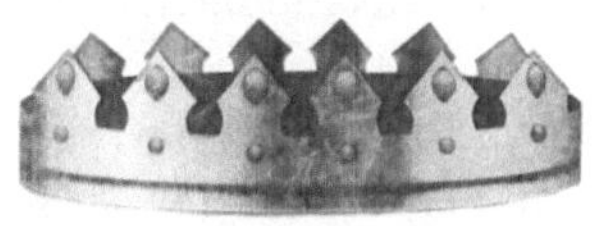

Epilogue

SUMMER 964 MC

The cathedral was packed with well-wishers as the initiates, all three of them, stood in a line awaiting the commencement of the ceremony. The choir's voices, singing the praises of Saxnor, echoed in the vast cavernous structure until the final word was sung, and then all went quiet. Everyone present, save the initiates, craned their necks to watch the entrance, knowing what would come next.

Dame Beverly Fitzwilliam, Knight Commander of the Order of the Hound, entered the great chamber, her footsteps echoing on the marble floor. Behind her strode Dame Hayley and Lord Arnim Caster, the only other members of the order. They made their way down the nave, taking up a position in front of the three assembled men, facing the altar.

The Bishop Supreme himself called on Saxnor to bless all present, a rare occurrence, and then Beverly turned to face the new initiates.

"Sir Heward," she commanded.

The man moved to stand before her, his towering frame looming over hers as his face held a look of amusement. She struck him on the arm with the flat of her sword, a solid blow that echoed off the metal plates which guarded his upper arms. He swayed slightly with the force, though she knew he only did it to emphasize her blow.

"I pronounce this man worthy," she said aloud.

Heward returned to his position in the line.

"Sir Preston," she called.

The knight walked forward, standing before her much as Heward had.

She struck him lightly on the arm, noticing his flinch as she made contact.

"I pronounce this man worthy," she announced in a clear voice.

Sir Preston returned to his position beside Heward.

"Lord Fitzwilliam," she called, "you stand in proxy for Sir Rodney this day. Step forward, that you may represent him."

Baron Fitzwilliam stepped up, standing before his daughter.

She lay the sword gently on his shoulder. "We deem the late Sir Rodney worthy of this honour."

Her father returned to the line, then Beverly knelt, the initiates doing likewise. The Bishop Supreme stepped forward and began extolling the virtues of bravery, honesty and fealty. When he was finished, a horn sounded, sending its clear sound echoing off the walls. Beverly stood, but the initiates remained kneeling, as Queen Anna entered the chamber, dressed in all her glory. Hayley carried the Dwarven sword, resting on a cushion, while Arnim bore the standard of the order, depicting the head of a great mastiff. The queen halted in front of Beverly, and the Knight Commander bowed deeply, then moved to the side.

"Since the time of our ancestors," the queen began, "many have come forth in times of need to defend that which is ours. We stand here today to welcome these new initiates into the Royal Order of the Hound, to serve their kingdom, their queen, and to protect those that cannot protect themselves."

She turned to Hayley, who held out the cushion. Anna lifted the sword, pulling it from the scabbard, its runes reflecting the light of a thousand candles that lit the cathedral. Moving towards the first of the initiates, she placed the blade on Heward's right shoulder.

"Recite the oath," she commanded.

"I do solemnly swear," said Heward, "to serve my kingdom, my queen, and the people of Merceria, until the end of my days."

"Arise, Sir Heward," said Anna, "Knight of the Hound."

Sir Heward did as he was bid, eliciting a round of applause from those assembled. It was a breach of etiquette, but Anna ignored it, nay encouraged it, by smiling at the crowd.

Next, she moved to Sir Preston, again placing the sword upon his right shoulder.

"Recite the oath," she commanded once more.

Sir Preston did as he was ordered.

"Arise, Sir Preston," said Anna, "Knight of the Hound."

Lastly, she stood before Baron Fitzwilliam.

"This day," she said, "we honour those who have fallen in service to the crown. Sir Rodney, who died in the Siege of Wincaster, is hereby declared to be worthy of this final honour."

She placed the sword on Baron Fitwilliam's shoulder. "Arise," she said, "and let it be henceforth known throughout the land that Sir Rodney was a Knight of the Hound."

Fitz stood, tears streaking his face.

"Be it also known," the queen continued, "that these brave and honourable men have been inducted into the Royal Order of the Hound. From this day forward, I call upon them to uphold the laws of this land and to serve the kingdom faithfully."

The crowd broke into applause, Anna joining in, and the whole cathedral echoed with the sound. The choir began to sing once more as Beverly led the queen down the nave, Arnim and Hayley following. The new knights fell in behind them until they reached the relative privacy of the atrium.

Anna turned. "Congratulations to you all," she said, less formally.

"I must thank you, Majesty," said Fitz. "Sir Rodney would have been proud."

"As are we of his service," said Anna. "We shall not forget our dead. Nor fail to reward where such is earned."

Fitz bowed deeply.

"Are you ready to return to the Palace now, Majesty?" asked Beverly.

"In a moment," said Anna, "we're just waiting for Gerald and Tempus. In the meantime, I'd like a private word with you, Beverly, if I may."

"Of course, Majesty," she replied, moving to the side of the atrium.

Anna waited until they were out of earshot of the others before speaking. "I wanted to talk to you about what happened at the trial," Anna began.

"There's no need," said Beverly.

"I was ready to throw away everything for Gerald," the queen confessed, "and I appreciate that you were willing to aid me in my efforts. I shall never forget that."

"I live to serve," Beverly replied.

"There's more," said Anna, grasping for the right words. "What I planned is not something I'm proud of. I'd like to keep it a secret between just you and me."

"I understand," said Beverly. "It will be as you wish."

"Good," said Anna, looking relieved. Returning her voice to a normal level, she asked, "Now, where are those two?"

Beverly knew they'd been watching from the balcony, along with the rest of the Royal Party. They didn't have long to wait though, a bark soon echoed into the atrium.

"Here they are," called out Hayley.

Tempus ran forward, wagging his tail, Gerald following along, slightly out of breath.

"He's faster than he looks," he said.

Anna laughed, "Come along, you two, we've got a dinner to celebrate the new members of the order."

The great hall had been scorned in favour of the dining hall, a much more intimate surrounding for such an august group of warriors.

Gerald sat, as was usual, to the right of Anna while Tempus lay to her left. The other knights, save for Hayley, were seated along either side, dressed not in their amour, but in more comfortable attire.

Gerald looked about the room. The order was only six strong, but Anna had declared them the senior order, relegating the Knights of the Sword to second place in the hierarchy of such things.

"I still don't know why I'm here," said Gerald, "I'm not a Knight of the Hound."

"You could be," said Anna, "I've offered to let you in."

"No," he replied, "it wouldn't be right, I'm the marshal now."

"That alone gives you the right to be here," reminded Beverly. She turned to Sir Heward. "Well," she asked, "what do you think? Do you feel any different?"

"It is a little strange," the great man reflected, "no longer being a Knight of the Sword, but I'm in good company."

"You are indeed," added Arnim, "a very select group."

"I shall have to get a new tabard sewn," said Heward.

"As shall we all," said Beverly, "but only for official ceremonies. The queen's more interested in how we fight, not so much how we look."

"Will we eventually have more in the order?" asked Sir Preston.

"Doubtless," replied Anna, "but we'll take it slow and only bring in the most trusted warriors."

"And what of the Knights of the Sword, Your Majesty?" he persisted.

"They'll still be a fighting order," answered the queen, "but their emphasis will be on fighting, not looking pretty at court."

"So we are to guard the court?" asked Sir Preston.

"No," said Beverly, "we have highly trained guards for that. We'll perform whatever duties the queen desires."

"Where is Hayley?" asked Beverly. "I thought she'd be here."

"She'll be along shortly," said Gerald, "she just wanted to check in with Revi. She said he was looking a little under the weather of late."

"If she doesn't get here soon," warned Heward, "there'll be none of this beef left!"

They all chuckled as the giant man stabbed out with his fork.

"Eat as much as you like, Sir Heward," said Anna, "there's plenty more where that came from."

The door flew open, revealing a dishevelled looking Hayley.

Beverly was immediately concerned. "Hayley," she called out, "whatever's the matter?"

"It's Revi," she replied, "he's disappeared!"

<<<<>>>>

REVIEW BURDEN OF THE CROWN

~

CONTINUE WITH MERCERIAN TALES: THE MAKING OF A MAN

~

If you liked *Burden of the Crown,* then *Ashes,* the first book in *The Frozen Flame* series awaits.

START ASHES

A Few Words from Paul

When I first envisioned the Heir to the Crown series, I saw it as three grand stories. Fate of the Crown finished off the first part, while Burden of the Crown launches into the second of these stories. Although it is complete on its own, it hints at greater dangers to come. Many stories tell of a quest for a crown, but few deal with what happens when that task is complete.

I wanted to tell a political story, but don't read any of our twenty-first-century politics into it as this is not a comment on current affairs. Instead, it is inspired by events in our own planet's history. One only has to look at something like the Wars of the Roses in England to see how plotting and counter-plotting can work. The struggle for the crown is more than just winning a war; it's about holding onto it once you're done, and I have endeavoured to show that in my own way.

In Burden of the Crown, I have resolved some plot lines, and I dare say more than a few readers will be happy to see Beverly and Aldwin finally together, but of course more is on the way. As hinted in this story, a royal wedding is approaching, and who knows what might happen then?

As usual, I must thank my wife, Carol, for her tireless efforts in the production of this tale. She is an invaluable part of this series, and her influence is seen throughout the series. I would also thank Christie Kramburger once again for her artwork, along with Amanda Bennett and Stephanie Sandrock, for their support and encouragement. Also, a big thank you to Brad Aiken, Jeffrey Parker, and Stephen Brown for their inspirational characters.

I also owe a debt of thanks to my BETA team that did an outstanding job catching mistakes and questioning some plot points. It is because of you that the book reached its final form. Thanks to Rachel Deibler, Tim James, Mark Tracy, Phyllis Simpson, Don Hinkley, James McGinnis, David Clark, Stuart Rae, Michael Rhew, and Dianna-Lynn 'Dee' Lundgren.

As always, I look forward to what you, my readers, think. Your feedback on the series inspires me to continue writing.

About the Author

Paul J Bennett (b. 1961) emigrated from England to Canada in 1967. His father served in the British Royal Navy, and his mother worked for the BBC in London. As a young man, Paul followed in his father's footsteps, joining the Canadian Armed Forces in 1983. He is married to Carol Bennett and has three daughters who are all creative in their own right.

Paul's interest in writing started in his teen years when he discovered the roleplaying game, Dungeons & Dragons (D & D). What attracted him to this new hobby was the creativity it required; the need to create realms, worlds and adventures that pulled the gamers into his stories.

In his 30's, Paul started to dabble in designing his own roleplaying system, using the Peninsular War in Portugal as his backdrop. His regular gaming group were willing victims, er, participants in helping to playtest this new system. A few years later, he added additional settings to his game, including Science Fiction, Post-Apocalyptic, World War II, and the all-important Fantasy Realm where his stories take place.

The beginnings of his first book 'Servant to the Crown' originated over five years ago when he began running a new fantasy campaign. For the world that the Kingdom of Merceria is in, he ran his adventures like a TV show, with seasons that each had twelve episodes, and an overarching plot. When the campaign ended, he knew all the characters, what they had to accomplish, what needed to happen to move the plot along, and it was this that inspired to sit down to write his first novel.

Paul now has four series based in his fantasy world of Eiddenwerthe, and is looking forward to sharing many more books with his readers over the coming years.